7TH SOUL

by Michael N. Ruggiero

Blue Print Productions, LLC
11852 Eden Estates Drive
Carmel, IN 46033
Visit our website at *www.the7thsoul.com*

ISBN: 979-8-9937731-0-0
eISBN: 979-8-9937731-1-7

There are so many people whom I'd like to dedicate this book. Raoul DeSota planted a profound seed in my mind when I told him my Mother had six lost babies then she had me. He asked, "do you think the six lost souls are in you?"

To Tammy Gross who held my hand and mentored me during the writing process. And most importantly my partner, friend, and wife, Carol Ruggiero who cheered me on at every page.

PREFACE

"Energy can only be changed from one form to another."
—Albert Einstein.

Einstein theorized that one can neither create nor destroy energy.

A family surrounded the deathbed of an eighty-eight-year-old man. A priest administered the last-rites sacrament to the man. Feeling helpless, the nurse checked various meters and confirmed to herself the man was dying.

The man's daughter held his left hand in her right. Her left hand held her brother's hand, and he held the hand of the man's niece. The niece's other handheld the right hand of the dying man, finishing the chain of hands.

The room was quiet except for the murmuring of an oxygen machine, the occasional beep from the machine registering each heartbeat, and the low-toned Latin coming from the priest as he anointed the man's forehead, lips, and chest with holy oils. All eyes were on the man whose labored breathing was a sign of impending death.

Then the last breath.

With the final puff of air expelled, the heart monitor registered a single tone with no beat. At that time, the family, united by the holding of hands, felt a strange sensation as it traveled through the connected chain of hands through their arms.

The daughter said, "Did you feel that?"

Her brother nodded. "Like a mild electrical charge?"

The niece confirmed, "I felt it too."

The sensation left as quickly as it arrived.

What just occurred? No matter what one might call it, the electrical current felt was real. Afterward, the family insisted it was energy leaving the man at the moment of death. Just energy? Or was it the soul leaving for a location of eternal existence?

Theologians, scientists, and doctors have debated and theorized for ages to try to answer the question:

Do humans have souls?

This story took us on an extraordinary young woman's journey. Coby Rodriguez was a fighter from birth to death, defying the odds from struggling to be born to saving the world. She encountered situations of staggering odds and fought every one of them. She did it alone, or did she?

IN THE BEGINNING

In the late 1920s, Naguabo was a sleepy fishing village on the east coast of Puerto Rico. Artists from all over the world came to capture the idyllic blend of beaches, palm trees, and the ocean lined with silhouettes of traditional fishing boats. For centuries, men there had only one trade: fishing. The role of the women was split between taking care of the family and creating and mending fishing nets.

Alberto Ferdinando Rodriguez, born in 1926, lived where the sun shone 318 days a year with water temperatures hovering in the eighty-degrees-plus range. Most of his schooling was in the school of fishing. As a young handsome teenager, Alberto and his six brothers were up before the sun rose, then went to the docks and readied the boats for another day or two of fishing. They spent their days on the fishing vessel captained by their father, Jose. Sometimes the catch was bountiful, and when they returned, nets of largemouth, yellowtail, peacock bass, shrimp, and dozens of varieties of edible seafood were readied for sale.

Upon return to shore, the fish were packed in ice and driven to Loiza, the collection point for fishermen throughout the island. The merchants from all sectors of the island converged to buy the fish to stock their shelves for the busy markets in San Juan, Havana, and Miami.

Alberto's mother, Conchetta, had attempted to teach her boys English and basic math. She figured that if they appeared to be educated no one would know the difference. The daily chores were a dichotomy of being the same yet never being the same. Yes, stringing the nets, and polishing the boat were mundane, but once at sea, it was never boring. Every condition of the sea was unpredictable, and each pull of the net was exciting to know that the fruits of their labor yielded such wonderful delicacies for many to enjoy.

All was going well until the Second World War energized the United States to beef up its military status to fight wars on two continents. It seemed the Army and Air Force had the means to stage military exercises on land and in the air in secluded areas, but the Navy needed water, land, and sea to exercise their military prowess. The Navy searched all the friendly seas to find a spot to test old and new armaments without interruption. A place where the marines could land amphibious boats. A place where Navy airmen could perform target practice on land and in the air.

After searching the US and its territories, an island, Vieques, forty-five kilometers east of Naguabo, became the Navy's whipping boy. Beginning in 1941, day and night the strafes and bombing never stopped. On the shore, the fishermen saw the sky light up. Some called it July Fourth fireworks every night of the year. Pretty to watch but devastating to the local inhabitants in the fishing villages on the eastern shores of Puerto Rico. If a fishing boat mistakenly approached the island, the Navy would send patrol boats out to chase them away. If the patrol did not get there in time, the Navy scrambled planes out to scare them away. The aircraft would swoop down to around five hundred feet then ascend with the rapid response of an eagle.

There was one incident when Alberto's brothers, Hector and Filipe, tried out one of the speedier new boats and crossed the danger line near the island. The brothers saw the incoming war planes and reacted with fear and anger. Filipe jumped in the water and Hector did a sign of the cross, and, as a contradiction, raised his fist and cursed the jets, "Loco hijo de puta!"

The pilots saw the action and considered it to be humorous. "Guess they'll never come around these parts again."

"Roger that!"

When the brothers reached the shore, they told their story to the entire family who was already peeved that the Navy was hurting their ability to fish in abundance. All of them took this in and reacted negatively, except for Alberto. He was always impressed by the strength and agility of the United States military.

One afternoon, Alberto entered the cucina where his mother was busy preparing the evening dinner. "Momma, sit down please."

Concerned that Alberto was in some type of trouble, she pulled out a chair and sat.

"We cannot make a living fishing, and for that matter, making boats will fail because there is no money for the people to buy them, and after they buy them there is no fish to catch to make the money to pay it off. I have made a decision. Momma, I will soon be seventeen. I must go to the mainland to search for my destiny. I dream to be in America, and I have but one life to live. As I make a good living, I will send you money to use for a good living too." Alberto was amazed at what he heard next.

"I understand, Alberto. I will not stand in your way. You must seek your fortune in America, find a Puerto Rican girl, have children, and settle there. You can always visit." Tears welled up in her eyes. "Your family will be here for you."

Alberto threw his arms around his mother and lifted her from the chair. "Momma, I will always remember these words of encouragement. I will not disappoint you. My first baby girl will be named Conchetta after you. Please give me Aunt Gilda's phone number in Philadelphia. I will visit her first. I'll contact her and tell her I am coming."

"I am sure she will welcome you. She writes me and says she is alone in a big house. I am sure she will find room for you to stay. I am proud of you for making such a bold move. When you are settled there, I would like to visit the United States. Alberto, let us have one more night of celebration with the entire family before you leave."

The celebration lasted two days. Alberto said his goodbyes

and was driven to San Juan's airport where he bought a one-way ticket to Philadelphia, Pennsylvania. As the plane left the ground, Alberto looked out the window to say farewell to home. He looked up and said a prayer that he was doing the right thing.

Around the same time, on another side of the Earth, some six thousand miles away, in Jubayl, a very old village located north of Beirut, Dina Murad, fifteen years old, experienced horrifying sights. Although there were signs of change, it was changing at the speed of a glacier. To be a woman in Lebanon was to constantly fight for freedom and respect. Dina watched her mother be tormented by her father. He never laid a hand on her. He did not have to resort to physical punishment to inflict pain. He would beat her down with his words and tone.

Dina wondered why females were not allowed to vote or drive. It just did not make sense to her.

Whenever possible, Dina would meet up with her female friends at a coffee shop in the local village and discuss every subject possible, even politics. The most progressive of her friends, Leisha, would sneak copies of Western magazines for the group to look at and laugh at the crazy dresses, drool over the dreamy male celebrities, and get a vicarious taste of Western freedom. The magazines were all in English. The one Dina liked the best was "World View." They covered stories from around the world.

Dina attended a nice school where the students were taught English, economics, and cooking. She excelled in all her subjects. She was so proud of herself when she won a prize for the best kibbeh, meatballs that were the favorite dish in the Murad household.

Dina would find herself daydreaming over what it would be like to raise a family in the Western world. Could she do it? Could she wear provocative clothes, go to clubs, dance, drive a car, and vote? Basically, be free to do anything she desired? Dina was always a dreamer.

She and her family were devout Maronite Christians, which was closely affiliated with the Roman Catholic Church. Her daily solace came in the local church. At one point she even thought of becoming a Maronite Sister of the Poor. She knew she had the fortitude to accomplish anything she wanted.

As she became older, the treatment of women became more onerous. Many were frightened to walk the streets at night. Crimes against women surged. The number of rapes and beatings climbed every year during her teenage years. Many of the women her age and older moved to Beirut where the climate was more liberal for females.

Islam was the primary religion in the country, and although Christian, she did feel a certain comfort hearing the Muslim evening prayers amplified by speakers in and around the area.

As her heart yearned for Western ideals, Dina was losing affiliation with her country. She felt imprisoned in her village.

One morning doing a chore, she left her home to go to the bakery to buy some fresh bread. After, she walked to the outdoor market to select good fruits and vegetables for her mother and father.

A large commotion caught her attention as a group of people had formed a large circle in the center of the dirt street. Her curiosity took over, so she walked over to see what was attracting so many people. When she was close enough, she witnessed three men in white robes lashing the body of a woman who was accused of adultery.

Blood was everywhere. Dina wanted to scream, "STOP!" but caught her emotions when she saw in her mind her own body in the street subjected to dozens of lashes.

This is barbaric! she thought. *I cannot stay here. I must go to a place where this barbaric violence is not allowed.*

The next day with her friends at the coffee shop, she tore out the page of the "World View" that had the names and contact information of the magazine publishers and staff in New York City. That evening she wrote a letter, went to the library, and mailed it to the address provided on that page.

To whom it may concern:

My name is Dina Murad, a teenager in Lebanon. The women in my country are not free and are desperate to be safe. Just yesterday, I saw a woman lashed near death for adultery. I know there is a better life for me. Can you help?

Dina would run to the library twice a day to see if she had a reply. Twelve days later, she received a letter response:

Dear Ms. Murad,

I shared your letter with my Editor who sat down with the publisher. They discussed sponsoring you to visit the United States on a special Visa. We would like to do a story on you and the life of a young woman in Lebanon. If you are interested, we can ask the US Consulate to arrange the travel documents and have them ready for you at their offices in Beirut. Please respond within 14 days.

Sincerely, Jane McCarthy, Manager, World View Magazine.

Dina could not believe her eyes and immediately approached her father and mother and told them the amazing news.

To her dismay, both parents vehemently said no with unending excuses: "Too young," "They will eat you up," "There is a crime on every corner," and "Only the rich survive." In all, they contributed more than a dozen reasons to stay put and remain among the oppressed.

When she needed solace, she went to the local church and prayed in front of the statue of the Blessed Virgin Mary. "Blessed Mother, I love my parents, but they do not understand. I have one life and I do not want to spend it here. There is a better calling for me. I know it. I feel it. Please give me a sign."

Out of the silence, a fluttering noise disturbed her attention. Behind the altar arose a white dove, a symbol of peace. In her young years, she had never seen anything like this. She immediately took it as a sign.

Dina ran home, took out the letter from the magazine, scurried over to the library, and mailed Jane McCarthy the following:

Dear Ms. McCarthy,
  I am on my way. Please alert the consulate.
  Respectfully,
  Dina Murad

The United States Consulate in Beirut was a small white building in the heart of the city. Smartly dressed Marines guarded the building holding automatic weapons ready to be used at any time. Dina observed how every car was checked from underneath the chassis for explosives. A pole with a mirror was swept under the car and the underbelly of the car was visible in the mirror.

When she arrived, she presented the letter to a guard positioned in a small sentry building to the side of the gate.

The Marine called a number and discussed the situation for a minute then gave the signal to open the gate to allow her entry to the property.

Dina followed Ms. McCarthy's instructions, and since she spoke English, it was easy to navigate through the corridors of the building. A female Marine pointed her to the correct office.

Inside the plain office, Dina showed the letter to a local woman behind a counter. The woman was Lebanese and conversed with Dina fluidly. The woman left for a moment and returned with a file folder with Dina's name printed on a white tab affixed to it. At the top of the paperwork were the words "IMMIGRANT VISA." The woman behind the counter looked surprised when issuing the visa. An Immigrant Visa was not the same as a non-immigrant visa. Her Visa meant she was in line to become a full-fledged American citizen.

"Good luck on your journey to becoming a citizen of America."

At first, Dina did not absorb the words until she was handed a booklet: "WELCOME TO AMERICAN CITIZENSHIP."

Making the sign of the cross, Dina looked to the Heavens. "Thank you, Blessed Mother!"

The plane ride to New York City was magical. She became an artist by giving form to the white billowy clouds. She chuckled to herself when she realized that most of the forms resembled sheep. After customs, she was greeted by the people from the magazine, headed by Jane McCarthy. Dina and Jane hugged each other. "Are you hungry?"

In her broken English, Dina said, "I had some peanuts on the plane."

"Follow me." The entourage went to a waiting limousine.

"My baggage?" Dina worried.

"It is already taken care of and is in the trunk of the car."

Impressed by the professional courtesies, Dina exhaled a deep sigh of relief.

And with a sense of accomplishment, she looked upward and said, "I'm here!"

Dina observed wide-eyed the size of the buildings, the expanse of so many bridges, and the broad rivers. The bumper-to-bumper traffic looked the same as it was in Beirut.

The limousine pulled up to the swanky 21 Club. Dina chuckled at the little statues of small men in different color shirts that lined the front of the building. Not yet accustomed to sports, she did not recognize that these tiny men were jockeys.

Inside, the decor was extraordinary. Every table was occupied with businessmen in white shirts all talking over each other.

Jane had arranged a separate room where it was quiet. They sat around the table, and they had an extraordinary lunch. Jane noticed Dina getting sleepy, and after lunch, she was escorted to the New York Hilton on the Avenue of the Americas.

In her hotel room on the thirty-fourth floor, her bags were delivered. She looked out the window and saw the hustle and bustle of a city that she called controlled chaos.

During the next two weeks, Dina was interviewed three times by reporters and taken to many sites: The Statue of Liberty, Saint Patrick's Cathedral, the World Trade Center, Broadway shows, and more.

What really impressed Dina was the air of freedom. Women seemed to be able to come and go whenever they wanted. Some wore skirts, some wore dresses, and some even wore pants. *Pants in the homeland could get you arrested*, she thought. This excited her. She began to see a rebellious side of herself. A new woman waiting to burst out of her body. She was becoming Americanized overnight.

During one of the interviews, Dina said she was an excellent seamstress and was able to cook chicken "a million ways. I even won a cooking contest for my kibbeh."

For the next fourteen months Dina did odd jobs at the magazine.

Jane McCarthy, a native Philadelphian, was a graduate of Saint Maria Goretti High School in South Philadelphia. In an Alumni newsletter, she read there was an opening for a substitute home economics teacher. The regular teacher was ill, and they would need a replacement during the times she was home ailing.

Jane knew Dina would receive a good Catholic school experience and she knew Dina would excel in home economics. Jane was anticipating that if accepted, Dina would have a good beginning with her new start in life. Thinking this would be perfect for Dina, as a big donor to her Alma Mater, Jane contacted the school and enrolled Dina in the assignment. Her donations paid off. Dina received the substitute position. The youngest teacher in the school. Some Seniors were the same age. That did not bother her since she always felt she thought like a much older person.

Jane and Dina were like sisters. Jane helped her find a small studio apartment near the school in a nice Italian neighborhood. She attended school every school day and sat in the teachers' lounge patiently waiting for the chance to substitute teach.

As time went on, the teacher's health worsened, and the principal, not knowing how long the teacher would be missing, promoted Dina to full-time and assigned her to the position of Home Economics teacher until the regular teacher returned. Dina was thankful that she learned English at a young age.

Teaching a class like this required very good communication. She was so good that when the regular teacher resigned, Dina was given a job with a better salary. Jane McCarthy felt that everything to this point had been worth the effort.

That night after prayers, Dina celebrated her new, better-paying employment. She looked in the mirror and thought to herself, *When I turned eighteen two months ago, I was wondering if my life would ever amount to anything.*

By this time, Alberto was now living with Aunt Gilda in a row home on the 1600 block of Bancroft Street in South Philadelphia. He did many chores for Gilda, and the two of them, being close in age, became very good friends. Alberto picked up a few side jobs as a handyman which brought in over a hundred dollars a week. He was extremely happy with his new life. Gilda introduced him to American Music. His favorite television show was American Bandstand, hosted by the ageless Dick Clark. He tried never to miss a show. He and Gilda would dance to the songs every afternoon.

Gilda was involved with the Sodality of Our Lady, a group of Catholic women who met regularly at the church and prayed the rosary with the open-armed statue of the Blessed Mother present. She would attend mass at least three times a week and always at the eight o'clock morning mass on Sundays.

Alberto would go with her to mass at St. Thomas Aquinas Church three blocks from Gilda's house. One Sunday in May, the high school seniors from Goretti attended mass at St. Thomas, wearing their uniforms with a ring of white baby tea roses worn on their heads. Catholics around the world celebrated the Blessed Virgin Mary during the month of May.

The inside of the church was beautiful: Frescos, stained-glass windows, pure Italian marble altar with statues on the sides of Saint Thomas, Saint Anthony, and Saint Michael. The hand-painted "Stations of the Cross" plaques adorned the side walls.

The hymns were equally beautiful. "'Tis the Month of Our Mother" was one that everyone knew the words to without looking at a book.

Alberto was dressed in a suit without a tie. He and Gilda looked like the perfect pair, although they would never think of anything else but being close relatives. Anything else would be considered scandalous.

Dina, who also attended St. Thomas, wore a light blue uniform with her own ring of flowers nicely resting on her smooth black hair. She looked angelic. Though she was an instructor, because she was still a teenager, she wanted to dress like her classmates.

Alberto knelt at the pew. He changed positions from kneeling to sitting and in the time that action occurred, he glanced to his right and saw Dina. He did not straighten his head and kept a leering eye toward her as she first walked into the church processional with her students. Something changed in him. His pulse increased, and he felt beads of sweat on his forehead. Those feelings doubled when she caught his eye and smiled.

After mass, the congregation was milling around the front of the church. The Spring weather was ideal. One might say love was in the air.

The high school girls were standing in an orderly line with two nuns and Dina stood in the front of the line. Alberto was waiting nearby until they would be given the okay to break ranks. To be ready, Alberto meandered over near the girls and as soon as they were able to go freely, Alberto approached Dina.

Gilda began walking home and saw Alberto frozen in his tracks in front of the church. "I'll see you at home, don't be long."

Alberto did not react to Gilda since he was now hypnotized by the beauty of Dina. "Hello, my name is Alberto. What is your name?"

"Dina."

"You are very pretty, but I can see you are not like the rest."

"I am Lebanese, and I am the teacher. They are showing me respect. That is what you see. I must be proper."

"Wow, that is interesting." He tried to search for words. "The flowers on your head make you look like an angel."

One of the students overheard Alberto. She whispered to her classmates, "This guy wants to get close to our teacher." The girls giggled.

"Well, thank you." Dina looked around and saw the girls giggling and she realized they were finding this humorous. "I am a bit shy, but thank you for talking to me."

"I will be at the eight o'clock mass every Sunday. I hope to see you again."

"I'll try to go. Promise I'll try, and thank you again for saying hello."

It was not long before they were dating. The meetings on Sunday mornings at mass were perfect. Since Alberto was always short on cash, a big date was taking the SEPTA public transportation bus into downtown Philly. Chestnut Street and Walnut Street were a block apart, and in the late Spring were lined with trees that gave this inner-city street a touch of color and nature. Both streets ran **east** and **west** and at one point the street boundaries seemed to merge and gave birth to a patch of green grass, pathways, dozens of pigeons and chirping birds, and benches for one square city block known as Rittenhouse Square. Dina and Alberto felt this was their favorite spot. They really loved feeding the pigeons sitting on the park bench, holding hands, then going to Horn and Hardart's automat for coffee to talk about the future.

They fell in love.

They'd laugh and talk about what they wanted for the future. Not all the dreams were alike except one: raising children. They both wanted a large family.

Alberto would tell her, "I'm not ready to marry until I can find a good-paying job. And buy you a nice ring."

Dina's immediate response was, "Money isn't everything, you know."

"I know, I know. After living with a large family in Puerto Rico, you need a good income. It is one of the reasons why I left. I saw how my momma struggled."

Teasing him, Dina said, "Maybe you will find a rich wife who will spend large amounts of money on you?"

"Great, I'm in love with a comedian!"

Alberto and Dina were a perfect match made from two totally distinct parts of the world.

Alberto found a job as a taxi driver. He learned the streets of Philly like the back of his hand. When he was out with his taxi-driving friends they would share stories.

Alberto's favorite story was when he picked up a sailor who had just returned from six months at sea. The sailor wanted to get home fast in the worst way. Alberto was very obliging and cut every corner to speed up the trip: Running red lights, jumping sidewalks, and of course speeding.

They cut over to a four-lane street with a center divider and got stuck behind a very slow truck taking up two of the lanes and holding up traffic. Alberto blew the horn. No reaction. The horn was sounded again and again until the man driving the truck suddenly stopped, exited his truck, and approached Alberto with rage in his eyes.

Seeing this, the sailor opened his door, exited the cab, and walked up to the angry man who was ready to fight Alberto, but in one right cross punch from the sailor, the man went down for the count. The sailor got back into the cab and instructed Alberto to jump the sidewalk and get him home. Alberto obliged with glee.

In September of 1946, Alberto and Dina were married in St. Thomas Aquinas Church. The wedding was beautiful. Dina's mother was able to attend, but her father had disowned Dina when she went to America. It broke her heart every time she thought of her father. She prayed that someday he would better understand.

All of Alberto's brothers attended with his mother and father. Hector was his best man. There was no honeymoon, but traditional wedding pictures were taken at the far southern extreme of South Philadelphia in an area called "The Lakes." A large expanse of trees and dozens of little lakes with many picturesque spots to guarantee the best photo memories of the special day. Limos were too expensive, so Alberto asked his taxi-driver friends to be the transportation. The line of a dozen yellow cabs winding through the streets of South Philadelphia caught the eye of many who could not believe what they were seeing. The Philadelphia Daily News even posted a picture of the yellow caravan on the front page.

Alberto and Dina had combined their saved money and placed a deposit on a home on 17th Street in the heart of South Philadelphia and in the St. Thomas Aquinas Parish. The fourteen hundred square feet were plenty for the newlyweds, but when used to house all the relatives who attended the wedding and reception, the elbow room was at a minimum.

Soon thereafter, at the housewarming party, the newly married couple lived up to their dream of having a large family and announced to all that Dina was pregnant.

The two struggled to pay bills. The fact that they were from two entirely different cultures sometimes caused a few flare-ups that never lasted more than an hour. There was no doubt that they were in love.

Aunt Gilda hosted a baby shower where all the neighbors assembled and gave Dina and the baby a crib, playpen, diapers and diaper pail, a mobile, and an assortment of blue and pink clothing.

Alberto was thankful that the Yellow Cab union negotiated a new contract that paid the medical bills which allowed Dina to get regular medical checkups then pay for the delivery.

Around the eighth month, Dina was very big and labored to do as much walking as possible, which the doctor ordered. So, they took a car trip to Wildwood, New Jersey.

CHAPTER 1

THE FIRST BIRTH

In 1946, Wildwood, New Jersey, a sleepy coastal village ninety miles east of Philadelphia and thirty miles south of Atlantic City, New Jersey. was the summer retreat for those who enjoyed the beautiful beaches, a myriad of things to do, and the food to eat while walking on the boardwalk. The extraordinary phenomenon was that the neighbors in South Philadelphia coordinated to find sections in Wildwood where they could all still be neighbors when they vacationed. It was not odd for neighbors who lived next door to each other fifty-one weeks a year to be living next to each other for a week in Wildwood.

This was a true blue-collar vacation mecca that was cash-rich with a boom after World War II. It boasted the cleanest and safest beaches on the East Coast and a five-mile boardwalk. Wooden piers large enough to hold amusement rides, including a one-mile roller coaster, Tilt-a-Whirl, and bumper cars, jutted out over the ocean. There were many carnival-type stands to win kewpie dolls by throwing darts at under-inflated balloons or flipping nickels on glass trays, praying they wouldn't roll off. Pizza and ice cream were the main food places, and although a New Jersey delicacy, Taylor Pork Roll sandwiches were always a treat.

Dozens of hotels and motels with enticing names like The Jolly Roger, The Bolero, and Diamond Beach lined the streets. In some ways, they all looked alike. There was an L-shaped footprint at the corner of the street, with a parking lot on the property across from a pool, complete with a Coke machine and an ice bin. Some even had a mini coffee shop.

On the Fourth of July, the town grew by the thousands with families who flocked there from New York, Philadelphia, and all points in South Jersey.

Dina and Alberto Rodriguez were two of the many people descending on this sunny day "down the shore." They had planned on being there for only a few hours to walk the beach and inhale the fresh sea air.

Sea birds filled the deep blue sky. Their moving shadows cast images on the sand, while the two-foot Atlantic Ocean waves awash with foam crashed never endingly on the beach. The little sandpipers were going through their ritual dance of avoiding the waves. Their little feet moved so fast it looked as though they were wind-up toys.

Dina and Alberto walked hand in hand near the ocean's edge with their bare feet being lapped by layers of water that lessened in power with each roll.

Dina was very pregnant. Their slow walk stopped when Dina felt the baby moving. "Alberto, I can feel the baby kicking really hard, so hard I think it is dancing the *dabke* inside me." Alberto had participated in the Arabic folk dance at their wedding reception and made a spectacle of himself. When he tried too many kicks in too short a time, his feet went under him, and he landed on his bottom. He did not get hurt, except for the embarrassment.

Alberto placed his hand on her belly and felt the kicking. "I think this baby wants to be born."

Dina took a couple of steps out of the shallow waves onto the dry beach. Reacting to a warm flow of liquid on her upper legs, she exclaimed, "Alberto!" They both looked down at her feet watching a puddle of fluid dampening the sand.

"Oh my God, Al, I think it is time. My water has broken."

Nervously Alberto told Dina, "Stay here. Don't move. I'll go get the car."

Alberto, ran through the sand tripping every third step to the street where the car was parked. He got in the car, fumbled with his keys, started the car, and drove erratically to a wooden barrier constructed under the boardwalk so cars would not enter the beach area. He maneuvered around the barrier and passed a large red sign: "No Cars Allowed On the Beach!"

The car swerved, winding through the sand to Dina. People on blankets scattered. Nesting seagulls were disturbed and seemed to take flight all at once. The car pulled up next to Dina. Alberto jumped out of the car to help her in. He then frantically followed the tire tracks he'd made to get back to the street, kicking up clouds of sand in the air with his spinning tires.

The closest hospital was Holy Redeemer. For Alberto, the ten-minute ride seemed like an hour. He honked the horn and flicked his brights on and off. He never stopped for a stop sign or red light. In one cross street, a bread delivery truck and their blue Chevrolet came very close to a collision. His driving reflexes, honed by driving taxi cabs, saved them from a horrible accident. For Dina, the ride felt like an eternity.

George Carlin once described drivers as either idiots or

maniacs. Alberto's driving would have given Carlin another adjective: lunatic.

Dina panic stricken yelled, "Slow Down!"

He shouted back with nervous excitement in his voice. "I'm doing the driving Here. You have the baby!"

When they reached the hospital, Alberto had one mission: get Dina into the hands of the professionals. The large red and white sign that screamed "Emergency Entrance" served as Alberto's beacon. He saw the goal line and it was under a concrete awning. Never removing his foot from the gas pedal, the car was moving too fast for the surroundings. Two people saw the car careening toward them, and their leisurely walk across the driveway turned into a sprint. Alberto never lost control. At the entrance, the brakes screeched for a second or two, a lot shorter than one would think considering the speed. With the car running, he jumped out, still barefoot and sandy, when he saw an unused wheelchair and commandeered it.

The intended wheelchair recipient came outside ten seconds too late.

Alberto helped Dina into the chair. Which was not easy since she was experiencing severe cramps. Once in, he turned the chair toward the open glass door, whizzed her through the hospital, past the security man, and directly into the emergency room. They were met by two nurses, who whisked Dina away. Alberto, shaking like a leaf, had to sit down for a bit.

CHAPTER 2

THE HOSPITAL VISITS

Dina lay in agony in the delivery room on a bed with a white sheet covering the bottom half of her body. Her feet were in stirrups and sweat poured from her forehead. Her screams could be heard from the room into the hallway. "God help me!" echoed throughout the halls over and over again.

Dr. Chandler was working on the delivery while the nurses and nuns were doing their best to comfort her.

Alberto paced in the waiting room. He was not alone. Two other fathers were pacing. They glanced at each other now and then with similar looks of impatience. The bond created among strangers ended when their respective babies were born.

Thirty minutes later, Dr. Chandler entered the waiting room and removed his skull cap revealing his red hair. Alberto had forgotten what the doctor looked like until then, but he remembered the fire red. He met him with excitement and a smile, which waned when Alberto saw that Dr. Chandler had a rather grim look on his face.

"Well, Doctor, is it a boy or a girl? I'll be happy either way."

"Mr. Rodriguez, Dina is fine and resting. Unfortunately, the baby was stillborn. It was a futile attempt to revive the baby. I am so deeply sorry."

Alberto morphed from happy to shock. He covered his face with his hands and sobbed loudly. Between the sobs, he exclaimed, "We want to have a baby. This is the worst day of our lives!" He gasped for air between each word. "Can I see her?"

"Yes, the attending nurse will tell you when the time is proper. Dina went through much. She is a strong woman. I am very sorry. The good news is you are both young enough to try again. Please sit. There is a water cooler outside the door, and, if there is anything you need..."

"Thank you, Doctor."

The doctor left the room feeling as though he had hurt a close friend.

A short while later, a nurse in blue scrubs and a cap covering her hair, entered the waiting room and approached Alberto. "Mr. Rodriguez, you can see her now."

Alberto followed her out of the room into Dina's room. He walked to her bed. Their eyes met and both began to cry. Alberto and Dina embraced.

CHAPTER 3

11 MONTHS LATER
ST. AGNES HOSPITAL – PHILADELPHIA

Alberto left his taxi driving when a friend introduced him to an executive at a sheet-metal company that worked with big companies like Kellogg's. They bent metal to make the housing for dryers, which roasted the billions of cornflakes that eventually journeyed to the breakfast table. His weekly pay doubled, and the health benefits were better.

Not too long after being at his new job, Dina became pregnant again. Once again, their hopes were elevated. At delivery time, Alberto found himself in the waiting room pacing. He repeated the rosary, which he held tightly in his right hand. The trip to the hospital was even more chaotic than the time in Wildwood.

Dr. Marra entered the room and took Alberto aside. "Mr. Rodriguez, we did all we could do." Although the doctor continued talking, Alberto, in disbelief, did not hear a word. Tears rolled down his cheeks.

Over the next six years, Dina and Alberto would experience four more babies lost to miscarriage or stillbirth.

The third loss happened in the second trimester.

The fourth loss was a stillbirth, and they were the only two at the cemetery beside a priest.

The sixth was a miscarriage, which occurred while Dina was in the bathroom. Her blood spilled on the floor and the toilet was splattered with blood, and the water in the bowl was crimson.

Death took the couple down deep paths of despair. In each tragic case, this couple of faith would enter the baby room they'd created and look at the empty crib. They knelt together in front of the crib and prayed to the Virgin Mary to please take care of the baby they just lost in Heaven with God. Mary in the painting seemed to listen to their pleas. This became a sad ritual.

They desperately wanted a baby, a child who would grow up with the finest cultural education. The best of three worlds: American, Lebanese, and Hispanic. A child who would make them proud and carry their love forever.

January 1965 was an exceptionally cold month in Philly. The civil rights riots of the summer of 1964 were threatening the safety of residents, especially in the north and downtown sections of the city. It seemed that the city was brewing for war. Frank Rizzo, the "law and order" cop, had basically told Mayor Tate to put the city in lockdown. Rizzo would eventually become the Police Chief then mayor.

The climate for people of color was ominous. The police frightened them. Crime began to rise in the Black and brown neighborhoods. The Rodriguez couple wanted to move from Philadelphia and escape the threat, but their finances forbade that desire. Fortunately, their neighbors all shared the same sentiment which formed a strong bond between them. *I will watch your back. You watch mine.*

The sheet-metal bending was extremely demanding work. However, Alberto mastered the ability to bend sheet metal into any shape the customer needed. The job was steady, and the pay was decent. His day started at six a.m. and ended at four p.m. He would take the Broad Street subway to and from work. His only bad habit was smoking cigarettes.

His doctor at the factory ordered him to stop smoking after he developed a chronic cough thanks to three packs of unfiltered Lucky Strikes a day.

On Fridays, during lunch breaks, Alberto played poker with his buddies at work. It was the only time of the week he had a social life with male friends. One day, while holding a full house, he held his chest and, panting, said several times, "I can't breathe!"

His co-workers thought he was having a heart attack and took him to Jefferson Hospital in Center City. He was placed through a series of tests and given oxygen. After a few hours, he was released. The consistent cigarette smoking had scarred his lungs to the point that they almost quit on him.

When he got home, he made a promise to Dina that he would never touch another cigarette. At the next poker game, he kept his promise. No cigarettes.

He switched to cigars.

In the late winter of 1965, early one morning around three a.m., Dina was awakened from her sleep by feelings of anxiety and shortness of breath. After a while, she recognized the signs all too well, she was pregnant again.

At her age, her gynecologist had warned her about any

more pregnancies. She was told the chances of having a baby were almost even with the chances she would die during the delivery. Her Rh-negative blood and previous lost carriages had weakened her uterus to the point that the growth of another baby could lead to internal bleeding that could lead to sepsis and potential death.

Being devoted Catholics, she and Alberto pledged to each other to have the baby, but this would be the last try. With another miscarriage, the doctor said he would perform a hysterectomy. They prayed that God would care for them no matter the outcome. Just follow the doctor's order to take vitamins, take walks for exercise, and rest, rest, rest, and pray, pray, pray.

Being pregnant during summer was very uncomfortable for Dina. Everyday chores made her uncomfortable in the heat of the city. Alberto would flag down the milkman on his truck who had ice that did not melt during the day. He would then come home with large blocks of ice to place in front of a fan hung in the window. The air from the fan would ride over the ice which in turn cooled the air. As summer passed into fall, the couple decided to take advantage of the cooling weather and take the hour car ride to Atlantic City. The breezes coming off the ocean were always refreshing. The salt air was invigorating.

In September of 1965, a very pregnant Dina and Alberto strolled along the same boardwalk in Atlantic City that saw many beautiful ladies representing states and territories of the United States vie for the coveted Miss America crown. Here, men would push carts for patrons too tired to walk, and

Alberto hired a cart so Dina could rest her swollen feet to enjoy the sights.

Atlantic City was quiet. The summer virtually ended for all the seaside businesses after Labor Day. Fudge and saltwater taffy shops, penny arcades, and the Steel Pier remained open yearlong to serve those who visited Atlantic City in the off-summer months. The Steel Pier was a big attraction. The biggest celebrities of the time would perform there, including Philadelphia favorites Frankie Avalon, Bobby Rydell, Fabian, and other pop stars like the Temptations, Count Basie Orchestra, and more.

But the perennial favorite was the "diving horse." At the end of the pier, there was an outdoor theater with a very large pool of water. At one end was a ramp where the horse would leave a stall and climb to the thirty-foot peak overlooking the pool. A lady dressed in cowgirl threads would mount the horse and on the count of three from the audience, the horse and the rider would plunge into the pool. People loved it. Five performances a day and at every horse splash the audience would give a standing ovation.

As they were being pushed in the cart on the boards, past the Mr. Peanut man hawking Planter's Peanuts, Dina noticed a sign on a storefront that read in dark red letters, "MADAME ZYRK, MYSTIC."

Dina tugged on Alberto's sleeve. "Let's go in."

"Where?"

"Here."

"A fortune teller?"

"Yes."

"Why?"

"I need to know."

"Need to know what?"

"If I am going to have this baby or another loss."

Alberto shook his head. "Waste of money. These people are charlatans. You will know when the time comes."

"Please, Al, I need to know."

She told the man behind the cart to stop and wait. She and Alberto exited the cart. The man explained he could not wait. Alberto understood and gave him money. The man continued along the boards with an empty cart waiting for the next set of tired feet to hire him.

Dina entered the store while Alberto found a bench near the railing with his back to the ocean. The back of the bench could be moved so one could swing it one way to face the ocean or the other way to face the stores. Alberto chose the stores, so he'd know as soon as Dina left the mystic's establishment.

Dina was greeted by Madame Zyrk, a forty-year-old woman with graying hair covered with a babushka. The room had the distinct aroma of incense. A black cat lounged in a corner of the room.

Madame Zyrk spoke with a heavy Eastern European accent. "Please sit down."

"Thank you, Madame Zyrk."

The room was dark with a preponderance of maroon, red, and black colors. The walls were covered with lace and frills. In the middle of the room was a small table with an olive-green marble incense holder. To the side was an even smaller table with a pitcher of water and a stack of small paper cups.

Dina noticed a rather large painting of an eye in a sea of pastel colors on one of the walls. For a moment she found herself staring at the giant eye while the eye seemed to stare back. She wondered if this was a trick to hypnotize her into believing everything she was about to be told.

Madame Zyrk broke the trance by offering Dina a seat at the table. "Please sit here."

Dina's pregnant belly made it difficult to sit.

Madam Zyrk adjusted the table to make extra room.

Dina took the now roomier seat at the table and gave Madame Zyrk her fee.

The mystic neatly folded the bills and placed them in her blouse pocket. "Are you comfortable?"

Dina was smiling and a little out of breath. "I'm more than seven, maybe eight months in. My doctor will not commit."

"I am a midwife, just in case, so relax."

This brought a slight smile to both ladies' faces.

Zyrk lit an incense stick and placed it in its holder. The room was eerily quiet. The smoke permeated the air.

"You are very troubled."

Dina answered emphatically, "I am."

Dina took a deep breath.

Madam Zyrk reached for her trembling hands.

"I'm a little nervous. My husband thinks fortune tellers are phony. So, you know, I feel a little silly, you know, telling a stranger my inner secrets."

"I am a mystic. Fortune tellers are gypsies. I already know you are curious about the baby."

Dina held a look of amazement. "How did you know that?"

"Well, you come into my sacred room very pregnant. I have many curious expecting mothers come in to see me and ask the same question. Is it a boy or a girl? But I sense you are different."

"You are right, Madame Zyrk. To get right to the point, I have had many miscarriages and I am scared to death that this baby will be born, you know, dead. We want a baby really bad, but my doctor said no more trying after this. You understand?"

Madame Zyrk nodded then lit another incense stick, placed it in the holder, and closed her eyes.

This stick was heavy with a cinnamon aroma. It mixed well with the first incense stick of frangipani.

Dina looked around the room. She was caught for a moment by the eye on the wall again. She shook her head and turned away when she felt the floating eye itself gaining her undivided attention.

Madam Zyrk went into a trance, meditating. An oscillating fan made the beads and lace on the wall sway, and when it targeted the beads, they hit the wall making a strange rippling noise. Nothing happened for a few minutes when suddenly Madam Zyrk came to life and looked directly into Dina's eyes.

Dina stared back with anticipation.

"The energy is telling me that for sure your baby will be born healthy."

Hearing this, Dina wiped tears of joy from her eyes. Excited she exclaimed, "Oh my God!"

Madam Zyrk closed her eyes again and smiled. She looked around the room, to the left then to the right, then at Dina. Gesturing with her arms, she said, "They are here."

"They? Twins?"

"No, much better."

Dina looked around the room again. Madame Zyrk spoke. "The souls of your six departed babies are in the room."

Dina responded quickly. "How did you know there were six?"

"I can see them. They are moving in and out of your body as tiny balls of energy." She stared, fixed on Dina's pregnant belly, then suddenly laughed, "Ha, ha, ha, ha, ha!"

Dina placed her hands on her belly. "What is so funny?"

"The souls are very playful, and I can see good traits in all of them. You are truly fortunate."

For a split second, an image moving so fast that it lacked definition darted out of Dina's body, past Madame Zyrk, and back into the body of Dina. Only Madame Zyrk saw the apparition. "This is remarkable. They really are all inside your body, inside your womb." She waited a minute. "They are quiet now."

Dina rubbed her hands over her belly. She felt nothing unusual. There was movement inside, but she had had those feeling before.

Madam Zyrk smiled. Then she paused as though she heard something, taking her into a trance. She said, "These souls are telling me they will protect your child for a lifetime. Like guardian angels watching over the good and bad choices in life. They will instill a spark that your child will always show. The spark is contagious to everyone who meets your child and when meeting people, the other person will become energized. However, I do see many challenges for your child."

Dina was puzzled. "Challenges?"

"Every human experience challenges and so will your child. The souls will protect the child." Shaking her head, Zyrk said, "I have never seen anything like this before. I have been told by my mentors that this is possible."

"I don't understand."

"A soul is what guides the mind. Bad souls can result in bad people, and conversely, good souls can result in good people. I have seen people where past miscarriages contributed to good and bad souls that cause an inner conflict. Those conflicts lead to uncertainty when the person is challenged. For an entire life, the good souls and the bad souls find it difficult to achieve harmony. It is a constant fight between good and evil.

"Fortunately, defying great odds, the six souls in your baby are of the same good nature and they will bond and blend with the baby's soul to form a spiritually heightened seventh soul. The number seven is very mystical. Very mystical indeed."

Madame Zyrk passed out.

Dina wiggled out of her chair. "Madame Zyrk, wake up! Please wake up!"

The mystic awakened. "I am sorry, I did not want to scare you. Sometimes I become..." madam Zyrk's head once again slumped into unconsciousness.

"Wake up! Madame Zyrk, come to. Here, have some water." Dina moved to the table with the pitcher and cups and poured water into one of the cups.

Madam Zyrk woke up and took the paper cup and a sip. "I am so sorry I passed out. When I feel there is something special, well it took up all my energy. I will be fine."

"Be assured the baby will be born healthy. Bless you and your family."

Dina was elated. "Thank you so much!"

Dina hugged Madame Zyrk. "I have to tell Alberto the good news."

Alberto saw Dina exit the store and got up from the bench to meet her.

Dina shouted, "We're going to have a healthy baby!"

They embraced and both cried tears of joy.

"She said the six souls of the miscarriages will bond with the baby's soul and the seven souls, working together, will protect our child's entire life."

They continued to embrace. Alberto looked to the heavens not knowing whether to believe her or not.

They resumed their walk when they heard Madame Zyrk in the distance yelling.

"Dina, Dina, I forgot to tell you. The baby is a girl!"

Dina and Alberto hugged and kissed. They looked into each other's teary eyes, smiled, and hand in hand they continued their stroll on the boardwalk in Atlantic City.

CHAPTER 4

OCTOBER 9, 1965
MYSTICAL INTERLUDE #1 – THE BIRTH

St. Agnes Hospital sat at the corner of two very busy streets in South Philadelphia. Founded in 1929 by the Sisters of the Holy Cross. Almost everyone from South Philly was born in St. Agnes.

The same obstetrician who was the doctor on the delivery of the second miscarriage, Dr. Marra, was in the process of delivering Dina's baby. The beginning of the delivery seemed normal. Then there was a complication.

"The baby is not cooperating. The umbilical cord is wrapped around the head." He turned to his nurse assistant. "We will have to cut her out. We don't have enough time to take her to O.R. Someone put out an alert for assistance!"

Dina was given an injection and passed out.

Alberto was standing in the waiting room when the hospital intercom system called out a booming message, "Code blue, code blue. All blue team members available to delivery room two, stat!"

Shaken, he ran into the hallway and down to the elevator bank. He entered the elevator and pushed the third-floor button five times. The slow elevator finally arrived, and the doors took an eternity to open and close.

On floor three, Alberto exited the elevator and was greeted by two big security orderlies working double shifts.

In the delivery room, Dr. Marra was preparing for the Caesarean section. "What is the baby's heart rate?"

The nurse said, "It is fluctuating between weak to none."

"I'm not going to lose this one." Turning to the delivery team, which included two nuns, he said, "Please start praying. The mother, the baby, and I need all the help we can get."

A second doctor entered the room with her hands held up with gloves on and surgically clean. "Where do you want me?"

"Once I remove the baby, please tend to the mother. Sew her up and watch her vitals." Dr. Marra reached for the baby and yelled, "This girl is alive, and I am going to keep her that way!"

The baby was removed, and a nurse cut the umbilical cord.

Alberto was forced to sit and wait for word from the doctor. He was anticipating the worst.

He looked at the clock on the wall and prayed to himself as the minute hand went around and around. He said the Our Father, which took fifteen seconds from beginning to end. He was on his twentieth Lord's Prayer, yet no sign of the doctor.

Dr. Marra now had the pale baby girl in his hands. She was not moving, barely breathing, and taking on a blue hue. He began to compress her chest with enough force to activate the involuntary muscles of her lungs. No reaction.

Not seen by anyone in the room, an eerie, transparent figure with no defining shape covered the baby like a cloud. Twinkling, star-like lights emanated from the figure.

Oblivious, the doctor placed the blue-toned oxygen-starved baby on a table and administered oxygen to her using two thin tubes flowing directly into the nostrils. A nurse wiped away the sweat on the doctor's forehead.

The unseen, ghostly figure completely engulfed the baby until it was absorbed into the infant.

The baby stirred. The doctor cleared her throat with his finger and miraculously, the baby began to breathe on her own and slowly turned pink. The doctor was ecstatic. "She's going to make it, thank God. She is going to make it." He handed the baby to the nurse. The tubes remained in the baby's nose.

The second doctor who was working on Dina shouted, "Good job!"

The little girl was sponged off and before being placed in an incubator, she began to cry. Dr. Marra remarked, "What a beautiful sound."

In the hallway, Alberto had switched prayers to Hail Marys, losing count after 117.

The praying stopped when Dr. Marra turned the corner in the hallway. Alberto ran to him. His heartbeat was rapid.

The doctor had a broad smile on his face. "Congratulations, Mr. Rodriguez, you are the father of a healthy baby girl."

Alberto fainted.

Two nurse nuns ran to him with smelling salts. They waved the salts under his nose, and when he revived, they helped him up, and with each nun supporting his arms, a wobbly-kneed new daddy was helped to Dina's room.

Dina was holding the little girl in her arms. Alberto saw the two and regained his strength.

Dina petted the tiny face of the baby. Alberto smiled and made the sign of the cross.

"Thank you, God, and my amazing Dina. Cannot wait to see the guys and finally pass out cigars."

"Al, she is beautiful. Conchetta Beroni Rodriguez."

CHAPTER 5

MYSTICAL INTERLUDE #2 – THE TRAIN

The first three years of Conchetta's life were those of a princess. Dina was an excellent seamstress and made sure Coby, which is what everyone began to call Conchetta, was the best dressed. Alberto was very proud of Dina's tailoring talents, and it saved him money. The Christening dress was taffeta and chiffon. Out of all seven of the babies ready to be set free of original sin, baby Coby stood out.

One of the other mothers asked Dina where she bought such a beautiful dress. When she heard it was handmade, she suggested Dina open a business making children's clothing. Dina took her advice and took on clients but only once a month. There were so many requests that Dina could have opened a store. The two hundred dollars plus material costs helped the family meet their monthly financial obligations.

Every year on Coby's birthday the family gathered and celebrated. When the Lebanese and Puerto Rican cultures gathered and mixed for a party, it could go on for days. Coby's first birthday celebration did go on for days. Dina and Aunt

Gilda baked cakes and pies. People slept on the sofa and floors. The laughter and spontaneous singing seemed endless. The highlights were many, but the levity hit the top of the charts when they found Uncle Lenny sleeping in the bathtub. Others had to use the bathroom, and they ignored him. He was out like a light.

Back when Coby was two, Uncle Lenny rode down the street on a brown-and-black pony. All the kids on the block got a turn riding the pony. Every neighborhood parent ran home to get a camera to capture this fun event. Even coming from a low-income family, Coby was spoiled.

When she turned three, everyone showed up but Alberto who was in Florence, Alabama on a sheet-metal assignment.

Everything had been set up for another rousing party. The banjos were tuned and ready, and so were the food and wine. The table was so filled with food that there was no place to even lay down a glass.

Friends and family were filing into the house when the phone rang. It was Alberto calling from Alabama. "Dina, honey, I will be returning late and will miss the party. The airlines messed up my schedule. They told me that a lightning storm is headed their way, so they canceled my flight. They placed me on a later flight after the storm passes. I am not sure how late I will be."

Dina lamented, "There is nothing you can do. We'll miss you here. The gang is beginning to arrive. We will have a big group here all missing you."

"This is why I love you so much. Thank you for calming me down."

The news disappointed the partygoers but only for a half hour or so. Uncle Habib took Alberto's role in strumming the banjo and singing the songs. Even Bingo, a black poodle puppy, was ready for another round of dancing the Bunny

Hop. Throughout the evening, the family would form a conga line, and Bingo, on his hind legs, would join. When the verse in the song said "hop, hop, hop," everyone in the conga line would take three short hops, including Bingo.

However, some of the fun nuances owned by Alberto were missing, like when he would act out, in pantomime, to the recording of "Some Enchanted Evening," and when he would hold the note at the end of a Sinatra song until he was blue in the face which was not easy for a brown skinned Puerto Rican.

When he finally arrived at the house at one in the morning, two taxi cabs pulled up to the curb. One cab for Alberto and one cab full of toys for Coby. It took a half hour to unload the toys into the house. All the while, Dina laughed, holding little awakened Coby, telling her she was lucky to have the best daddy in the world.

The next summer, Dina took Coby on a train trip to Atlantic City. Dina loved Atlantic City and loved to see her cousin, Rita, who had a house there. In the family, Cousin Rita was the rich one. She was married to the best mechanic in the city.

The train was the best way to go. No traffic, and no hassle, plus one could see the wooded pine forests, better known locally as the pines. Even though there was a fictional story that a human monster roamed the forest, the acres of lush green pine trees were beautiful.

"Train five fifty-nine is approaching track number eight. The stairs to the platform are now open."

"Here we go!" Dina took Coby's hand from the air-conditioned station out onto the sunbaked platform.

Dina futilely fanned the summer heat from her face as she stood on the train station platform. She plucked her damp blouse away from her sticky skin, embarrassed by the inevitable sweat stains forming. Any other day she wouldn't have minded much, but Cousin Rita was bound to notice such a thing. Dina had never doubted that she had married well when she married Alberto, but Rita had married wealthy. While Dina didn't fault her cousin with any snobbishness, she still couldn't help but feel that familiar, unwelcome twinge of inadequacy whenever she fell short of being presentable. An unruly lock of hair that wouldn't stay pinned up, a missing coat button, a scuffed shoe. All commonplace defects were amplified next to the opulence afforded to Rita.

It wasn't the screech of the approaching train that jarred Dina from her thoughts back to the platform, but the sight of Coby precariously walking the back of a bench like a tightrope.

"Coby! Get down from there!" Dina flung her bag to her other shoulder as she rushed over and plucked Coby up with experienced dexterity. She set her down and smoothed her daughter's new dress. Blue and white. A fine fabric. Hand-sewn by herself. Dina ran her fingertips over the seams to make sure no stitches had ripped. She'd wanted Coby to look stunning when she exited the train.

Coby was every bit of three years old: curious, bright-eyed, and ever in motion. She squirmed away when her mother licked a thumb and wiped a smudge from Coby's cheek.

"Where are we going?" With her fun interrupted, a pout clouded Coby's brow like a looming storm.

The train squealed to a stop beside them. Dina straightened. "I told you. We are going to Cousin Rita's house."

"In Lantasity."

"Atlantic City."

Coby balked at the steps to the train car and held back when Dina tried to lead her up them. Dina stopped. "You love Cousin Rita! She'll be so happy to see you!"

Coby wasn't swayed. She ducked behind Dina to hide from the train.

Dina twisted around to find her. "And this is your first big-girl train ride. What a wonderful day! In a short while, you'll be in a whole other city." Dina softened. She kneeled so she and Coby were face to face. "You know when I was a little girl, all I ever wanted was to travel far away. I loved being home with my momma and poppy, but the world was so big, and I wanted to see all of it. And yes, I was scared. But I wasn't going to let a little fear stop me from seeing everything there was to see."

Coby mulled this over.

Dina kept trying. "And if I had stayed home, I never would have met your daddy. And we never would have made you." Dina smiled. "So, you see? The most amazing things can happen. It just took a few steps to get there."

Coby reconsidered the steps up to the train car, then leaped up them as if it had been her idea all along. Dina followed with a smile.

The train car they entered was clean with brown leather benches that faced each other. The car was only a quarter filled with passengers. Dina was amazed that so many seats were empty, especially on the only train that started in Philadelphia and terminated in Atlantic City.

The last time Dina was in Atlantic City, she and Alberto learned that their seventh baby would be born healthy. She remembered that day as one of the special days of her life.

On top of the soft leather benches was a rack to place any baggage. Dina carefully placed her valise on the rack, but in true three-year-old fashion, Coby wanted to keep her Minnie Mouse suitcase next to her. "Mommy, my coloring stuff is in there and I might want to color."

Dina's response was, "Sure, sweetheart."

Dina sat on a bench with her back to the front of the train. Coby sat next to her. The train began to move slowly at first then picked up speed after it crossed the Benjamin Franklin Bridge.

Halfway to the destination, a fidgety Coby decided to get up and sit on the bench opposite her mother. Dina gave her a coloring book and some crayons thinking that would keep Coby occupied for a few minutes, but, as with most children, the quiet lasted fewer than ten minutes. Coby was tired of sitting. There was too much to miss not looking out the window.

Bored and restless, Coby stood up on the bench.

"Coby, baby, you have to sit. If this train makes a sudden stop, you will be tossed forward and could get hurt."

The scenery passed by so fast that the trees began looking like a green blur. When the train passed a family of deer dining on the grass near the tracks, the still-standing young Coby pointed. "Look, Mommy. Deer. Do they belong to Santa?"

Those words placed a smile on Dina's face.

Coby paused for a moment. "Momma, will we see Cousin Carol while we are there?"

"Yes, dear, Cousin Carol, Aunt Rita, and Uncle Willie. Now please sit down."

Unseen by all, one of the same apparitions that had entered the newly born Coby exited the tot's body and created a wall between her and the end of the bench seat. The cloud pushed up against Coby so that even if she had wanted to, she could not sit down. Coby could not see the force, nor could Dina see the force, but it was there.

A sudden loud popping noise broke the rhythm of the train's "ka-chunk" cadence, while simultaneously the loud unmistakable sound of glass shattering next to Coby was followed by a loud pop of the window directly across the train aisle.

The noise caused people on the train to look back to the end of the car to where Dina and Coby had been.

An older conductor ran up the aisle to their bench. He saw Dina clutching Coby in her arms on the floor. Broken glass was on the bench and the floor.

"What happened here?" the conductor said.

In a nervous response, Dina replied, "My daughter was standing on the seat when an object—maybe a bullet? —flew through the window and went out the other side."

There was a clean hole through the window on the other side of the car, but on their side, the glass was shattered.

Dina sobbed. "If she was sitting, she would be dead!"

The conductor shook his head and inspected the damage by running his finger over a piece of glass still attached to the frame. The wind howled into the car. The gray-haired conductor told everyone to move into one of the adjoining cars.

The conductor, dumbfounded at first, soon realized a small child was involved. Bending down, and looking at Coby, he said, "You okay, child? You and Mommy can move, and everything will get back to normal."

Dina wasn't so sure. She was still on the floor clutching onto her little girl and stroking Coby's head. "Are you sure you are all right?"

"Yes, Momma."

They and the passengers from the damaged car moved to the next car. Dina wasn't taking any chances. She removed her rosary beads from her handbag and quietly prayed for the safety of her daughter. The rest of the train trip was uneventful.

CHAPTER 6

MYSTICAL INTERLUDE #3 – HOLIDAY PARK

The urban street where the Rodríguezes lived had fifty-eight row homes. One of the City of Philadelphia's nicknames was "The City of Homes." The myriad of streets in South, West, and North Philly were all lined with two-story row homes. So, a fifty-eight to sixty-home block was the usual measure in Philadelphia.

For a child, Halloween trick-or-treating was always a bonanza. One bag was never enough. Fill the bag on one street, go home, empty it, and back at it again around the corner for another fifty-eight homes. Everyone participated. The neighborhood businesses stayed open just to give the kids items they knew they would like.

The sidewalks were concrete. The streets were asphalt with trolley tracks embedded. Big metal poles spaced on each side of the street held the overhead electric lines that fed the trolley cars electricity. If the asphalt wore down, it exposed the cobblestones that had formed the streets in the late 18th century.

In the summer, there were no swimming pools to be had. The yards were too small, and the public pools were over a mile away. Any chance for a city person to be near water where they could sunbathe, and swim was only reachable by driving. The closest one to them was Holiday Park, about a forty-minute ride over the Ben Franklin Bridge into New Jersey. The alternative would be the Jersey Shore.

The Rodríguezes' street was diverse with Latinos living next door to Blacks, next door to Whites, and so forth. Everyone played together, held block parties together and Dina, who was proud of her spaghetti sauce, would take tomatoes grown in the backyard of next-door neighbor Mr. Smith and turn them into the tastiest spaghetti sauce.

Dina never knew Mr. Smith's growing secret, but his "jersey beefsteak" tomatoes were the best she ever tasted. At the end of July and all through the month of August, Mr. Smith would give Dina bushels of those bright red tomatoes every two weeks.Dina would take, strain, and jar them for the oncoming fall and winter months.

She would thank him by giving him back a dozen jars filled with the thick, red, pulpy nectar. Then Dina would thank Mr. Smith even more by making him a pot of "Sunday gravy" with meatballs, pieces of beef and pork, sausage, and braciola. It was truly a wonderful symbiotic relationship.

On many of the summer nights, Alberto would sit on the step listening to the Phillies game broadcast on the radio with bottles of Schmidt's beer yapping about the world's problems with Mr. Smith while they smoked their Philly-brand cigars.

Coby and Dina could hear their hearty laughter, or the cuss words directed to the umpires from inside the house. "God-damn umps, they are as blind as a bat!"

This was radio, so they did not "see" the play but reacted

to the announcer's "Cloooose call at first. I don't know. I think the runner beat the throw."

One day, Coby, age seven, asked permission to go with the Cardillo family to Holiday Park for a picnic.

Alberto said yes right away.

Dina was more reluctant. "You know how much I worry."

"I'll be fine, Momma. Stevie, Chuckie, Marie, and Roberta are going too."

"Well, okay. Just do not go anywhere alone. And if you need to use the restroom, ask Mrs. Cardillo to walk with you."

"Okay, Momma."

"Promise?"

"Yes, Momma."

Holiday Park had a man-made lake in the center. In the middle of the lake were a deck with diving boards and a spiral slide that would toss swimmers into the lake. The total trip down the slide lasted only ten exhilarating seconds.

The Cardillo family car no sooner pulled up to the place when the kids, already in swimsuits, dashed to the lake.

Stevie yelled, "Last one in is a rotten egg!"

For Coby, up to this point, the only water-fun environment was under the spray of a fire hydrant or the garden hose in the tiny backyard. The lake looked immense. The deck in the middle was so far away, she knew it would be a risk to even attempt the swim. She now saw all her friends in the water. Marie, Stevie, and Chuckie had a good head start over Roberta and her. They had learned how to swim years ago on similar Holiday Park adventures.

Gaining courage, Coby ran into the water and began to take strokes that propelled her body toward the diving boards. Gaining more courage, she stroked even faster then suddenly her body began to sink. Her strokes became faster and faster, but it seemed the more she paddled, the less forward momentum. The strokes turned into flailing arms in the air.

Losing confidence, her brain reasoned that she was in trouble and tried to stand at the bottom to no avail. She was literally and figuratively over her head.

Her arms flailed wildly, and she swallowed water. She managed to scream "Help!" but the noise around her muffled her pleas.

She went under so deep this time she could feel the bottom. She gave herself a boost with her toes. Her head surfaced and she yelled again, "Help! I'm drowning!"

Chuckie who was halfway to the boards heard the cries and turned his head to see that Coby was in trouble. He was now on a rescue mission. He reached her as she sank a third time. Chuckie submerged and saw her body. In no time he was holding her, but Coby was fighting him to stay on top and not go under again.

"Hold on, grab my shoulders." He told her. In doing so, she placed her right hand on Chuckie's head which gave her lift but submerged Chuckie to the point that he was in trouble of drowning.

A lifeguard had just come down from the life stand and was positioned on the beach ready to take a break.

But he felt compelled to climb back up on the stand when the cloudy non-descriptive images of souls left Coby, traveled to the shore, and began pushing the guard back to the stand, unseen and unknown to him. If asked, he would not be able to describe the force, but it was strong enough to head him toward the lifeguard stand.

Once he reached his perch, he immediately noticed the troubled pair and blew a whistle alerting the other guard that there is trouble in the water. He took a surfboard and paddled to the two. He reached for Coby and placed her on the board.

He dropped his hand in the water and grabbed Chuckie by the hair. By this time the second guard was there to lift Chuckie, and the two guards brought their victims to the shore.

CPR was administered to both, and after they spurted out water, the two were left resting on the beach to regain their strength.

Unseen by all, Coby's guardian souls reassembled and reentered her body.

Mrs. Cardillo wrapped Coby and Chuckie in blankets that were used for the picnic. "My God, Coby, you had us all scared."

They all decided the scary incident ended the day of fun, and they returned home.

Coby told her parents about the incident. Dina's thoughts traveled to the words of Madame Zyrk about the other six souls. It was time to tell Coby about her mysterious internal strengths. Coby sat and listened to Dina's story. As difficult as it was to comprehend the supernatural phenomena her mother was telling her, Coby reasoned that the incident on the train and now the rescue were all orchestrated by something odd but real.

CHAPTER 7

MYSTICAL INTERLUDE #4 – A BORN LEADER

One of the fun things to do in the hot city during the summer was just hanging around doing nothing. There were street games to play, such as hopscotch, dead-box, wall ball, and pitching pennies, but after the first few weeks of summer vacation, those games wore themselves out.

Now nine, Coby and her friends, Marie and Roberta, loved hanging out outside Cannuli's candy store. It was around the block from their homes, close enough that parents did not worry, yet far enough away from home that the girls felt some independence.

Aside from an array of every candy on the market, Mr. Cannuli's store had a sliding-door refrigerator full of sodas, including Yoo-hoos, the popular watery chocolate drink, Hires root beer, and an assortment of Frank's fruit-flavored sodas.

The fad at the time was to buy Mallo Cups and save the paper coins found in each package for a prize.

The store also had an illegal pinball machine used for

gambling. The children were not allowed to play with the machine since it was without flippers and if the player was lucky enough to use the right body language to get the five balls in a row in a checkerboard of holes, Mr. Cannuli would pay out money. Sometimes as much as five dollars. Not bad for a nickel.

Occasionally, a police officer would visit the store and place his police cap on the counter. Dutifully, a five-dollar bill would find its way into the hat. A small price to pay to have the police look the other way while they knew illegal gambling was being conducted in the store. They looked at it as a victimless crime. Mr. Cannuli looked at it as a cost of doing business in South Philadelphia.

On a hot mid-August inner-city day, Coby and her friends were sitting in the shade under the candy store awning chatting about boys and sharing a cold orange soda.

Coby, in a dreamy manner, said, "Tommy and Stevie are cute, but nothing like Mikey. He has such beautiful dimples."

"Coby, what do you think about Tony?" Marie asked. "He's the one I want to marry."

"Marry?" shouted Coby and Roberta in unison.

In the middle of the boy talk, a red beat-up car pulled up on the corner across the street and two masked men exited the car, crossed the street, and entered the store.

Surmising the situation, Coby barked orders to her friends. "Marie, you run home real fast and call the police. Those men are going to rob Mr. Cannuli's store. Hurry!"

Marie took off running as fast as she could.

Coby turned to Roberta. "Take the chalk and write down the license plate number of that red car over there. I'll go see if Mr. Cannuli is okay."

Roberta pulled a piece of hopscotch chalk out of her pocket and wrote down the number on the sidewalk.

Coby walked around to the private side entrance of the store and, through the screened door, looked in. She was horrified at what she saw.

Mr. Cannuli was lying on the floor with a trickle of blood running from his forehead to his cheek. The two masked men were behind the counter taking money from the register. One of the thieves took out a gun.

"This guy knows who I am. He's old. Better him than me."

Coby quietly opened the door and moved inside to the back of the store, calculating the danger. She saw a tray of glass ice cream dishes balanced on a counter against the wall. At first, she hesitated then reached under the tray, upending the dishes, causing them to crash to the floor so loud that it even startled Roberta who was standing outside.

The surprised thieves looked at each other and took off after Coby who had already left the scene and was running down the street as fast as she could.

The men were in fast pursuit when they heard sirens and stopped to head back to their own car. The money they took from the cash register was flying out of their pockets and spilling onto the pavement.

The police arrived and arrested the two men and their driver.

Coby ran back into the store to check on the condition of Mr. Cannuli. He was semi-conscious. "Mr. Cannuli, you'll be okay. Help is coming and the bad guys have just been arrested."

The souls inside her were jubilant.

Coby had done this all on her own. A sign of leadership that would be useful later in life.

The neighbors rushed to pick up the bills that were scattered on the street. Mrs. Coangelo collected all the retrieved money and returned it to Mr. Cannuli.

Later that week, in front of a sea of TV cameras, the Police Chief of Philadelphia awarded certificates of valor to the three girls. The city was introduced to Coby Rodriguez.

CHAPTER 8

MYSTICAL INTERLUDE #5 – VOTE MERLINO

As Coby grew older, she began to have intense emotions and strong opinions in life. The family was deeply patriotic. Poppa would display the American flag on every holiday, even Easter. He said that he was blessed to be American and wished he had served in the military to show his love for the United States. He would always talk about the Navy fighters he saw fly over as a teenager.

On Veterans Day each year, the family would travel to the Veterans' cemetery to plant tiny flags on the graves of the brave soldiers who gave their lives.

Coby felt a certain kinship with the men and women in the graves. She did not truly understand why she felt this way.

As a teenager, Coby would read history books about war heroes and could not understand why there were no female generals of any color. Her pride, knowledge, and patriotism reached a level that triggered a dream to be the first female Hispanic-Lebanese general in the US Army. After much research, in her heart and mind, the only real path to her dream was to graduate from West Point Academy.

Her school grades were always at the top of her classes. She joined the Forensic Union and came in second in the City of Philadelphia for declamation speaking and first in debating. She joined the glee club, the photography club, the prom committee, and of course the military club. Her rifle marksmanship was always precise, earning her the nickname "dead eye." That moniker was with her forever.

When she hung around the boys in the neighborhood, she picked up the habit of cigar smoking. Her first romantic boyfriend smoked them. She never inhaled but the aroma was intoxicating. As she grew up, she seemed to like men who smoked cigars. She was never sure why. Maybe it reminded her of her father or just of a man of status or possibly her first love.

During her high school years, Alberto was stricken with colon cancer. Coby came home early one evening from spending time with her friends. When she entered her house, she discovered her father on the floor in the living room in a fetal position, racked by pain. Shocked, she screamed, "Momma, Momma, Poppa is in trouble!"

Dina ran from the back kitchen and saw Alberto on the floor. He was moaning from pain. Dina knew what to do. She called for an ambulance. Within ten minutes, Alberto was on his way to St. Agnes Hospital. Coby and Dina rode in the ambulance with him. During the ride to the emergency room, the two sobbed. Dina held Alberto's hand the entire time. The EMT had given Alberto a strong sedative to quell his pain. His face turned ashen, and his skin was cold.

At the emergency room, Alberto was immediately registered, assigned a room, and operated on within one hour. The doctors deemed it was an emergency. They were afraid that the obstructed colon would create toxicity that would cause his death.

Dina and Coby waited for hours in a room outside of the operating room. When they saw the surgeon exit the OR, they moved to the hallway and witnessed something they would never forget, no matter how long they lived. The doctor entered the hallway from the operating room holding a clear plastic case and approached Dina and Coby.

"Alberto is recovering from the operation. We removed two feet of his colon." At this point, the surgeon lifted the plastic case. Through the lid, one could see the colon that was removed. It was a mix of dark pink and red with what looked like small white roots embedded in the colon. "This is what cancer looks like," said the surgeon. "We think we got all of it. We sewed the ends together so for the next few weeks he will need to rest and definitely not pick up anything heavier than a toothbrush."

Coby could not take her eyes off the bloody mess of her father's body inside the see-through case.

"We will keep him here for four to five days to monitor his systems."

"Thank you, Doctor," Dina said with her voice quivering. "How will we know if you did not remove the cancer one hundred percent?"

"I know it is a worn-out phrase, but time will tell. He could live another thirty years or less than five. It depends on the hands of God. His age and the damage from smoking is a negative, but his heart and vitals are strong. I'd say on the plus side of five years."

Coby learned a lesson on mortality. It emboldened her

desire to attend West Point and help save the world. If the world was a better place, many more sick people could be helped. She was determined to make a positive impact on society. She had to do it for the love of her father.

As a young teenager, she did not date much. She was never really attracted to the "immature" boys. She took part in many charitable and community projects. Every Thanksgiving, Coby and Dina displayed their hearts of gold to help deliver turkey meals with all the trimming to Philadelphia families, shut-ins, and the sick who would consider that such an act of charity made them feel wanted. The Rodriguez women became their family for the day.

Alberto treated his daughter as the most precious person in the world.

One day, Coby took their 1980 Oldsmobile on a drive. When she returned and had to maneuver that tank of a car on a sharp corner on a narrow South Philadelphia street, she side-swiped a parked car. The Oldsmobile suffered the worse of the damage.

Shaken up, she told her dad.

Alberto hugged her and said everything would be all right.

The next day, Dina was walking down the street and noticed the dent and scrape on the driver's-side door. "Khalas!" She lost control of her senses and was ready to yell at and punish Coby. Later, Alberto walked in the door after work and saw Dina pacing in the kitchen. He knew what was about to happen. Dina wasted no time getting into his face. "Did you see the car?"

"Yes, it is difficult to ignore."

"I told you not to give the keys to Coby. She is not ready

for this driving shit. When she comes home, I will punish her. She will be locked in this house for months."

The unusual use of a cuss word coming from Dina's mouth upset Alberto. "Dina, please watch your mouth."

A heated Dina shouted, "Don't tell me to watch anything. She has to be held accountable for this!"

Alberto, in a calming voice, said, "Dina, I was the one who caused the damage. I took a turn too sharply. I'm taking it to John's Auto Repair. He'll fix it up like new, and he's cheap."

Dina placed her hands to her face. "Oh my God, Al, I was ready to kill her. Why did you wait to tell me?"

"I knew you'd be upset, so I planned to take it to John's this weekend praying you would not see it."

Shaking her head in disbelief, she scolded, "That's dishonest."

Alberto tried to pick up her spirits. "I'll solve this for you! We'll sell the car. We are still paying for the surgery not covered by insurance. We can pay off that amount and have change left over to put in the bank. Coby will get married one day, and I want her to have the best wedding."

Dina became immediately placid and hugged Alberto. She kissed him gently and wiped away a tear from his eye. "Yes, let's do that, Al."

On most Friday nights, Coby would take the Philadelphia subway to Olney Avenue, the stop before the end of the line, to meet Alberto. It was a ritual. The first stop was Max's Seafood House for oyster stew. Coby found the combination of oyster crackers, horseradish, and a bite of pickle that was tasty. Around the corner on Chew Avenue were the "Chew Bowling" alleys. There she would watch Alberto bowl with his team of fellow workers from the shop. After bowling, the men and Coby would move to a game room to play poker.

As she grew older, Alberto would let her sit in his place every once in a while. That became more often when she would consistently win. She had the perfect poker face and was darn lucky too. She became brazen one night and lit up a cigar and drank a beer while playing. As long as she was winning, Alberto turned his cheek.

Aside from her desire to lead and save the world, Coby was a teenager with normal raging hormones. At one of the Saturday night school dances at a Catholic boys' school, Coby and a few of her girlfriends went to enjoy the music and, hopefully, meet boys. The school gymnasium was decorated with flood lights behind color wheels that revolved and cast changing hues on the walls of the gym. Being the one social event for teenagers, it was no doubt that the dance was well attended.

At seventeen, a group of girls could find many normal things silly. Coby and her friends were hanging near the metal stands yakking away with each having the floor to discuss, school, movies, and the like.

Their conversation was cut short when a young man approached Coby and introduced himself. "Hi, I'm Russ."

Coby was quick to respond. "Hello, Russ. Having a good time?"

Without hesitation, he answered, "I am now."

The giggling girlfriends chimed in together, "Oooooh, good answer."

An embarrassed Coby quickly jumped in. "Don't mind them. Want to dance?"

Russ again did not hesitate. "Sure!"

Later that evening, Coby and Russ were in a 1982 red-and-white Chevy Impala embracing and kissing. The windows were steamy. "Uh, Coby, do you have a date for the prom?"

"Are you asking me?"

"Well, kinda, yes."

"Since I am part of the team putting the prom together, I have to be there anyway, so y-e-s, yes."

After a few more kisses, Russ asked if she had a car, then added, "This is my uncle's, and I was hoping you'd have one we could use."

"My poppa became very ill, and we had to sell the car to pay off the hospital. They were having trouble paying for the car insurance anyway."

Russ perked up. "We'll get a cab!"

She laughed. "That sounds like a plan!" Still, in an embrace with occasional kisses, Coby asked if Russ was going to college.

A blush-faced Russ confessed, "My parents took out a loan and filed for grants to pay the tuition."

"Where are you going?"

Proudly Russ said, "I hope Villanova. What about you?"

Equally as proud, Coby said, "That's easy. I'm going to West Point. I'm going to be the first Lebanese-Hispanic five-star general."

Russ reacted quickly. "Wow, that's a tall order. From what I hear, it is not easy to get into West Point, and very few become generals."

Coby raised her index finger. "That is a very true statement. First, you have to excel in your classes. Then you fill out a ton of paperwork, which I have already done. And then you need someone to vouch for you. But not just anybody. It has to be a mucky muck in the military or somebody like that."

Russ blurted out, "You mean a sponsor?"

"Yes, something like that."

Russ' voice escalated. "My uncle was in Vietnam!"

Coby looked at him with laughing eyes and they resumed embracing and kissing. During the time exercising their teenage right to make out, Coby saw Russ as a very nice person. *I've known this guy for an hour, and he is already trying to help me fulfill my dream to go to West Point.* Breathless, Coby murmured, "Happy you have bench seats." She pulled him down. They disappeared below the window line. The rest was what the kids in her school called "going to the submarine races."

Coby and Russ became a couple and saw each other on school nights to study together, and on weekends to go to the movies and the Saturday night school dance. Coby always had fun with Russ. She felt that he was the type of person who would make a wonderful husband for someone, but not for her. She was smart enough to understand that when they graduated and left high school, that will be the end of their romance. He'd be attending a swank college on Philly's "mainline" while she will be in upstate New York many miles apart.

As seniors in high school, Russ helped Coby send out a letter to every military college in the country, including West Point. She was accepted by two of them, but she never heard from West Point. This discouraged her, but it did not discourage her drive to fulfill her dream.

The Rodríguezes' row home was positioned in the middle of a city block. The brick-façade, two-story home was modest like every other house on the street.

In Coby's home, most of the action was done in the

kitchen. Dina was proud of her cooking skills and spent a great deal of time cooking and cleaning in her *cocina*. Her teaching of Home Economics was a great basis for her being in command of the kitchen. Dina's range of cooking spanned from traditional Lebanese food to Italian, Mexican, and Puerto Rican specialties.

Having Coby late in life, Dina was now fully grey. In the kitchen was Coby's favorite aunt, Gilda. The two were preparing the house for Coby's surprise birthday party. A large chocolate cake sat in the center of the kitchen table. Written in yellow icing were the words "Happy 18, Coby." Brightly colored presents and envelopes were piled on one end of the table.

Dina became frantic after a glance at the clock.

Recognizing Dina's anxiety, Aunt Gilda comforted Dina. "Relax, Dina. Everything looks great."

A nervous Dina said, "I hope so. Nobody is here yet, and she is off from work in less than an hour."

Gilda reassured Dina, "Everyone will be here on time. Jeez, all the guests live in the neighborhood only minutes away."

In the distance, the two women heard music. Dina said, "Gilda, it sounds like a marching band."

Gilda agreed. "Yes, it is coming from the front of the house, and it is getting louder."

They ran to the front door and opened it to see where the music was originating.

Heading down the street was a marching band with fancy convertible cars led by a red fire truck with a sign tied to the hood that read, "Vote Merlino."

Dina recognized the parade. "It's Congressman Merlino. He does this every two years or so."

Gilda chuckled. "So, it's obviously working."

"Looks that way. He's been doing this for as long as I can remember. The people around here love him."

Down at the end of the block was Foti's Grocery Store where Coby was pricing cans of food and placing them on the shelf. The aisles were small and could barely fit a mini shopping cart.

Now a high school senior and beautiful, with dark eyes, dark hair pulled back in a ponytail, and a well-cared-for and mature body, Coby kept fit by exercising whenever she was not studying, working, or going out with friends. She knew that a military school would prefer their attendees fit and ready for years of being pushed mentally and physically to the limit.

The parade had reached the Rodriguez house and was approaching the corner store where Coby worked.

Coby placed the last can on the shelf from a cardboard box. Hearing the music aroused her curiosity and she ran to the door, tossing the empty box behind the register counter.

"Not your everyday sounds of the city," she remarked.

As if on cue, the fire truck blew its siren.

"That's more like it." The sounds became louder and louder as the parade reached the store. "My gosh, a parade!"

The band, marching with uniform vigor, although not entirely in tune, played patriotic songs. Cheerleaders tossed their batons. Most they caught, however, some dropped in the street. One careened off a parked car.

Some of the neighbors hung outside their windows, waving hands and American flags, while some stood on the front stoops cheering for the olive-skinned, white-haired Congressman.

Merlino was a young-looking fifty-five-year-old with pure-white hair, seated on the trunk of a brand-new white Cadillac convertible waving to the crowd.

Coby was positioned outside the store on the highest step to get a good look at Merlino.

The Congressman turned his head and caught the eighteen-year-old's beautiful dark brown eyes. He waved to her and blew a kiss.

She laughed and returned the gesture.

He was taken by her stature and attractiveness and motioned to her to come over to the car.

The unseen, transparent apparition of one of her souls exited her body, swirled around Merlino's car on a reconnaissance mission and upon reentry gave Coby the courage to respond, "Why not?"

Coby hesitated with a reflection on what her mother told her about the souls. *"Protect and Guide."* She darted out into the street, keeping pace with the convertible, and shook Congressman Merlino's hand. He motioned for her to jump in.

She pointed to herself. "Me?"

"Yes, you. I want to show the world how close I am to the young people." The car slowed down enough for Coby to get on board.

She was helped to the makeshift seat on the top of the trunk next to the congressman. "I cannot drive with you for more than a block or two. Today is my birthday and my mom expects me home."

Merlino looked the other way and in a loud voice said, "Start waving and smile a lot." They both waved from the slow-moving car. "Birthday, wow! Can I give you a present?"

"Not really, it isn't a good thing, I mean—"

"Seriously, if you had a magic wand, what would you wish to have for your birthday?"

Coby responded instantly, "Having a sponsor for West Point. I must become a cadet. It is my destiny. Someday, I will save the world."

"How old are you today?"

"Eighteen."

The waving continued. From the car behind them, someone tossed candy on the sidewalk. Kids scrambled between the parked cars to harvest as many pieces as possible of candy as they could.

Merlino's tone of voice became a bit more serious. "What is your name?"

"Conchetta, but everybody calls me Coby."

"Well, Coby, do you know who I am?"

"Yes, you are our congressman. We just talked about you in our civics class."

"Well, I am honored. What did they say about me?"

"That in August two years ago, the FBI—"

"Coby, before I ran for Congress, I was a colonel in the US Army. I have a Purple Heart from Vietnam and a Bronze Star. How are your grades?"

"Very good, sir. I am always number one in my class for everything."

For a moment, Merlino became solemn, the waving slowed down, and he looked into Coby's eyes. "Coby, will you please give me the honor of being your sponsor?"

They both stopped waving and looked at each other.

"Huh? Are you saying you'll be my sponsor for West Point?"

"Yes, but you know there are no guarantees. I will do my best to help you get to your very noble dream." Merlino, a softy at heart, wiped a tear from his eye. The Congressman touched the shoulder of the man sitting in the front seat to get his attention. "Please take this young lady's name and information. I will contact her tonight."

Coby thanked him and kissed him on the cheek. She

jumped in the front seat, took a pen from the man's pocket and on his hand wrote her name and phone number.

The car had barely stopped when Coby leapt from it. Running as fast as she could, she darted over to the front step of the grocery store where Mr. Foti was standing. Coby enthusiastically shouted, "I'm going home, Mr. Foti! And I'm going to West Point!" She ran up the block toward home.

Mr. Foti waved goodbye. "Happy Birthday, and I'll see you tomorrow!"

Inside the Rodriguez house, everyone was hiding, waiting for Coby to enter. As soon as Coby ran into the kitchen, everyone shouted in unison, "Surprise!"

They were all there. All the people she loved and idolized as good folks. Aunt Gilda, Uncle Lenny, Mrs. Gagliardi and her son, Chuckie, who once saved Coby from drowning, Mr. Smith, Miss Teresa, the other next-door neighbor who ran a shelter for abused children, Uncle Habib, Aunt Salome, Stevie, Tommy, Roberta, Marie, and, of course, Mom and Dad.

Dina stood at the entrance of the kitchen with an apron on. Alberto was sitting at the table nursing a glass of beer.

Aunt Gilda tugged on Coby's arm. "Look, look at the beautiful cake your mom made for you on this very special day. I helped with the decorating."

Coby broke away and hugged her mom. They both had tears fall from their joyous eyes. "Momma, you really got this one over on me."

They laughed.

Coby went to Alberto. "Poppa, I have a surprise for you that will make you very proud of me."

Whenever the very proud Alberto heard Coby talk like this, tears swelled in his eyes. "My baby girl, you make me proud every day."

Coby turned to Dina and Aunt Gilda. "The cake is beautiful, and my favorite kind too."

Dina, Alberto, and Coby embraced in a group hug. The guests cheered and saluted the birthday girl.

Aunt Gilda attempted to get into the group hug. After dancing around for a few seconds, she barged in and all four were now in.

Alberto broke free and stood on a kitchen chair and announced, "I am so proud of my little girl!"

Gilda pointed out, "I helped decorate the cake."

Coby smiled and hugged Aunt Gilda. "I love you, Aunt Gilda. You have always been there for me and our family."

Gilda blushed and lovingly responded, "Thank you, sweetheart. You are my favorite niece. You know I helped raise you?"

Glancing over to Dina, whom she caught rolling her eyes, Coby replied, "Yes, Aunt Gilda, I know, and I love you. We all love you."

Alberto motioned for Dina to join him. He helped her up on the chair. For a moment they lost their balance and almost tumbled onto the table with the cake. Thankfully, Uncle Lenny was there to give them a hand to retain their steadiness. What made it more amazing was he was holding a full glass of beer and never spilled a drop.

It was now Dina's turn to address the guests. "Next year, our dear Coby will be the first one from our family to go to college."

Cheers erupted, then from the guests came a bevy of questions.

"Have you picked a college?"

"Are you going to a local school?"

"West Point still in your dreams?"

"Pick one that won't bankrupt your parents!" That one

brought a chorus of laughs.

The wine and the beer were now flowing heavily.

Coby waved everyone to form an audience. Alberto stepped down from the chair and now she stood on the kitchen chair and shouted over the din, "All of you, quiet now!" There was still some murmuring, so she begged for quiet. "Please, I have an announcement to make!" Finally, the group was quiet. "I have a surprise for all of you. You came today to celebrate my birthday and for that, I love each and every one of you."

Mrs. Gagliardi yelled, "We love you too." That comment elicited a round of applause and a few hoots.

"You all know my dream is to attend West Point. I feel like if I had a sponsor, they would accept me. Well, I just met Congressman Merlino in the parade that just passed by." A gigantic smile erupted on her face. "Ready for this? He's going to sponsor me. I'M GOING TO WEST POINT!"

The room erupted with cheers and the celebration really began. Hugs, kisses, and music...sheer jubilation. The wine and beer never stopped flowing. Dina and Gilda filled plate after plate of delicious food from the table.

Alberto opened a cabinet door and took out a bottle of Four Roses whiskey, something he kept for special occasions. Into shot and water glasses he poured enough shots for all the men. Raising his glass in the air he shouted, "To my daughter, Coby. The world will be in safe hands with her leading the US Army!" With that, he and the men swallowed their shots. "Let's party 'til the cows come home."

Uncle Lenny and Alberto strummed on banjos trying to harmonize to "Dark Town Strutter's Ball." Cousin Jose sang "Mack the Knife" wearing a straw hat and swinging a cane. Bingo, now old and slow but still the family's loyal black poodle joined a conga line to "The Bunny Hop." Bingo managed enough energy to hop on cue.

Although many of the friends and family had passed, and the parties had become shorter and shorter over the years, this party lasted for two days.

The next day, Congressman Merlino was in his stark South Philadelphia office on Castle Avenue, discussing Coby with his secretary, Anita.

"Anita, that girl who was with me in the car is going places. Please send for the sponsorship papers and while at it, check to see if the zero-tuition program is still in place."

"Wow! Yes, sir, right away."

Merlino, smiling, said, "I'll call her tonight and give her the news."

In the evening, Coby was in her room reading a book about Pearl Harbor when the phone rang. "Hello?"

"Hello, Coby?" asked the voice on the other end.

"Yes."

"This is Congressman Merlino."

Coby's heart began to pound so hard that each beat was amplified in her throat. Her fingers automatically crossed, wishing this call would be positive.

The Congressman told her, "I am a man of my word. I can tell you now all the paperwork has been sent to West Point. You should receive a letter from them soon. Being late for these types of requests, I'd give it a fifty-fifty chance. Good luck."

"Congressman Merlino, I cannot thank you enough for doing this. You have given me hope."

"As I told you in the car, there is no guarantee. Let's pray they have the space. As you can surmise, there are many who want to become cadets."

"Yes, sir," snapped Coby as though already in the Army and the voice on the other end was her commander.

They said their goodbyes. Coby, who occasionally found herself daydreaming, envisioned herself, leading a battalion of proud and strong men and women defending the freedoms only found in the United States of America.

The anticipation mounted, and every day Coby was eager to greet the postman and receive the good news in writing.

Day after day she met the mailman to see if the letter had arrived. One day, the South Philadelphia Review arrived. This weekly neighborhood newspaper gave all the local highlights that the big papers like the Inquirer, Daily News, and the Bulletin had no room to print. On the front page of this edition was a photo of Coby riding in the car with Merlino. This would not be the first time her picture would grace the front page of a newspaper.

A week after her birthday, Coby did receive a "Special Delivery" letter from West Point. Hands shaking, she opened the letter and read.

WEST POINT ACADEMY

Dear Ms. Conchetta Rodriguez,

Congratulations! You have been accepted in the freshmen cadet class on our fully paid scholarship program. Your acceptance will be verified at orientation. Please report at 0700 August 11, 1983.

Sincerely,

Dean Brigadier General Shane Reeves

With tears in her eyes, she said aloud, "Congressman Merlino, I will never let you down!"

CHAPTER 9

MYSTICAL INTERLUDE #6 – THE EXPLOSION

Civilization did not know it yet, but they needed Coby Rodriguez. Whether she knew it or not, every major international event added to her future and the future of the United States.

The world in the 1980s was amid an arms buildup. The United States, Russia, and China were in a battle to build the biggest and most destructive hydrogen bombs to ensure mutual mass destruction.

Iran held sixty-six hostages for 444 days. The Iran-Iraq war was at a fever pitch. Over time, the region would heat up and eventually lead to the Persian Gulf War when Iraqi tyrant Saddam Hussein invaded Kuwait, an American ally. That gave way to operation "Desert Storm."

Somalia was a mess. U.S. soldiers were dragged through the streets and their bodies were savaged. The light at the end of the tunnel was that US President Ronald Reagan was determined to end the Cold War. He met with Russian President Mikail Gorbachev in Geneva in 1985. That paved the way and planted the seed for better relations between Russia and the United States.

The Geneva convention gave way to hope that nuclear proliferation was now in check. The two biggest superpowers agreed to begin the de-escalation of the building weapons stockpiles. The "Cold War" was officially coming to an end.

Even with this hope, there was the issue of foreign and domestic terrorism. Racial riots sprung up when Rodney King was beaten on the street in Los Angeles, Unabomber Ted Kaczynski mailed and concealed sixteen homemade explosive devices killing three people and injuring twenty-three. Special postal stations were established to examine mail with the fear that anthrax could be present in envelopes addressed to the leaders of the country, and the Ku Klux Klan was recruiting an army of white supremacists.

Internationally, Bosnia and Herzegovina, the Middle East's religious sects, were at each other's throats, and groups of rogue maniacs were planning ways to conquer the world. It seemed like the "best of times and the worst of times."

During these trying times, Chi-Lah and Fahid felt emboldened that their plan to annihilate the infidels was overdue. The world held a collective breath that a new world war was inevitable.

Coby and her fellow cadets saw the disruption of the world's stability and imagined that this was the stage where her education and duty would be needed the most.

WEST POINT ACADEMY

The iconic university and academy boasted being the world's premier military school. It was beautifully nestled in the woods off the banks of the Hudson River in New York State.

Coby took the train from Philadelphia to ensure that she would arrive early for her orientation the next day as a cadet. Ironically, train platform number eight was the same one where her mom, Dina, held her hand and gave her words of wisdom to see Aunt Rita which helped shape Coby's mindset forever. All during the train ride to West Point, Coby was excited knowing that this ride along the beautiful Hudson River would be the beginning of a new life for her. The beauty of the passing scenery was a sharp contrast to the concrete and clay of the big cities.

The train arrived right on time. Coby grabbed her suitcase and exited the train, then grabbed the first bus that clearly stated, in back-lit letters, "West Point Academy."

At orientation, the class was told that their time at West Point was carefully designed to expand their minds, boost their morale, and teach the art of leadership. The speaker also let them know that more than forty percent of this class would drop out for a variety of reasons.

That sobering information did nothing to dissuade Coby's enthusiasm. She was beyond excited to learn military history, how to take and give orders, algebra, armaments, languages, and more. She wanted to be a part of the body of cadets more than anything in her life, attending football games at Michie Stadium. As a sophomore and junior, she traveled to Philadelphia to see the Army-Navy game which gave her a chance to visit with her family.

She became best of friends with her barracks roommate, Cindy Raymond, a perky short-haired blonde from Sioux City, Iowa. Her father, Dr. Douglas Raymond, an orthopedic surgeon, was credited with using his skills to cure many miracles. People walked who never thought they'd be able to walk again, and athletes with severe injuries played again. Cindy's mom, Margaret, was a part-time bookkeeper who never cared about anything in her life except her children. Cindy was always special to her. Margaret was one of those parents who bragged constantly about their kids. Cindy once told Coby that her mom would always embarrass her.

Cindy was a daredevil, and since Coby always considered herself somewhat of a tomboy, together they liked to do adventure trips. When they had time off, they would travel to the Catskills, canoeing and white-water rafting in the spring and fall, and riding snowmobiles in the winter. They became pretty good at trail-blazing in many feet of snow, barreling through fields, then steering to the icy lakes abundant in the area.

One night, they ventured out on a large frozen lake. The moon was dark. The clear skies gave way to a canvas of twinkling stars. It was pitch dark. The only lights came off the nose cones of the snowmobiles. The weather was frigid, almost always in the sub-zero territory. To offset the cold, they both had a bottle of "Snowshoe Grog," or, as Cindy called it, human anti-freeze.

Cindy hit fifty miles per hour while Coby lagged behind. In the darkness, Cindy, being a practical joker, turned off her light, leaving Coby in a sea of utter darkness. Coby, being no slacker would not be deterred. Working up the courage, she sped her craft even faster, pushing it to the limit.

"These Artic-Cats can fly!" She jumped the snow moguls that formed on the ice from snow and wind. She felt exhilarated when the snowmobile hit the mogul and for a few seconds, she was airborne. She did not like the landing. One time, she thought she bruised her tailbone.

Coby was fully cognizant of the danger. It was just a year

ago when one of the male cadets on an adventure trip with fellow cadets hit a mogul speeding in the daytime. The vehicle did a 180 flip and landed hard with his helmeted head hitting the six-inch-thick ice. The hit shattered the windshield into a hundred pieces. It wasn't the fall that killed him. A shard of plastic from the windshield had cut into his throat. From what Coby had heard, it was an eerie sight to see the sun's beam on the ice with a stream of blood snaking through the warming rays.

One night while on the frozen lake, Coby and Cindy saw what appeared to be a cabin on fire. They steered toward the red glow. Their curiosity kicked in when they saw the cabin had no flames. The air was so cold, the cabin wood was burning without flames. They moored their snowmobiles and walked into the cabin. The fact they could enter a burning cabin and feel no fear fascinated them. Coby, being a cigar smoker, made an analogy. She pointed to the embers. "Look at the edges all around. They're burning like a slow-burning cigar red, ember and all."

"Speaking of cigars, I have some Macanados in my sack," Cindy said while giggling. The two lit up and laid down on the floor staring at the ceiling of the slowly disintegrating cabin, smoking their cigars, blowing smoke rings, and laughing like two giddy teenagers.

On her first day, Coby learned that West Point was no ordinary school of learning. During classes, free time was at a premium. Even lunchtime was kept to a minimum with just a half hour to stand in the food line, fill their dishes, get to a table, eat, then take the dirty dishes to the conveyor belt. Tums became a big seller in the drugstore area at the Post Exchange (PX). Everything was done on the clock no one dared be late lest they be subject to disciplinary punishment like washing dishes, peeling potatoes, or cleaning the bathroom floor with toothbrushes.

As a regular practice, the officers would punish everyone in Coby's homeroom whether they violated the rules or not. One time, Coby and Cindy were both ordered to scrub the women's restroom with toothbrushes. They both took their assignments seriously until they made eye contact. That optical connection was all that was needed to show a slight smile at first, a larger smile if the eye contact continued, this time with teeth, then seconds later, the outright burst of laughter. That was another violation that got the two of them, and their class, doing forty push-ups later that same day. At the Academy, the cadets said, "You learn something new every day."

At breakfast one morning, Coby said to Cindy, "Wanna walk with me over to the PX? I want to buy something light to read. Maybe a magazine or two?"

Cindy was always upbeat and happy to follow Coby. "Sure, I need a few things too."

At the PX one could find almost everything. Coby was examining the magazine section when she looked up and saw Cindy holding a black onyx cross on a thin, gold chain. Knowing it was Cindy's birthday in two days, Coby revisited the PX later that day and bought the cross. She then sprinted across campus to the chaplain's office to get the cross blessed by a Catholic priest.

On Cindy's birthday, Coby gave her the onyx cross which immediately brought Cindy to tears. "This is so very thoughtful of you. I have never had a friend like you. I am a very lucky lady."

They became the best of friends and vowed to be friends for life. They even pinky-swore to it.

On one of Coby's visits home, before returning to West Point, Coby was able to have a private talk with Alberto. It was important to spend time with her father. She knew her dad was in health trouble due to the regular medical reports from her mom. All she could talk about was her dad's health.

Alberto was nestled at his favorite spot on the sofa. Coby sat next to him and held his hand. The coldness of the hands sent chills down Coby's spine. Why isn't his blood keeping him warm?

"Daddy, been with the guys lately?"

"I have, sweetheart, and they always say such nice things about you."

"They are kind, wonderful men. I was sorry to hear about Phil."

"Yep, one of a kind. He must have told the story about you getting your finger caught in the pinball machine about a thousand times."

Within one hour of returning home, Dina saw Coby in her room and entered. She pulled her aside to give her the sad news. "Coby, the chemo is not working on Daddy. The doctors are going to try radiation." A stream of tears flowed down Dina's face. She had trouble uttering outright that Alberto was dying. "Baby, your daddy is leaving us."

Scared, Coby asked, "How long, Momma?"

"A year. Maybe eighteen months."

Coby bucked up and made an offer that was not expected. "Maybe I should drop out and stay home to help you help him."

Sternly and immediately, Dina barked, "Don't you dare. He is counting on seeing you in a uniform in the military of the country he loves. He says the world needs you."

The next night, they all went out to dinner at a favorite South Philadelphia restaurant, the Melrose Diner, at 15th Street and Snyder Avenue. This iconic place was where people of all colors and creeds met to talk business or just practice the art of gabbing. They talked and laughed for hours, enjoying apple pie with vanilla sauce after dinner. That was one of Alberto's favorite food cravings. They would talk about it all the time. Coby noticed Alberto could not take more than two bites of his favorite dessert, and it saddened her. In better health, he'd eat the entire slice with two scoops of vanilla ice cream on top.

Coby learned how to be brave even though Mr. Cannuli would say he never met anyone braver. Coby proved herself to be a stellar student, passing every course with flying colors. West Point's US Military Academy's mission was "To educate, train, and inspire the Corps of Cadets so that each graduate is a commissioned leader of character committed to the values of Duty, Honor, [and] Country."

As a junior, Coby was called into the office of Dean Brigadier General Shane Reeves. That either meant a merit or a demotion. General Reeves was too busy a man to just have a casual talk.

Coby entered the office with a tinge of apprehension.

"Cadet Rodriguez, please sit down. Many cadets have excelled in a myriad of categories taught at this Academy. President Dwight Eisenhower and General Schwarzkopf are just two examples of the greatness associated with West Point. I am proud to say you possess some of the same qualities. Your grades and attitude are only outperformed by your military awareness. I have asked our training group to give you an important assignment."

Coby ran from the Dean's office to a phone to call her parents.

"Momma, I'm so excited. As a junior, I've been given the assignment to take a team of artillery cadets to Georgia for night-time artillery practice."

"Coby, you need to be careful."

"Yes, Momma, I'll be careful. Love you. How's Poppa?"

In a feeble attempt to put lipstick on a pig, Dina responded, "He's looking good."

Coby could detect a modicum of despair.

The Army had specialized fields throughout the world where soldiers could practice various weaponry. Forty miles west of Macon, Georgia, was one of those fields. This particular grassy field was over six square miles. The targets this night were two miles away. Sixteen long-range cannons were positioned ten feet from each other. Only four were active that night. The artillery cadets took turns firing the shells. The practice included firing in a pitch-dark environment. The shells used were not fully loaded to capacity with explosives. They used special shells that would not fly greater than two miles. On impact, they had very little powder to explode. This was mostly a test of accuracy.

There were teams at the target area to score the accuracy of the artillery weapons. The twenty-four-pounder howitzers could hit a target eight miles away. The weight of the powder that projected these shells was calibrated according to the predicted trajectory.

Coby stood behind the cadets and made notes on what she saw. After an hour of training, she would rest those cadets and order four different cadets to the practice site. They were scored on how well they worked together, the length of time to load the shell, the accuracy of the projectile, and most of all, safety.

Everything was going smoothly. Coby had seen what she needed to make a full report and drove over to the field tent to write it. Before leaving she gave the order to the last shift to fire all the unused shells. That would keep them busy for a while. The khaki tent was about forty yards from the cannons and a similar distance from the motor-pool garage.

Project Captain Cadet Rodriguez studied maps and evaluated the cadets involved in the test from inside the field tent, the sounds of artillery fire shattering the silence every fifteen to twenty seconds. The night was illuminated with each launch of the cannons in flashes that lasted half a second. Outside the tent were two buildings. One was the motor-pool garage and about a quarter mile away was the office and barracks that housed the commander and the NCO fire-safety team.

The platoon sergeant ran into the field tent, out of breath. "Cadet Rodriguez, one of the shell casings lit a fire in the grass, and it's spreading through the dry grass and headed to the garage and propane tank. Hurry!"

"Thank you, sergeant." Coby picked up a large mobile phone and dialed the commander. "Commander, notify the NCOs to assemble the fire-safety team and get over to the artillery field A-SAP! In the fire's path is a three-hundred-gallon propane tank. If it blows, the motor pool is toast."

In minutes, Coby arrived in a Jeep at the scene minutes before the NCO fire crew arrived. The shelling had ceased. The fire was ten yards from the propane tank. Coby jumped from the Jeep, and when the NCO team arrived, she instructed the firefighters, "hook up the hose and hit the tank. If that blows, we'll lose everything in the garage! Everyone evacuate the area!"

One of the firefighters took the hose to the pump. He turned on the water, but nothing came out. He shouted, "no water in the pump!"

"Turn the handle clockwise."

"I did!"

"Is it stuck?"

"No, it turns but no water is coming out. I'll follow the line to see where the flow is jammed!"

Two cadets seeing what was happening approached the tank now engulfed with flames. With fire extinguishers, they began to spray chemicals on the tank.

Coby saw this and ran toward the fire shouting and waving her arms. "Get out of there!"

The cadets did not hear her and seconds later the tank exploded with a force that immediately destroyed the walls of the motor pool. The two cadets were engulfed in flames and died on the scene.

Miraculously, the souls appeared to form a wall that shielded Coby from the fiery force of the explosion. The invisible figure pushed Coby away from the inferno kill zone, knocking her ten feet in the air and away from the blaze.

Those who witnessed Coby's flight through the air wrote of it as *if she was being lifted in the air from the force of the explosion.*

Coby lay unconscious on the ground with the fire raging in front of her. The garage was on fire and the cars inside began to explode. The dark Georgia sky was now illuminated with fire and explosions.

The base commander arrived and stopped his Jeep where Coby lay lifeless on the ground. He jumped from his vehicle, lifted Coby's head, and repeatedly slapped her face. She was out cold. Frantic to save her, he ran to his vehicle and removed a canteen of water. He ran back to the lifeless body of Coby and emptied the entire canteen on her face. After a minute, she opened her eyes and looked at the commander. The first words out of her mouth were, "I thought I was dead."

When she returned to the Academy, she asked for a week's furlough to visit the families of the two dead cadets.

She was amazed at how understanding the families were considering they would never see their sons alive again.

Coby entered a period of despair. Even though she knew it was an accident, she could not reconcile the fact that she might have made a difference. Clear the field? It was known that hot shells can ignite materials and that the water pump should have been checked before the firing.

In her mailbox, she received a notice to appear at the military court off-campus in Rochester, New York. Could this be the end of a career that never even got off the ground?

When she entered the courtroom, she noticed how different the room looked when compared to all the courtroom dramas she had watched on television and in the movies.

The jury box consisted of three chairs, all occupied by military brass. The prosecutor was seated at a wooden table to the right of the jury box. She and her Army-appointed attorney sat at a similar table to the left of the three-person jury.

At the inquisition, Coby was ordered to take the stand. Her testimony was articulate and very descriptive of what happened that night.

"Cadet Rodriguez, how did you come about this assignment?"

"General Reeves felt it would broaden my knowledge of weapons and exercise my leadership skills."

Coby continued to describe all the details exactly as she remembered.

"Cadet Rodriguez, do you believe that if the water pump were working, the two deceased cadets would be alive today?"

"Yes, I do."

"Do you feel that part of your duty was to check the fire-fighting equipment?"

"That was not in the manual I was given, but in retrospect, I wish I had."

"The initial report from the JAG officials labeled the unfortunate incident as an accident. Do you agree?"

"Yes, sir."

"Is there anything else you'd like to add?"

"Yes. Nothing is sacred and it would be nice to pray to God to take care of the maintenance. Routine **safety** checks of equipment **are imperative**."

After two intensive weeks of cross-examinations and deliberations, the three-person military jury found that the mishap was nothing more than an unfortunate accident.

Because of the incident, the Army issued a directive that before any future field tests in all the testing fields under their command, teams would be required to clear the building of any growth that would feed a fire and be doubly sure all fire equipment was in working order.

After that date, no similar accident occurred in peacetime.

For the first time, Coby recognized that she was pushed out of harm's way by an inexplicable force.

In her own time, she explored the "mortalism doctrine," the belief that the soul died when the host body died. This doctrine was not reconciling in her head. Her mother had instilled in her the seven souls prediction from Madame Zyrk. She recalled Dina insisting that the mystic saw things in the room and in her body that were described as souls from previously lost deliveries.

"Coby baby, Madame Zyrk saw those souls. She counted

them. Six of them she said. Coby, I never gave her a number of the babies I lost at birth, but she knew. She saw them. I know she did."

Dina told her that she was blessed because the souls were all good souls and that was very rare. "Many times, in my dreams, Madame Zyrk would tell me never to be afraid. The souls would never harm me. That they would protect me from harm and open the doors to the great opportunities that life can offer."

Dina never came to a conclusion but did theorize that the human body ran on energy. She followed Albert Einstein's theory that energy cannot be created or destroyed. The existence of souls then was plausible, and seven of them were inside her body or mind or both. Dina repeated the words of Zyrk which emphasized that there were seven good souls, and that "seven is a very mystical number."

Coby spent the final year at the Academy excelling at all her assignments. She could speak many languages including Arabic and Russian. She found Russian history to be extremely interesting and took every course she could to enrich her mind on the subject.

On graduation day, Coby and Cindy, in their white officers' uniforms, proudly walked down a path in the middle of the quadrangle. Both smiled broadly. Standing in the middle of the quadrangle they threw their arms and hats in the air and shouted with glee, "WE DID IT!"

Over the years following her graduation, Coby was deployed to South Korea, Tokyo, and Germany. She also received a promotion for excellence. She became First Lieutenant Conchetta Rodriguez.

At least once a week, Coby and Cindy would exchange letters. The last letter explained that Cindy was going into combat on a clandestine mission in Libya.

Coby did not feel good about Cindy's deployment. She wrote her:

Dear Cindy,

I miss you and all the things we did together at WPA. Please be ultra-careful in Libya. There are some mean people there and especially, since you are female, they will treat you like shit. Are any of the other cadets from our class assigned to the same detail? I just have some bad feelings about this. Of course, I could be feeling this way because my poppa is very sick, and my momma is holding back information about his health. Just learned that our precious dog Bingo passed. I'm very sad. Wish I wasn't so down, but then again, that is what friends are for. I am being moved to Germany. The Army always said I'd see the world. I'm due for a furlough and would like to meet you somewhere, preferably in Philly. This way I get to spend some time with Poppa too. Just let me know when you are Stateside again.

It's a small world. I met an orthopedic surgeon from Sioux City. I told him about you. He's single and gorgeous. The two of you would get along famously. Let me know if you are interested. I would love to be the matchmaker. For me, I have yet to meet a man who can sweep me off my feet. But I confess, I am looking.

Love, you.
Be extra careful.
Coby.

. . .

Months passed and Cindy never wrote back.

One day in the mess hall, Coby picked up the latest edition of the "Stars and Stripes" newspaper. And there it was: "First Lieutenant Cindy Raymond killed in the line of duty."

Coby vomited after reading the horrible news.

Later, she wrote Margaret Raymond a letter to express her deep grief:

Dear Mrs. Raymond,

I cannot fully express the pain I have over Cindy's demise. In my mind and heart, she is alive and will remain alive until the day I die. She always spoke so highly of you. You meant the world to her. I hope to meet you someday and I apologize for not being there for the funeral.

I keep her picture close to me all the time and even talk to her late in the night like we did at the Academy. Please take care of yourself.

Love, Coby.

CHAPTER 10

ABDUL BIN FAHID

Abdul bin Fahid was born in a village near Orumiyeh, a town that sat precariously close to the border of three countries that had been at war with each other for centuries. At one time or another, the people there were overrun by the Turks, the Iranians, and the Iraqis.

Although he came from a large family of four sisters and seven brothers, Fahid witnessed the brutal death of two sisters and four brothers.

He was recruited by a Kurdish army to fight the Turks and later to fight the Iraqis. Death and famine were everywhere. The people in the region saw that there could be some hope in the newly elected female Prime Minister of Turkey who was educated in the United States. Tansu Ciller was the first Prime Minister of Turkey and promised great reform in her country and the neighboring countries.

During this welcomed time of peace, Fahid met and fell in love with Katia, a beautiful woman ten years his younger.

Their wedding was taken from a page from a classic fairy tale. The idyllic setting resembled a painting by one of the Masters. The bride was decorated in white lace and yellow flowers. The two took their vows on a serene hill overlooking a spot where the river branched out into three tributaries.

Fahid was optimistic that his life would get better with upgraded living conditions, increased work at decent wages, and freedom. They had three children, two boys—Adil and Abdul—and a girl named Lidia. He was very much in love with his children and showed it as a very good and attentive father.

However, over time, the gap between the rich and the poor grew, and the people revolted, looking to find a better life and, in some cases, food to eat. The uprisings led to counterattacks and raids.

Fahid's family was not immune to the raids.

Fahid returned home after a merchant trip to find his house leveled to the ground. Walking through the rubble of the place he held so near and dear to his house—the place where he and Katia raised their children in an air of love and happiness—brought tears and anger. A homeless Arab, who lived off the scraps of food left by people in composts, and who was always in the neighborhood, told Fahid that he witnessed the destruction of his house. He said the soldiers came in with grenades and tossed them into the house. He saw Fahid's son running from the house engulfed with flames. After the invaders left, a band of holy people went through the town and collected the dead, and brought them to the center hall for loved ones to claim their remains.

Desperately Fahid asked, "What about the rest of my family? Do you know anything about them? I saw no bodies in the debris."

The stranger, shaking his head, said, "I only know about the boy."

Fahid ran to the hall, and when he entered, he saw dozens of bodies on the ground all covered with white sheets. The holy woman at the entrance sat at a table with a ledger book opened on the table.

She knew why he was there and asked, "Where is your home?"

Fahid told her. She looked at the ledger, turned a page, and ran her finger down columns of names. "Oh Yes, here, aisle three, tag numbers forty-five and forty-six."

Shocked Fahid asked, "Two?"

The holy woman bowed her head. "Yes, very sorry."

He was now on a mission, walking up and down the aisles of death. Then he came upon the aisle that had numbers that were close to the tag number given to him by the woman. This strong man was now leveled as a mere mortal looking for the bodies of his loved ones. Taking a deep breath, he knew he was close. He went in front and stood over the body only identified as number forty-five. He kneeled and carefully lifted the sheet to expose the body underneath. He cried out, "Abdul!" and reached down to pick up the charred head of his eldest son. There was just enough of a face remaining that Fahid knew it was his son. "What have they done to you?"

Gently placing his son's head down, still kneeling, Fahid turned to look under tag forty-six. Another deep breath, preparing his mind to see what other member of his family was now shrouded in white linen. Under the sheet, Fahid realized his worse fear was now real. "My love, Katia. Why did they do this to you? You are loving and peaceful. You are not a warrior. The pain I am experiencing is great. I will live the rest of my life avenging your death. I promise I will avenge your death."

He prayed for both and returned to the lady at the desk

and paid a fee to take the bodies away. Nearby, a cart only used to take the bodies away from this horrible place smelled of piled bodies rotting from the heat. Fahid, with the two bodies, returned to the leveled home where he dug two graves. No one could tell him about Adil and Lidia. He prayed they were alive and safe from the ongoing violence.

Fahid felt trapped with nowhere to go. He knew he could not continue to live under those onerous conditions. Fahid changed overnight. He abandoned his two-remaining offspring. He knew that to survive, he'd have to take matters under his control. To determine his true destiny.

In his first offensive, he commandeered a truck, slitting the throat of the driver, and headed west to Syria.

Damascus was a metropolitan section of Syria. Its name meant the "Pearl of the East." Ironically, his home was two hundred kilometers east of the childhood home of Dina Murad.

North of the capital city, Syria was overrun by armies of merchants whose philosophy was to burn everything they touched. That was after looting everything of wealth and raping the women.

Fahid was self-educated, especially in economics. He was well aware of the riches of America and the Western World and envied the opulence. Frustrated, to feed his revenge he needed to make money and lots of it. He tried to amass his fortune through stealing. That was futile since there was very little to steal.

One of his friends introduced him to an extraordinarily wealthy arms dealer. He learned the business of death quickly and began making connections to the point that he needed more and more inventory to keep pace with the competition. His supply was not keeping up with the demand. At one point there were over two dozen armed conflicts going on just in the

Middle East. Through his nefarious dealings, he heard that a Chinese merchant named Chi-Lah was the head of a very successful importer of weapons of all sizes and shapes. It was rumored that Chi-Lah had access to dirty bombs that could wipe out a large segment of populations with a double-edged sword. The blast would vaporize a radius of one kilometer, killing everyone in the radius instantly. Then the radiation would kill those another two kilometers in its radius from cancer and burns while destroying all reproductive organs. None of the devastating results deterred him from going deeper into the arms-dealing business. Taking a calculated risk, he set his business aside and ventured to Nepal to try to arrange a meeting with Chi-Lah.

Searching dark alley after dark alley, Fahid eventually found his way to an associate of Chi-Lah. It was then he learned that the Chinese master had a cache of weapons larger than that of many armies in the region. As fate would have it, Chi-Lah's most productive connection to the armies in the Middle East was found hanging in a monastery in Tibet, the result of people who did not trust him to give them the weapons they needed in a timely fashion. This left an opening for someone ruthless to fill the gap. Fahid sent a message to Chi-Lah that he had the connections to bring the merchandise of death to fill the void left by the murdered associate.

It did not take long for the two to meet.

Chi-Lah had amassed billions of dollars in arms dealing and opium trading. He surrounded himself with beautiful women highly skilled in martial arts. Their beauty was deceiving until someone tried to touch their Chinese master. It was said that one time, six armed assassins charged the home of Chi-Lah, and when confronted by the deadly beauties, never penetrated more than ten meters into the home. The women's swift action and nimble moves destroyed their intentions in less than two minutes. The woman who kept the beauties of death in line was named "Alwardat Alsawda," which translated to "Black Rose."

Word of the female guards capable of producing one-sided fights spread from town to town. The end result was that Chi-Lah led a safe and untouchable life.

Fahid would meet him in a park near the Buddhist cemetery. The surroundings were idyllic, the air fragrant with osmanthus and white Chinese wisteria vines. The sun cast a glow on the white frock Chi-Lah customarily wore. Fahid was kept at a distance until he was thoroughly frisked and examined by heavily armed guards. The female guards formed a circle around Chi-Lah until they were given the safe signal by the armed guards.

Fahid slowly approached Chi-Lah so as not to cause any misunderstanding of his peaceful intentions. When he was six feet in front of Chi-Lah, Fahid bowed his head, and the bow was returned by the Chinese purveyor of death, who spoke first. "I hear you have connections to the myriad war zones in the Middle East."

"Yes, sir," Fahid said.

"You do understand that the available position will make whoever is granted that position an extremely wealthy individual. The amount of wealth sometimes makes greedy men foolish in thinking they can move me out of the key role. To date, seven have tried, and seven are dead. I am surrounded by watchful eyes who will kill first and ask questions later. Fahid, I am considering you to fill the vacancy open due to an unfortunate misstep by one of those greedy people. Therefore, you will be tested."

"Yes, I understand."

"When you leave here, you will be instructed to drive to a place where you will meet one of my associates. You will be blindfolded and taken to a building that currently has fifty surface-to-air missiles. You will load those missiles onto a cargo van, again be blindfolded and taken to a road, where your blindfold will be removed. Then you will be given directions to take those weapons to a designated warehouse in Baghdad. The journey will be hot and dangerous, especially when others learn about the cargo you will be transporting. The exchange must be quick. The missiles are unloaded, and you will be given fifty kilos of gold for each missile. You will take the gold back to me and your reward will be ten kilos of gold for each missile delivered."

Fahid's economic and mathematical brain calculated his take to be well over twelve million dollars. It took him three seconds to accept the job.

"This is the first one that I will set up for you" Chi-Lah continued. "You will be on your own to represent me everywhere weapons are needed. You will become a very wealthy man. There is even a greater reward once I gain confidence in you." On that note, Chi-Lah turned and walked away with his entourage of trained female protectors.

Almost a year to the day later, Chi-Lah arranged every meeting with Fahid in his palace. This was the first time Fahid got to see where his leader lived. The streams of crystal-blue water leading up to the place were filled with rare black swans. The door was pure jade. Dozens of white birds flew around free from any harm. Chi-Lah, although ruthless, cared for animals. Toward the back of the palace was a zoo of exotic creatures. Fahid was led to the zoo where he saw Chi-Lah petting a golden-colored emu.

From out of nowhere a voice rang out, "Welcome, Fahid."

Fahid looked around and followed the direction of the recognizable voice. "Thank you, Chi-Lah, for the ability to collect wealth that is a fortune for someone as unworthy as I am."

Chi-Lah spat back, "Never say that you are unworthy again. Surely the millions you have made on the job have changed that primitive thinking."

Humbly, Fahid said, "Yes, sir. I will always consider myself worthy."

Chi-Lah motioned with his hands, and said, Come with me. I want to show you a plan I have constructed to make what you have amassed so far look like a few shekels."

They entered a dimly lit room where Chi-Lah asked the female guards to leave the two of them alone.

They obeyed, and Fahid curiously asked why he dismissed his protection.

"What I am about to show you, not even they can see."

"I am humbled to know your trust in me is deep. I will never abandon you. Your trust in me is sacred and I intend on keeping it intact."

"That is good." Chi-Lah walked to the side of the room, flipped a switch and the dim room turned into a well-lit big room with paintings and sculptures at every angle the eye could see. Fahid was never knowledgeable about art, but he could recognize that some of the paintings were originals of Picasso, Dali, Matisse, and Van Gogh, and he recognized a sculpture to be an original Bellini. He found himself staring at the marble piece.

"An original Bellini that was given to me in exchange for a dozen handmade artillery cannons to protect a palace in Mongolia."

"Handmade?"

"Yes, we have the ability to manufacture weapons made to order, so to speak. For some reason, our client felt it was worth the exchange of priceless art for the satisfaction that he now possesses cannons capable of firing low-level nuclear projectiles if invaded by an unfriendly army. Yes, along with conventional armament, we were able to deliver the nuclear payload too. Nuclear weapons are a Godsend for me and my operation. You will understand better in a few minutes." Chi-Lah picked up a remote-control device and pushed a button.

The wall in front of him pivoted around to reveal a map.

Fahid immediately recognized the shape of Turkey.

Chi-Lah took a pointer and circled a tiny island to the west of Turkey sitting in the Aegean Sea. "This is an island resort called Denali Island. I now own it and there are no inhabitants there." He moved the pointer slightly to the right toward the east end of the island. "In less than two weeks, construction of a control room and ten silos will be made right here. Those silos will contain intercontinental ballistic missiles capable of flying undetected for up to eight thousand kilometers. The missiles are currently being constructed in a place that I do not even know by dozens of scientists who have the same desires I have: to destroy all the capitalist centers of the world."

"Incredible. Genius. But what can I do to assist such a grand endeavor?"

"You will find and bring to me ten sophisticated nuclear warheads to arm the missiles. Weapons that when detonated will send off up to thirty smaller bombs to cover an area as large as the city of New York. Each mini bomb can deliver more than fifty times the destruction of the A-bomb set off in Hiroshima."

"I presume you know where these warheads reside?"

Chi-Lah gave a sinister laugh. "The two biggest nuclear powers in the universe have decided to play nice with each other and eliminate the bulk of their arsenals. Fools. They are out there just waiting to be taken. In Russia, there are arsenals filled with warheads that are left to rot. You will devise a plan to steal ten of them. That's all, just ten. Once in our hands they will be fitted on the rockets, fueled, and armed. You and I will be the ones who launch these weapons of mass destruction into the free world. Each ICBM has a target where the economic heart of the capitalistic free world lies."

Fahid smiled, and said, I like it."

CHAPTER 11

THE CONSTRUCTION

The construction began right on time. Regularly, cargo ships carrying workers from Turkey arrived on the shores of Denali Island. The island was small consisting of three areas.

The western side was the resort with its one hundred suites, a large infinity pool that appeared to overflow into the ocean, an eighteen-hole golf course, and a central hall with a bar, restaurant, gym, and a wing with two meeting halls.

The eastern shore was where the control room and silos would be erected.

In between was a narrow jungle that acted as a buffer between the two shores.

A fifty-foot electrified barbed-wire fence was constructed on the perimeter of the resort separating it from the nuclear intercontinental ballistic missile (ICBM) silos. A smaller fence separated the resort from the jungle.

The workers slept in makeshift tents as a part of a tent city that also had a medicinal tent, a kitchen, and a mess hall. Once in the morning and once in the evening, the men were bused to the resort for sanitary purposes, but they were not allowed to sleep there. When the buses returned, everyone was counted, and the list was checked twice. Violators would be escorted to the north end of the island and executed. The others were told the missing were sent home, and, in some religious beliefs, that was a very true statement.

After the men arrived, the heavy equipment was received on barges on the east side. Ironically, all the equipment was made by Deere, a one-hundred-percent American company. Materials shipped in included a small concrete mixer used to solve many problems, such as in-ground craters to house the fuel for the missiles and control building.

The control room and the chain-link walls around the area were finished in three weeks. The main construction was erected within the jungle and forest for natural cover. Those construction people were then moved to the construction of the silos.

A problem was discovered that could have destroyed all their plans. The silos needed to be forty meters deep to be able to place a cover over the hole in inclement weather to hold and conceal the loaded ICBMs, but the water table was thirty meters.

The silos were built in the ground. Concrete was poured into molds that extended the silos by ten feet. It did not matter if the sites were destroyed after the rockets were ignited and sent off on their missions of death. They would only be used once.

Fahid was given a progress report by a few hand-picked people who showed loyalty and ability. Those who did not contribute their part were taken to the north shore and disposed of.

Of the three dozen workers, a select fifteen were chosen to man the control tower. The remaining were taken to the mainland and housed in a makeshift prison. Once the annihilation was over, they would be released, given high positions in the government and more gold than they could spend in a lifetime.

The last to arrive were the scientists, the people with knowledge of rocketry and nuclear weapons. One was American Dr. Peter Torey, who spent many years teaching nuclear science to students at USC Stanford. In close and secret association with the University of California Davis, he devised experimentation on animals and their exposure to various levels of radiation. Being somewhat demented, he was thrilled to be a part of a venture that would enable him to examine the immediate aftermath of nuclear bombs and the ongoing effects on people during the nuclear winters.

At the resort, a concrete helipad was constructed that would be strictly used for Chi-Lah's needs. The helipad was painted black to not be noticed by satellites or overhead spy planes. Chi-Lah was paranoid and had an excellent reason to be.

To fund this project, Chi-Lah contacted his top customers. With wars taking place in so many zones, the arms business was brisk. His black book consisted of a rogue's gallery of assassins, saboteurs, greedy oil sheiks, traitors, and cold-blooded murderers. They all had one thing in common: the love of gold. That would be easy prey for Chi-Lah due to his promise of giving thousands of kilos of gold that would appreciate in value by as much as one hundred times after the capitalistic world was annihilated. The entry fee would be twenty billion dollars each to get a seat at the table.

Once seven participants were secured, all that was needed were the warheads.

Fahid had researched the arsenals in Russia. He determined it would be easier to steal the bombs from Russia than the United States although the US weapons were more dependable and slightly more powerful. The silos they were constructing were designed for ICBMs that would transport the Russian warheads with greater reliance and accuracy.

In reviewing the information on a dozen arsenals, Fahid's eye caught one particular name: Major Burka. A Ukrainian-born officer in the Russian Army, Burka was commanding the Russian Arsenal Kapustin Yar in the western mountain range in Russia. Burka lived in a mansion near the arsenal with his niece. His wife died from incurable breast cancer.

Kapustin Yar was the largest Russian arsenal. The types of warheads included the deadliest of Multiple Independent Reentry Vehicles (MIRVs) capable of being programmed to deliver a nuclear payload to twelve targets in a single blast.

The United States had three monitors positioned at the arsenal to keep Russia honest. Their assignment was to periodically count the warheads and take action if any were missing. These monitors all came from the US Army. They would need to pass a battery of loyalty tests before being shipped to the various arsenals spread throughout Russia.

Fahid planned a way to get into Russia and approach Burka. He would be offering payments of gold to bribe Burka to turn away while he stole the warheads. If bribery was not the answer, he reasoned there could be other methods of persuasion.

CHAPTER 12

WESTERN RUSSIA – 1995

Lieutenant Timothy Jeffries was an action man. He loved fast dice, cards, vodka, women, and especially cars. The Maserati he was driving could reach 150 miles per hour in a very short time. The sun was setting as he headed toward the nuclear base with his lover, Natasha Burka, the niece of Major Burka.

Natasha was one of those stunningly beautiful Ukrainian women with pure skin and the kind of striking eyes that seemed to pop out of ads on the internet, which begged American men to adopt them as wives. The mail-order-bride business was very much alive, and Lieutenant Jeffries was falling in love with someone who could be their poster child. Her long brown hair and green eyes hypnotized him, and he loved being controlled by her, especially in sex.

Jeffries was appointed out of an elite group to act as a monitor at the Russian nuclear warehouse base named Kapustin Yar. Kapustin Yar held 348 large nuclear multiple warheads, the kind with the capacity to destroy multiple targets in a city with one missile. Each multiple missile packed the power of many megatons of force. The amount of the blast and the radiation left in its wake was equal to fifty times the one that instantly killed eighty-four thousand people at Hiroshima.

After the Cold War was over and the Berlin Wall was torn down, the United States and Russia entered into an agreement to monitor each other's nuclear warhead stockpiles. Strategic Arms Limitation Talks (SALT) eventually morphed into a treaty whereby each nation would send a select number of military personnel to keep an eye on each other's arsenal. As President Reagan would say, "TRUST BUT VERIFY!"

Lieutenant Jeffries was one of those hand-picked monitors. He was the cream of the crop. His friends would make fun of him. He was only thirty-two, unmarried but with an out-of-wedlock child who lived with the baby momma in Chicago. Many of his fellow soldiers would tease him that he should move to Hollywood with his striking good looks.

The drive from Major Burka's estates was thirty kilometers to the nuclear base. The night of the accident, driver Jeffries and passenger Natasha had been partying at Major Burka's house. Alcohol could have played a role in the accident since the major had his own distillery and distilled vodka for guests, though mostly for himself.

The Maserati was in a gear that allowed a speed much too fast for the damp Russian roads, especially when wet.

The road's many curves were designed to follow the base of the mountains. When it rained, the water would come down off the steep hills and onto the asphalt road.

Natasha also loved the speed. Many times, when the car was at full throttle, she would yell, "Faster, faster!" and Jeffries would obey.

A warning sign on the road indicated a sharp turn ahead leading in and out of a tunnel. Jeffries' instincts were to hit the brakes to slow down and navigate the turn under control. This night, that was not enough. The car entered the tunnel at breakneck speed, and when the car exited the tunnel, the second sharp turn applied too much centrifugal force for the car to remain on the road. It swept the couple toward the guard rail. The Maserati did a 360-degree spin. If the brakes were pressed at all, it did not help. The speed was so great that the car crashed through the rail, took flight, flipped in the air, and landed on its side, careening through trees, rocks, and dirt, causing multiple turnovers until the flames appeared and engulfed the car and the occupants inside.

The next day, Inspector Yablochkov of the Russian Police stood on the ridge where the car had gone airborne. There were several uniformed police and firemen on the scene.

One of the inspector's men shook his head. "Inspector, have you any idea what might have happened? There is nothing left of the automobile and its passengers."

Yablochkov looked over the road and commented, "Foothills in these mountains become eerie around dusk. The combination of the evening mist, water from the mountains, and the glaring sunset plays tricks with the eyes. The moment you lose vision, you lose control. It happens in seconds."

A uniformed policewoman with a notebook in her hand and a camera slung around her neck walked up to the inspector and the policeman. "Sir, there are no marks on the road. No other cars were involved. He must have been blinded by the setting sun and took the turn too fast out of the tunnel before he lost control. It is my belief it happened so quickly that the car was doomed as soon as it exited the tunnel."

The inspector, rubbing his chin, admitted, "I haven't seen one this bad in a long, long time."

CHAPTER 13

DENALI ISLAND, TURKEY

It had taken less than a year to construct the ICBM launch facilities. All that was needed were the rockets and the warheads. The rockets would arrive by barge from Iraqi secret factories, and the warheads were in the Kapustin Yar arsenal.

Most of the construction crews became key people in the manning of the launch complex and silos. The other non-important people had disappeared. Nowhere to be found.

The rogue evildoers knew the price of gold would increase in value by over one hundred times once they destroyed key capitalist sites. Each one of them held thousands of gold ingots. Each ingot would be worth a fortune, plus they were all enticed with the offer to earn five hundred thousand pounds of gold for their twenty-billion-dollar entrance fee.

Inside one of the convention rooms was a large conference area. In the center of the room was a long mahogany table that was occupied by seven of the world's most dangerous criminals. Rajani Singey, responsible for car and bus bombings in London, was the chief architect for the TWA

Catastrophe which murdered 344 innocent people over the Atlantic.

Alfred Conners was a former executive with MI-6. He was associated with and wanted for the assassination of two world leaders. He was paid ten billion dollars to eliminate a high-profile sultan.

Eddy Farrow was wanted in Australia for the largest diamond heist in modern-day history. That theft caused the death of six people, two of them at the hands of Mr. Farrow himself.

The oldest member of the group of seven was an old Arab named Fisal. He was said to own most of the land in the untapped Iraqi oil fields north of Baghdad. The land was conservatively estimated to be worth six trillion dollars.

Jambo Mgawi, called the most dangerous person on the African continent, was pure evil. He and his team of cutthroats had commandeered tons of gold from the mines of Tanzania. They had no limit to the amount of gold they would love to own. They murdered many to prove that.

Prisca Perks—at least that was what she called herself—held control over several wealthy men that together easily eclipsed a total net worth of two trillion dollars.

To round out the who's who in the evildoer's hit parade, Vladimir Ivanavitch, disavowed by the Russian government as a traitor, had held some of the richest nations hostages over weapons, amassing a fortune. Over three hundred thousand deaths were attributed to his actions. His most daring project was in Damascus when he and five others destroyed his adversary and all his friends when they demolished the roof of a hotel while a party was in progress. The act was executed to perfection. At the right time, two cars painted to look like Damascus taxi cabs pulled up in front of the hotel. Three men jumped out of each vehicle wielding bazookas, which they fired from the street to the roof of the hotel. It took only one minute to do the damage. The target and his friends were all transformed into ashes. Vladimir and his team of murderers left the country as they had entered: two large helicopters held the taxis, the men, and the sleeper cell that were employed for a decade just for a moment like this.

The members of the rogue group were all extremely wealthy and wished to get wealthier no matter the human price. They knew that once the industrialized world was destroyed, gold would increase in price tenfold or maybe even a hundred times its current value. With that wealth, they could build new financial centers and control one hundred percent of the world's commerce. They would be able to fund huge militaries to make sure they stayed in charge.

At the head of the table, slightly elevated to provide a sense of stature, dressed in a customary Asian elder's white outfit, was Chi-Lah. To Chi-Lah's right was Abdul Bin Fahid, dressed in a white thawb, an Arab tunic.

Seated side by side, Alfred Conners and Rajani Singey spoke to one another in a low tone so only they could hear each other. Conners told Singey, "Chi-Lah was responsible for the bombing of the Imperial Palace in Athens. That day, the Russian and American spy agencies lost over a dozen agents each."

Singey retorted, "They make what we have done look like child's play. I know many stories about Fahid and his association with the Al Qaida group. No one in this room is safe." They laughed.

Fahid stood to address the group. His face displayed a broad grin. He purposely waited until there was complete silence in the room. "Welcome, my friends. Welcome to this beautiful island." The group politely applauded. "Welcome to the beginning of the end of capitalism. I am Abdul bin Fahid.

Thank you for your generous contribution to the project. Our ten silos are poised to deliver devices to the major financial and political centers of the world: London, New York, Amsterdam, Rome, Moscow, and for good measure, Washington, DC.

"Each intercontinental ballistic missile is state-of-the-art, constructed by friends in support of our cause. Many of the best rocket scientists helped design super-fast speeds and extremely accurate guidance systems. They can travel over nine thousand kilometers and deliver a payload to a targeted location within three hundred meters.

"The warheads we have on hand will deliver a nuclear hydrogen bomb warhead that, when it reaches its target, bursts into thirty smaller missiles in thirty directions. This will guarantee the destruction of the world's financial backbone along with at least one hundred million instant deaths. The ones who survive will eventually perish due to their weak western cultures. Drinking supplies will be poisoned and so will the air they breathe.

"Our plan is right on track. The launch has been set back by a short period. There was a minor incident in the north. We have a backup plan to alleviate the setback, and in two days, we will be ready to launch hell. Hell like no species on earth has ever caused or seen."

That generated very loud and vigorous applause from the seven members. Chi-Lah smiled.

"Your families will be safe as long as they remain in shelters in your homelands. Connors, you can relax. Your family has been moved to the Middle East for safety."

Connors acknowledged, "I trust you have taken extra care in the move. My wife knows nothing about our plans and is not a threat."

Chi-Lah remained smiling, and said, "Mister Connors, it is very clear the love you have for your family. Trust me, after we implement our plan, you will be overjoyed to know they are safe and not vaporized. My reports tell me the move was accomplished with no trouble at all."

The room filled with chatter.

Fahid waited for quiet again. "I hope you like it here. It has taken much planning and money to secure this haven. Before I turn this over to our leader, Chi-Lah, are there any questions?"

Old Arab Fisal stood, cleared his throat, and began to speak in Arabic, his native tongue.

Fahid stopped him immediately. "We all agreed that we will speak in English, so I hope you have followed your instructions and know the language."

Fisal answered in English, "I do. Since we had a setback, how many of the warheads do we have in our control?"

Fahid smiled. "I am not at liberty to tell you. You know the rules. If I tell you, then I have broken my own rules and that would be hypocritical."

Fisal quickly responded with a stronger voice. "Pardon me, Fahid. We have each contributed twenty billion dollars, taken unbelievable risks, and have committed to staying on this island possibly for the rest of our lives and *you cannot tell us?*" Fisal changed his tone. "I am sure everyone here wants to know the answer."

Growing angry internally, Fahid was silent outwardly, so he continued letting the old man rant.

"I insist that you answer. I cannot speak for the others, but I would like to hear their opinions. Fahid, you *must* be more cooperative."

Fahid took a deep breath. "My friend, your wish will be granted." He turned to the group. "Any others who would like to join Fisal? I will personally take you to see the cache." Fahid then faced Fisal. "As you can see, we are able to disagree, but we are friends toward a bigger goal."

He turned back to the group. "So sorry for the interruption. Now, my dear friends, our leader, Chi-Lah."

At the head of the table, Chi-Lah, not intimidating to look at, not tall, nor muscular, nor even wise looking, stood and gently removed the brown cowl from his head. In a soft voice, he said, "Everything will come together. We will meet our schedule." Chi-Lah slowly looked over his audience. "Please take all our resources to insure your ultimate pleasure and comfort."

Chi-Lah extended his arms toward the door. In walked seven very sexy female assistants all dressed alike in see-through black-mesh coverings. The women were scanned by the eyes of all the men present. Doing his homework, Fahid even arranged for a lesbian beauty to be Prisca's assistant. They took their place behind each assigned member.

"Here at Denali Island, we can accommodate your every desire. Each of you will have a personal assistant who will show you to your suites and take care of whatever needs you may have." Chi-Lah gestured toward the door.

The women left through the same door.

"You understand that you cannot go back on the plan. You must not leave the island until the plan is complete. Then, and only then, can you return to your homeland very wealthy."

A round of applause filled the large room.

"At that time, we will build a coalition to pool our gold to fund the birth of our own style of capitalism." Chi-Lah sat.

Fahid stood and turned his attention to Fisal. "Those of you who want to go with me now, please remain behind. The others may leave and meet your assistants on the other side of the door. I will see all of you at dinner. Five o'clock sharp."

Bodies stirred, and one by one they left the room. The only

one remaining was the old Arab, Fisal. In a quivering voice, he said, "Well, I guess it is only me who had a wonder today."

Fahid answered, "That is fine. Please walk with me."

"Where is my assistant? I would like her to go with me."

"Your assistant, sir, has been ordered to your room to unpack your valise and run your bath water. I believe you like your water rather tepid at eighty-two degrees."

"Yes, something like that."

Fahid and Fisal walked outside to a golf cart parked in the front driveway. Fisal sat in the passenger seat, and Fahid took the driver's position. The cart was energized with the turn of a key and the two were off to the east, toward the silos. The cart started slowly through a winding road. Then the cart picked up speed.

Fahid never said a word. He pressed his foot hard on the pedal accelerating the cart faster and faster so that each bump in the road acted like a catapult to the bodies inside the vehicle. Fisal gripped the handle next to him in a death hold. Fahid navigated a radical S turn which made Fisal nauseous. He grabbed Fahid's arm while rubbing his stomach.

"Stop this thing now!" I will be sick if you do not stop now! I am sorry I questioned you in there. Please, Fahid. I do not want to see the stockpile. Turn this back, please."

Fahid said nothing. He drove the cart to a clearing inside the jungle. To the right was a chain-link fence that towered thirty feet in the air. He took a small remote-control device out of his pocket and aimed it at a gate in the fence. The gate opened. Fahid drove the cart one hundred feet into the secured area. He stopped the cart, removed the key and jumped out, and ran back to the open gate. While running he engaged the device, and the gate began to close. Fahid barely escaped into the safe area outside the fence.

The gate closed shut leaving Fisal and the cart inside the chain-linked walls.

Fisal screamed, "don't leave me here! Fahid let me out!" He exited the cart and walked to the gate where he could see Fahid walking away from the area on the same path they used to get there. Fisal tries to force the gate open but to no avail.

"Let me out!" Fisal then tried to climb the fence but fell from a quarter of the way up. He landed on his back. He tried again but stopped when he heard a strange growl coming from the jungle behind him.

Out of the green brush on the edge of the tall jungle trees emerged two mature, very muscular white tigers. Seeing this, Fisal jumped off the fence and back in the cart. He tried to start the vehicle, but the key was missing. The tigers slowly circled the cart five times. Fisal never took his eyes off the circling tigers.

The animals were lean and hungry. In a zoo, they would no doubt have been the main attraction.

Suddenly, one jumped into the cart, sniffing the man's face, and gently licking it.

Fisal was petrified. Then the tiger in the cart viciously attacked the old man. The huge deadly claw batted at his head, drawing blood. The second tiger jumped onto the cart and bit into Fisal's neck and dragged him off the cart and into the jungle.

Fisal screamed and tried to fight off the two beasts. In seconds, the screaming stopped. The cart was now covered with blood.

Fahid turned just in time to see the animals carting Fisal's lifeless body into the jungle heading toward their lair. He let out a maniacal laugh.

CHAPTER 14

PENTAGON

Seated at the head of the Joint Chiefs of Staff was fifty-five-year-old Five-Star General Cliff J. Matthews. His office at the Pentagon was simple with a great view of the Washington Monument through the window behind him.

The general had worked his way through the ranks. When the Vietnam War began, he enlisted, even though his "lottery" number was 360.

He had become a military scholar. As a private, he attended military school in hopes that the extra education would get him recognized by those who could issue promotions. He excelled in all courses and his non-stop work gave a stunning representation of himself to those above him in rank. Recommendations for promotions were common.

President Reagan promoted him to Brigadier General, and in the next seven years, he climbed the ladder to a Four-Star General rank.

He was born into a fairly well-to-do family in Vermont. People got to know him as a thinker rather than a doer, although he received three medals for bravery in the Vietnam War. No doubt he was considered an exemplary military general.

A "TOP SECRET" envelope was placed on his desk by his assistant with the words "Open Immediately" across the head of the package. After opening and reading the contents, he picked up the phone and called his assistant back into the office. "Please call Team V to the conference room for an emergency meeting at fifteen hundred hours."

15:00 PENTAGON SITUATION ROOM "V"

The conference room was large with three big projection screens and a mahogany table that could seat sixteen people. Each seat had a desk area with a telephone. At three o'clock, the room was filled with military brass from every service. No one dared be late.

General Matthews took his seat at the head of the table and cleared his throat. "Welcome, everyone. Today I've been informed that the NSA has intercepted a coded message that an unknown enemy has plans to raid the nuclear arsenal in the Kapustin Yar nuclear arsenal in western Russia. They have their eyes on capturing nuclear warheads with the intent of selling them on the black market or, worse yet, using them."

An officer seated to the right of the general spoke up. "That is impossible, General. That base is one of the most secure in the entire Russian arsenal system."

Matthews retorted, "That's not saying much. Most of the soldiers there have been moved to other Russian lines."

A second officer was skeptical. "It would take a coordinated army to break into that fortress."

The general answered both comments in one statement. "As I said, the forces guarding that base have been removed. A small company remains."

The second officer asked if this could be a dirty trick from the Russians. He then asked if NATO had been notified.

Before hearing an answer, a third officer asked if this could be caused by inside operatives.

Matthews answered, "That is possible. We are running a security check on every person there. Major Burka is the top Russian authority at the base. The odd thing is he is not Russian, but Ukrainian."

A military soldier entered the room and handed the general a note.

After reading the paper, Matthews said, "Burka used to be on our payroll but vanished for three years. Then he shows up at Kapustin Yar." Matthews removed his reading glasses. "According to what I was just handed, there is nothing new on the Jeffries accident near Burka's estate. The NSA is looking into the coincidence of Jeffries' death and the top-secret alert.

"Back to Burka. Before he vanished, he gave us very actionable data on rogue Russian agents. He saved many NATO operatives. He left on rather good terms. What I just told you is extremely confidential. If the Russians ever find out, there would be no Major Burka."

"General, do our monitors at the base have a good grip on the situation?"

"One would like to think so. How many do we have there now?"

"General, sir, with Jeffries gone, two."

"We will need to replace Jeffries immediately. We'll need to find someone we can trust and be able to get close to Burka. I will place into the proper channels a message to all the remaining twenty-nine monitors in the system to stay at their assigned bases until they hear directly from me."

A third officer, Major Haus, spoke up. "Sir, at first hearing about the news of Jeffries, I began a replacement-candidate search."

The general was pleased. "Good thinking, Major."

"I narrowed it down to two qualified candidates. Of the two, I'd like to nominate an outstanding prospect: First Lieutenant Coby Rodriguez."

"What do you know about him?"

"He's a she, sir."

Everyone at the table grinned, including the general. The women at the table were not smiling.

"I pulled her file for you, sir. I'll have it brought in." The officer picked up a phone from the center of the table. "Please bring in the Rodriguez file."

The general looked around the table. "Kapustin Yar is not the type of place you'd find yourself yearning to visit. The winters are abhorred. The people act and dress like the weather: cold and gray."

Air Force Commander Jeanne Smith added, "Yes, sir. I've been there. Little activity. The once-Russian base I visited is now a ghost town. Security is questionable. You are correct. Most of the forces pulled out with the START treaty, then more were deployed elsewhere with SALT. That leaves that base vulnerable to attacks."

A soldier entered the room and handed over a zippered satchel to Major Haus, who removed two files and handed both over to the general, who did not immediately look inside as he continued, "Timothy Jeffries was one of the elites chosen to watchdog the stockpile of nuclear weapons in Russian arsenals. I remember him. A sharp officer who knew how to handle most situations. His tragic death leaves a hole that needs to be filled post-haste."

One of the people at the table asked, "General, do you believe Jeffries' death was no accident?"

"The Russians have already cleaned up the area. There is nothing left to investigate. That is why we need to get someone close to Burka." The general opened one of the files. Coby's photo was on the inside cover of the file. The general read from the dossier. "Hmm, number one at West Point, speaks five languages fluently, including Russian, and holds a master's degree in Russian History." He hesitated, then read out loud, "She has aspirations to be a general someday." The general brought out a smug smile. "Be careful what you wish for."

Everyone at the table chuckled.

"Says here she is currently in Kaiserslautern, Germany." He turned to his assistant. "Get in touch with her now while it is still early there."

CHAPTER 15

KAISERSLAUTERN, GERMANY, ARMY BASE

After ten p.m. CET at Kaiserslautern US Army base there was not much to do. During the day the base was hopping. Tanks rolling, helicopters hovering, jets arriving and departing, and dozens of soldiers marching in unison. In her room, First Lieutenant Coby Rodriguez, now thirty, exercised to "The Rhythm Is Gonna Get You." Her ringing phone startled her.

"Hello?" a female voice on the other end asked.

"Lieutenant Rodriguez?"

"Yes."

"Please hold for General Matthews."

"Yes, sure." Coby took her towel and wiped the sweat off her face. She extended the phone cord so she could reach the player to turn off the music. Wondering why a high-ranking officer would be calling her, under her breath, she murmured, "The general?" She took a deep breath and gathered herself as a deep voice broke the phone's silence.

"Lieutenant? General Matthews here. How are you? Please forgive me for calling late."

"Hello, General. I am fine. This must be important." Coby's eyes widened while the general spoke. She listened intensely.

"Are you okay with me calling you Coby?"

"Yes, sir."

"You have been recommended to take on a position that is vital to the security of our country."

"Yes, sir."

"At oh-six hundred you'll need to report to the NATO air base with your bags packed."

Coby responded to authority. "Yes, sir!"

"Hope this doesn't cause you any problems?"

"No, sir!"

"Good. Your command of the Russian language, history, and politics convinces me you are the perfect selection."

Coby nodded. "Yes, sir!"

The general told her, "The details will be given to you in a written report before you board the plane. It is so very highly classified, I cannot tell you any more about the assignment over the phone. When you arrive at the base, proceed to the blue gate and report to Security Officer First Lieutenant Zappile. He will have an attaché with an envelope inside with the details. This is extremely top secret. Only Q-level clearance can see it."

Coby grew somber.

"Kapustin Yar is the largest Russian warhead arsenal that is covered by SALT. We monitor them and they monitor us. Our man, I mean, one of our inspectors, met a tragic death when his car crashed through a guardrail in the Russian mountains. Two remaining inspectors are sharing the detail at the arsenal, but they need a third to help mitigate fatigue."

"I understand, sir."

"Upon your return, you will be rewarded and on your way

to a higher rank. This assignment is extremely dangerous, but it is needed to secure the freedom of the world."

Coby hung on the general's words and pondered. "Er, yes, sir. Oh-six hundred tomorrow, er, that was tomorrow, correct, sir?" Coby realized that this mission for her was to begin in just a few hours.

"Yes."

"What was the name of our inspector that was killed?"

"Lieutenant Timothy Jeffries." In a lower tone, he added, "Coby, I will not mislead you. The living conditions are not the best and are not set up for a woman. You would have to share the quarters with two men, but you will have a private room and bathroom."

"Yes, sir!"

"You will be moving into Jeffries' room. Your first assignment will be to clear the room of his personal effects and send them directly to the address found in your orders."

"Yes, sir."

"Good luck and know you have our total support." The general hung up.

Coby hung up the receiver and stood still rather stunned that her world was about to dramatically change. An excited Coby immediately called her mom in South Philadelphia.

Dina was in the kitchen mopping the floor when the phone rang. "Hello?"

"Hello, Mom, it's me." Coby talked on the phone while she packed.

Dina dropped the mop and sat down. "Coby, it is so good to hear your voice. Are you okay? Do you need anything? I have so much—"

"Mom, Mom, wait, wait, I don't have much time."

Dina nervously responded, "Okay, okay, what's wrong?"

"Nothing is wrong, Mom. I'm going on my first major

assignment that will keep me from calling you as much. Just didn't want you to worry."

"I pray for you all the time. How can I not worry?"

Coby chuckled. "Besides I still have some guardian angels to spare."

"Don't make fun of that!"

Coby changed her tone, and asked, "How's Daddy?"

"He's the one we should be worried about. I don't know, Coby. He is just not his same self. Seems to be getting weaker by the day. He's down at the tavern with the guys. Cancer has not stopped his love of beer and cigars. The doctors have given up."

The tears began to flow down Coby's cheeks. "Please tell him I love him very much. That I'd much rather be with him smoking cigars and playing poker with the guys. If I have a chance to call again, I will. Just don't worry if you don't hear from me over the next few weeks."

Worried, Dina said, "That's a long time."

Coby assured her, "It will go by fast. Love you, Mommy. Please give Daddy lots of kisses for me." Coby kissed into the phone then hung up.

For the first time in her life, she wondered if she had taken the right path going to West Point. Maybe she should have been a real daughter staying home tending to her father's last days.

CHAPTER 16

GERMANY - GILENIKERCHEN –
NATO AIR FORCE BASE – 6 AM CET
MYSTICAL INTERLUDE #7– EYE CONTACT

The base was huge with large military planes in a row. Coby parked her Jeep and proceeded to the "Blue Gate." As she approached, a military vehicle pulled up beside her. An officer exited the car with an armed soldier by his side. Coby walked toward them. "A Lieutenant Zappile is to meet me here with my orders."

Zappile saluted and handed Coby the attaché. "That is me, ma'am." He proceeded to clamp the case to her wrist with a chain then snapped the lock in place.

Coby secured the case under her arm. They saluted one more time, and Coby was directed to a waiting airplane.

Zappile handed her two keys: one for the lock on the chain and one for the lock on the case.

She placed both keys in her left blouse pocket. Keys seemed to get lost in the pants, she thought. Didn't know why, just did. Having a slight sinus problem she inherited from

Poppa, tissue was always in the pocket. Runny nose? The hand automatically went into the pocket, pulled out the tissue, and along for the ride was the key.

From inside the plane, forty thousand feet above the German terrain, Coby watched the sunrise from the transport's window. She removed one of the keys from her pocket and unlocked the attaché and removed an envelope with red lettering— "Only Q level Clearance"—and cut the security tape with a pen knife.

She removed a file from the envelope and studied the dossier of Jeffries. Coby noted that he had graduated from West Point two years before her. The instructions showed an address to send Jeffries' personal effects to a "CESAR THOMAS, PADDINGTON PLACE, LONDON, ENGLAND." She studied Jeffries' photo and thought to herself that she was replacing a handsome James Bond stereotype. A film casting agent would grab him in a heartbeat as the star of a major spy movie. He had never been married but did have a child in Chicago. She also wondered why she was to send his personal effects to England and not his home. Coby removed another file from the attaché.

She studied the first page with much interest, but the words found on the second page—"COMPLETE ANNIHILATION OF EARTH"—caught her eye. She read on and discovered the NSA was 98.6% certain there was a plan to steal warheads at the base she was headed to. There was no intelligence on when this was to occur. There was a possibility it already had happened. She then removed a file labeled "BURKA." She thought it was a strange order to get close to Burka to determine if he was friend or foe. *"Why don't we already know?"*

The plane landed at a military base close to Moscow. As she left the plane, a Russian Officer approached Coby. "Welcome to Russia."

In Russian, Coby thanked him, "Spasibo."

"You speak Russian?"

"Ya, ochen' svobdo."

"You speak it very well. You will have another plane ride to an air force base and then a hop aboard a helicopter transport to Kapustin Yar."

"Dosvidaniya."

LENINGRAD RUSSIAN AIR FORCE BASE

The adrenaline surges, flights, and lack of sleep were beginning to wear Coby down. Upon landing, she was whisked to her next flight. Coby was directed toward a parked mammoth Russian helicopter revving its rotors. The whooshing sound was hypnotic. Examining the aircraft, she couldn't help but think, *Can this thing actually fly? Suddenly, I do not feel safe in something not made in the good old USA.*

The safety instruction card in the craft showed it was a Mil Mi-26 class, designed to lift heavy weights. She thought, *This big thing for me?* The helicopter's interior was stark with what seemed like fishing nets hanging from the walls. To herself, *I'm sure the nets are there to grab when you are thrown around in this flying tin can.*

The helicopter ride was noisy. The eight blades slapping the wind called for earplugs, which she did not have. Coby looked out the large side-door window at the Russian landscape. She whispered, "This could be the Dakotas or Wyoming."

The Russian pilot turned to Coby. He waved to her to come closer to the cockpit. Wobbly, she managed to get close, but the pilot still needed to elevate his voice to be heard.

He shouted in a heavy Russian accent at a decibel slightly above the whir of the rotors, "The last time I was in Kapustan was to pick up the remains of Lieutenant Jeffries' body. it was a mess!"

Coby glared at the pilot for the insensitive information. The craft was flying into the sunset. Coby checked her watch. "We should be landing in less than an hour. Maybe I can get a little shuteye." She saw a mound of foam rubber near the cockpit and lay down.

Close to an hour later, the pilot extended his arm and politely shook Coby's arm. "Lieutenant, Lieutenant, Lieutenant Rodriguez."

Startled, Coby awoke. "Are we here?" She clutched the attaché and checked that the lock was in place. From the air, Coby could see the clearing where the base was located, carefully nestled between two rather large hills.

Waiting on the tarmac were two very nicely appointed Russian soldiers. One ran to the copter once it landed and assisted Coby into a van. The other stood erect as though standing for a president or head of state. "Good day, Lieutenant. My name is Private Corsky. Please follow me." He motioned to the other officer to take her duffle bag and place it in the van.

The Chevy van, which Coby found humorous, took them all to a metal Quonset Hut illuminated by a single bulb swinging in the breeze under a hanging chain.

The three walked side by side through the chilly hut. Not a word was said. Coby and the two Russian soldiers exited from the rear door and proceeded to a big brick building about ten feet away, with two big unfriendly looking, marred wooden doors.

Coby ran her fingers down the door and murmured, "Maybe it's prettier in daylight."

Private Corsky said, "Excuse me, Lieutenant, did you say something?"

"Just commenting to myself about the décor." *Nice start, Rodriguez. Try not to embarrass yourself."*

Coby and Corsky entered the building. The other soldier left them, placing her duffle bag on the floor. Coby then took possession of the bag. The two walked down a short, badly lit hallway. Coby and Corsky walked toward a flight of steps at the end of the hallway.

"This is the building where you will be living." Corsky took Coby's duffle bag and began to climb the stairs. "Lieutenant, this upstairs area is for the Americans. We have worked on knocking down a wall and adding a few walls to give you a girls' bathroom."

Coby noticed a smirk on the soldier's lips, which she interpreted as sexist. Then shook her head.

Corsky continued, "You are our first woman. We watch many American movies and are you like Private Benjamin?"

"Ah no."

"Your room is on the right. Captain Cowboy and Lieutenant Mark stay over there." The soldier pointed to his left. "We built special privacy for you. A woman." Again, a smirk.

"Cowboy? The papers said Captain Boyd."

Corsky smiled.

Coby noticed. "Does the other guy dress like a construction worker? Could be the beginning of the new Village People."

Corsky asked, "The who?"

"That's a different group." The line did not register any humor from the Russian.

Coby, in her best Rosanna Dana voice, uttered, "Never mind."

After a moment of awkward silence and a few more steps, Corsky broke the silence with, "They will be happy to see you."

"Do you know both of them well?"

"It is my job. We will get to know each other also."

Smiling with her hand held out, Coby said, "Glad to meet you, Private Corsky."

He shook her hand vigorously. "Thank you. The base closes lights-out at twenty-two hundred. The wake-up bell is at zero-five hundred."

Coby took in every word.

The private opened her door and the two entered her new living quarters. "We are here. I am speaking low. One of them is asleep now. Since Lieutenant Jeffries died, one goes on duty while the other sleep."

Coby placed her bag on the table.

Corsky headed toward the door and said, "The base kitchen is open for twenty more minutes. Do you wish to eat? I can walk you over."

Fighting brain fog and hunger, Coby thought, *My first big decision is to sleep or eat.* She stepped outside and said, "Food wins!"

With the attaché still chained to her wrist, she followed Corsky to the mess hall. He led her to a flight of cold, metal, gray stairs with matching railings.

A Russian guard in his mid-thirties, uniformed and handsome, passed her on the stairs. "Hello."

For a moment Coby was connected to his eyes. "Hello, zdravstvuyte."

The guard stopped and looked back.

Coby returned the look. They exchanged the slightest of smiles. Then he continued ascending the stairs to the Russian guard level. Her heart skipped a beat.

They reached the bottom floor where there was another dark hallway. An opening halfway down the hall emitted light. Coby and Private Corsky walked toward the light. Coby took this opportunity to begin her investigation of Major Burka. "Where is Major Burka's area?"

"He lives about thirty kilometers west of here." Corsky pointed toward what Coby assumed was west.

"Does he come to the base often?"

"I think he does. I have seen him here inspecting the safety devices."

"Do you think I could meet him?"

"I do think it is possible. I have seen him talking to Lieutenant Jeffries a few times."

Coby puzzled over that statement.

They reached the mess hall. Private Corsky led Coby into the room. "Well, here we are." Coby and the soldier looked around the very dark and eerily quiet room. Again, Corsky broke the silence and said, "Hope you like borscht?" They headed to a lone server behind a counter partially obscured by steam billowing from below.

The borscht was better than expected and so was the slab of unidentified meat on a plate. But Coby was tired and could not finish the gravy-soaked mystery meat.

Later, in bed, she thought about her assignment. A habit she developed at West Point was to recreate the day in her head. The long flight, the monster helicopter, the Q-level assignment...

Coby reminisced about the Russian soldier she had passed on the stairway. That made her smile, but she was not close to falling asleep. She kept repeating "Five a.m. will be here too soon" over and over. Finally, after an indeterminate length of time, she dozed.

CHAPTER 17

DENALI ISLAND - CHI-LAH'S MANSION – NIGHT

The only light on the island was from the partial moon. The property was exquisite. In its heyday, only the top one percent of one-percenters could afford the rent. All suites started at thirty-five hundred dollars a night. On some occasions, one person would rent the entire resort. Since there was no empirical proof of the rumors that festive sex orgies were held at Denali, many of the famous people who participated were protected. Young girls and boys were rounded up, drugged, and let loose on the clientele. If the swaying palm trees could talk, there would be dozens of scandals revealed.

The trees danced in the breezes and were noticeably in unison. There were some lights on in the mansion.

Inside an elaborate suite, Chi-Lah paced the floor. Dinner on the table was untouched. There were three raps on the door. Chi-Lah opened the door to Fahid. "Welcome."

Fahid entered the room. Bowed his head. "Good evening."

Chi-Lah walked over to a set of crystals on a marble table. "Would you like some fine Ningxia wine?"

Fahid declined.

Chi-Lah fondled the wine bottle. "This is a very rare bottle." Chi-Lah closed the door and headed toward the bar.

Fahid asked, "Where is your assistant?"

Chi-Lah always spoke softly. "She placed the food and wine and left. I could not take the chance that what we have to say would be heard by other ears." He poured the open bottle of red nectar into a fine crystal glass. "My friend, we have a serious problem. What is happening at Kapustin Yar is unacceptable." On a rare moment, Chi-Lah raised his voice. "This should have been done without a problem. YOU SWORE TO ME!"

Fahid tried to interject, "Chi-Lah—"

Pacing the floor, in the same raised voice, Chi-Lah said, "Allow me to finish. We are three warheads short of our goal. The death of Jeffries has caused much unneeded attention there. We have five partners here who may be inquisitive like our tiger-lunch friend. The clock is ticking. If we fail now, we will never have this opportunity again."

Fahid responded in a subservient tone, "Burka got nervous, and Jeffries panicked. I will never let you down. The silos are ready, and the targets are chosen. We will have the remaining warheads here in a day or so. If not, we should launch with the seven we have."

Chi-Lah's quick reaction was, "NO! Fahid, we must stay with the plan. All ten targets are important. Falling short by three will not weaken the enemy enough. We must make them extinct."

Changing the tone, Fahid said, "Chi-Lah, we have good news. I have been notified that Jeffries is being replaced by a woman without experience. She may be too busy fixing her nails and might not even notice any crates are missing. Do not fear. I have doubled our forces to conduct the mission to take the three remaining warheads. It will happen on her first shift. The chaos and her newness will be fatal to her and her world."

"Fahid, when we meet in the morning, you will tell them everything is good." Chi-Lah took a sip of wine. "Tell them Fisal had an emergency and had to return to his homeland. He has forfeited his share. Tell them his share will be divided equally to those who remain loyal and faithful to our cause."

"Yes, with pleasure." Fahid bowed his head.

CHAPTER 18

KAPUSTIN YAR – DAWN

The sun was making its daily rise casting an orange hue on the rustic buildings on the base. If it weren't for the warehouse of enough destructive material to level the Earth, the scenery was beautiful. The mountains and the lakes were worthy of an artist's touch to paint the view on canvas.

Inside Coby's pitch-black room, Coby lay half-awake in her bed. Sleep was not as relaxing as it should have been. She was obsessed with beginning her assignments. The attaché case was causing some discomfort on her wrist. She finally closed her eyes in the hope of getting at least a short rest. The hour or so passed in a flash and the five-a.m. wake-up alarm bell rang. It was deafening.

Coby was completely startled. Hands over her ears, she jumped out of bed. "Will it ever stop?" When the noise finally ceased, she made a mental note: *Pack earplugs*. "I hate it when I don't get enough sleep. Let's see. I managed to get about four hours total in over two days. I wonder if the mess hall has coffee and oatmeal with blueberries and honey. Ha, I must be joking. I'll settle for coffee."

After a visit to the bathroom and some stretching exercises, somewhat of a morning ritual, Coby's attention was taken by the boxes of Jeffries' effects ready to be shipped to an address in London. Coby walked over to the desk in her room and noticed some of the boxes were packed with Lieutenant Jeffries' books, clothing, and personal items. Some boxes were empty waiting to be filled.

"I need a pot of coffee to handle this today. Wonder if there is anything in the desk." She opened the top drawer and the first item she saw was an unopened pack of cigars. Just the kind she liked. "I am so tempted. My brand. I'm keeping them just in case I get the urge." She removed papers, matchbooks, and a notebook. Upon opening the book, on the first page she saw the number seven in a circle. The rest of the book was blank.

A knock at the door startled Coby. "Yes, who's there?"

"It's Captain Cowboy."

Coby conjured up images based on the name and the timber of his voice. Adonis, Tom Cruise, Brad Pitt, boots, definitely boots.

Again, he knocked. "Hey, y'all, I gotta get to duty and relieve Mark. I wanted to meet you before I left."

Coby slipped on her jeans and Army sweatshirt and walked over to the door, took a deep breath, exhaled slowly, and before she opened the door, a mind game was played called, "Who has the voice?" She conjured up Captain Cal Boyd, aka Cowboy, thirty-four, who was tall with dirty-blond hair and a strong west Texas accent, definitely wearing boots, but Army issued. When the door was opened, her virtual description was pretty close.

"Hi. I'm Cal Boyd." He extended his hand. "Sure, glad to see you here."

Coby responded, "I understand you need the relief...pardon me." Remembering her military protocol, she took his hand and shook it firmly, then saluted. "Lieutenant Coby Rodriguez reporting for duty."

Cowboy, returning the salute, asked, "Did you rest okay?"

"Not really. Guess I'm a little nervous. When I was finally able to doze off, Big Ben practically knocked me out of bed." Coby covered her ears for a moment.

Cowboy laughed. "Yeah, I think they are trying to raise the dead. You'll get used to it. May I come in?"

"Sure."

Cowboy entered the room.

Coby, embarrassed, said, "I did not have the time to go through and totally clean up Tim's room. I just put stuff in boxes." Cowboy looked everywhere but at her.

"Thanks, I see that." Coby firmly stated, "I was planning to start that process today."

Cowboy looked over toward the area near the desk. Then his eyes scanned the desktop and stopped to stare at the number seven circled in the open notebook. "I didn't get to his desk." Changing subjects, Cowboy said, "Did you bring sheets?"

Coby quipped like a seasoned comedienne, "Sheets!? I'm lucky I have my toothbrush."

Cowboy, being honest, said, "You have a good sense of humor, I like that in a woman, er, I mean person."

Coby stayed in the mode. "The show starts at eight."

"You are a hoot!" Cowboy answered with an "aw, shucks" accent. "Listen, I need to relieve Mark. Here is a pamphlet on our job responsibilities here. It is not interesting reading. You'll need to commit much of it to memory. The assignment is rather darn simple, actually downright boring. They'll have you going to a checkpoint before you enter the vault. Don't let the size of the place intimidate you."

Coby was waiting for him to call her little woman. Somewhat relieved, she said, "Thanks. I'll have some time to finish packing Jeffries' personal effects and study the pamphlet."

"My shift ends at eighteen hundred. If you can drive over an hour earlier, I can show you the ropes that aren't in the pamphlet."

Coby smiled and said, "Thanks, I appreciate that."

As Cowboy left the room, he made a rather feeble salute. "See y'all later."

The sun began to eat up the morning fog revealing the base to another day of existence. The sun's rays worked their way through the windows in Coby's room.

With an open box in front of her, she was carefully placing Jeffries's items into the container. It did not look like Jeffries was much of a reader. There were only four books to pack. She wondered if the titles gave a peek into his personality. "The Catcher in The Rye," "Catch 22," "Brave New World," and "1984." *There is a theme here*, she thought, but it would take a psychologist to figure out what it was as it was related to a First Lieutenant in the US Army.

Not much in the clothes selection either. The way ol' Timmy was described, it wasn't his clothes that made him a ladies' man. Nothing here, except for a deck of cards. Not sure what that indicated.

Coby decided to keep the deck for herself. She could get lost playing solitaire for hours.

She stood and looked around the four walls. The dust was everywhere. *Wonder if they have a maid here to help with the cleaning.* She took a second look at the thickness of the dust and answered her own question. *Nope. Not even a feather duster to be had.*

Coby relaxed on the bed to rest her eyes and fell asleep. She awakened to a friendly aroma filling the air. "Coffee?" She took another sniff. "It *is* coffee!" She got up, opened a door from her room, and entered a small common area. At a table in the corner by a barred window sat a coffeemaker with a half-full carafe of java. "Must be the construction man who made the coffee."

Coby looked around the room. "Where do they hide the cups?" She searched around the coffeemaker. No cups on the table, on the sink, or under the sink. *Hmm, everything here seems to be a mystery. Right now, I'd settle for a straw.*

To her left stood a large wooden cabinet. Coby tried to open the door, but it was locked. Another mystery to solve. She turned toward the window and noticed three empty green plastic flowerpots. Picking them up, she examined one and concluded that these would make fine coffee cups. Coby took one of the pots to the sink and turned on the water. A rusty color of water flowed from the spigot. Coby turned the water off and waved her hand in front of her face. *Yuck, sulfur. If they are making coffee from this, then maybe I don't want coffee anymore.*

The rustling of the doorknob in the room disturbed her thoughts. In walked Lieutenant Mark Thompson, thirty-nine, African American, handsome, six foot, with cropped black hair and an Adonis body.

"Good morning, Lieutenant Rodriguez. Cal told me you were here. Welcome, we—"

Smiling, Coby said, "I know, you are glad to see me. I never felt so wanted." While grinning, she was thinking she may have said something girlish or stupid.

"Coffee?"

"I was trying to find a cup."

"We all keep our cups in our rooms. You can get one of your own from the mess hall. They don't like it when people take things so be sly."

"Thanks for the warning."

"You can probably find Timmy's somewhere in his box of stuff."

"I didn't see one. Maybe it is in one of the desk drawers. If not, I come from South Philly. I can easily sneak one out of the mess hall."

"I have great friends from Philly. My Dad sold restaurant equipment and always visited Philly. I'll never forget the time I spent Spring break traveling with him. He took me to the Phillies' opening day game. It was the first game that Pete Rose was a Philly. The fans went wild when they announced his name. Funny how some things are. When Rose played for Cincinnati, the Philly fans hated 'Charlie Hustle.' Now the same fans adore him."

"Kind of like us. Our team is from the USA. We love our allies but if one goes over to the other side, they become our enemy."

"Ain't that the truth!? I'm from the South, and the only team we can root for is Atlanta. Hank Aaron was my hero."

"Ah, Lieutenant Thompson, do we make the coffee with the water from—"

"No! No! Bottled water. Uncle Sam sends supplies to all the monitoring sites every two weeks or so. The water comes in gallon bottles, and we usually get two cases. Believe me, you'll find yourself drinking the water or the vodka. There is plenty of that stuff. Major Burka has his own distillery. They drink his concoctions just like water. Gives me a headache. He even makes his own alcohol from potatoes. Whoo-ee, it will send your head spinning."

After disappearing behind the door to his room, Mark returned with a clean cup and filled it for Coby. "I have a spare one."

Coby's first sip was delightful. She grinned. "Not bad."

"I swear it's psychological. Word of advice: don't drink Cowboy's coffee, that is unless you don't mind chewing it." They both laughed. "You'll find clean water in the shower. They collect the rain for sanitary reasons, and if luck is shining on us, the water is even hot." Snapping his fingers, Mark amended, "Well not exactly hot. You'll get used to it."

"Good advice."

"Best to take the shower at the end of the day when the water is exposed to sunlight longer. The next US delivery is in three days. If you have anything to send out, that would be the time."

"So, I better get Jeffries' things ready by then." She pointed to the closed closet door. "What's in the big closet?"

"Our personal arsenal of weapons. For defensive purposes only. We've not had to use any of it. Things are noticeably quiet around here."

"How do you unlock it?"

"The key is hanging on the wall over there. Believe me, Lieutenant, you'll never need to use any of this."

"What makes you so sure?"

"The Russians don't want to be here either, and this is their turf. You'll see."

"Can I look inside?"

"Sure." Mark took the key and opened the doors. On the wall were grenades, incendiary bombs, rapid-fire armor-piercing attack weapons, and an array of side arms neatly placed on the side wall of the cabinet. Mark stepped up to the closet and removed a crossbow.

Coby was amazed by the number of weapons. "And this is for three people? It would be like the Alamo. Right? Are you worried the Russians would come in here and take the weapons?"

Mark said with confidence, "They are not allowed in here."

"Oooooh, that'll keep them out," Coby said with a heavy dose of sarcasm.

"Look there has to be some trust. We don't go where we're not supposed to go, and they don't come in here."

"What about the workers who built my bathroom? Didn't they have to come in here?"

"Yes, but they are workers, not soldiers, right?"

"I see. I wonder if we are as loose with their inspectors at our arsenals. I'll bet those Russkies are kept under a microscope. I would have thought the same here."

"It's the same here, you just don't see it." He pointed to the light on the ceiling. Then to the smoke detector.

Coby took another sip of coffee not saying another word.

After a few minutes of silence, Mark broke the ice. "Anyhow, Cal says he's going to stay with you for a brief time tonight. You are in for a big treat with the count."

She detected sarcasm.

"That is due tonight during your watch."

Coby looked at the smoke detector. "I'm goin' to take a nap. Can you keep yourself occupied?"

"No problem there." Mark went on, "The truck keys are

on the table. See you later. Get some rest. Get ready and study the manual. I'll leave the coffee pot on."

"Lieutenant Thompson, who was the last one to count?"

"Jeffries was the last to count. A day before his accident."

"What kind of person was Jeffries?"

"Quiet. Never really intermingled with Cowboy and me. This is the second time I was monitoring with him. He had changed."

"How do you mean changed?"

"When we were in a different arsenal, he was the life of the party. Everyone liked to be around him, especially the Russian women. He was always one to crack jokes and laugh at them even though they were not funny. His laughter was contagious, so you found yourself laughing, not at the joke, but at him."

"Who got here first?"

"He did. When I first arrived, I saw him when I walked through the door. I was so happy. I ran to him and embraced him. You could just tell he changed. The return hugs were weak like he did not care to see me. Then he met Major Burka and went to the mansion often. Ironically, he drank so much over there that when I heard about the accident, I wasn't surprised."

"He lost his sense of humor?"

"Yes, like overnight, he became very serious. He met a Russian beauty and spent most of his spare time with her."

"Have you ever met Major Burka?"

"Yes. He gave Jeffries and me a lesson about what these warheads could do. Scary shit. Oh, he gave us bottles of homemade vodka. There are bottles in the cabinet above the sink if you care to imbibe."

"Thank you, Lieutenant."

"I'll wake you up before I leave. I'll drive over with you to show you the way. Just have to make sure you sign into each sentry station in order. Very simple. Then to what we call the vault. That is where they keep the warheads. Wear a sweater or coat in there, it is freezing."

"Roger that."

CHAPTER 19

FIRST DAY ON THE JOB

Coby's first day on the assignment began with Mark taking her to the warhead arsenal building. She thought it was very nice of him to drive her over an hour early. The people assigned to her seemed very nice. They could become good friends someday but not here. Cowboy could be a pal and Mark a friend for life. However, an assignment was at hand. An order so important that there was a possibility of annihilation. An order was personally given by one of only five people directly under the president of the United States, their Commander-In-Chief.

Things were not adding up the way Coby had hoped. All she learned so far was that Jeffries was a drunk, the Russians seemed too loose with all that there was at stake, and Burka had a distillery and supplied everyone with Vodka. The Ford truck Mark was driving was very old and looked beaten.

Coby thought the American vehicles would be recognizable to use especially with the steering wheel on the left and the manual-shift transmission.

The building that housed the warheads stood alone with a fifteen-foot cyclone fence with another two feet of razor-laden barbwire. Large towers had been constructed around the perimeter for lighting and video surveillance.

Mark said, "Only takes ten minutes to get to our luxurious office. I like driving this thing. It reminds me of my days at Camp LeJeune."

Coby, in the leather-worn seat next to Mark, said, "This thing is decades old."

"Yep. They told me we'd be getting a new truck in two weeks. That's Russian Army speak for anytime this year."

Coby could see the guard station ahead. A gray concrete building with a sliding door. On the roof was a display of antennas and a small satellite dish that Coby recognized as a Ku Band receiver. The truck stopped at the gate and was approached by two Russian guards. Mark, being instantly recognized, did not have to show any credentials. The taller of the two Russians walked around the truck and approached the window where Coby was seated. He had a rifle strapped around his shoulder. She recognized him as the guard she had seen on the stairs. Coby turned to Mark. "That's the soldier I passed on the stairs yesterday."

The guard looked directly into her eyes.

She tried to lower the window, but it was stuck. The guard opened the door and motioned for her to get out of the vehicle. "We need to see your ID."

Coby glanced over to Mark. "What do they want?"

"It's okay, they need to see your identification."

Coby reached into her shirt pocket, unlocked the attaché, and extracted a manila envelope. She ruffled through the papers and pulled out a white envelope with the words: "Orders – for Q-Level eyes only."

"Mark, it reads for my eyes only."

"It's okay, please act cool. You are looking shaky."

Coby was taken aback by his choice of words.

Mark, realizing he may have embarrassed her, said, "Just show him your identification. He did not want to see your orders. It is in there."

Coby exited the truck and handed the guard a white sheet of paper with writing and an ID badge paperclipped on the top. He took it over to the guard house. He perused the letter and stamped the paper, then signed it and walked over to Coby, handing it back to her with a radiation badge in his hand.

"Thank you. You need to wear your picture ID, Lieutenant Rodriguez. And here is your radiation badge. If this part turns red, then you must find shelter immediately."

"Yes, sure."

The guard said, with a smile, "Your presence will liven this place. Welcome."

Coby immediately recognized a flirting comment. "Since you now know my name, what is your name?"

"Sergei. Next time we pass each other on the stairs, at least we will know each other's names."

Coby smiled and took her picture ID badge and radiation badge and pinned it on her uniform. She re-entered the truck.

Cleared through the gates, they began the short drive to the arsenal. Mark apologized, "I'm sorry, I should have told you about the ID. I apologize."

"I was a little shaky back there and it showed. Guess I got off on the wrong foot," she said quizzically.

"You're fine." They reached the parking area. Mark parked the truck and the two of them entered the building, a very large field house with a parking lot in the front with two gates, one in the front and one in the rear of the building. After a short walk, they entered the building through the front gate, went up the stairs, then opened a large door.

A uniformed woman sat at a table to the right of the entryway. Major Alexis Stipenoff, fifty-two, with broad shoulders, stood when Mark and Coby entered. Extending her hand, the stern-looking woman said in perfect English, "Welcome to Kapustin Yar arsenal. My name is Major Alexis Stipenoff. This is the largest of all the arsenals held by the Kremlin."

Coby grabbed Alexis' extended hand with a firm grip. "Thank you, Major. My name is Lieutenant Coby Rodriguez."

The blackboard behind her had her name written in white chalk. It was misspelled. There were many ways to misspell Rodriguez and she had seen them all.

Alexis said, "Captain Boyd said he will show you the area. He's in the office waiting for your arrival. The routine is not complicated. However, it must be done by the rules."

"Yes, ma'am," Coby said reassuringly.

"You will address me as sir, okay?" Alexis was steadfast in teaching the rules. "Please understand that our countries have agreed on several courtesies. You are compelled to report anything that may appear to compromise the treaty to me or Major Burka. Anything else is not important to you here."

Coby nodded. "Yes, sir." *I wonder if calling her sir is the norm, or is she reading Cosmopolitan or other US magazines?*

"We will need your fingerprints." Alexis pointed to the ink pad and cards to capture the prints. Being in the Army, getting one's fingerprints was a common routine, so Coby knew the procedure. Coby registered her prints. Alexis then ordered them, "Follow me."

All three left the room and entered an office where Captain Cal Boyd was seated behind a desk. The walls were adorned with maps and signs in Russian. In the corner were two flags, Russian and the USA. Cowboy stood and all four were standing in a circle with only the desk between them.

Alexis told them, "Be prepared for unannounced lie-detector tests, drug tests, and auditing your reports. For count days, your team was issued a key for the warhead vault door. No single key will open the door. You will be met by a soldier at the vault door with the second key. When they change the locks on a random basis then you will be issued a new key."

Mark pointed to Coby. "It's all yours now. Let's go, Cowboy. Rodriguez is a grown soldier and can learn the rest on her own."

Cowboy wanted to live up to his promise to help. "I'm going to stick around. I want to make sure she is all right. I'll hitch a ride back."

Mark and Alexis left.

Cowboy sat on the chair in front of the desk.

Coby said, "Thanks, Cowboy, but I got this down. You can leave with Mark."

Cowboy reminded her, "The next planned count is today, and it is on your watch."

"Cal, er, Cowboy, which do you prefer?"

"I never liked Cal. Short for Calvin. In high school, I always wore a cowboy hat. The nickname began then and never ended." He rose from the chair heading for the door.

Coby, not wanting to ruffle feathers, said, "Okay, then Cowboy it is! On second thought, stay for a bit. I do have a question."

Cowboy gave his full attention.

"Where was Jeffries going the night he died?"

Cowboy had been waiting for these Jeffries questions to come sooner or later, so he was ready. "He was returning to the base from a party with his girlfriend."

"Party?"

"Yeah, at Burka's place."

"Oh. Does Burka throw parties often?"

"Every once in a while."

"Did the term 'conflict of interest' ever surface?" Coby acted like she had taken the bad cop role.

"I've been to one of the parties. No big deal," Cowboy answered.

"Did Mark and Jeffries attend the parties?" Coby was motoring.

"Yes."

"Were you all there the night Jeffries died?"

"I was but left early to take over my shift from Mark."

Coby was making headway in putting pieces of the puzzle together. "So, Mark was not with you that night."

"Nope."

"Was Jeffries drinking?"

"That is an understatement." Cowboy's face looked like he just ratted on a friend.

"You took the truck?" Coby asked.

"Yes, and Tim took Natasha's car," Cowboy recalled.

"And she went with him, and we know where that ended," stated Coby in a somber tone.

"Timmy musta been goin' more than 125 miles per hour in the Maserati," Cowboy commented.

"All this in less than sixty days?"

"You gotta know Tim. He is a fast mover."

"He was the last one to take a count.

"Did he file a report?"

"If he did, it would be in the filing cabinet."

"Did you review it?"

"No."

"Why not?"

"He can count and if there was anything unusual, he would have brought it to my and Mark's attention."

"Not very buttoned up, is it? Where are the keys to the cabinet and the vault door?"

"I've got a feeling in my stomach you are not going to like my answer. Both are in the top desk drawer."

Coby opened the unlocked drawer and saw a large and small key. She removed both keys. "I take it the large one is for the arsenal?"

Cowboy nodded, accepting the chiding.

Coby frowned. "This is rather sloppy if I say so myself. The pamphlet clearly states that the arsenal key should be in our quarters except on count days. I'll hang onto both keys."

Cowboy retorted in a superior manner, "Relax, I had it in my pea-picking pocket when I left our quarters. I know the rules."

CHAPTER 20

THE BREAK-IN IS PLANNED

Three hundred yards behind the back gate of the arsenal, six figures, all men, camouflaged, moved carefully through the jungle. A semi followed another hundred yards on the main road. They knew the routine. They had just done it a short while ago when seven warheads were lifted, placed on forklifts, and driven onto the semi-truck on its way to the ship waiting to take the weapons of mass destruction to Denali Island.

The rogue army leader raised his right arm. The others halted. Seconds later, the semi stopped and cut off the ignition. All was quiet. The lead soldier spoke softly into a communication device to the base command on the boat. "We are a couple of hundred meters from the capture point. The new American will perform her first count soon. She will want to be accurate. If we don't act before she counts, she will see that seven were already gone. That will prompt an alarm that will stop our mission to capture the other three." The leader looked at his watch. "It is now 18:40."

The base commander on the ship acknowledged the update. "Roger. It is a go here."

The rogue leader turned to the second in command. "We have a go. Set your clocks now. On my mark, we have twenty minutes to make this a reality. Turn the semi into position. Pull the forklifts out and get them in position."

The driver and the passenger of the semi exited the truck and opened the back doors. In the back of the semi, the forklift drivers started their engines, and the three forklifts slowly emerged from the semi and began their short journey over the moist dirt road toward the arsenal.

The skies over the warehouse were crystal clear. The crescent-shaped moon cast off a little moonlight but in the clear skies, it was enough to cast light to see clearly once the eyes were adjusted.

The floodlights inside the fence filled up the yard. The contrast was remarkable. Inside, the fence looked like daytime, but outside the fence it was nighttime.

Inside the American security office, Lieutenant Rodriguez stood by the filing cabinet.

Cowboy walked over to her. "The count log is in the upper drawer. After the count, you write in the count and sign it on the line."

Coby reached for the drawer when Cowboy's voice stopped her.

"You'll have time for that. It is usually the last item on the checklist. If you have any questions, call. You have our contact numbers."

"Are the landlines secure?"

Cowboy gave a "What, are you kidding?" glare.

Coby, realizing the lack of freedom, asked, "Cell phones too?"

Cowboy, with a sarcastic mocking, responded in his deep Texas drawl, "Right! Golly, you have a lot to learn." Cowboy pointed to the attaché. "Must be something special in there."

"Unless you are Q level, please don't mention my briefcase again."

"Yes, ma'am."

"Thanks for your insights. Please go, get some rest. If I have a question, I'll call the house phone."

"Catch you later. Adios!" Cowboy exited.

In Russian then in English, an amplified voice announced the beginning of the count.

Coby's heart jumped. She put down the brochure on the assignment and looked around the office. *Can't make the count with the briefcase attached to my arm.* She moved her hand into her pocket and pulled out a key. She unlocked the wrist lock and placed the attaché in a cabinet drawer labeled "Jeffries." Although tempted to see the last entry book, Coby locked the file and exited the office. She was caught in a conundrum. Could she leave the attaché case in the office, or back at the apartment? She decided to leave it in the office under lock and key. With a flashlight in one hand and a chart in the other, Coby headed toward her assigned security step one.

CHAPTER 21

THE WARHEADS ARE STOLEN

There was very little clearing outside the rear exit fence. Inside the space, were empty barracks and, after the clearing, there was nothing but dense forest split by a dirt path that over years of heavy trucks evolved into well-packed dirt roads. The rebel leader received various reports from the advance team in his earpiece. He was worried that the team was not ready and that they would lose their window of opportunity. "Get those three warheads before the American woman replacement counts the inventory."

"Yes, we know. We are waiting for the all-clear signal." Their window of time was now shortened by two precious minutes.

Finally, the words he had been waiting to hear were happening. "Sir, the alarm was disconnected, and the rear gate was unlocked."

The leader ordered the lift into the clearing. Three forklifts drove through the opening and into the warhead warehouse. The sentry guards disappeared following an order signed by Major Burka.

Inside the arsenal, at the first checking station location, Coby took a key hanging on a chain and inserted it into a keyhole in the wall and turned it clockwise to record her presence at the site. A little red light turned green. She then initialed the paper on the clipboard hanging next to the keyhole. She noticed that the last initials were "TJ."

Inside the arsenal, the three forklifts had loaded up the three large crates and were leaving the compound. Each crate was labeled "RADIOACTIVE STAND CLEAR" in English, and in Russian as "RADEOAKTIV STOYAT' V STORE."

The semi's rear doors were opened and one by one the forklifts motored up a ramp into the truck with the crates.

Speaking into the communication device, the leader said, "Phase one is complete. Reset the alarms and re-lock the gate. Alert HQ the goods are on the truck."

After completing step two's key check, Coby was now ready for the count. The vault door was a short walk away.

On the wall outside the warhead storage area was a speaker. Coby pushed the button, then waited for someone to acknowledge her presence at the door. A female voice from the speaker announced, "Da, I'll be right there."

Coby peeked in the vault window and saw the crates of nuclear warheads in the large warehouse. They were all piled in neat rows and columns. She thought to herself, *There is enough firepower in here to send the Earth out of orbit.*

A metal door to her left opened and a tall young female Russian soldier entered the arsenal entrance area. "Hello, I am Private Koslov. Do you have your key?"

"Yes, right here. I'm Lieutenant Rodriguez."

Private Koslov did not react. Nothing but a blank look.

Coby, with a smile, said, "Glad to meet you."

Still no reaction.

She thought, *Robots.*

Together they inserted the keys in the double keyholes in the door and turned them simultaneously. A buzzer sounded and the light on the door illuminated green with the word "ACTIVATED." A countdown clock began a fifteen-second countdown.

"Are you coming in with me?"

"It is forbidden. You need to quickly place your thumb on the pad here to verify it is you."

Coby placed her thumb on the pad. A second green light illuminated, and the door slowly opened. The door was as big and heavy as a bank vault door.

"There will be another pad inside for you to shut the door. You will not need me here to reenter this area. You will have fifteen seconds to close the door."

"What happens if it closes without my fingerprint?"

"The base goes in lockdown and the soldiers are alerted."

"Oh. Don't want that, do we?"

"It has never occurred before."

Coby entered the warhead storage area and placed her thumb on the pad inside. The door closed slowly. She went down a flight of metal stairs to the storage area. She checked her badge for radiation. Each step was answered with an echo as her boots hit the metal step on the staircase leading to the arsenal hall.

She opened the notebook and began to count the wooden

crates. She checked her badge again to be sure it was safe to continue. Then she resumed counting. Each crate was numbered and the sheet she was using had corresponding numbers with boxes to check off. Coby proceeded to count and check her list. As she approached the large hangar doors to the outside, she felt a cold draft. The draft alerted her to the giant doors being ajar. *This cannot be normal.* She wrote something in the notebook and examined the doors but did not notice anything unusual until her eyes caught the fresh tire tracks on the floor.

She squeezed through the open door and stepped outside to examine the tracks that led to the back gate. *I think they would have alerted me if something was being removed or added to the arsenal.*

Back inside, Coby followed the tracks to an empty section in the corner. *This is not right!* She compared the number of crates on the clipboard from that section. One two, three, four, five, six, seven, eight, nine, ten...

Crates 00233 through 00243 were *gone*. None of the spaces were filled.

"Let me double-check." Coby walked to the area where the crates should have been and verified that all ten were missing. "Shit, there are missing crates, or did I mess up? I need to report this to Major Stipenoff right away."

She ran to the office and stopped at the door to register her thumbprint. Impatient, waiting for the heavy door to respond then open, she ran down the aisle to the American office, turned the corner, had a momentary slip, caught her balance, entered the office, and called the apartment.

Mark answered the phone. He was half-asleep.

"Mark, there are ten missing warheads. Alert the Pentagon and contact General Matthews. I'll contact Stipenoff. Put Cowboy on."

"What do you mean... He's not there? I thought he was with you."

"And he has the truck. Great! I need you here now. I don't give a crap how you get here. Walk if you have to."

A quarter mile behind the arsenal on the dirt road the semi was moving slowly, and a military truck with the rogue army followed close behind. Not to make any unnecessary noise, the two vehicles crawled. Once a good distance from the arsenal, the semi and truck picked up speed. As the semi accelerated, dust was kicked up and illuminated by the faint moonlight.

At the arsenal, the entire area was now awash in floodlights and a klaxon filled the air.

Alexis Stipenoff was on the phone.

Coby opened the locked cabinet and removed the count log. Coby and Stipenoff looked over the log. Coby said, "The last count is missing. Seems Jeffries did all the counts. The page is gone. G-O-N-E, gone."

Alexis put down her phone. "I have alerted all units. Whoever stole the warheads entered and left through the back gate. We are processing the videotape now. What we do know is they seemed to have used forklifts. The video does not show where they go after they left the vicinity. We have placed the sentry guards in lock-up."

Coby deduced, "They must have loaded the crates on a large truck."

Alexis added, "They only took three."

Coby realized, "They, whoever *they* are, already have *seven* warheads."

Coby thought back to when she opened Jeffries' notebook from his top drawer and remembered the circled number seven written on the paper. Coby looked at the clock. This all came down ten to twelve minutes ago. Turning to Alexis, Coby said, "Major, please give me the keys to the fastest vehicle in the motor pool."

"Come with me." Alexis took Coby by the arm to the parking lot and gave her the keys to her personal car. "Here are the keys to my Uza. It is speedy."

Coby got into the Uza, revved the engine, and took off like a bolt of lightning toward the main gate.

Sergei, who was on duty, saw her barreling toward the barriers, stepped out, and waved her to stop. "Halt!"

On the other gate at the guard house, a personnel truck entered the area with a group of armed Russian soldiers. They were there to stop any further thefts.

Coby shouted to him through the window. "Open the gate!"

"The base is in lockdown. No one leaves!"

"They are gaining ground and must be stopped!"

Sergei recognized Alexis' car and didn't hesitate further. He opened the gate.

Coby revved the motor, threw it in gear, and began to take off.

Running, keeping pace with the car waving his arms, Sergei yelled, "Stop the car, I'll go with you! Move over, and we'll change seats. I know these roads. Besides this was done on my watch!"

Coby stopped the car and slid over to the passenger seat. Sergei got in, fully armed, revolver at his side and a rifle strapped to his body. Once inside, the car sped behind the facility. "You will get us both imprisoned."

Coby responded quickly, "This is a matter of global security. I am given orders to fix this situation. If we do not stop this, many innocent people will die."

The semi entered a curve at a great speed and almost turned over. Its passenger was hanging onto the open window frame for dear life. "Slow down, slow down! You will kill us! Easy, easy remember we are carrying nuclear bombs!" The semi continued at full speed.

"Relax, comrade, they can only be exploded when they activate the little bombs in a ring around the nuclear weapons. Drink some more vodka, relax." The driver reached under his seat and removed a bottle of vodka. He unscrewed the top with his teeth and placed the bottle on his lips. He drank a hardy swig from the bottle and passed it over to his sidekick who swallowed two mouthfuls.

"Ah much better now."

CHAPTER 22

THE PENTAGON

Nothing seemed unusual as exterior lights illuminated the giant Pentagon building. Many American and military branch flags were waving in the breeze. Just another day at the office.

General Matthews was on the phone with President Jonathan Waters, the first president elected as an Independent. "They have ten, Mr. President. The CIA says they believe the thieves are not associated with a nation but a rogue group of international criminals." The general listened and responded, "Yes, sir, the Russians are deploying helicopters in search of a large speeding truck we suspect to be carrying the three warheads. We have two soldiers in fierce pursuit. A Russian and one of our monitors." The general listened. "Coby Rodriguez. Yes, sir, we will keep you posted."

The general quickly put down the desk phone and pushed the red speakerphone to the other side of the desk. "This is General Cliff J. Matthews 'star 17 cavalry N DASH 771.'"

A female voice said, "Voiceprint activated, General Matthews."

"Activate Def-Con 3 status."

The robotic voice responded "Def-Con 3 status activated. An alert will go to all facilities. Thank you, have a wonderful day, General Matthews."

The alarm at Kapustin Yar never stopped ringing. The floodlights surrounded the complex. Spotlights were focused on the forklift tire tracks in the area behind the building. The Russian soldiers formed a ring around the complex with rifles in their hands. Two helicopters were revving their engines on the helipad. Two men jumped into each machine with grenades and bazookas. Their mission was to catch up with the truck and destroy it. The helicopters were awaiting further orders.

Major Stipenoff was in command after many futile attempts to reach Major Burka. She called the airbase in Leningrad for assistance. "This is a code red situation. We need assistance. Ten warheads have been stolen." Two more troop transport vehicles entered the complex. Major Stipenoff met them and ordered them to go around the complex. One took the dirt path to the north, and the other took the path to the south.

Coby and Sergei were making excellent time in the very fast Russian-made sports car. Coby asked Sergei, "Can you drive this thing any faster?"

"I'm going as fast as I can with all these curves!"

"For God's sake, try slamming your foot on the gas pedal."

Sergei pushed his foot down and the agile sports car accelerated even faster. The two were making excellent time.

The semi and the rogue team in the army truck reached the docks. The leader jumped from the truck and ordered the men to unload the forklifts from the tractor-trailer. The giant back doors were opened as wide as they could go. The forklift drivers entered the semi and one by one drove off the truck and onto the dock. The warhead crates were being prepared for transport on a large fishing boat. Each forklift was positioned next to the boat's hull. Ropes were wrapped around the crates and a large hook was carefully placed inside the top of the crates then slowly lifted onto the ship.

The crew topside then gingerly guided the crates onto a board which was then anchored securely to the deck. Once all three were loaded, all the men abandoned the semi, the truck, and all the forklifts, and got on board the boat. The precision was remarkable. In under ten minutes, the semi was emptied, and the boat readied. The ship's captain, with a dark complexion and wearing a captain's hat, had watched all the action. The fifty-foot boat, *RODINA*, had its motors running. The captain had observed the loading project. He shouted, "Good! The last crate is on board. Cover them with a tarp. We may run into some wet weather. Squalls are being reported tonight." On the boat, all three warhead crates were covered with gray tarps. The captain barked, "Lift anchor!"

The large fishing boat slowly pulled away from the dock. On the bridge, the first mate took orders from the captain. "We will be at full speed in the open waters, then several hours to our destination. Just in case, prepare the defensive weapons. For now, we will take it slow and not cause any attention."

"Yes, Captain." The crew member ran to a battery of three missile launchers and removed the protective coverings. The surface-to-air (SAM) missiles were not state of the art, but the ones on the ship were capable of taking down anything that had heat emanating from the engines.

From the arsenal base, two Army helicopters received their orders and took flight from Kapustin Yar. The intercom lit up with a destination. "Copter 657, follow the road south leading to the river. Second copter, stand down and wait for orders."

In the Uza, Sergei focused on driving the winding dirt path. He heard the words "That means this road will lead us to the river" shouted over Coby's radio.

Mark's voice came over the radio. "A Russian helicopter from a different base has located the semi. It is hovering at the river port, Helena. The copter will wait for you there. There is another copter on its way from here."

"Makes sense. Moving the warheads by air, radar would pick them up in a second, but on the water it is smart."

Sergei said, "That is where this road ends."

"What is our ETA?"

"My guess is ten minutes."

"How much ammo do you have?"

"One hundred rounds."

"Good. But I have a feeling we'll need more."

CHAPTER 23

DEF-CON 4

A dozen security vehicles entered the Pentagon's main north gate. Most of the cars were black and had the flags of the United States flapping in the wind next to the flag representing the branch of the military the vehicle served.

Due to the urgency of the situation, they were waved through the north gate without checking credentials, which would be done once they enter the massive office building.

In the Pentagon's Situation Room, every seat in the room was occupied. On the screen in the room were projected the words "DEF-CON 4."

This room was different from the White House "Situation Room" since it was only three levels underground and the White House was six levels below ground. The Pentagon was sitting on a rather low water table and could not go any deeper than three floors.

Once the Joint Chiefs of Staff were seated at the horseshoe-shaped table, General Matthews stood to address the elite group.

"The pouches you have on your desk have a complete recap as to where we were with the stolen warheads." Reading from a printed report, Matthews said, "We have received intel on Jeffries. He was not alone in the car. He was returning from Burka's home." Now from the heart, he said, "This news gives us all great concern since there are ten nuclear warheads in the hands of a mercenary group determined to destroy us and our allies." With the general's face turning red, he raised his voice in a tone of disgust. "And our guy helped make this happen!"

The general sat to look at a notepad then stood and moved to a second screen with a pointer in his hand. Pointing to the map at a spot east of Greece, Matthews said, "Per reports, we are ninety percent sure the warheads are on their way to this shaded area." The pointer was moved from Ankara to a tiny island in the Aegean Sea. "The Russians are working with us to verify the location so we can destroy the area."

Quiet in the room.

The general, in an assuring tone, said, "We have alerted NATO and every one of our partners is on a high state of alert."

Bruce, a second general, approached Matthews. "All bases are readied, and the Civil Defense personnel are in touch with all the parties to notify the public based on your command, General."

"Thank you, Bruce. Notifying the public now will only cause a panic."

Bruce assured General Matthews, "I agree, Cliff. You say the word and we will have the message in every corner of the country in five minutes."

Matthews said under his breath, "In five minutes those nukes could be flying over our heads." Then Matthews uttered what may have been the most sincere words of his life: "God help us."

THE RIVER DOCK

At the end of the road and over the river's edge, a dimly lit dock for fishing boats was rocking with the unsettled river waters. At the end of one of the piers, under a single light coated with hundreds of flying insects drawn to it was a fuel pump. Coby and Sergei arrive to see the unloaded semi, the abandoned forklifts, and the military vehicle all neatly parked next to each other. The Russian helicopter was hovering overhead.

At the dock, an old fisherman with a full beard was pointing. He said in Russian, "I watched the whole thing."

Coby, understanding the language, answered back in Russian, "What did you see?"

"Forklifts carrying big wooden boxes. They were hoisted onto the large fishing boat." The fisherman pointed. "They headed south, probably to the bay."

"Spasibo."

Another smaller boat entered the docking area. Sergei jumped on board and told the pilot to give up his boat. "As you can see, I am a Russian soldier. I order you to give us the use of your boat. You will be handsomely rewarded."

The pilot refused.

Sergei removed his revolver and aimed it at the pilot's heart. "I will not hurt you. Just leave the boat. Do you not understand? I am a Russian soldier in pursuit of an enemy. Do this for the Motherland."

The old fisherman reluctantly stepped off the boat.

Sergei was now alone in the unoccupied thirty-foot wooden boat. The motor was running.

Inside the hovering helicopter, the copilot pointed to the dock. The pilot nodded. "The team has arrived. The two down there must be the two soldiers chasing down the criminals."

"Should we land and pick them up?"

"No, they'll let us know the next step." The pilot spoke into the radio microphone. "Base, this is chopper L-23, repeat, L-23."

Over the speaker, a voice said, "We hear you five by five. There are two more birds fully loaded about ten minutes behind you."

"Roger. Shine the spotlights on them. They are working practically in the dark."

Coby and Sergei saw the helicopter, which was now overhead. Coby from the shore, shouted over the roar of the blades, "Motion the pilot to fly down the river, south." Looking at Sergei in the commandeered boat, she said, "We'll use the boat to catch those creeps. Hope it has enough fuel."

Sergei put the boat in idling gear, jumped back on the dock, secured the boat to the dock, and stepped into the helicopter's spotlight. The wind from the blades had all the clothing on Sergei flapping. Water from the river was sprayed on the Russian soldier. The spray was accented due to the searchlight. He arm-gestured for the helicopter to fly south.

Coby ran to the hijacked boat and jumped in. The helicopter took off south following the river leaving everything illuminated by the moon and the single bulb swinging in the breeze. "Sergei, grab that gas can over there. Fill it up and jump on board."

Sergei filled the can, untethered the boat by lifting the mooring rope from the staff and tossing it into the boat, then jumped on board with the can of fuel tightly held in his hand. Coby was piloting the boat. She went full throttle. The boat accelerated leaving a large wide wake in her pursuit of the vessel carrying three nuclear warheads.

KAPUSTIN YAR

The floodlights were on, and the alarm had ceased. Inside the American security office, Mark was left by himself with no communication as to what was going on. He was aware that the two US monitors were missing. Curiosity steered him to the filing cabinet. He tried to open the drawer with pure muscle. After two attempts he then looked for a tool that could help. Going to the desk he opened the bottom drawer where there might be a screwdriver. No screwdriver but a thick wooden ruler. He took the ruler to the filing cabinet and placed it in the space on top of the drawer and with his brute force pushed the stick only to have it snap into two pieces. Now he was determined more than ever.

Mark exited the office and stood back from getting trampled by three Russian soldiers in a hurry. He remembered that in the hallway there was a janitor's closet that might have the tool he needed to force open the filing cabinet drawer.

Luckily the janitor's closet was unlocked, and inside the dark room, Mark felt something hit his face. Unflinching, he grabbed the object and could feel it was a chain. He pulled the chain and the bulb attached to the other end of it lit up.

On one of the shelves, he spotted a toolbox. Inside the array of tools, there was a sixteen-inch heavy gauge screwdriver. He ran back into the office and with the long screwdriver, he forced the drawer's lock to disengage. With one hearty yank, he opened the drawer. He removed Coby's attaché case and picked that lock open. He rifled through the papers.

When he came across a file labeled "Q clearance." He opened the file. He could feel his ears and face blushing. He knew he had broken a sacred honor. Inside the file was a photo of Major Burka. Under the photo were the words "Double Agent," "Mercenary Background," and "Former CIA." Mark closed the file and placed it back in the drawer then locked the drawer. He was sweating profusely.

On the river, Coby was piloting the boat. There was a light moment when she shook her head and wondered why an Army person was piloting the boat.

Sergei was checking his weapons.

Inside the helicopter pursuing the fishing vessel, the pilot ordered the copilot to open the side door and ready the weapons. The co-pilot pointed to the escaping vessel. "I see the ship down there."

"Looks like they are removing the tarp from a battery of SAMs. We need to hit them before they hit us. I'll fly low and buzz them while you get ready."

The captain of the Rowina had seen the copter coming from a distance and had ordered the missile batteries to be ready to fire.

"They think we are unprotected. They are coming closer. Do not fire until I give the word!"

The Russian Airman leaning out the door initiated the shoulder missile carrier and aimed it at the ship.

"Get closer, they are still— Shit! They are in firing mode right now. Pull up! Pull up! I can get a good shot out but act fast!"

The helicopter made a radial upward and to-the-left motion sending the co-pilot back on his legs. He managed to get one shot off and it was right on target. The missiles dug deep into the hull of the ship and exploded, rendering the boat dead in the water.

The enemy soldier was thrown to the deck from the explosion. He struggled to get to the missile bay and fired one blast.

No one knew what the people in the helicopter uttered as their last words. The armaments from the boat hit the engines and fuel tanks of the copter.

The commandeered boat was at top speed. Wind and water spray were all around causing Coby to shelter her eyes. Fortunately, the river had calmed which gave them the speed advantage of skimming on the water. Her vision was impaired and yet she reacted to a flash in the sky.

Coby pointed to the sky and said, "Out there, look! The helicopter."

Sergei computed. "I think we are three to five kilometers behind. Hopefully, the copter slowed them down. They must have some serious weapons on board."

Coby mustered up some sarcasm. "A handgun and a rifle versus artillery shells and handheld missiles."

The helicopter dropped from the sky as a ball of fire.

Turning to Sergei. "Hope you are a good shot."

He responded quickly with pride, "Number one in my

class at Frunze. We should catch them in less than twenty minutes. If the copters slowed them down, maybe sooner."

Coby looked down at the boat's dashboard. "We're getting close to empty. How full is the can?"

"Enough to catch them but forget getting back. I filled the can the best I could." Sergei picked up the can and shook it. "It's almost full."

"Good job."

CHAPTER 24

PENTAGON DECISIONS

In normal times, the area around the Pentagon was still. But tonight was anything but normal times. The sound of sirens filled the air. Military vehicles were in numbers greater than the civilian cars on the street. The sky was filled with helicopters, none of which were owned by the local TV news. They had been told not to fly near the Pentagon.

With all this activity, a line of military vehicles blocked all the gates. The Army trucks were loaded with artillery cannons of every shape and size. Under Def-Con 3 protocol, they were protecting the Pentagon as though Washington DC was being attacked.

The Situation Room was five floors under the floor of the Pentagon. It was secure from the rock foundation below and to the four walls around the room. The ceiling was made of concrete and steel. The Joint Chiefs entered with Vice President Donner, forty-five, salt-and-pepper hair, very fit.

General Matthews stood. "Good evening, Vice President Donner." They shook hands.

A second elevator door opened, and the head of the CIA entered the room. Gloria Smith, fifty-four, five-foot-four, matronly, wore a blue pants suit.

The vice president and Gloria embraced. Donner said, "Right on time." Worried, he added, "From what I hear, things look bleak."

General Matthews answered, "Yes, sir. However, we have one of our monitors and a Russian soldier chasing down the stolen warheads."

Gloria added, "No word from them."

"How many warheads does the breeched arsenal hold?"

Mathews answered, "Three hundred and forty-eight. That only represents about five percent of their capabilities."

Gloria added, "That five percent alone is capable of overkill."

"Have we heard anything from the other arsenals?" Donner seemed to be getting a grasp of the vulnerability and danger facing the globe.

Matthews said, "Reports are still coming in, but so far so good. The Russians are good actors here. They have fortified all the arsenals."

Vice President Donner reassured the people there, "The president is on his way from Arkansas." Turning to the general, he said, "How much time does it take to activate our Air Force? We could easily take down the ship carrying the weapons."

Matthews shook his head and said, "Not without permission from the Russian president. I'm afraid this is their show. Let's hope they are effective."

Donner asked, "What about the CIA?"

Gloria was pessimistic. "I've been briefed, and this does not look good. Our operatives are too far away."

The vice president, now reaching for straws, said, "Do we have any people in the area?"

The general responded, "There is a team of Navy SEALs headed to what we believe is their base of operations. A resort area called Denali Island off Turkey." He pointed to the map again.

Donner asked, "What if we are wrong?"

The general, in a lower tone, said, "Let's pray we are not."

Donner turned to Smith and said, "What is the SEALs' mission?"

She responded, "To completely destroy the complex, including the silos, and all the buildings on the island."

President Jonathan Waters was listening in on a dedicated line, and speakers embedded in the ceiling interrupted, "Silos?"

Gloria wasted no time answering, "Yes, sir."

He quipped, "And if the warheads are armed?"

"Sir, they cannot explode unless they are armed. My guess is the enemy knows how to arm them. As they are removed from the arsenal, they are not armed and probably will not be armed until they are on the rockets and the rockets are fueled and ready to fly." Having done her homework, Gloria added, "However, ten nuclear-armed warheads would be detonated, and the force of the explosions would destroy Turkey and its neighboring countries. It would create a tsunami in the Aegean and Mediterranean Seas to wipe out all towns and villages on the coast. Then there is the radiation." Looking at her notes, she said, "The immediate kill rate would be ten to twelve million people vaporized, with another fifty million by intense radiation."

Waters asked, "How would we know if they are armed or not?"

Gloria, in an authoritative tone, said, "That is what the SEALs will determine once they penetrate the launch complex."

Matthews quipped, "NATO, however, has been notified about the island compound."

DENALI ISLAND

Outside the mansion, the balmy temperature, when combined with fine champagne, loosened up many of the evil guests. Two of the guests and their assistants were swimming in the lit pool naked. Prisca and her female assistant were being more than friendly. Their erotic and exotic shadows were gaining the attention of the other two watching from the edge of the pool.

The two took turns diving and surfacing inside the spread legs of her partner. Prisca yelled with pleasure. It was a turn-on for the two other voyeurs, and they began to pleasure each other orally as well.

In Chi-Lah's suite, Chi-Lah and Fahid were seated at a desk with a CRT screen's green glow casting an eerie color tone on the conversation.

Fahid reported, "The warheads are close to our seaplanes outside of Russian control. We had to shoot down a helicopter, but they were able to stop the ship, dead in the water. The world now knows we need to act quickly."

"Are you suggesting we launch the seven we have?"

"Yes, we will not see the remaining three. I can put the order out to fuel and arm the devices. They will be ready in forty minutes."

Chi-Lah said something in Chinese that sounded like an

angry leader who was frustrated. "Be sure they target Washington, New York, and London. We shall soon see how sophisticated these rockets are. By the time they realize they are coming, it will be too late."

"Yes, Chi-Lah"

CHAPTER 25

THE ICY WATERS

Coby and Sergei's boat was close enough to take on fire. The boat was on a collision course with the much larger fishing boat carrying the warheads.

"They're not moving. The copter must have hit them too," Coby yelled.

A bullet soared through the plastic shield in front of Coby. For a moment she reminisced about the bullet on the Atlantic City train with her Momma, how close it was then and now.

The team answered with their gun and rifle, but it was no comparison to the high-powered weapons from the boat they were chasing. Coby yelled to Sergei, "How well can you swim?"

"Not bad, but I'm pretty good with a vest!"

Sergei opened and searched the white bench lockers on the boat. Then he looked in the center near the bilge and said, "no vests!"

"Sergei, listen carefully, secure the wheel and set our boat on a collision course toward the engine room, then jump in the water and swim as fast as you can!"

"Are you serious?"

"Trust me!"

Sergei took a rope and tied it so the wheel aimed the speeding thirty-foot boat toward the enemy ship, then he jumped in the cold water. They were only fifty yards from a collision. Coby moved to the aft railing and aimed the rifle at the fuel can and repeatedly shot into the gas. After three shots, the can ignited into a fiery ball, and Coby was thrown into the water from the force of the ensuing explosion.

She hit the water hard. Her motionless body sank deeper and deeper into the river.

Seconds later, the flaming boat crashed into the enemy boat at full speed. On contact, it exploded causing more damage. The calculated risk worked. Flames were crawling up the side of the fishing boat soon to lap onto the deck. The fishing boat with the warheads was not only dead in the water, but it was also completely on fire.

Three of the crew jump into the water and into a life raft that had preceded hitting the water moments before them.

Sergei was treading in a river that was a mixture of water and fire. When the fuel spewing from the damaged ship hit the water, it ignited into flames. From a distance, it resembled a large bonfire somehow resting on a body of water.

Through the sea of flames, Sergei searched but did not see Coby. "Coby! Coby!" No sign of her.

Sergei took a deep breath and went under the surface to look for Coby. Out of breath, Sergei returned to the surface. Hoping she had surfaced, and he just couldn't see her through the smoke and flames, he shouted, "Coby! Coby! Where are you Coby?"

He went under for the third time. Eyes burning from the fuel on the water now free flowing from the engine compartment on the enemy ship that was now totally ablaze and listing starboard.

Coby's body was in a free fall sinking farther and farther into the depths, and she was unconscious. The silhouette of her body contrasted the backdrop of fire on the water's surface.

The still of the water was broken when an unusual shape left her body, then another and another until the seventh shape emerged and united with the six to form an eerie blanket that resembled a jellyfish, which began to lift her body to the surface.

In seconds, her body rose to the surface. The souls held her in place until she could be rescued.

The water was extremely cold. If it weren't for the heat from the flaming vessels, hypothermia would have set in by now, killing both Coby and Sergei.

In the light from the flames and through the smoke, Sergei noticed Coby on the surface twenty yards from him. He frantically swam to her. When he reached her, he wrapped his arm around her like a seatbelt. He looked into her face, and she had both eyes closed. There appeared to be no sign of life. He frantically swam toward shore with her lifeless body in tow. The blanket of souls never left her, now forming a pod around her.

Swimming hard, Sergei navigated through debris and flames headed toward land.

When they reach the shore, he placed her body on the sand and began to perform CPR. No response. Sergei pinched her nose and breathed deeply into her mouth, lips to lips. No response.

The cold was bitter, and Sergei could feel his fingers going numb. He stopped for a moment and breathed into his cupped hands. The numbness subsided for the moment.

The eerie form of souls separated and one by one, they reentered Coby's body.

Sergei resumed the rescue maneuver on her, and time after time, when most would give up, Sergei continued, never quitting.

Now the frigid air was beginning to penetrate wet clothing on Sergei. He repeated a mantra over and over in his head, *Russians are strong. Russians can endure.*

He spoke to the unresponsive Coby Rodriguez. "Please don't leave me."

Again, he pinched her nose and breathed into her mouth, praying his air could bring her back to life.

After what seemed like forever, Coby showed a weak sign of life with shallow breathing. Sergei pushed his hands and applied great pressure down on her chest. Water rushes from her mouth.

Coby opened her eyes and saw Sergei smiling and crying at the same time.

"You are breathing." He picked her shivering body up and held her close to him. Sergei sobbed with relief.

Coby held him tight.

In the skies above them, the roar of many helicopters permeated the air.

The enemy vessel was listing with the captain's perch now parallel to the water. The flames, however, had not subsided. To the couple's benefit, the flames cast enough light for the Russians in one of the helicopters to spot them on the shore.

The Russian helicopter carefully maneuvered between the forest and river and landed on shore. The crew jumped and ran to rescue Coby and Sergei. Coby slowly regained strength and walked to the waiting copter. Sergei was helping her stabilize.

Moments later, the remaining Russian helicopters blasted the enemy boat into oblivion. The flashes of firepower revealed the survivors in the rafts just before they too were destroyed.

CHAPTER 26

DENALI ISLAND

Four Navy SEALs were lying low outside the perimeter of the compound where the silos were located. They were covered with camouflaging leaves and twigs.

Lead SEAL Captain Tony Di Martino led SEAL Two, Captain Gallo, to the edge of the silo area. They entered the area by crawling under a wire fence they had cut. They detected activity with the technical teams fueling the huge seven rockets. SEAL One had a communication device. "They are fueling now. They appear to be using kerosene and liquid oxygen. If they follow the handbook, the warheads will not be activated at this point. That is if they are following the handbook."

At the moment he signed off, a voice sounded: "Stand up and drop all your weapons." An enemy soldier revealed himself, aimed his rifle at SEAL Two, and executed him point blank.

Di Martino reacted by looking after the fallen comrade.

He realized that death came instantly to his partner in arms. Standing, he was now ready to accept his fate.

Inside Chi-Lah's mansion, Fahid heard the unexpected shot and, in fear, left the building and ran toward the heliport.

At the fence standing over the corpse of SEAL Two, the enemy soldier asked SEAL One, "How many of you are there?"

"Just the two of us," Di Martino lied.

"Come with me." The enemy soldier led Di Martino on a path through the thick forest to the resort.

SEALs Three and Four heard the shot and surmised something was terribly wrong. SEAL Three, Azteca, said, "They should be back by now. The planes will be here in minutes. I'll go take a look."

Inside the rescue helicopter, Sergei and Coby sat and shivered. Sergei was holding Coby close to him exchanging body heat. They were heading back to Kapustin Yar.

Coby said through chattering teeth, "I never thought I'd be thankful to the Russkies for anything."

Sergei smiled and they tightened their hold on each other.

Coby said, "I want to pay Major Burka a visit."

Inside the Pentagon, the activity was heightened. Gloria Smith said, "We must make a decision quickly. The ground team has located the site of the silos. The warheads are not armed. We need to destroy the warheads before they are to avert the single greatest disaster created by man."

The president entered the Pentagon Situation Room

through the elevator doors, dressed in a sport coat, no tie. Everyone stood. "Please be seated. I heard what you said, how much time do we have?"

Gloria responded, "Minutes, Mr. President. I suggest you take to the bunker."

Shrugging, Waters said, "If the launch compound is destroyed, won't that keep them from arming the weapons?"

General Matthews answered quickly, "Not necessarily. The weapons are armed manually by technicians at the silos. Even so, my guess is they could be launched by a timer. You know, a doomsday trigger. I'm afraid the only way to be sure is to send in our bombers."

In a very commanding voice, the president said, "I pray I am doing the correct thing. Blow the God-damn thing up! All of it! NOW!"

Outside the silo perimeter, SEAL Four, Honcho, transmitted to the Situation Room, "This is Navy SEAL Four reporting that the ICBMs are in the fueling process. We did hear a single shot about two minutes ago. SEAL Three is on a search mission to locate our two missing men."

From Command, he heard Donner say, "POTUS says light it up. I say get your fucking asses out of there A-SAP!"

"How much time do we have?"

"At the most seven minutes."

Azteca returned with the bad news. "Captain Gallo was killed, and Tony is missing."

"Come on, we have to find him," SEAL Four said.

"I think I know the path they took." SEAL Three and Four ran as fast as they could through briar and thick bramble.

Di Martino stopped walking in the forest when he saw the

resort buildings. The enemy soldier poked the rifle into his back. Big mistake. "Keep moving!"

Di Martino turned and grabbed the rifle and twisted the gun, which caused the soldier to lose grip. Now the soldier's fate was in the hands of a United States Navy SEAL.

SEALs Three and Four arrive at the site. SEAL Honcho snuck from behind the soldier and made eye contact with Di Martino. Stealth-like, with his knife, Di Martino slit the soldier's throat. The three SEALs then scurried to safety. SEAL Three said, "We should go back and get Captain Gallo's body."

"It's too late," De Martino said. "The planes will be here in minutes."

Within two minutes, the sound of jet bombers was overhead. Seconds later the compound, silos, forest, resort mansion, and remaining buildings were destroyed. From a distance, the entire island was ablaze in fire and fury.

A minute later, out of the fiery sky, a lone helicopter flew away from the turmoil.

CHAPTER 27

MAJOR BURKA

The rescue helicopter carrying Coby and Sergei landed on the helipad on the grounds of the arsenal. The two ran from the copter to the American office in the arsenal.

Coby and Sergei entered the American security office, clothes still damp with blankets wrapped around their shoulders. Neither Mark nor Cowboy was there. Coby wondered, *Who's minding the store?* She examined the lock and realized someone had opened her case.

Mark entered the room.

Coby opened the cabinet drawer and took out the attaché and examined it. "Did you open my case?"

"Sorry, Coby, but you were on a suicide mission, and I had to know what I was up against. I'll take the court-martial."

Coby asked Sergei to leave the room for a few minutes. Once he cleared the room, she asked Mark, "So, what have you learned?"

"That you were assigned to recon the situation. See if there is a connection between Jeffries' accident and the stealing of the warheads. That you are to find out what side Major Burka is on as a possible double agent."

"What else?"

"That there is a sixty-eight-percent probability that Tim, Cal, or I are involved in a conspiracy to help the enemy destroy selected targets or to sell the warheads to a hostile nation."

"I assure you I am one-hundred-percent American. I have never missed an election," Mark said.

"We'll revisit this later. Sit down," Mark suggested more than ordered. "There is more I have to tell you. We knew the warheads might be stolen."

"Who is we?"

"General Matthews, the CIA, NSA, and intelligence from twelve different agencies."

"Oh, those. So, you knew about this the entire time?"

"We were not sure when it would happen or who was behind it or how the warheads might be used. Washington suspected Jeffries. In his car that night was Jeffries' Russian girlfriend who was collateral damage in the murder of Jeffries."

Intrigued, Coby asked, "Murder?"

"Yes, the way I see this is Burka and Jeffries were working together.

Burka had done his job. He can control the alarm system and other surveillance from his house."

"So, is this a Russian plot?"

"No," Mark said with some confidence.

"And Burka?"

"As you read in the top-secret file, a possible double agent. Well as I see it, he is. He was being blackmailed. They dangled his loving niece in front of him. He did find ways to back-channel info to our command through various friendly spooks."

Coby thought a moment. "I'll need a vehicle."

"You're going there?"

"My orders, sir. See if Stipenoff can get us another vehicle. Yes, tomorrow I am paying a visit to Burka."

"Roger."

Perfectly timed, Major Stipenoff entered the security room, picked up the phone receiver, and dialed. She did very little talking but was intensely listening to the person on the other end of the call, nodding her head.

After the major hung up, Coby asked, "Major, do you know where Lieutenant Boyd is?"

Mark commented, "With what is going on, Cowboy should be here."

"No, I do not. Have you checked the apartment?"

"He's not there," Mark responded.

"It seems you have a discipline problem. I was just told a compound on an island near Turkey was completely destroyed. The enemy was only minutes away from launching other rockets. The immediate threat is over."

"Great!" Coby said, relieved. "Good news! Major, we need a vehicle, and why are you saying the immediate threat is over? Do you know of more breaches?"

"There are many more arsenals here and in your country that must refine all security protocols. Well, since my car is on a riverbank, the only thing I can get you is a truck. Tomorrow there will be a horde of inspectors crawling over the base. I fully expect to be relieved from my post."

"I doubt it. You are too valuable here."

"Except ten of the warheads under my watch are gone," the major quipped. "Where is Private Billicoff?"

Coby looked around. "He is here somewhere. He came in with me. Maybe he left to go to the guard house."

"I will get a key and give it to him. I will order one of the soldiers here to drive you back to your apartment."

"Thank you."

The next day, after a welcomed night's sleep, Coby showered, dried herself off, then draped her body in a towel, and lay down on the bed. This was the day she was to visit Major Burka, and although she had some aches and pains, she was mentally prepared for whatever may occur. A knock at the door prompted her to put on a bathrobe over the towel, and she answered the door.

Sergei was standing there smiling.

Surprised, Coby told him, "You can't be here."

"Had to see you. Make sure you are okay."

"How did you get here?"

"Major Stipenoff gave me one of the newer pickup trucks. I drove over to pick you up. Too bad you guys still get to drive the antiques."

Coby looked outside the door both ways. "Come in."

Sergei entered Coby's room.

"I have nothing to offer you."

"Yes, you do." With that, he pulled her close to him and they kissed passionately.

The towel under her robe fell to the ground as they move to the bed. He undressed in a passion and Coby removed her robe. Together they made passionate love.

Later, Coby and Sergei lay in bed. She stroked his face. They kissed. She whispered, "You never left my side. You brought me back to life."

"Coby, back there in the water, I thought you were dead. You went under and I could not find you. My heart was sinking too."

"I don't remember much. Just hitting the water hard."

"The water was so cold. But the fire... It heated the air enough to save us both I think."

"Not just that. A mystic once told my mother that the souls of her miscarriages are in me to keep me safe."

He slapped the top of his head. "That is about the craziest story I ever heard."

They both burst out laughing.

CHAPTER 28

EVIL HAD THE UPPER HAND

Coby dressed and met Sergei outside where he waited in the pickup, and they drove to the arsenal.

In the security room, Mark was asleep at the desk. Many people were milling around. Some were taking photos in the hallways. Stipenoff was being interviewed by a Russian secret service officer.

Coby entered the room. For privacy, Stipenoff and the agent left the room.

Sergei decided to walk over to the guard room to stay for a few minutes then returned to the truck where he patiently waited for Coby.

"Wake up, Mark." She shook him. "Wake up, wake up."

A groggy Mark awakened and looked at Coby. "Glad you are here. This place is full of Russian agents. They interviewed me and I am sure they will want to talk to you. I'm going back to the apartment, shower, and—"

"You got to stay here, big boy. Tough it out even though

you absolutely need to shower." Coby, with a smile on her face, cleared the air with her hand.

Mark retorted, "Funny ha, ha. When I get nervous my body odor turns to skunk."

"I was only kidding, although..." After a pause, she said, "I am going to talk to Burka."

"What? Are you sure you want to do this? It is borderline insane. The worst is over. Our guys leveled the bad guys. When will you be back? Have you heard from Cowboy?"

"No, but I have a hunch where to find him."

"Be careful, Coby."

Coby exited making sure she was unnoticed by the agents.

In the parking lot, Coby saw Sergei waiting for her in the truck. When he saw her, he flashed a large smile, and Coby entered the passenger side of the vehicle.

In unison, they said, "Off we go."

Coby and Sergei drove to Burka's very large house. They passed the spot where Lieutenant Jeffries and Burka's niece had hit the rail flying out of the tunnel headed for their one-way trip to eternity. Large orange and green traffic cones mark the spot.

They reached Burka's place and stopped at the front gate next to a white stand that held a black box with a phone. Coby picked up the phone and pushed the only button to announce herself. However, surprisingly, the gates opened without anyone saying anything on the phone.

They drove up the circular driveway to the front door of the house. As Coby exited the pickup, the house door swung open. She checked the revolver under her coat and the grenades she had in her pockets.

A tall, rather obese, uniformed man stood alone in the foyer, then staggered out to the top step leading to the entrance.

Sergei leaned out the window to tell Coby, "That's Burka."

Coby yelled out to the man, "Major Burka I presume."

Burka didn't answer and collapsed face down with a knife freshly embedded deep in his back.

Coby rushed to his side and placed her fingers on his throat and determined that Burka was dead. She removed her revolver and looked around. She motioned to Sergei to move out of sight. Sergei exited the vehicle and walked around the right side of the house.

Carefully, Coby backed up to get a full view of the house. She then removed her phone to call Alexis for backup. As she placed it to her ear, Cowboy stepped out of the house onto the step with Burka's lifeless body at his feet. Less than five feet away, he pointed a gun at Coby. "Put the phone down, Lieutenant, and do not make any stupid moves."

Coby stared at Cowboy and the gun, and with venom, she shouted, "You fucking traitor." She spat at him.

"Just put the gun down and tell your accomplice to come around here. If he makes any offensive moves your life will be the price."

She tossed her gun to the ground.

"What is in your pockets?"

Coby reached into her pocket and grasped the two grenades. She thought, *What is the risk of pulling the tab and setting these grenades off?* Surmising the situation, she determined not to and just followed the orders to drop them on the ground. Coby shouted, "Sergei, come around here, unarmed."

Sergei dropped his gun on the ground and walked around to the front.

Cowboy ordered the two of them, "Now follow me."

Coby and Sergei followed Cowboy inside the house to a dark hallway, stepping over Burka's body to do so.

They walked down the corridor to a door. Inside the dark space, a click was heard, and the room was visible and so were the people inside.

When the light came on there were three other men. Fahid and two henchmen were standing by a table.

Fahid spoke first. "So you are the little lady who temporarily ruined our plans. We underestimated you."

Coby turned to Fahid and said, "Who the hell are you? Guess what? Whomever you are, all your plans and you are doomed." Coby turned to Cowboy. "Cal, why?"

"I'm a rich man now."

An angry Coby emphatically stated, "I will personally see that you are hanged. You killed Jeffries too."

"He panicked and stopped the operation when he was three short on the count. He came directly to Burka. He threatened to quit the operation. Unfortunately, the girl was with him. She was the leverage we used to get to Burka. He refused to help anymore. He became dangerous. She was collateral damage."

Fahid was pacing the floor.

Cowboy continued, "With the girl gone, Burka knew it was either continue with the plan or face a very painful death. Besides, we knew the alarm codes. That was easy to get. We poured enough vodka in him to get him to a point of telling us everything."

Fahid was ready to burst. "STOP NOW!"

Cowboy turned away from Fahid and tried to persuade Coby to betray her country. "Fifty thousand pounds of gold. Think about it. Join us and have all the riches you could ever dream of."

Coby, still angry, said, "You think those riches will buy your way out of hell?"

Fahid turned to the two henchmen. "In case we have visitors, I'll drag Burka's body inside. Take these two to the distillery. Tie her up, but don't kill her. We might need her as currency. The Americans are known for paying high ransoms. I don't care what you do to the Russian."

The henchman ordered them to follow him at gunpoint. They reluctantly acquiesced.

Coby and Sergei were taken to Burka's private distillery.

The dimly lit room had tanks of liquids spaced apart crudely labeled "Water," "Vodka," and "Alcohol." Pipes with valves were connected to each tank. Against one wall were open shelves with dozens of filled vodka bottles. Opposite the bottles, on the other side of the room, was a coal bin loaded with potatoes. Next to the bin was a vat with a roaring fire with steam billowing, cooking up the next batch of hooch. A bottling machine was in the foreground. There were two windows, one louvered with a slowly turning exhaust fan, the other closed.

One henchman tied Coby to a chair. Another henchman had a gun in his left hand and pointed it at Sergei.

Sergei lunged to his right and was shot two times in the chest and once in the thigh. He fell to the ground motionless.

Coby screamed, "Whyyyyyyyy!?"

CHAPTER 29

THE TRAITOR

Major Stipenoff and Lieutenant Mark were in the security room. Stipenoff said to Mark, "Seems the agents have found a connection to the alarm system. It was overridden by Burka remotely or someone here who knew Burka's codes. I have tried to reach him several times. The phone rings but there is never an answer, so I have ordered a team to drive out to his house."

"I need to go with them!" Mark insisted. "That's where Coby is."

"Why is she doing that? It is suicide!"

"Major, Coby is under orders to get close to Burka."

"Why?"

"I am not at liberty to say. The US agencies are evaluating him now. It is way above my pay grade."

"This is very upsetting. He is a man I trust. He would never act against the Motherland."

"He is Ukrainian, no?"

Stipenoff left the room shaking her head and talking to herself in disbelief.

On the road to Burka's house, four black official cars were speeding in a row. Mark was positioned between two agents who did not say a word. One of them tried to move closer to the window as he got a whiff of Mark's dank body odor. He cranked the window down to get some fresh air. Mark subdued a chuckle.

Inside the distillery, Coby was tied to a chair, and Sergei was motionless on the floor. The henchmen were gone. Coby was trying frantically to break free. But it was futile. Her hands were tied so tight that all she could feel was nothing since her hands were numb. Her legs were not as tight, but still not easy to break free. However, she used a hostage training tactic to relax the legs while being tied to allow a little wiggle room.

Sergei made a weak coughing sound.

Coby enthusiastically said, "Thank God. I hear you, Sergei. Stay strong."

Sergei coughed again.

"Can you move any part of your body?"

No answer.

"Think about any part of your body you can move."

In a weak utterance, he said, "I feel paralyzed and my left leg, it hurts so bad I think I can cut it off."

"Try, Sergei. Try, dammit! I am tied to a chair and need you to break free."

Sergei's weak voice said, "Had my vest on. Too bad there isn't one for the thigh. I'm slowly getting my breath back."

Outside the front of Burka's house, the four Russian cars entered the property grounds. The armed men exited the cars along with Mark. There was a Russian truck parked to the side. The house door opened, and facing them was an unarmed Fahid, hands in the air.

The lead agent barked an order to stand down.

Fahid said, straight-faced, "No need to panic. Burka is dead. He caused all the trouble."

The lead agent, automatic weapon in hand, ordered his team to slowly move in closer.

Fahid raised his hand. "STOP! You need not advance."

The Russian team stopped in response to a hand gesture from the lead agent. The agent said, "Where are Lieutenant Rodriguez and Private Billicoff?"

"Don't know of a Rodriguez or Billicoff."

"Identify yourself."

"I am the housekeeper."

Mark pointed to the truck. "That's Major Stipenoff's truck. Coby used it. She's here. He's fucking lying."

The lead agent asked Fahid, "Who killed Major Burka?"

"I did. I did not want millions of people to die because of a sick mind. He is a maniac and a traitor."

"How do we know he is dead?"

While Fahid turned to get Burka's body, now unseen, Mark moved around the left side and to the back of the house. He noticed a parked helicopter in an open space in the backyard. Mark entered the house through the back door. He proceeded down a dark hallway and opened the door to the "dark room." With his pistol in one hand and a flashlight in the other, he checked it out. No one was there. In his mind he said, *Clear.*

Sergei was responding slowly and got up on all fours. Coby struggled to get free. She moved her body from side to side. With each move, the chair tilted. With one large effort of body movement, the chair tipped over to the side, and Coby, using her feet and body motion, managed to maneuver over to the tank marked "ALKOGOL." She extended her foot and tapped the valve near the floor. The alcohol trickled onto the floor. She mustered up the energy and kicked the valve harder. The flow increased. A stream of pure alcohol was now covering the distillery floor and gaining volume.

At the front of the house, Fahid dragged Burka's body out the door and onto the steps. The knife was still protruding from his back. His uniform was soaked with blood. Upon verifying it was actually the dead body of Major Burka, the lead Russian agent approached Fahid. In Russian, he barked, "You murdered a Russian officer. Lie down on the step with your arms extended! You are under arrest!"

Fahid began to bend down in a feigned attempt at obedience. Instead, his hand moved quickly to retrieve a revolver, and he shot the lead agent in the head then ran inside. A firefight ensued.

The Russian agents outgunned Fahid's group. Nonetheless, the enemy rogue army was holding its own. Burka kept his own arsenal of weapons and ammo. In fact, it was more than the agents combined.

Inside the distillery, Sergei worked his way over to Coby's chair crawling on all fours. With all his strength, he managed to pull her and the chair away from the stream of alcohol. The trickle became a small river of alcohol.

Gunshots sounded nearby to break the silence. Dozens of blasts could be heard.

Sergei untied Coby. The alcohol was close to reaching the two as they moved to the door. The alcohol fumes were beginning to have a reaction to the exposed flames under the vat cooking the potatoes.

With the intent of exploding the tank of alcohol and taking out the bad guys, Coby calculated that the fumes and an accelerant would surely do the trick. She ordered Sergei to stand by the door. "Be ready to open it on my word."

On the shelf was an old rag. She dipped the rag into the alcohol on the floor. "We've got to get out quick! The flames are going to ignite the alcohol tank!" Making a calculated, risky decision, Coby ran to the window and turned the exhaust fan off. "We need to build the fumes in here!" The pair was beginning to feel faint from the fumes.

The gunshots ceased from the front of the house. The two gave a look of curiosity over the sudden silence. Sergei's first impulse was to open the door to see what was going on.

Coby pulled him back. "We need to keep the door shut to build up the fumes. There just aren't enough fumes yet to ignite."

Mark, who was working his way to the distillery, heard voices and ducked behind a wall. He peeked around the corner and saw Fahid and the two henchmen running out the back door. Thinking he was clear, he took a step out from the cover and was suddenly grabbed from behind. Cowboy, with his right arm, had a choke hold on Mark. With his left hand, he disarmed his former friend. "Bad day for you, Thompson."

The two exited the house through the back door and headed for the detached garage.

When there was no more firing, the Russian agents slowly approached the house. Fortunately for them, they immediately entered the room where the shots had been fired from and searched the room for Fahid and his men.

The alcohol fumes were transparent but deadly and permeated the air. The liquid was now near the vat of boiling potatoes. In a matter of a minute, the flames from the vat ignited the transparent fumes, which in turn set a trail of fire to the tank.

The scene in the distillery was chaotic. Coby held up Sergei and the two exited the room as fast as they could. Coby made sure the door was closed tight. Anticipating an explosion, they lay prone on the floor immediately outside the distillery.

The tank exploded with a force so great as to blow a hole in the wall and propelled the metal door off its hinges.

Sergei and Coby were in a prone position as the shock of the explosion blew behind them. The heavy steel door was now airborne and fell two feet in front of the pair. They quickly crawled over the hot door through the hallway and out to the back door. The hallway behind them was on fire. The flames were close to touching their bodies. The heat was intense.

From their vantage point on the back porch, Sergei and Coby saw Cowboy forcing Mark into the detached garage from the house.

Coby ordered Sergei to stay put. "Lie down on the ground. Give me your gun."

"I don't have it. It's on the ground in the front toward the side of the house."

"I'll get it." Coby left in a hurry to the front of the house to retrieve Sergei's gun.

One of the agents, in a case of mistaken identity, fired on Coby. She managed to roll on the ground, pick up Sergei's gun and run back to his side in the back of the house.

The agents ran out the back door coughing and rubbing their eyes from the smoke inside the house. One of the agents had his sleeve on fire. He rolled to the ground to extinguish the flames. Another agent attended to Sergei who was on all fours at the end of the step attached to the back porch. They saw Coby running toward them and began to chase her. In Russian, Sergei shouted at the agents, "Leave her be, she is with me." He then asked the agent for a weapon. The agent took a revolver from his inside jacket and gave it to his comrade. Still sitting on the ground, Sergei checked to see that it was loaded. He ripped off his shirt and removed his bulletproof vest. His chest was black and blue from the impact of the bullet.

The detached garage was located twenty yards behind the house. Inside the garage, Fahid was faced with the decision to either make a run for the helicopter where he would have to face a hail of bullets or jump inside one of the two cars in the garage. He opted for the car, which was facing the garage doors. He desperately looked for the key to start the car.

Cowboy was holding Mark with a gun to his temple. "You understand I cannot allow you or Coby to live. You two are the only ones who know the truth."

Smaller explosions could be heard in the distance as the flames began to cause each of the bottles of vodka in the distillery to explode.

Everything was happening in rapid motion.

Coby snuck up to the back of the garage and peered through a window. She saw a shadow of a man and did not recognize the profile as Mark which gave her the impetus to aim and shoot.

A gun blasts.

The bullet exited her revolver and broke through the glass pane.

The effect was a clear shot to the head of one of Fahid's henchmen. The "dead eye" kid in high school rode again.

The henchman fell, and the other henchman jumped into the car with Fahid. Fahid, in the driver's seat, finally found the key behind the passenger's visor. He started the car, thrust the transmission into "drive," stepped on the gas pedal all the way, and crashed through the garage door.

Coby ran to the side of the garage and opened fire. No bullets hit Fahid, although one did penetrate the back window.

"I think I hit one of them."

Inside the car, the man next to Fahid slumped over from the impact of the bullet from Coby's gun.

Cowboy was not fazed by the bloody remains of the henchman and continued to hold Mark at bay. He looked down at his pant leg and could see some of the remains of brain matter from the shattered head.

The house fire now reached the gas pipes and caused the house to explode with debris and embers filling the air.

The agents dropped to the ground.

Cowboy flinched at the loud sound of the explosion.

Mark could see the explosion from where he was standing. The shock from the explosion broke every window in the garage.

Coby's quick reflexes caused her to escape the flying glass by covering her face, then she entered the garage where Cowboy was still pointing a gun at Mark. Her Russian-issued revolver pointed directly at Captain Cal Boyd. From inside the garage window, Coby could see the agents and a limping Sergei approaching the garage.

Cowboy, tightening his hold on Mark, said, "Well, isn't this cozy? The Americans were the only survivors."

Coby, in a determined voice, said, "Cal, there will be an army of Russian agents ready to charge this garage. There is no way you will survive even if you kill both of us. Put the gun down and spare all our lives."

"You said you'd personally see me hang. So, what is there to live for?"

An agent shouted in Russian, "Come out with your hands in the air!"

Mark said to Cowboy, "What is wrong with you, man? Money made you a traitor."

"I will not hesitate to kill you like I did Jeffries. He panicked and went to Burka, who informed the CIA. I cut his brake line. The little sports car could not handle the sharp turns."

The agent, in Russian, said, "Last time, come out with your hands in the air!"

Coby returned a shout in Russian, "We are being held hostage!" She added, "don't do anything crazy!"

The agent in Russian responded, "we want the man who shot Burka and our captain!"

Coby, in an excitable voice, said, "He left five minutes ago!" the second agent in command ordered to four of the agents, "Get the cars and chase him. Bring him back alive. The others stay with me."

Four of the agents ran to the front of the burning house and cleaned the windshields from the black soot caused by flaming embers landing everywhere. They entered two cars and took off after Fahid. The cars screamed around the back and onto the same road Fahid took during his escape.

Inside the garage, there was an eerie silence.

From Coby's point of view, she could see Sergei looking in the glassless window that was behind Mark and Cowboy.

Their eyes met for a split second and a connection was made. The figure in the window raised a gun from his side and aimed it at Cowboy.

Coby yelled, "Mark, don't move!"

One shot was fired through the window, and Cowboy's head shattered.

Mark fell to the ground and crawled for cover.

Coby, in a relieved voice, said, "Mark, it is all clear."

The agents entered the garage.

Coby dropped her gun and raised her hands.

Mark stood with his hands in the air.

Sergei entered the garage and limped to Coby. They embraced.

The remaining agents stood down.

Coby looked up at Sergei. "What took you so long?"

Sergei snickered, "I thought you could do it alone." They both laughed. The excitement of being together this close led to a very romantic kiss.

CHAPTER 30

LOVE CONQUERS

The two became a couple, and they fell deeply in love. They flew together to Moscow and were greeted by many of the Russian officers who lauded their bravery. Sergei was admitted to a hospital. The medical report was broken ribs and contusions in his chest over his heart. An operation extracted the bullet from his thigh, and he was ordered to stay in the hospital for a week.

Coby walked into his room, and, smiling, she bent down, and planted a kiss on Sergei's forehead. "How's my hero doing today?"

"Sore."

"I have a question. Thank God, but I don't remember you wearing a vest when you left my room. When did you put it on?"

"When I was waiting for you in the truck. I ran to the guard house and put it on."

"Nice."

"Coby, I have been thinking. Come closer please." Sergei extended his hand.

Coby reached out and held his hand.

"Coby, every time I think about you drowning that night, a deep feeling inside me causes me to shiver over the thought of losing you. Together we are strong and can defeat anything in our way. Please be my bride."

"Sergei, I have been thinking too. Being independent my entire life, when with you I feel ten feet tall. I can imagine building a life together."

"Are you saying yes?"

"Yes, yes, yes!" She bent down to kiss him.

The nurse entered the room and asked Coby to leave because he needed his rest.

After a long life-changing visit, Coby returned to her hotel room and saw the red message light illuminated. She walked across the off-white shag rug to the blinking light and accessed the voicemail.

"Hello, sweetie. This is your mother. Coby, call me when you receive this message."

Coby knew from her mother's tone it was bad news. Her heart sank while she was waiting for the phone to be answered.

Dina answered the phone.

"Momma?"

"Coby, Coby I am so glad to hear your voice. Something sad happened... Poppa died last night. He left us peacefully."

Coby was in shock. "I'll get home right away. Are you okay?"

"I am fine. Coby, his last words..." She stopped to regain her composure. "Tell Coby I am dying a happy and very proud poppa."

Coby fell silent. She reminisced about her childhood and how wonderful Father Alberto was to her. Her heart was aching, and she was angry that she was not there to hold his hand during his last breath.

She hailed a taxi to visit Sergei in the hospital to tell him about Alberto and her plan to fly back home and be with her mother during the funeral.

Sergei understood and told her how he wished he could be with her.

She gave him a warm tight hug. Sobbing, she said, "I'll miss him so much. I am sorry you did not get to meet him."

"Coby, my love, I may not have met him, but I know his daughter. His legacy is you. I am one-hundred percent sure he passed so very proud of your bravery."

She told him the last words. The tears were falling on his bed sheet.

It took a day and a half to get to Philadelphia on military transport. The Philadelphia Airport was difficult to maneuver. Coby saw signs for the taxi and limo stands. There were only two people ahead of her in the taxi line.

The taxi wound its way heading for its South Philadelphia destination. "Cabbie, can you just once take a drive around the block?"

"Sure, miss."

The trip around the block was important to her. She knew she would be passing by Mr. Foti's grocery store and Mr. Cannuli's candy store. Her heart pounded. To her dismay, the grocery store was now a sandwich shop and Mr. Cannuli's was now a twenty-four-hour dry cleaner.

"Guess nothing lasts forever."

The rest of the trip was mostly the same with major and minor changes. The clothing factory looked the same except for a new sign. As they turned the corner heading south on her street, Coby noticed all the houses looked the same. The cab parked in front of the house. She gave the driver an extra tip for the nostalgic experience and because Alberto drove a cab many years ago.

She was greeted by Dina and Aunt Gilda. No words were exchanged for a long minute. Only hugging. Gilda broke the silence with, "The viewing is tomorrow night. Father Joe will perform the funeral mass."

Coby looked deeply into the sad eyes of her mom and asked, "How are you doing?"

In a sad tone, Dina explained, "What can I say? I've lost my best friend. My life is empty now. Take my hand, we'll go inside."

"I made a pot of freshly brewed coffee," Aunt Gilda said.

Coby thanked Gilda then turned to her mother. "How are you?"

"The doctors say I'm as healthy as a horse. Guess I should be careful and not break my legs."

Coby realized she meant it exactly as she said it. So, she didn't laugh.

They entered the kitchen. Coby noticed that everything except the refrigerator was the same. The kitchen chairs were reupholstered to a pleasant shade of green. She sat in one.

Dina went into the updated refrigerator and took out a white cake with yellow butter frosting. Gilda set the table and took the coffee pot off the stove and walked to Coby.

"Here, have some coffee."

"No thanks, Aunt Gilda. Mom, does he have a nice suit and tie?"

"He has no suits. The ones he had we gave to Goodwill. None of them would fit. The funeral director said he will provide that."

"Hell no, I will go and buy him a suit and tie. I need to do this. Do you want to come with me?"

"I don't think I am able. Gilda will go with you."

Coby and Gilda spend part of the afternoon at Mancuso Men's Shop and purchase a fine blue suit. Gilda picked out a matching tie with very faint polka dots. Together they took the clothing to the funeral parlor.

Inside the hallway at the funeral home, Mr. Leonetti took the clothing and said, "These are beautiful."

"Blue was his favorite color."

"The tie. I know this brand. It is very expensive."

Gilda chimed in, "I picked that one! Money is of no matter at moments like this!"

"I see you have good taste, and the tie will complement the suit."

Coby handed him a white paper bag with Mancuso's printed on each side. "There's a white shirt in this bag."

"No problem."

"I have one final request. Can I see him alone?"

"We frown on this. We have so much to do."

"Please, I was away when he passed, and I need to tell him something alone."

"Hmm, just give me a minute. I'll come to get you."

"See, I told you I have good taste." Gilda couldn't resist.

Mr. Leonetti returned and gave Coby hospital gloves. "Please put them on and follow me."

They turned down a hallway and stopped in front of a wood door labeled "DRESSING ROOM A."

"Coby, you will have only five minutes, and please do not remove any part of the covering sheet."

Coby modestly nodded.

"And refrain from touching the body."

Another nod.

"I trust your military training helped give you discipline, and on that note, I trust you and will see you in five minutes."

Coby entered the room, and her eyes focused on the corpse

covered with a white sheet up to the neck. From a distance, it did not resemble her father. She approached the body and stared into the lifeless face. It was at this point she began to sob.

"Poppa. Oh, Poppa. I love you so much. For giving me so much in life. For showing me the way to be an amazing parent. Many times you told me I made you proud, Poppa. Oh, Poppa, you are my hero. I will always miss you."

She turned away, exited the room, and was greeted by Mr. Leonetti and Aunt Gilda. Coby exhaled and for a second or two smiled then handed the funeral director a pack of cigars and a book of matches. "Can you please tuck these into his pocket before you close the casket?"

"My pleasure."

With that, in her mind, closure was accomplished.

The viewing line went out the Leonetti's Funeral Home and down the street. Coby was grateful for the number of people wanting to say goodbye to her dad. All his friends and co-workers, poker and bowling friends, and neighbors who loved him came to say their final farewell. Coby was in her dress-white uniform. Standing erect and properly was a challenge since she was falling apart inside. She was one hundred percent a trooper.

The mass at Saint Thomas Aquinas church was soulful and beautiful.

This church was the religious center point for the Rodriguez family and hundreds of families in the parish from births to deaths, baptisms, weddings, celebrating May and October with mass every day to honor the Blessed Virgin Mary, and of course, funerals. Coby and the family-maintained dignity throughout. They finally broke down crying at a beautiful and moving rendition of "Ava Maria," sung by an angelic soprano operatic voice in the organ loft. Everyone in the church was emotionally affected.

On the way to the burial ground, Coby made an effort to keep the situation light. "Momma, I cannot wait for you to meet Sergei. Our eyes connected at first glance. Oh, and he smokes cigars."

Even with the grief, Dina managed a chuckle. "I do think the souls were working overtime for me over there."

"I know they were. I believe it."

Looking directly into Coby's dark eyes, Dina said, "I'm so happy for you and Sergei. I cannot wait to meet him."

Both Mother and Daughter saw the burial spot outside the window as the limo stopped behind the hearse.

Father Joe gave a deeply personal eulogy about Alberto. Then he asked the assembled crowd to raise their hands if Alberto did anything for them and asked nothing in return. Every hand was raised. He went on to say that Alberto, out of his own time, helped construct the sanctuary in the church. He then blessed the coffin. Everyone placed a flower on it. And the ceremony ended.

In Moscow, Sergei was recuperating nicely. He would have to get used to using crutches for three or four months. He and Coby talked two or three times a day. Together they planned their trip to Washington, DC, to meet the president and accept their recognition for helping to save the world.

Three days later, Coby met Sergei at the Dulles airport in Virginia near Washington, DC. They taxied to the Hotel Washington and dropped their bags off.

Coby put on her imaginary tour guide cap and took Sergei around Washington in a taxicab. He had heard and seen pictures of Washington, but never realized the majesty of seeing the monuments, the Capitol, and the White House in person.

Pointing to the White House, Coby said, "We'll be in there tomorrow. Can you believe it?"

"No, it looks so powerful. I'm a little nervous."

They spent a wonderful evening together at the Hotel Washington.

Sergei poured two glasses of champagne.

Coby shouted first, "I want to make the toast!"

She took Sergei by the arm over to the window where the Washington Monument could be seen all lit up.

"To my friend forever, welcome to America!"

They clinked glasses, took a sip, and looked out the window to gaze upon the beauty of the capital city.

CHAPTER 31

WASHINGTON DC - THE WHITE HOUSE

At dusk, the building was lit by giant flood lights beaming from several angles which accentuated the alabaster color of the building. The view was breathtaking for the heroic couple.

Inside the Oval Office were the president, General Matthews, Gloria Smith, Coby, Mark, Sergei, dignitaries from Russia and the USA, the families and friends of Coby and Mark, and the Press pool.

Sergei, Mark, and Coby were center stage on a portable stage constructed in front of the Resolute Desk. Red, white, and blue piping surrounded the stage. A podium was in the middle with the presidential seal. The top of a microphone over the podium edge could be seen by the audience.

There were flags on both ends of the stage. The flags of the USA and Russia stood side by side, with the American flag slightly higher.

President Jonathan Waters was seated in the front row. Secret Service agents were scanning the room with their eyes even though each person had been thoroughly vetted. He rose and climbed the three steps to the stage. Before he spoke, he looked out at the audience to make sure the vice president and the CIA director were present before he addressed the people in the room. "Ladies and gentlemen...for today that includes the press..."

A smattering of chuckles could be heard in the crowd.

"Seriously, I am honored to present the U.S. Freedom Metal with three examples of the best representations of freedom in America, Russia, and the world. I want to thank President Mikail for giving me permission to honor a soldier from Russia with this revered American medal. A first in history."

Applause from the audience.

From a silver tray, the president removed one of the medals on a lanyard and walked over to Sergei. "Captain Sergei Billicoff, I am honored to award you with this freedom medal of bravery."

The room exploded with applause.

Coby proudly looked at Sergei.

The president repeated the removal of the next medal and placed it around the neck of Mark Thompson. Mark's family was joyful and proud. "First Lieutenant Mark Thompson, not only did you show great bravery but loyalty to your service and the peoples of the world." Mark broke out with a wide smile. His family stood and hooted and hollered with joy.

His seventy-year-old grandmother ran past the guards to give Mark a personal hug and kiss. That special moment was the number one newspaper front page photograph distributed by UPI, AP, and Reuters the next day.

The president then stood behind Coby. Dina was crying tears of joy. She was wearing a US flag pin that belonged to Alberto.

The president draped the award around Coby's neck.

"General Matthews sensed you were the right person for the assignment from the moment he spoke to you on the phone. We are all so very proud of you!" He placed the award around her neck.

Coby had a beautiful smile that one would expect from a hero.

"General Matthews, I understand you have a special message for Coby."

General Matthews approached the podium. "Coby, please move closer. I have a star to pin on your lapel. As Commander-In-Chief, I can promote those who deserve a higher rank. I am pleased and honored to promote you to the rank of Major. You are now Major Coby Rodriguez."

Congressman Merlino, now in his seventies, watching from a wheelchair, wiped tears from both his eyes.

Aunt Gilda shouted, "I watched her grow up!"

President Waters continued, "You are the youngest female major and the highest-ranking Hispanic female in the Army." Applause filled the air. "It is with special people like you, America's finest days are ahead. You are an inspiration to all young women around the free world."

The general pinned the star and saluted her, and Coby returned the salute. The audience applauded. The family smiled and cried with pride and joy.

As soon as the ceremony was over, Coby ran to Dina pulling Sergei along with her.

Dina, trying to hold back the tears of joy, said, "I am so proud of you. I only wish your father were here to see this."

"Momma, please meet Sergei. We are in love and getting married." Dina extended her arms and all three embraced in a group hug. They could feel that the spirit of Alberto added a fourth to the embrace.

Dina broke away and looked Sergei in the eyes. "You saved my daughter's life. I so welcome you into our family."

Coby and Sergei exchange loving looks. The group hug grew as Aunt Gilda wound her way in the middle.

As they were walking away, an attractive woman over seventy years of age touched Coby's arm. "Excuse me. I'm sorry, but I need to give you something."

At first, the older woman looked familiar. "Do we know each other?"

"No, but we know of each other. I am Cindy's mother, Margaret."

"Oh my God, you and Cindy have the same eyes." Coby wrapped her arms around the lady, sobbing while saying, "I loved her."

Margaret took a step back and with her right hand, she motioned to hold Coby's hand. Coby extended her hand.

Mrs. Raymond opened her left hand and revealed the black onyx cross Coby had given Cindy on her birthday back at the Academy.

Coby took the cross and kissed it.

Cindy's mom, with tears flowing from her eyes, said, "Cindy always talked about you. Even in her last letter, she mentions that someday you and she were going to take an RV from one coast to the other."

Coby squeezed the cross and upon releasing her fist, she asked, "Would you put the chain on me?" Coby turned her back and Margaret fastened the chain.

After this, the cross was hanging alongside the Freedom Medal. Coby embraced Mrs. Raymond once again. "Oh, excuse me. Please meet my fiancé, Sergei. Oh, and let me introduce you to my mom, Dina."

The positive feelings of chemistry were so strong that an

outsider would have recognized the beginning of an ongoing new family of friends.

Newspaper headlines around the world told the story on the front page and most of them had the photo of Mark Thompson's grandmother hugging him on the podium. Coby, Sergei, and Mark were found on page two.

The Mayor of New York proclaimed, "WORLD HEROES' DAY" in New York City and ordered a celebration.

On the great white way in New York City, the three were honored with a ticker-tape parade. In the lead cars were Dina, Margaret, and Congressman Merlino. The Times estimated three million people lined the streets. The ticker-tape confetti was three inches deep.

The wedding was a simple one. Aunt Gilda walked Coby down the aisle and gave the bride to Sergei. The reception was equally simple. Friends and family gathered at the modest South Philadelphian home. The buffet table was set with a pot of meatballs, trays of fresh Italian hoagie rolls, several varieties of cold cuts, and a dish of broccoli rabe.

The bride and groom and the wedding party gathered down at the "lakes," the same area where Coby and her boyfriend made out. On the way over, Sergei took Coby's hand and said, "You have worked hard to gain the status of Major. You will always be known as Coby Rodriguez-Billicoff between us and our friends and family, but to the world, and as an honor to your father, I am very okay if you just use the Rodriguez name.

Coby was slightly taken aback by the words, bowed her head, and thanked Sergei for his generosity and love.

CHAPTER 32

THE SIMPLE LIFE?
TWO YEARS LATER

Sergei was given an honorable discharge from the Russian Army with full benefits and was one of the first to receive the newly commissioned "ORDER OF COURAGE."

Once they found out they were pregnant, the Army granted Coby maternity leave and some extended time she had earned. She remained ready for activity and could get "called up" at any time after she had the baby.

ATLANTIC CITY BOARDWALK – 2001

Coby and Sergei were dressed in civilian summer wear. She was very pregnant. Looking at all the boardwalk businesses, they came across a sign: "Madam Zyrk Mystic."

Coby motioned Sergei to wait for her as she entered the store. "This is the mystic my Momma met before I was born. I want to do this alone, okay?"

She was greeted by the now elderly Madame Zyrk. White

hair with a babushka, Madame Zyrk flashed a wide smile when she saw Coby.

Coby extended both her hands. "Hello, Madame Zyrk, my name is Coby."

Zyrk held Coby's hand with two of her hands and warmly greeted Coby. "I knew who you were as soon as I saw you. Your momma and your seven souls stand with you."

Coby said softly, "She passed away last January."

Zyrk remarked with a smile, "She will never leave you. Please have a seat. We have much to discuss."

Coby's curiosity quieted her while she sat at the table. The table needed an adjustment for Coby's pregnant tummy. "My mother told me about you many times in my life."

Without notice, Zyrk went into a trance for a minute or two. Coby found herself looking around the room. From what her mother described; nothing had changed. Then she caught the giant eye on the wall. After a second or two, she found herself mesmerized by the eye.

Without notice, Madame Zyrk stopped the trance. "I remember her well. Why do you come to see me? Are you also concerned if the baby you are carrying will be born healthy?"

"No, no, I did not plan on this, but then I saw your sign." Coby, with sincerity, said, "Momma told me you knew her better than anyone. She felt bonded with you. Trusting, she used to say. Madame Zyrk, I feel like I should be dead." Coby explained in detail the ordeals she encountered. She went on to explain that it was the souls who saved her.

"Yes, go on, this all makes sense."

"Mother told me your story about the seven souls. I believe they have been with me through my entire life."

"Have you had any other unexplained experiences?"

"Yes, that is a concern of mine. There is a total of six times."

Madame Zyrk was now seated on the edge of the seat. "Fascinating. Please go on."

"There are more unexplained events. After surviving a difficult birth, I had six unexplained experiences that either saved my life or helped me in a strange way like 'divine intervention.' Not all were negative. Finding my sponsor for West Point. Meeting my husband."

Zyrk nodded and said, "Yes, miracles orchestrated by one or more of the souls. I am sure of it." Zyrk continued, "This is remarkable. I am so glad you came to see me today. Hmm, are you concerned that you have only one soul event remaining?"

"Yes, so I better be extra careful, yes?"

"I do not think so. I can see the souls are still with you. Also, your mother is now watching you too."

Madame Zyrk sat back in her chair and entered a trance. "That is all I can say now."

"Is that a bad thing?"

"I just cannot explain it. If it is not clear to me, then I should remain quiet."

"You are scaring me."

Madame Zyrk stood and placed her arms around Coby when she also stood. "I can see your husband is waiting for you through the window. Go to him. He will give strength during all times good and bad."

"Madame Zyrk, what do you see? I MUST know!"

"It is not necessary—"

"I can take it, just let me know."

"I do not see the seven souls in your womb like I saw when you were inside your mother's womb."

"Are you saying the guardian angels are gone?" Coby asked.

"They are there, but not active."

"And the baby?"

"Yes, the baby has a soul, but it is alone. I do not understand and don't know why."

"So, my baby will not have the protection that I was blessed with?"

"Maybe so," Zyrk conceded. "After all, what occurred in you is extremely rare. I cannot see the future in the baby, who by the way, is a girl. I wish I could tell you more. It is not clear to me right now. After you have the baby, perhaps you can bring her in to see me."

"I will, I will." Coby hugged her. After a few quiet moments, Coby left.

Sergei met her at the front door. "You don't look good."

Coby was tearing up and hugged Sergei. "I'm okay."

"You're upset. What is it? What did she tell you?"

"It's not what she told me. It's what she didn't tell me. Is she being truthful or is it because she doesn't want to scare me?"

"Well, she certainly has you worried."

"Really, I'm okay. Just things will be different from now on. I just need to think differently. Suddenly I feel alone."

"Thanks. What am I? Chopped herring?"

"Sergei, you make me laugh. It's chopper liver. And the baby is a girl, but I already knew that." She smiled.

"Yes, little Coby."

A kiss on the lips and Sergei flagged down a cart and off they went being pushed down the boardwalk on a beautiful day in Atlantic City.

CHAPTER 33

TWO MONTHS LATER
THE BIRTH OF BABY DINA
ST. AGNES HOSPITAL - SOUTH PHILADELPHIA

A gray building with little outside activity. The Emergency Entrance was unusually calm. Catholic nuns in a variety of habits—blue, brown, and white—were entering and exiting the building using the front steps with rosary beads dangling at their sides.

Broad Street was relatively quiet. The rumbling sound of the subway lasted for ten seconds or so, then all was quiet again.

In Delivery Room Two, Coby was in intense labor. Her husband Sergei was holding her hand. In blue scrubs, an older Dr. Marra, the same delivery doctor from St. Agnes during the lost second birth, attended to Coby alongside two nurses and two nuns.

The nurse stated, "Blood pressure just spiked." Dr. Marra turned to a nurse. His hands were not visible as he was delivering the baby under sheets. "Nurse, please escort the father out of the room."

A confused Sergei questioned the order to remove him from the room. "Why? We've been through much together."

"That was then. This is now. Please leave."

"But Doctor?"

Now enraged, the doctor again order Sergei out of the room. "I am trying to save two lives here. Now leave or I will have you forcibly removed." The two nuns began to walk toward him.

Sergei, not wanting any confrontation, voluntarily walked out of the delivery room.

Now in the waiting room, Sergei was pacing the floor. He dropped to one knee. "Dear God, please protect her. She is a very special woman." Sergei clasped his hands together. He was sweating and his hands go to his face. Sobbing, he said, "God, oh, God, please hear my prayers. Please, please..."

After a long and excruciating hour, Dr. Marra entered the room where Sergei now sat. The other fathers gave them needed space. Sergei stood. The expressionless doctor removed his cap. Sergei stood at attention, bracing for the bad news. "Coby and your baby girl are both doing fine." Sergei hugged and kissed the doctor on the cheek. "Coby is a true warrior. We had some scary moments when we did not think she or the baby would make it. Congratulations!"

THE SUMMER OF 2000

Coby and Sergei were pushing a stroller with little Dina inside down a park path. Birds chirped, soft summer winds surrounded the family, and all seemed good in the world.

MALAGA, COSTA DEL SOL, SPAIN - AUGUST 2001
COUNTRY SHACK IN THE VILLAGE

In a small field was a two-room shack surrounded by trees and brush. The shack's aging thatched roof appeared to need mending. Inside, the place was dark, with a winding hallway that connected the two rooms.

At the end of the hallway, a glow from a light was shining from a room casting an eerie spotlight on the wall. Inside the room, a door led to the bathroom. A figure could be seen as a man standing in front of a mirror illuminated by a single forty-watt bulb dangling from a chain. The figure was Abdul bin Fahid, with a sinister and angry look. His eyes were red, his hair was wiry, and his face was covered by a large, black, unkempt beard. He appeared to be tired and had aged from his ordeal and failure to the people who had paid him to destroy the free-enterprise world. His voice was strong and got stronger each time he said to his mirror image. "This is not over. This is not over. This is not over."

CHAPTER 34

9/11

On September 11, 2001, the World Trade Center was destroyed when two hijacked heavy planes rammed into the sides of the buildings. Two hundred miles to the south, the Pentagon was heavily damaged when a plane crashed into the north side façade. A total of over three thousand died. A fourth plane was on its way to either the Capitol building or the White House but was thwarted when a brave group of patriots charged the pilot's cabin and brought the plane to a fiery end in Shanksville, Pennsylvania.

Coby, just like many Americans was shaken to the core. Instinctually, she picked up the phone and called the assignment officer to volunteer for active duty. His last words on the call were, "Let's roll!" in homage to one of the heroic passengers of the thwarted plane.

Malvern, Pennsylvania, was a beautiful, pastoral, sleepy suburb of Philadelphia. It was the type of area where many country roads passed green-pastured horse farms, older stone homes, and new-money modern homes. The area was not considered the "mainline" of Philly since that was made up of one-hundred-percent old money: the Pews, the Biddles, the Kelly's, and other famous names of wealth. The Kelly's made their money from bricks. A large sign on the Schuylkill River touted "Kelly for business." The Kelly's were always in the midst of the Philadelphia social life. However, they reached true royalty status when their daughter, Grace, married Prince Rainier of Monaco.

When Coby and Sergei returned from Washington, they rented a house in Malvern, Pennsylvania. They heard that the schools there were exceptional, and they wanted the best for little Dina. Coby was receiving payments from the Army and Sergei was receiving a monthly stipend from Mother Russia. That was a part of the award given to him for saving the world. The couple chuckled, "Rubles for life!"

They decorated the house with furniture that Alberto and Dina had in their home that had been held in storage. It was somewhat dated, and the table legs had chew marks from Bingo the poodle, but nothing a little paint, sanding, staining, and varnishing couldn't cure.

In January 2002, Little Dina was in her playpen while Coby and Sergei were watching their favorite afternoon game show "Family Feud" when the phone rang.

Coby answered, "Hello?"

The voice on the other end said, "Please hold for General Matthews."

Major Coby Rodriguez sat down. Deja vu set in.

Two weeks later, Coby found herself back in Germany waiting for her orders.

On a call back home, Coby said, "Sergei, I miss you and the baby very, very much."

"Do you have an idea where you are going next?"

"The scuttlebutt around here is Afghanistan. Seems Osama bin Laden is hiding, and we will need to assemble several squadrons to look for the bastard."

"I don't feel right about this. Not like me to worry. That is not good for a Russian."

"Not good for anybody, although Puerto Ricans worry all the time. What are your plans today?"

"Nothing today but taking Dina to the aquarium tomorrow morning."

"Huh?" Coby puzzled. "Honey, she's too young to appreciate that!"

"Then why is she always coloring the fish in the coloring book? She likes them, especially the dolphins. We'll have a good time. The weather is getting warmer. I'll send you pictures."

"Ha ha, that is the right answer. I guess I am feeling lonely. That is new to me. The last time I was here I did not have you and Dina in my life, and now that is rough. I promise I will resign from the service when I return home."

"I will not allow that!" Sergei insisted. "What about your desire to be the first Hispanic Lebanese general?"

"I don't know. Just not the same. For example, one of the contacts in the field speaks Arabic. I am the only one who can interpret the communiqués for him."

"Sounds like you are very much needed there."

"Except that the contact is asking for soccer scores."

"Well, that's important too. Morale and all that!" He chuckled.

"It's time to get some reading and exercise in before they shut out the lights here. With each day there is a new direction. I'll keep you posted. Have fun at the aquarium. Is she awake?"

"Yes." Sergei picked up little Dina and placed the phone to her ear. "Dina, Mommy wants to say hi."

"Mommy?"

"Yes, sweetheart. Are you being a good girl for Daddy?"

"Daddy is taking me to see fish."

"Be a good girl for Daddy. When I get home, we'll all go to the zoo to see all the animals. Doesn't that sound good? Ask Daddy to play the Crawford the Cat video for you again."

"Mommy, I love you."

"I love you too, baby doll. Please put Daddy on the phone." After a few kisses, Sergei got back on the phone.

"She misses you too. Love you, Coby. Please be careful. Hope those guardian angels are still with you."

Coby hung up the phone and stared at the floor and sighed deeply.

Inside the Billicoff house, Sergei was feeding little Dina oatmeal. The little girl was teething and therefore placed on a softer food diet.

After her breakfast, he climbed the stairs and walked into the baby's room. On the crib mattress the cover filled with little pastel bears had a spot that he knew if Coby saw this, she'd change the sheets immediately. But, in Mother Russia, children were brought up the hard way. "Teething? Here, let me rub some vodka on your gums." *American children are spoiled,* he thought. At five, he was responsible for making sure there was enough firewood in the bin for the evening. There was no time off from chores.

He decided the sheet was not dirty enough to change. "If she finds out, I'll just tell her that reducing the use of hot water helps the environment. I don't think she'll buy it."

He walked to the top of the stairs and shouted, "Dina baby, you okay?" No answer.

"Dina honey, Daddy wants to know. Are you okay?"

This time he did not hesitate. Thinking the worst, he flew down the stairs with strong heartbeats pounding through his chest and ran into the living room and into the sight of the baby. There she was, safely in the playpen. Baby Dina was fast asleep. It occurred to Sergei that he would never lose sight of her again. Even when going to the bathroom. She'll have to suffer through it.

Sergei took Dina upstairs, took a shower, and through the steam, there was baby Dina watching. As he was brushing his teeth he glanced over at the little girl. Their eyes met for a long second. She blinked, he blinked, and they both let out a giggling laugh. He gathered his clothes for the day and took them and Dina to the living room, placed her in the playpen, and dressed in front of her.

While putting on his sneakers, his cell phone rang. "Hello?" After a few seconds of silence, he again said, "Hello?" He disengaged the phone and thought, *Strange.*

He positioned the playpen so he could see her while in the kitchen making coffee and toast. Baby Dina was comfortable and fell asleep.

Baby Dina later woke up and saw her daddy. "Where's Mommy? Is she making us safe?"

Sergei looked into her big brown eyes and said, "Yes,

sweetheart. Okay, Daddy is going to dress you, then we are going to see the fish."

"Will the big green one be there?"

"Honey, that fish is green because that is the color you made it."

"Oh, I see."

"You are one smart little *pechenye*. Dina baby, Daddy will teach you the greatest language in the world: Russian."

In less than a half hour, the baby, the stroller, and Sergei were all in their efficient SUV off to the aquarium in Camden, New Jersey. The sun was shining and the temperature in the early morning was quite delightful. The SUV exited the driveway and headed south on the asphalt road toward the main highway.

Two blocks north of the house was a black, late-model Mercury Lincoln parked on the road. Inside the car were two men dressed all in black. The driver was smoking a cigarette when the passenger pointed to Sergei's car leaving the driveway. "There he is."

The driver dropped the transmission gear into drive and pulled out of the street trailing Sergei and little Dina.

When driving from Philadelphia to Camden, there were very few choices. The most direct route was to cross the Ben Franklin Bridge into New Jersey. The exit off the bridge was only ten minutes from the aquarium. The black Mercury was now four car lengths behind.

"Daddy, are we close?"

"Yes, Dina dear. I have an idea. Let's sing a song and by the time the song is over, we'll be there."

"Can we sing 'Itsy Bitsy Spider'?"

"Okay, you ready?" Together they sang, "The itsy-bitsy spider crawled up the waterspout. Down came the rain and washed the spider out. And the itsy-bitsy spider went up the spout again."

Dina squealed, "Are we there?"

"Guess that wasn't such a long song. Let's try 'Twinkle, Twinkle Little Star.' That's a little longer." The two sang and laughed together. Sergei thought this was a wonderful little outing for Daddy and his daughter.

In the black Mercury, the driver said, "My mother is from New Jersey. Exit three on the Turnpike."

"Don't really care," the passenger muttered. "We have a job to do." Then he lit up another ciggy.

Sergei's car turned into the aquarium parking lot and steered toward the parking ticket booth.

"That will be a dollar."

Sergei paid and proceeded to find a space close to the front doors.

The Mercury followed suit but did not park. It waited on the path leading up to the front entrance.

The sun broke out from the clouds. Sergei smiled at the kindness of the weather gods.

After he parked the car, he exited the car to open the hatch to remove the stroller, humming to himself the Itsy-Bitsy Spider tune. Then he wondered, *Why would the spider run up the waterspout again? Stupid spider.* He removed the stroller, unfolded it, walked to the side of the car, and unhooked little Dina from her car seat, lifted her up, and placed her in the blue vinyl carriage. Closing all doors, he pushed the stroller to the cement walkway on a path to the front gate.

As they approached the crossing street to the path, the driver in the black car then revved its engine, and the vehicle headed on a direct death course to Sergei and the stroller. The car picked up speed.

Sergei heard the car, turned his head to see the approaching vehicle, and in a quick move, just before impact, he pushed the stroller up the curb onto the sidewalk. The stroller hit a post and turned on one side. Baby Dina was screaming.

The speeding car hit Sergei with such impact that his body was thrown ten feet in the air. The black weapon on wheels braked hard.

Sergei was lying unconscious on the parking lot asphalt, bleeding from his head.

Little Dina was screaming "Daddy, Daddy" from the stroller which was lying on its side.

The passenger got out of the car and ran to the stroller and removed little Dina and took her back to the Mercury. The culprits revved the engine again, this time heading to the exit.

Visitors to the aquarium gathered around Sergei. One good Samaritan covered him with a jacket. One witness shakenly wrote down the license plate of the car. Another witness called the emergency number and calmly told the person on the other line, "I am calling from the Camden Aquarium. There has been a terrible accident, and what looks to me like a kidnapping. Please send an ambulance and the FBI at once. Please hurry!"

The police arrived at almost the same time the ambulance showed up. Witnesses were being interviewed by the police while the EMT attended to a battered Sergei. "He's alive," said one of the attendees.

"We'll need some support to lift him on the gurney."

One of the policemen assisted.

"His neck is not broken, but I am afraid that may be one of the few bones that are not broken." Carefully, they lifted Sergei onto a board, then to the gurney. With full lights and sirens, the ambulance took him to Cooper Hospital in Camden.

The police sergeant on the scene entered the police car and began to report the situation to dispatch. "A late-model black Lincoln Mercury with partial Pennsylvania plate number A-S-N at the beginning, maybe E-3-B at the ending, is headed north from the Camden Aquarium. Please note that they have with them a little girl with dark hair and a pink dress and white shoes. Witnesses say she could not be older than three. So be very cautious when apprehending the vehicle."

The forensic team arrived and began to scour the area looking for clues. They were measuring the tire tracks and assessing how fast the car was going when it struck Sergei.

The FBI was inside the aquarium security room looking at two different angles of the incident. They ran the video at a slow speed. They could see Sergei pushing the carriage and at that point, they stepped into the street aligning to the front of the aquarium's first building. The black car was certainly waiting for Sergei and his daughter to enter the "kill zone." In horror, they watched when the car accelerated and drove straight at the father and daughter. It was reasoned that if Sergei failed to push Dina's stroller over the curb and into a post, she would have received the full brunt of the two-ton murder weapon.

The lead FBI agent turned to his underling and said, "This is one hundred percent premeditated."

The Mercury headed back to Philadelphia over the Ben Franklin bridge, paid its toll, and sped off. It turned on Vine Street. A minute later, the toll booth operator received an audio message on the speaker announcing the crime and the car.

"Hey, that's the car that just went through here." He notified the New Jersey authorities who then contacted the Philadelphia Police force.

A squad car was parked on Vine Street when the black

Mercury sped by. The officer alerted dispatch, "I have in sight the suspect's car. It is heading east on Vine and just turned south on Delaware Avenue. We are in pursuit!"

Three more police cars joined the pursuit with sirens blasting and lights flashing. Delaware Avenue paralleled the Delaware River from North Philly to the South Philly docks. The avenue was not paved too well which led to a very bumpy ride with many potholes.

In the Mercury, the abductor was in the back seat with baby Dina. The driver saw the police in hot pursuit through the rearview mirror.

Bump by bump, pothole by pothole, the chase was now at a furious speed. To accentuate the roughness of the road were the myriad train tracks used to haul materials unloaded at the docks.

The Lincoln driver said, "I know these streets. I can lose them. Watch me." Just as he said that two more police cars were now up ahead charging toward them. "They won't ram us. They know we have the girl."

The Mercury took a hard right turn on one-way Tasker Street, going west, throwing both Dina and the passenger against the car wall. Dina was scared and began to cry.

The streets in South Philadelphia were tiny. Some were so small it was like threading a needle maneuvering between parked cars on both sides of the street. At high speeds, the tires could be caught in the trolley tracks throwing the car wildly to the right or the left.

The Mercury driver saw the police cars through his rearview mirror, one by one in single file, forming a parade of blue-and-white cars in pursuit of them, a would-be murderer and a bona-fide kidnapper.

A hard right turn on Seventh Street. This was a shopping area with many neighborhood stores lining the street. They immediately turned into a parking lot reserved for shoppers and parked next to a van to obscure their car. The driver turned off the engine and turned to his accomplice, covered Dina's mouth, and stopped that screaming.

From his vantage point, he could see the police cars whiz by the parking lot. The three exited the car and casually walked to the sidewalk and hailed a taxi.

An hour later the police found the Mercury and began to perform their forensics of dusting and tracking down the car's owner through the license plate and VIN. Their discovery was quick. No prints, and the car was stolen.

CHAPTER 35

SERGEI FAILING

Inside the Cooper Medical Center Emergency Room, Sergei was fighting for his life. A swarm of medical personnel was working on him with tetanus shots, X-rays, wound cleaning, morphine for pain, and checking his vitals.

"Not promising," said the chief ER doctor. "Many bones were broken, and extreme blood loss will make this very difficult." Turning to one of the nurses, he said, "See if Dr. Meyers is visiting. He's the best Orthopedic surgeon in the state. This man is broken in so many places."

A nurse interrupted. "He's failing, Doctor."

Coby was in Germany, preparing to head out to meet her troops at an undisclosed point on their way to Afghanistan. At the time of the incident, she could feel a strange ping in her head and heart palpitations in her chest. She wrote it off as an anxiety attack. The chest feelings did not seem to lessen, however. *Something is wrong.*

Somewhere in the Philadelphia area, little Dina was being held in a dark room by herself. She had soiled her pull-up diaper and when the kidnappers entered the room, they exited just as fast once they got a whiff of the dirty diaper.

The adjacent room had an old brown sofa and a distressed coffee table with empty glasses on it. On either side of the sofa were stained brown tables and cheap lamps. Both lamps were lit. The two who perpetrated the crime were standing when a door opened and in walked two more men. One of them was Abdul bin Fahid.

The Mercury passenger, Oscar Fitzgard, in a sheepish way, said to Fahid, "I am so sorry we missed hitting the little girl. If you desire, I will go in there and kill her."

Fahid responded, "No, no, this will work out fine. Her mommy will be looking for her. I am more disappointed that the man is still alive. For that mistake, you will pay." Fahid took a revolver and shot the man point blank in the head. Turning to the others in the room, he said, "There is a price to pay if my command is not carried out to the fullest exactly the way I order it!"

The Mercury driver was now visually shaking. "Fahid, please spare my life."

"We shall see. I have a plan where I will use your driving skills."

"Yes, sir, thank you, sir."

"Now bring the little girl to me."

A man named Pinto went into the side room and picked up baby Dina under her arms. The odor was horrible, and he inhaled with no plan to exhale until the girl was far enough away.

He took the girl to Fahid, handed her to him, then took five giant steps backward.

"From now on, this child is an asset. I will bring my vengeance to fruition when I ransom the girl for her mother. Whom can we rely on to go and pay our Russian a visit in hospital?"

Pinto said, "I know local Philly people who will take care of that matter."

"Contact them right away. And you!" Fahid pointed to one of his men. "Take care of this girl. Change her, bathe her, feed her, and dress her."

"Sir, this needs a woman's touch. The perfect woman is a friend of my sister and can be trusted."

"If I have learned anything, women are trouble. When you let them in, they act fine, but when questioned by the authorities they sing like little birds. You are now in charge of protecting and taking care of..." his tone grew more sinister, "...her. And if you fail, you'll wind up like him." He pointed to the passenger's corpse on the floor.

While still pointing at the dead body, Fahid turned to one of the remaining men and ordered him to take care of "this mess."

Fahid lifted little Dina to his eye level. "Little girl, welcome to the team. I promise you that you will get to see your mommy one more time."

Extending his arms with the baby held in his hands, he handed the baby over to the newly designated nanny and said, "Take her."

CHAPTER 36

ASSASSINATION

From the outside, Cooper Medical Center was nondescript. The hospital administration prided itself on exceptional cancer treatments. In addition, being very close to three major interstate highways, they finished building a heliport landing platform for triage treatment on traffic accident victims Medacoptered in for care.

There was always a uniformed policeman stationed at the hospital's main entryway. However, if one wanted to get into the hospital there were unwatched entrances through the kitchen supply docks, the funeral director's special door that was accessed off the morgue, and a few less conspicuous doors that led into the main building of the hospital.

After the kidnapping, the FBI built a temporary control area in the lobby of the hospital. Included was a metal detector and an X-ray machine to make sure everyone who entered was checked for firearms and explosives. They were there for two reasons: to protect Sergei from further attacks, and to look for anyone who might be associated with the kidnappers.

At the employee entrance, two men in white orderly uniforms reported for duty. They bypassed the sign-in desk and headed to the elevator bank. Their intelligence report told them that Sergei was on the fifth floor—Intensive Care. Their mission was to kill Sergei in any way possible.

When they exited the elevator, they knew immediately where Sergei's room was located. In the hallway, in front of room 521, were six New Jersey State Troopers and two men in suits that fit the "FBI look" profile.

The two would-be murderers took a right turn which was in the opposite direction from Room 521.

An unsuspecting nurse saw the two fake orderlies and asked them to go to room 520 to clean up the mess caused by the vomit and diarrhea left by the patient in the room. Reluctantly, they obeyed but were pleased to see that room 520 was directly across the hall, exactly opposite 521. From their vantage point, they could watch and monitor the authorities providing Sergei's protection.

When they saw the two plain-clothed officials leave the room, they put their plan in motion. One began to clean up diarrhea on the bed, ripping the sheets off and throwing them in the trash. One then walked down the hallway and located a storage closet, opened the door, and to his pleasant surprise, saw a mop and bucket ready for the taking.

He took the two items and altered his path back to 520, bypassing room 521. As he passed, he gave a nod to the authorities, and they nodded back in return. Recognition had been made. The assassin returned to the room where his partner watched the transaction.

"I think it is time to clean 521, no?" he said with a grin.

The two slid the wheeled bucket and mop across the room and the hallway and approached Sergei's guards.

"Hello, gentlemen. We need to sanitize the room."

The State Trooper recognized one of the men, and let the two in.

One of the troopers walked in with them.

Everything looked normal until one of the fake orderlies revealed a knife with an eight-inch blade and plunged it into the belly of the trooper. The knife was removed and was now targeted for Sergei. The perpetrator was just three feet from the body in the bed. In a matter of a few seconds, the beloved husband of Coby and the father of baby Dina would lose his life.

The second man in the room was guarding the door so that no one would enter and spoil their mission. Less than one foot away, the evildoer raised the knife above his head to insure a cutting blow to the heart. Just as he was on the drive to plunge the blade, a shot was fired from the wounded trooper lying on the floor. The bullet was accurate, and the knife holder was thrown back and dropped to the floor.

The gunshot was heard throughout the fifth floor and the entire hospital. The remaining troopers outside rushed in, and the second man took the mop handle and swung it back and forth keeping them at bay, but only temporarily.

The troopers fought their way to him and tackled him to the floor. One of the troopers ran into the hallway and said, "We need medical assistance here. Officer down!" At first, no one was responding until he yelled, "It's all clear, no more danger!"

A group of nurses and two doctors rushed into the room to attend to the fallen trooper. One doctor ordered a nurse to take him to the OR right away. He was still alive but losing too much blood.

The second man was cuffed, and one trooper began to choke him, shouting, "Who are you, who sent you here?"

Another trooper separated the hands of the trooper choking the man. "We need to keep him alive. Keep your cool."

The third trooper knelt next to the severely wounded law officer, pressing on the point where the blade entered the body. "Dammit. The blood is not stopping."

A team of men in white uniforms entered the pastel blue room and picked up the wounded officer and placed him on a gurney. The officer, who was applying the pressure, had blood coating his hands. He accompanied the group as they left the room on their way to the operating room.

Two FBI agents entered the room and escorted the criminal to a car waiting in front of the hospital.

CHAPTER 37

THE SECOND DEPLOYMENT CUT SHORT

Bagram Air Base was in Eastern Afghanistan and was the command center of the Allied Forces. The Allies were there to work and train the Afghani army to defend themselves against the Taliban.

Major Coby Rodriguez's orders were to train a team of Army Rangers to hunt down the mastermind of the 9/11 attack, Osama bin Laden. The intelligence reported that he was held up somewhere in the Tora Bora caves. A huge network of caves created secret passageways inside the White Mountain near the Khyber Pass. It was once fabled that one could hide in the Tora Bora caves forever and never be found. So, Coby and the rangers had their work cut out for them.

The hope was that the relentless bombing of the north slopes by the Allies would drive Osama and his band of terrorists toward the south. The rangers and SEALs, in a coordinated assault, would start in the south and work their way north.

Two days before deployment, Coby received a

communique that she must return to the United States within forty-eight hours. The message was signed by General Cliff J. Matthews. The message also said her replacement would be on site the next day.

Concerned, Coby tried to find a way to respond and ask questions. However, she needed to find transportation to return home. Traveling to and from the States was not a big problem for military personnel. Military transports left every hour on the hour for Germany, and from there, planes to the USA were abundant. All a military person had to do was call, tell them they were coming, and hop aboard. Those who traveled via the military never expected comfort.

Coby was fortunate. A Boeing C-40 was dead-heading back to the States and she was able to hitch a ride. The seven-hour trip was smooth. Once it landed at Anacostia-Bolling Air Force Base she was able to get a ride to the Pentagon.

General Matthews was waiting for her as she entered his office. They saluted and Matthews offered her a chair. "You look worried, General, what is going on?"

"Would you like some water?"

"General, does this concern my family? I called home once I arrived and did not get an answer."

"Coby, Sergei is in the hospital, and it does not look good."
She stood up. "Dina?"

"We have the entire Military Special Forces on this."

"Excuse me, General, on what?"

"We are still trying to put the pieces together," Matthews said. We told her the details of the incident.

"My baby was kidnapped?!"

"We have all available military and FBI personnel on the case."

"Abdul bin Fahid. That fucker," she said. "He should have

228

killed him at Denali. I have a recurring nightmare he is still alive."

"That is what we believe. You and Sergei upended his plans of world domination. Our profilers believe that all of his actions have always been motivated by revenge with a 'Fuck, what do I have to lose?' frame of mind. And he had no problem taking down as many humans as possible who do not agree with his life philosophies. To cause his victims as much pain as he has had to endure during these past years. What we do not know is to what depths is he willing to go to even up the score."

"General, this is the worst day of my life. Are there any clues? Any ideas where Dina might be?"

"Sorry, Major, no."

Coby placed her hands on her face and sobbed. "I need to see him."

"He's in a well-guarded hospital in Camden."

"Camden? You can't be for real. Shouldn't he be moved to a more secure location?"

"Coby, let me get right to the point. His injuries are many and, simply said, he cannot be moved. We have a twenty-four-hour watch over him. You should know there has already been one attempt on his life."

"I must see him."

"I know, so I have arranged a bird to fly you to Camden, and under strict armed protection, an armored van will pick you up and take you to the hospital. Rest assured, Major, Camden's Cooper Medical Center is as protected as Fort Knox."

"Thank you, General."

"I know I am breaking protocol, but I need to give you a hug." With that General Matthews rose from his chair, and Coby stood in her place. The general wrapped his arms around a broken-hearted Major Coby Rodriguez.

The helicopter flight took eighty minutes. It landed at the New Jersey State Troopers' Headquarters where a team of military police and armed soldiers greeted the bird and saluted Major Coby as she exited the helicopter, while the rotor blades slowed down in a swirling motion. As she was escorted to the armored van, Coby looked up toward the roof of the State Police Headquarters to see at least six snipers positioned, ready to fire on anything or person that might be perilous to Coby. She thought to herself, *That won't stop Fahid.*

With a motorcycle escort, the van, along with a dozen vehicles, headed out toward Cooper Medical Center.

At the hospital, she noticed a cadre of military surrounding the buildings. The protection, in her mind, was over the top and reserved only for the President of the United States.

The entourage entered the hospital and wound their way to Sergei's room. There were no other patients on his floor nor the floors over and under his room.

As she approached his room, Coby's heart pounded, and beads of sweat formed on her forehead. With all her bravery and gumption, she entered the room.

The dark room had a strange sterile smell. The windows were blacked out with heavy bulletproof curtains. The only light was coming from the fluorescent light above the hospital bed casting a surreal glow in the room. Sergei lay in the bed with several tubes in his arm. Wires leading to all types of medical sensors were emanating from various parts of his body. His eyes were closed. As she approached his bed, tears were streaming from her eyes. The sight of a lifeless friend, lover, father, and hero was unbearable. An oxygen tent covered the top fourth of his body and the sounds of oxygenated air were heard along with the monitors tracking all his vital signs.

She broke away for a second to gaze at the monitor and recognized what the numbers represent. Oxygen levels eighty-three, blood pressure eighty over fifty-five, and heartbeat 105, which all added up to Sergei being in a very troubling and serious state of health.

In her mind's eye, she saw the glance in his eyes the first time they met at the guard house, and his leadership and actions during the ordeal chasing the bad guys on land and later on the river. She remembered the look on his face when he rescued her from the frigid river waters and the look in his eyes when he entered her room then kissed her with a deep conviction that he would be her soulmate for life.

Once the shock of seeing him in a coma was over, she turned to the trooper standing by her side and said, "Now I must find our daughter."

CHAPTER 38

THE HUNT

Little Dina, not aware of her perilous surroundings, was sleeping in a makeshift crib. Her "nanny," a six-foot-two man, was sitting next to the crib watching television. A soccer match grabbed his undivided attention. When the team he supported scored a goal he shouted "Goal!" so loudly it woke up baby Dina and she began to wail.

Fahid entered the room and slapped the "nanny" in the face. "You're a fucking idiot. You are very stupid. Now pick her up and change her diaper. There is a box of pull-ups on the kitchen table. Then feed her. I want her in good shape when she sees her mommy for the last time." Fahid exited the room and began to plan his scheme to lure Coby to his lair where he would torture her by torturing baby Dina in front of her eyes. Then killing them both.

Fahid left the room and called for assistance.

An hour later, six men, all in black, enter Fahid's apartment. One of Fahid's cohorts made espresso for the men who were seated around a table.

"Good to see you, my brothers," Fahid addressed them as he entered and took a seat. "It has been a while since we last met and planned the Denali ordeal. Today, we should be sailing on the Arabian Sea in our yacht thinking about ways to spend our newly found wealth. We should be sitting at a marble table constructing a worldwide government that will control what is remaining from the so-called free world. The economic centers would be in our control protected by the highest paid and best-trained army, navy, and air force the world has ever seen." His temper began to rise as he banged his fist so hard on the table that ounces of espresso splashed out of a couple of cups onto the table.

"It is laughable that a woman and ill-trained Russian soldier, weak and stupid, foiled our plans." Fahid faked a laugh while these words left his mouth.

One of the "brothers" spoke out. "Brother Fahid, yes, I agree that the riches we lost were disappointing to face. The plan that you and Chi-Lah created was a feat that would have changed the way the world operated, forever. But I have learned to put that in the back of my mind and focus on one item. My father was killed at Denali. And I want to see the major and her family destroyed. Revenge now!"

Fahid felt the need to remind his army why they were there at that moment in time. "Brothers, we are fortunate that so many of the children and friends who were attacked in Denali have pledged their support to me. Many are with this team today. Do not forget our focus: to find and torture Coby and Sergei Billicoff...and their baby. Then and only then can we consider this mission a full success."

The crowd of men in unison shouted, "Yes, sir!"

"There is one thing that could spoil our plan for revenge. One of our brothers was captured at the hospital and is in custody. They have him and are interrogating him. They will use every means available to get him to be disloyal. It is our assignment to eliminate him before he talks."

"What are you proposing, Fahid?"

"The best man for the job is now dead from a bullet fired by a New Jersey State Trooper, a disgraceful way to die. Therefore, I will do this myself."

The FBI's Philadelphia offices were located downtown near the Delaware River. From the outside, it was nondescript. In fact, it looked like a regular office building.

From the shaded window in the office of FBI Chief Roberts, one could see Independence Hall, the Liberty Bell display building, and many of the structures that were the basis of the American Republic. The chief had spent over thirty years in law enforcement. He had achieved Police Commissioner ranking in several American cities including Milwaukee, Des Moines, and Sacramento.

Chief Roberts was seated at his desk, looking over some papers when his assistant, Baldo, entered the office to let him know that Major Coby Rodriguez was in the guest room. In this building, there was the "guest" room, a nicely appointed room with a large gray sofa and a conference table with twelve gray chairs that matched the sofa, all surrounding the table. A Hollywood set designer could not do a better job.

Then there was the other "guest" room. Located deep in the bowels of the building, there was no sofa, a large two-way mirror adorned the wall, the table seated six people, and there was no chance in hell a set designer had anything to do with the décor.

In the nicer guest room sat Coby, New Jersey State Police Captain Sanchez, and two Army privates whose only job was to protect Coby. An attractive brunette was in the act of delivering coffee to all in attendance when Chief Roberts entered the room.

They all stood.

"Please be seated," Roberts said. "Thank you for the honor of standing and maybe someday when I am President of the United States, then I will be worthy of the honor." He immediately walked over to Coby. "Major Rodriguez, it is a pleasure to meet you. You are a hero and I speak for the entire bureau: we will find baby Dina. Our profile experts are extremely certain she is alive. Please forgive what I am about to say. She is their bait to catch you."

"Thank you, sir. I did not realize the price I might be paying for taking down the launch site at Denali Island. All I did was perform the way the Army wants their officers and line men and women to perform."

"Your story is fascinating, and I hope someday soon we can sit, and I can hear about the harrowing experience in its entirety."

"I look forward to that day too, but right now, I need to find my little girl."

In a tone that was gentle but direct, Roberts said, "We all need to find Dina. We have examined the video of the kidnapping. We could not get a good look at the face of the driver. However, the man who abducted Dina, his identity, through a newly developed facial recognition technology, is now known. The kidnapper's name is Oscar Fitzgard. He is from this area and has a very long rap sheet. He is known to have connections with a rogue group in Europe and must have slipped into the United States undetected. Interpol has been looking for him for years."

Dina was taking this all in. Her mind was processing every word and was staging in her mind a series of questions just waiting to be released the moment Chief Roberts stopped talking.

Roberts continued, "We have an agent in front of every house he ever touched including his mother's house in the Frankfort section of the city." He opened a file and removed a photo. "This is Oscar Fitzgard."

Dina could not remain silent any longer. "I suppose you have this photo everywhere?"

"Of course, but it is my guess he is laying low and in the same locale as Fahid."

"The FBI has verified that the black Lincoln Mercury had no prints except smaller prints which we presume belong to little Dina."

Coby deduced, "They wore gloves."

"Yes, and the videos confirm that both the driver and Fitzgard were wearing gloves."

"Where do we go from here?"

"We will escort you to our in-house jail cell. The man who was one of the two in Sergei's room was apprehended after his cohort was shot dead trying to plunge an eight-inch blade into Sergei. He's not talking, but rest assured, there are ways we can get him to talk."

Chief Roberts led Coby, the two military guards, and the state trooper to an elevator that transported them five stories underground. Exiting the elevator and walking down the gray hallway, one could hear the amplified and echoed steps of everyone's shoes touching the painted off-white cement walkway. The group stopped outside a closed metal door. Chief Roberts entered a code on the keypad and the keypad lit up bright green. A mechanical voice emanated from the box, "Please place your thumb on the pad in the space provided." Those words brought Coby back to the time she was at the arsenal vault door at Kapustin Yar.

Chief Roberts' thumb did the trick, and they entered a dark room with a glass wall covering sixty-five percent of the wall. On the other side of that wall was a table and two chairs facing the other. On the wall was a mirror the same size as the glass window in the observation room.

She recognized it as the interrogation room. The lights in the room became bright, and a door opened.

Chief Roberts double-checked that all the microphones were turned off.

An armed guard, an FBI agent, and Henry Fasbottom—the individual that came very close to assassinating Sergei Billicoff in his hospital bed—all entered the interrogation room.

The unshaven Fasbottom was in handcuffs and shackles tied around his waist plus another set around his ankles. Dark eyes were lifted by a series of circles on grey skin, indicating little to no sleep. Coby thought that may have been done on purpose. She knew one of the methods the FBI used to wear down their suspect was sleep deprivation.

The door was shut. The guard stood vigilant in front of the door, and the agent took the seat opposite Fasbottom.

Inside the observation room, the technician switched on the audio and video capture system for the adjacent interrogation room.

Once seated at the table, the guard secured the shackles from Fasbottom's waist to a metal ring secured on the floor of the room.

The FBI agent pushed a button on the table and firmly stated, "For the record, this recording is the second in a series labeled 'Hospital Assassin FBI 1117.'"

Coby was in a trance. She had a penetrating look into the face of the person who may have altered her life forever. She was thinking to herself that she had never been more emotionally torn. *I want to murder him so much, yet I know he can help me find Dina.*

The FBI Interrogator continued, "Please state your name."

"Henry Fasbottom."

"Where is your place of birth?"

"Leicester, England."

"Are you a citizen of Great Britain?"

"Yes."

"What was your occupation in Leicester?"

"How many times are you people going to ask the same fucking questions?"

"I'll ask one more time. Refusal to answer will identify you as hostile, and you remember the last time what happened to you when we believed you to be hostile?"

Without hesitation, Fasbottom said, "I worked in a machine shop."

"Explain in detail your line of work."

"You come in with a design, and I can make it out of nuts and bolts."

"Does that include ammunition?"

"Yes, we have had some special orders for that."

"Bomb casings?"

"No."

"When did you come to America?"

"About six months ago."

"Do you know an Alfred Conners?"

"He was my uncle. My favorite uncle."

"Do you know where he is today?"

"Yeah, in about a million pieces somewhere in the Aegean Sea or somewhere around there."

"Is your reason for being in the United States connected to your uncle's demise?"

No answer.

The agent asked again, "Is your reason for being in the United States connected to your uncle's demise?"

No answer.

"Do you know the names Sergei Billicoff and Coby Rodriguez?"

"Yes, the bloody bloke and his cunt wife who had my uncle murdered."

"Harsh words. Were you given an assignment to assassinate Billicoff?"

No answer.

"Who gave you the orders to kill Billicoff?"

No answer.

"Does the name Abdul bin Fahid sound familiar?"

Fasbottom reacted when he heard Fahid's name. "All I know, he was a friend of my uncle, and was going to make us rich while destroying the corrupt capitalistic way of life."

"Are you aware of the kidnapping of a little girl in front of the Camden Aquarium?"

"Only what I read in the newspaper. Too bad they didn't kill the girl too."

Coby took a deep breath upon hearing that remark.

The agent responded, "Seems personal to me. Is it?"

No answer.

"Mr. Fasbottom, do you cherish life?"

"That is a stupid question. Of course I do, but not those who are my enemies."

"You mean like Major Rodriguez?"

"Yes, and her Russian husband. For that matter, the child they brought into the world."

"You do realize that the crimes you have committed are Federal and subject to death with lethal injection?"

"You can't do shit. I am a British citizen."

"You can put that statement away. We have received

paperwork from London. Basically, we can do whatever we want with you."

"Actually, I'll save you time and money. Shoot me here and now!" With that, he struggled to get out of the shackles and became violent.

The guard at the door removed the club from his holster and twice whacked Fasbottom across the back and once in his face. Blood spurted like a fountain out of the bridge of his nose.

Chief Roberts, with his hand to his mouth, whispered to Coby, "This is the part the public doesn't see but only in movies."

The agent in the interrogation room offered Fasbottom a cup of water and a paper towel. "Here, wipe the blood off your face and drink some water. We are not done here."

"Fuck you!"

The guard removed his club and when Fasbottom saw this action, he calmed down.

"The little girl is innocent. Do you know where they are keeping her?"

"For all I know she's dead."

Coby made a move toward the door in an attempt to enter the interrogation room.

The Chief grabbed her arm and brought her back to the viewing area.

In the interrogation room, the agent said, "You said you cherish life. Do you cherish your own life?"

No answer.

"Our people at MI-6, the place where your favorite uncle worked then disgraced with his murderous actions, have a sheet on you a mile long. Your terrorist uncle is dead, and you are here on a vengeance adventure with Fahid. We also know you have a wife and three children back in Leicester. Henry, listen to me and listen closely. I will guarantee that you will live, and we will move your family to Terre Haute, Indiana, where they can have a new and rich life here in America. The United States has a federal prison there. Your family will have repeated visitor rights to sit with you, play games with you, have dinner with you and if you cooperate, we can also arrange conjugal visits with Nadine, your lovely wife."

No reaction.

The agent took a photo out of the case and placed it in front of Fasbottom. "Nice-looking family. The little boy kind of resembles you. Nadine is very attractive and will have you replaced in no time. She is less likely to do that when we move her and your children to Terre Haute."

Fasbottom stared at the photo. "You play dirty."

"What's the little girl's name?"

No answer.

"Sally, yes, Sally Fasbottom. My report says she is doing well in school. Too bad all she'll remember of her daddy is the picture we will send her of your body jacked up on chemicals that eat away at your brain. The last thing to go is your heart. Rest assured that all **your children** and Nadine will remember of you."

Fasbottom's eyes began to swell.

"Do you know an Oscar Fitzgard?"

"The only Oscar I know is a retarded chap back at home."

"We have identified him as the kidnapper. You better pray we don't catch him, and he sings before you help us. Then what I have offered you is rescinded. We will meet here again tomorrow, where you will be asked the same questions. That will be the last time you will be given the chance to determine your destiny, life, or death."

Inside the viewing room, Chief Roberts nodded to the technician.

Inside the interrogation room, the silence was broken by

the voice of little children in the cutest British accents. "We miss you, Daddy. When are you coming home?" A pause and the youngest child, a little girl, said, "I love you, Daddy."

The agent said, "You are excused now. I will see you here tomorrow. Rest tonight and think about how you can help save a young girl whom I believe is the same age as your Sally."

With that, Fasbottom was led out of the room with his head shaking from one side to the other.

Chief Roberts then escorted a very quiet Coby down the hall and back to his office.

She broke her silence.

"Why didn't you tell me that the man who attempted to murder Sergei could be pampered in prison."

"Coby, our goal is two-fold: to find Dina and find Fahid. Everything else is just fodder. You are invited to be back again tomorrow. I can have security detail escort you here."

"I'll be here."

CHAPTER 39

NOSTALGIA

Coby took her position in the armored limousine ready to take her to the hotel. Along with the armored vehicle were two black SUVs and a group of the finest uniformed Philadelphia motorcycle police.

The motorcycles were blinking red and blue lights and in the windows of the SUV, a series of blue lights adorned the front windshield and the rear window. The lights seemed to dance across the top of the car above the windshield.

Before they took off, Coby asked the driver to take a detour down 17th Street in South Philadelphia, the street where she had spent all her young and early teen years. "Officer, please make a left on 17th Street."

The two agents assigned to her were not pleased. "Major Rodriguez, our orders are to take you to the Four Seasons where your security detail is waiting."

"I understand, please just let this happen. Notify them at the hotel, let them know we'll be a half hour to forty-five minutes late."

"Yes, ma'am." The agent sent a notice to headquarters to notify the motorcade that there was a change of plans. In a flash, the motorcycles turned on their lights and sirens and headed west on Market Street, around the City Hall circle, three more blocks then turning left on 17th Street.

A curious crowd gathered on the street to see the motorcade.

As soon as they turned, Coby began pointing out places and talking to the agents like it was her tour of 17th Street, Philadelphia. Chestnut Street, Walnut Street, then South Street, Washington Avenue, and with Reed Street in sight, she knew she was close.

As they approached the block where she grew up, past Reed Street, they were just yards from her childhood home. She asked the driver to stop. "Please pause here for a few minutes."

The neighborhood people were curious and wondered who could be in the stretch limo protected by so many motorcycles and vehicles.

Major Coby Rodriguez reached for the door handle, opened the door, and exited. In a mystical moment, she transformed into Conchetta Rodriguez. The little girl was treated like a princess. She could imagine Poppa's cigar smell, the spot where she scraped her knees playing on the sidewalk, the call from the kitchen, "Coby, your poppa will be here soon. Come in and wash your hands for dinner." Coby caught herself looking down at her hands. They mimicked hand washing. She stopped when her intellect took over the fantasy.

Getting back in the car, she told the security people to continue to the end of the corner where Foti's Grocery store used to be. To her dismay, the grocery store was now a sandwich shop, and Mr. Cannuli's was now a twenty-four-hour dry cleaner.

The motorcycles and cars then continued south. When they passed Saint Thomas Aquinas Church, she took her right thumb and made signs of the cross on her forehead, lips, and heart with a silent prayer. *Please, God, Saint Thomas, and all the saints in Heaven, help me find my daughter.*

CHAPTER 40

THE FBI

The Four Seasons Hotel in Downtown Philadelphia was reserved for those who want to be in a five-star hotel yet be in the heart of the city. Tourists and basic everyday businesspeople could not afford the four-figure room rate. They usually bunked at the Independence Hall Inn or the nearby Ramada. The Four Seasons had an opulent presidential suite for the elite, celebrities, royalty, and very special guests, like Major Coby Rodriguez.

The suite consisted of three bedrooms and a common area big enough to hold a nice-sized celebration. A full bar and a service area were on one end of the common area. Three plush sofas and a large dining room table filled the center of the room. Opposite the bar area was a large credenza with a refrigerator and a granite surface that when opened, revealed a large digital TV set that rose for viewing.

The curtains on the windows were operated by remote control. Prior to Coby checking in, the curtains were replaced with materials that could withstand the largest caliber bullet.

On the dining room table, the FBI had set up a mini office with recording equipment, fax machines, an array of telephones, and sophisticated electronics which could monitor many frequencies with the hope that they could intercept a covert message sent or received by Fahid.

Before Coby arrived, the next shift of agents had meticulously gone over various plans to handle anything that might cause harm to Coby. They were anticipating the obvious call from the kidnapper, as was common in all kidnapping cases, except this was not an ordinary kidnap. The usual kidnapping had a ransom attached: money, gold, gems, etc. The usual kidnapping had the kidnapper calling to make demands like the place for the pick-up, the come-alone plea, and of course, the monetary reward for the safe exchange of the person kidnapped.

Here the exchange was not established, and the agents speculated that the swap was Major Coby for baby Dina.

The agents expected the trade-off to take place somewhere for Fahid to have a quick escape route, like a subway station or a mall during peak shopping times. They had appropriated 125 men and women in this case. Every agent took this case personally since Coby and Sergei's actions had saved all their lives. They truly believed they and their families would be dead if it weren't for the couple's heroism. Now it was their turn to repay them with undying loyalty.

Coby and her entourage arrived at the hotel and were whisked to a special elevator that was checked out from the top of the shaft to the bottom of the car. Video surveillance was installed inside the elevator shaft with the live feed sent to one of the screens on the dining room table in the suite. The elevator was rigged to go expressly to the top floor where the suite was located.

Upon reaching the floor, Coby noticed the number of

special agents and military people lining the hallway. She had not felt this special since the New York ticker-tape parade and the medal presentation at the White House.

The suite door opened in anticipation of her arrival. Entering the room, she was greeted by FBI Chief Roberts. "Welcome, Major Rodriguez. We have set up a mini office for added security and to intercept anything that aids us in finding your daughter."

"Thank you, Chief Roberts."

"Your room is that one there." He pointed to the main bedroom.

"I would like to visit my husband."

"I do not think that is a good idea. We are installing a video camera in his room so you can see him during his stages of recovery."

Coby nodded in total understanding.

"You might want to take time to rest and refresh yourself. If Fahid tries to contact you, this could be a very long night."

Coby walked into the room and saw the California-size bed waiting for her. She locked her door and began to undress down to her undergarments. She picked up a bottle of water on the table next to the bed, removed the cap, and took two very large gulps. The tiredness was growing. Still, she had enough energy to walk toward the window, spread open the ultra-heavy curtain, and gaze at the iconic landmark of Philadelphia's City Hall with the enormous statue of William Penn facing North Philly. She was startled when a helicopter flew past her window with the door open and she could see it was occupied by a sniper. Her reflexes caused her to jump back.

A knock on her door. "Major Coby, this is Chief Roberts. We were just notified by personnel in the copter. Please refrain from opening the curtains. I hope you understand."

"I do, thank you, and good night."

The moment her head hit the pillow; she fell asleep.

At 8:00 a.m. sharp the phone in her room rang and woke her up. At the same time, there was a knock at the door. "Unlock this door. This call might be from Fahid."

Coby jumped to the door, ran to a robe neatly next to the bed, and put it on. Then out to the hotel phone in the common room. The call was now in its fourth ring.

"Hello?"

A "click" with no answer.

A freshly awakened Chief Roberts entered the room. "Major, I am certain that was Fahid. Get yourself ready for a long day. If the phone rings again, answer it even if you are in the shower. There is a phone in the bathroom. We are monitoring it here and tracing the originating locale. I hope he does not call for a while so we can instruct you on how to handle the call. Please do not take long. Coffee and breakfast are ordered, and they should be here when you come out."

"I'm quick. I was always the first at the Academy leaving the showers."

In the common room, FBI technicians were adjusting an antenna that was tuned to a special frequency on a direct point-to-point contact signal with Cooper Hospital right over the Delaware River. The problem they were encountering was the curtain. The solution was to open the curtain for ten minutes to allow Coby to keep a vigil with Sergei.

In fewer than ten minutes, Coby exited the bedroom. "Coffee, Major?" was offered by one of the Army security team.

"Yes, please, thank you," she replied.

On the coffee table between the sofas, there were six metal covers that when the lids were lifted revealed the breakfast:

croissants, muffins, scrambled eggs, bacon, oatmeal, and a healthy assortment of fresh fruit.

Coby felt a bit guilty about being hungry. Her internal barometer said, "No time to eat. Find your daughter." Despite that, she did fill her plate with an assortment off the table.

Chief Roberts entered the room from the bedroom on the other side of the room.

Coby asked, "You slept here too?"

"Yes, Coby. You might get tired of looking at my face. I will try to be with you all the time."

"Don't you have a family?"

"Yes, but my sweet wife, Molly, totally understands the parameters of my job responsibilities."

"Kids?"

"Yes, a little girl."

"Are you concerned they may be in trouble, you know, because you are in charge of my safety, the number one enemy of a lunatic?"

"I have thought of that and have a detail surrounding my house."

"This man is crazy. What is on the agenda today?"

"We are hanging here for a bit. I fully expect him to call. Then we will move to the FBI building for the second round of interrogating Henry. He's had a full day to contemplate his choices. My guess is he is more afraid of Fahid than he is of us."

The two were interrupted by one of the FBI technicians. "Sir, the hook-up is made. Give us the ten-minute window we'll need to dial in the line of sight."

In exactly ten minutes, which was expected from a technician, he alerted Coby that the connection was made. "Major, we can have a point-to-point signal with your husband at Cooper Hospital. Once you are ready, we believe it will be safe to open the curtain for ten minutes and allow a clear signal and if all goes well, you'll have a live video of Sergei on the TV set over there."

Chief Roberts gave the hand signal and said, "Open the curtain, alert Cooper, and let's see if this can do what they tell me it can do."

Coby was staring at the TV set. She was behind the entry wall and had a clear view of the set. The screen was snowy. The curtains opened and in seconds a picture of Sergei, in a hospital room, appeared on the screen in black and white.

"Can he hear me?"

"Yes, the microwave signal carries audio."

Ignoring the safety concern by walking around the wall, she moved to the screen where she was as close as three feet. "Sergei, I am not sure you can hear me, I am being taken good care of. I am very secure. I miss you so much. I pledge to you, with all my heart, Dina will be found safe and sound." There was not any reaction. "I pray for you every chance I have. I—"

The phone rang.

Roberts barked out the order, "Close the curtains, turn on the recording and tracking. Major, use this phone on the table."

Coby picked up the receiver and placed it to her ear. "Who's there?"

"Good to hear your voice again," Fahid's voice came through.

"Fahid, is my daughter safe?"

"Good mother, good question. She is in a safe place. I have one of my best men taking care of her every need. We want to keep her healthy and happy. We have even found her tickle spots."

Coby did everything she could to hold her temper.

"I need to know she is alive, and you can have anything you want."

"She is not here. Like I said she is in a very safe place."

Coby turned her head toward Chief Roberts and saw him giving her hand signals to keep talking, the trace was happening, but they needed more time.

"I know what you want."

"We will talk again." On that note, he hung up.

The FBI technician was frustrated. "Just a few more seconds. We can, with certainty, locate the origination as North Philadelphia. The bad news is if it's from a phone booth he could move from one place to another."

"Let's go with what we have. He's a game player. An expert in psychological warfare. We cannot let him take control. Major, please get ready. We need to go back to the interrogation room."

It took over an hour to close things down at the Four Seasons Hotel, prepare the motorcade, and reach the interrogation area in the bowels of the FBI building at Market and Sixth Street in East Center City.

Henry Fasbottom looked different in his eyes, his walk, and his posture. He looked like he was good with himself.

The interrogator opened with the same questions in order to give official chronological validity. Then a voice from the walls began to echo in the room with Fasbottom, the guard, and the FBI agent...

From the viewing room, Chief Roberts decided to take the lead on this run. "Henry Fasbottom, this is Federal Bureau of Investigation Chief James E. Roberts. How you answer a couple of questions can determine how you spend the rest of your life. Do you hear me?"

"Yeah."

"Do you understand the offer that was made to you yesterday?"

"Yeah."

"Well," Roberts continued, "I am the only person in the universe who can approve the sweetest deal I have ever seen the bureau give. So how you answer the question is how this little meeting ends. Happy or miserable. Before you answer, let me define miserable. Solitary confinement for the rest of your life. You'll live with roaches and ants biting at your dried and wrinkled skin. Sunlight will be a thing of the past, and if you are thirsty, which I guarantee you will be after I will see that extra salt be added to every meal, you will only receive the minimum-by-law two cups of water."

"All I can tell you is what I know."

"I'm all ears, Henry."

"This guy, who calls himself Pinto, took me and the guy you shot to a bar in the northern part of the city."

"Do you remember the name of the bar?"

"Something like a Wet Spot or Wet something."

"Go on."

Chief Roberts flipped the switch to mute his voice, turned to a detective, and said, "Get me a list of bars in that area with the word 'wet' in it." Flipping the switch to on, he said, "Was there anyone else with you?"

"No, Pinto was alone."

"Can you describe Pinto?"

"Dark skin, not a Black man, I'd say more Greek or Italian. Wore shades, even in the bar. He had a package tied up with twine and gave it to us. He then gave each of us five thousand dollars with the promise of five thousand more when the job was done."

"What was the job?"

"Inside the packages were two white outfits usually worn

by hospital workers, fake badges, and money." Fasbottom filled them in on how they followed instructions to get past all the guards. "Luckily, we were ordered by a nurse to clean up a mess in a room down the hall from our target."

Coby shouted loud enough to be picked up by the microphone, "That target is my husband, you are a fucking piece of shit," but only half her message got through.

"Major, restrain yourself, please."

"I'm sorry."

Roberts commented, "The knife blade was porcelain, easy to get past the detectors."

Turning to Coby, Roberts said, "You okay, Major?"

"Yes." Coby was sweating from the vision being painted by Henry.

"Could you describe Pinto to a sketch artist?"

"Yes, I think I could. Did I live up to the bargain?"

"So far. Let's see what the sketch artist gives us. The other thing you have going for you is that the State policeman who was stabbed will survive."

"Thank you, sir. I am really a good person and a good father. I love my wife and hope she can forgive me."

Roberts turned to Coby. "Now let's get back to the hotel room and hope the bastard calls again and stays on the phone a little longer."

CHAPTER 41

THE WAIT IS ON

FBI Senior Officer Deborah Poore had been assigned to Coby's well-being. Anything Coby would need, Officer Poore would get it. The knock at the door was her. She had gone to various downtown stores to shop for Coby to get her some new jeans, sweats, and a variety of tops.

The military man in charge of the door let her in. She flashed an extraordinarily large smile when she walked in to greet all the people in the room. Her personality made her perfect for this role. "Hello, everyone. I am an FBI special assignment officer. I am here for a single purpose: to assist Major Rodriguez. Sir, please check these bags." She handed them to the man who opened the door. "Once you have cleared the merchandise, I'd like to meet the major."

"She is taking some quiet time."

"Did she have dinner?"

"The dinner looked great, but she hardly had a bite."

"I see. Is that her door over there?"

"Yes. Ma'am, our orders are to not disturb her."

"Well, I'm here now and what I am about to do, in no man's land, can be considered disturbing." Agent Poore gently rapped three times on the door.

"Yes?"

"Major Rodriguez, I am FBI agent Deborah Poore and I have some things I know you will like. Please let me in."

Coby opened the door and let the agent in the bedroom. "What do you need from me?"

"What I need most is your trust. Please sit over here." She pointed to a corner of the bed. Once they both were seated, Agent Poore took Coby by the hands. Poore looked deep into her eyes and said in a slow, sobering tone, "We will find little Dina and bring her back to you. You must have faith in the FBI and faith in your Catholic faith. Yes, I studied your history, and it is over-the-top amazing. I know more about you than you'd like to believe." Agent Poore's soothing Southern accent became more pronounced the more she spoke. "You are a hero, and your family did not ask for this anguish."

"Thank you."

Agent Poore stood up and picked up the two shopping bags and walked over to the other side of the bed. Coby swiveled around to see what was in the bag. "I hope these fit. I am a pretty good judge of sizes, but to tell you the truth, I cheated. I looked at your military records." They both smiled. One by one, Agent Poore revealed the articles. "Here are some nice jeans. Did not want to get two of the same, so here is a black pair and a white pair." Still digging in the same bag, she pulled out another bag with "Bonwit Teller" printed on the outside. "I saw these pullovers and bought a long sleeve and a short sleeve." From the second bag, she pulled out a shoebox and removed the lid, and pulled out the shoes. The very stylish walking shoes were beige with a very slight heel.

Coby remarked, "Very nice. You have good taste. Thank you."

"Wait, there is more." Placed on the bed came panties, two pairs of socks, two bras, and a bag from the hotel drugstore. "Here are some things you might need. You know, aspirin, candy bar, and well, you know, feminine things." She pulled out a small handbag.

"I like the handbag, especially the color and the handles."

"Open it up."

Coby opened the small handbag and saw a thirty-eight-caliber revolver with a box of hollow-point bullets designed to enter the body, break into many pieces, then not exit on the other side. She acknowledged the gun and closed the handbag. Sarcastically, Agent Poore remarked, "Should have seen me trying to tell General Patton out there that this piece was approved by somebody high in the Pentagon. He finally had to verify the order. Now tell me about your daughter."

"She is beautiful, at a very fun age, and very smart. She is a perfect clone of my husband and me. She has very similar features. Thank God she has my nose." With that, Coby stopped and needed to gain her composure before she continued. "I don't know, I just know she will grow up to be a very special person."

"How can she not, with parents like you and Sergei? Tell me something about him."

"He's right across the river, so close yet so far apart. He's all the man a woman could ever wish for. Gentle, loving, and cooks, and as I get to see how wonderful a daddy he is, I fall even deeper in love. If that is possible."

"Have you heard anything about him today?"

"Just that he's still in a coma. I got to see him for a few minutes earlier today on a television screen."

"I'll be back in the morning. Promise me two things: you

get a good night's sleep, and you'll eat breakfast when it arrives. Here is my card if you need anything day or night."

"Thank you, Agent Poore. You are a kind soul. I am a bit tired. I'll sip a little wine and that will get me drowsy. Wine does that, except I want to be alert if and when Fahid calls."

Agent Poore said her goodbyes and left.

Coby neatly picked up the goods and placed them on the credenza top. She removed the cellophane wrap from the top of a glass of red wine and took a nice gulp. She lay down on the bed, fluffed her pillow, yawned twice, then fell asleep.

"Coby, Coby."

She heard her name and ignored the calling. She shifted from the right side to the left side.

"Coby, I have come to help you."

Her eyes still closed, she managed to envision a human form. "Momma?"

"I thought it was time I came to you and tell you what I know."

"Momma?" Coby opened her eyes, and the blurred vision became very real. "Momma, is this really you?"

"I know lately you have been questioning your faith. That is understandable. Know that I have never left your side."

"But you have, you have. You let them take Dina."

"I was with you a world apart."

"I did not need you or any of the souls over there. Here is where I needed them."

"It is not too late, Coby. The souls are still inside you. You have not given them any reason to surface."

"I desperately need them now."

"They have not abandoned you. In the future, some may be called to help others, but right now all seven are inside you."

"Why would any of them leave?"

"It is the spark. Madame Zyrk told me you were gifted

with a spark. That when you meet people your energy reaches out to find the spark inside that person so the two could interact on a very high spiritual level. Well, when one of the souls detects there is a chance to make that person a better person by emboldening that person's soul, they leave and go with that person."

"Well, I hope that is a long time. How's Pop?"

"Resting well. Remember, Coby, I will always be by your side."

Both eyes were open wide as she observed the vision fade away. She was shaking because the experience seemed very real.

CHAPTER 42

FAHID WANTS IT ALL

Fahid had been recruiting men for the last two years. They all shared one common thing: all would have been extremely wealthy had not Coby and Sergei spoiled their plans. The house in Chestnut Hill, which was now their garrison, was an old one in an old neighborhood. Everyone in the area kept to themselves. However, when they heard a baby's laughter and crying, they become especially curious.

One of the next-door neighbors, Mrs. Ida Jones, paid a visit to the house with a stuffed teddy bear for the baby. She knocked, but no one answered. She knocked again, and after a few seconds, the door opened, and standing in front of her was a very tall man with a full beard, with a distinct body odor.

"Yeah," he said.

"Hello, I'm your next-door neighbor Ida Jones, and I wanted to meet our young neighbor and give this cute teddy bear to, uh, is the baby a boy or a girl?"

"She's not my kid."

"Can I see her?"

"Not right now. She is taking a nap."

Mrs. Jones became curious when she could hear a baby's cry coming from inside the house. "Uh, okay, I understand. You don't want her bothered."

A second man with a heavy beard came to the door and took the stuffed animal. "Thank you for the gift, I'll make sure she gets it. Look, we are pretty busy here so have a nice day."

"Oh okay, well, have a nice day. Oh, today would be a beautiful day to take the baby outside. I've never seen you take the baby outside."

"She's allergic to the sun."

"Oh, the poor darling. By the way, if you ever need a babysitter, I am a good one. You know, I have six grandchildren."

The second man told her, "Thanks, we will keep that in mind."

Ida returned to her house. Her husband, Kenneth, was sitting at the breakfast table with a cup of coffee and reading the newspaper.

"Ken, there is something strange I sense about our new neighbors."

"Oh, Ida, please. You know I hate it when you judge people."

"No, Ken. These two men were telling me the baby was sleeping when I could hear her crying. And the smell coming out of there was horrible, nothing for a baby's sensitive nose."

"What do you want to do about it? Call the cops because the place smells? That's no welcoming gift."

"Okay I get it, but I am telling you something is just not right."

Inside the Chestnut Hill house, Fahid was questioning the men who answered the door.

"Just a neighbor giving a gift for the baby."

"Let me see it."

The teddy bear was handed to Fahid, who proceeded to take a sharp knife off the table and cut into it, shredding it into many pieces. "One can never be sure. It is just what it seems to be."

He called everyone into the room and motioned them to sit around the table. "Amid, clean up this mess."

Amid gathered the doll's stuffing and threw it into the trash can.

"There are several things on the agenda. Plus, one more I am adding today. When someone is at the door, do not answer it. Do you all understand?"

They all responded, "Yes," except for Amid.

"By not answering, will that not cause suspicion?"

"My friend, never question me. Someday I will tell you a story about a man who would not trust my every word. Sometime after, that person became tiger shit."

"Sorry, Fahid."

"Next on my list is the baby. Pinto, it is your job to take care of the child. When I went into her room, the entire place smells. When was the last time you changed her?"

"Sir, we have no diapers."

"Then go fucking buy some. There are convenience stores close by. Take ten dollars out of the kitty and buy some diapers and baby powder, oh, and some milk and oatmeal."

Pinto took the money and started to leave when he was called back to the table.

"Hold on, you'll leave after I go through my list. Amid, get me a complete map of the subway system here with schedules. We will use the subway system to capture Coby. So, I will need three of you to work with me on this plan. The timing needs to be spot on."

Fahid was fortunate that he had surrounded himself with

loyal people. Josef, a middle-aged warrior, once told Fahid that he would sacrifice his life for him.

"Josef, you take a walk around the block and see if there is a car that you can steal. We will use that car to deliver Coby to me. The rest of you will stay in the house to protect our turf. The three I want to be with me when the capture is made are Josef as the driver, and Mo and Jacob, you will be my security if needed. Once I get the subway schedules, I will be more precise. We have no time to waste."

The men in the room all nodded in agreement.

At the Four Seasons Coby was trying on the jeans that Agent Poore bought. She thought to herself that it was a good fit. So were the tops and the walking shoes.

She exited her room and saw the full array of breakfast items on the serving table. Remembering the promise she made, she sat, took a plate, placed some scrambled eggs, bacon, and a croissant, and on another plate some fresh fruit.

Chief Roberts entered the room. "Good morning, everyone. Our friend Fasbottom has worked with the sketch artist, and this is our man, Pinto." He passed the sketch to all in the room. The drawing followed the description given by Fasbottom.

Coby stared at her copy and looked into his eyes. "He is evil."

"This drawing has been passed to every police precinct in the city. Being that he is so tall and unattractive, he should not be that difficult to locate. That is if he comes out in the public."

Coby inquired, "Where is Fasbottom now?"

"He's on his way to Lewiston to stay for a bit until we can settle this case in its entirety."

Chief Roberts' phone rang. He answered, and all the people in the room could hear was, "Good," "Positive," and "I am sure to tell her now." Roberts hung up and turned to Coby. "Major, Sergei has opened his eyes. He is awake and the doctors are elated. He is having trouble talking, but I believe they are ready for a video transmission at the top of the hour."

Coby began to shake. She dropped her fork and stood up to hug Chief Roberts for the good news. "Finally, something positive. Today, right now, I have more hope that we have turned the tide. I just feel it. I had a wonderful dream with my mother who stands beside me and has given me renewed strength."

Just before it was time to see and hopefully talk to Sergei, the hotel phone rang. Chief Roberts ordered everyone to stand by their post. He then gave a head signal to Coby to answer the phone. "Remember to keep him on as long as you can."

Coby picked up the receiver and said, "Yes?"

"I will make this short and sweet," Fahid said. "At exactly four o'clock today, I will send a messenger to you with the instructions on how to get your baby back. He will deliver it to the hotel in an envelope addressed to you, Major. He will then leave unharmed and unfollowed. If he is harmed and if he detects being followed, do you know what the consequence will be?"

"How is my baby?

The phone went dead.

"Not long enough, Chief," the FBI technician stated.

"What did he say?"

She told them about the 4:00 p.m. meeting and threats.

"I understand, but we will need to apply some fingerprint and toxicity tests before you touch the envelope."

The lobby of the Four Seasons was not very well lit. However, the FBI had three cameras set up to capture the messenger. These cameras were so very light sensitive that it made no difference in the quality of the lighting in the room.

By three o'clock, the cameras were set, and a forensic team was ready to analyze the envelope. Even the hotel agent behind the counter was with the FBI. All the helpers behind the desk were instructed to wear white gloves in case the envelope was tainted with anthrax, serine, or some other deadly toxin.

At exactly 4:00 p.m. a short-statured man wearing a baseball cap, large, rimmed sunglasses, and a surgical mask entered the hotel. The agents outside later deduced he came to the spot using public transportation and walked several blocks to reach the hotel.

The man walked up to the desk reached into his jacket pocket and handed the woman FBI agent an envelope. He quickly turned around and exited. None of the agents followed.

The envelope was given to the forensic team who cleared the outer casing as clean. The envelope was opened, and they examined the letter itself. It was also deemed clean and clear.

The letter was delivered to Coby's room. The instructions were very clear:

Tomorrow at 12:11 PM catch the southbound Broad street train at the City Hall platform.

Enter the second car.

I will meet you there. I will take you to your daughter.

If I should somehow not show up at my house with you at 2pm, I have instructed my men to slit little Dina's throat.

Fahid

"Jesus, this guy is crazy. That is lunchtime and those cars will be packed. He won't have the girl with him, and we cannot kill or capture him. He has us over a barrel."

Coby asked if there was a vest she could wear. "It saved my husband once and with this lunatic, anything could happen."

"Poore, fit her with a vest and a coverup so it is not obvious."

"Yes, sir."

"Donnelly, get the subway schedule and grab a partner, and be on that train. I know the stations. Get on at Erie Avenue. That's the end of the line and about twelve stops before City Hall. Make sure it is the Broad Street line. Place men at each station south of City Hall. We need to have eyes on him all the time."

"Wait, Chief, they will murder my daughter. I can do this alone. I have a weapon now. I can take care of myself."

"Major, with all due respect, we have ways of tailing him without being noticed. Right now, we are working in a vacuum. Please leave the FBI work to the FBI. We know what we are doing."

"We are talking about my daughter here. I'm not afraid of Fahid or anybody. I fought him and won before, and I can do it again. Now I want to see my husband."

Chief Roberts nodded to the technician who called his counterpart at the Cooper Medical Center. "We go live in two minutes. Open the curtains on my count." He looked at his watch. "Five, four, three, two, one, NOW."

With that order, the curtain was pulled back letting a burst of sunlight into the room. The television set flickered, then TV snow appeared and after a minute the form of Sergei in the hospital bed appeared. Although the picture was not clear, Coby could see his eyes and they were open.

"Sergei, can you hear me?" Sergei responded to the question by moving his head slightly. "Can you talk at all?" His mouth moved, but no sound came out. "I cannot wait to hold you in my arms again, I miss you very much. We are making progress on finding Dina." He blinked and uttered a sound that sounded like a grunt. She could see he was struggling to talk but to no avail. "The doctors say this will take time." Coby detected a smile and turned to the FBI technician. "Did you see that he smiled?"

The technician explained, "Major, we only have one more minute."

"Thank you. Sergei, one of the assassins from your room is talking and—"

"Major, please refrain from airing any facts from the case."

"Sorry Chief. Sergei, I must go now. Hopefully, we can get to see each other, and you will be strong enough to talk. I love you, honey, with all my heart. Bye."

CHAPTER 43

TO CAPTURE COBY

Fahid's curious next-door neighbor, Ida Jones, was now in her backyard stretching over the fence to get a good look at the strange new neighbors' backyard. She was not tall enough, so she grabbed a wooden box and climbed on it to gain enough height to see into the yard. Her old eyes took in a yard of unmowed grass at least knee high. Closer to the house under the porch were empty bottles and piles of broken glass. Next to the glass was a box with the word "Remington" in large print and the words "24 cases of .38-caliber hollow ammunition." She concluded that this was rather unusual for the community, and it fortified her suspicions that something was just not right.

Watching this from an upstairs window was Amid.

Ida returned to her house. "Kenneth, Kenneth there's something I have to show you." She went upstairs to the bedroom where Kenneth was taking a cat nap. *I'll get him to see it when he wakes up*, she thought.

She went downstairs to the living room and picked up a feather duster and began to dust the lamps, some knick-knacks, and the mantel over the fireplace. She exited the living room, and out of nowhere, Amid suddenly grabbed her around the neck and proceeded to choke the life out of her with a belt. In the process of fighting for her life, she managed to knock a sculpture off its base. The porcelain piece fell to the ground and shattered into a thousand pieces.

The noise awakened Kenneth. "Ida, Ida? Are you okay?" *Damn woman needs her hearing checked.* "Something broke. I could hear it." Kenneth got out of bed, walked into the hallway, and was greeted by three bullets fired from a pistol with a silencer. He dropped dead instantly.

When Amid returned to the house, Fahid politely asked if it was done.

"Yes, sir."

"What did you do with the bodies?"

"Nothing."

"Go back and bury them. The backyard is safe."

"Yes, sir."

Fahid returned to the table when the child began to scream. "Where the hell is Pinto with the diapers?" He then turned to his team and reiterated the plan.

"Now, everyone knows their assignment. When she is in the car, inject this into her." He was holding a hypodermic needle up to show everyone. He then placed the needle in a case. "Then we'll take her here where we can reunite her with her precious daughter. Josef, you will be the driver. After she is here, dispose of the car. Wear your gloves, leave no prints."

Josef responded, "Yes, sir, piece of cake."

"Let's go over the plan one more time."

Fahid opened a map of the Philadelphia subway lines. He pointed to City Hall. "I will get on the train up the line in the second car. The pick-up car will be here at the Spring Garden station on the west side of the street."

"Sir, that is north of City Hall, and you will be going on the southbound train."

"I know exactly what I am doing."

The FBI technician handed Chief Roberts a paper. "Here are some details on what we were able to discover about Pinto. Seems his father was killed in the Denali bombing, which verifies all this is about is vengeance with a capital V."

"Donnelly, all your men ready for this tomorrow?"

"Yes, sir," Donnelly said. "The subway schedule shows that the train reaches City Hall at 12:11 p.m. We will be at the end of the line, the Erie station, at 11:29 a.m. That is where Agent Pattison and I will enter the second car. We will see him when he gets on the train and put eyes on Fahid and make sure he does nothing to harm Major Rodriguez."

"Good. And the stations south of City Hall?"

"Yes, sir. We'll have men at each stop at each exit. The command for them will be stationed at the Snyder Avenue station. If they get that far, then the next stop is Veteran Stadium. We have a team ready there too."

Roberts pondered. "The difficulty here is not to kill him but to capture him so we have a chit to bargain for the baby. He'll put the major in a car at one of those stations. Tail them. Remember, do not engage until you receive backup support."

Coby interrupted, "Sir, that will not deter him. Captured or killed and my daughter dies."

"Major, as I said, let the FBI do what the FBI does best. He doesn't want to die."

That's all he wants, that is to kill the person I love the most besides the rest of his team will still be after me and Sergei."

"We shall see. Please keep the faith."

Later that afternoon, Coby asked Chief Roberts if she could see Sergei in person one more time. He declined and said, "He must rest, and we'll contact him before you head out to the subway."

Dinner arrived and the two military security men, Chief Roberts, and Agent Poore all sat down. Agent Poore said, "Before we touch the food, I'd like to say a prayer."

Chief Roberts said, "Sure, that would be nice."

"Dear Heavenly Father, we know you feel the pain in our hearts for baby Dina and her momma, Coby. Please, we beg you to watch over baby Dina and protect her with all the grace in the heavens. Please I implore you to watch over all the honorable men and women who will be in action tomorrow to catch the devil incarnate. As we partake of this food, we thank you for the many blessings you have bestowed on us. We love you and pray for peace. Amen."

In unison, everyone responded with an "Amen." The tension was thick in the room.

Coby finished and said good night and retired for the evening. Before bed, she knelt and prayed. *Dear Lord, you have sent your angels to protect me my entire life. For that, I have the deepest gratitude. What I am asking for now is a strange plea. A plea that the FBI fails on its mission, and that Fahid does take me to Dina. I will leave my fate in the hands of you and your army of saints and angels. Amen.*

CHAPTER 44

CITY HALL

The Philadelphia transit system was one of the best in the world. It was old and in parts, it looked its age. The system crisscrossed the city with Market Street as the focal point. Parts of the system ran into the suburbs and parts of it even traveled across the Benjamin Franklin Bridge into New Jersey. The Broad Street line was the busiest of all the underground segments. It ran from the southernmost point of Packard Avenue, where the Philadelphia Eagles and the Philadelphia Phillies played, straight up north under City Hall and to Fern Rock fifteen miles away. There were no twists or turns. Broad Street was known as the longest, straightest street in the world.

The trains were fairly punctual. At some times of the day, they ran more often. At lunchtime during a work week, the Broad Street line had a local and an express train that alternated. At lunchtime, the cars were usually crowded with all the seats taken with people standing and hanging on leather straps dangling from rails connected to the roof.

At precisely 11:29 a.m., the train pulled out of the Erie station. The two FBI agents were in casual clothing and took a seat.

"First stop Olney Avenue," came the announcement from the speaker inside the car. The train stopped to let in a horde of passengers. One passenger in a baseball cap and sunglasses boarded the train. After a second look, he was identified as Fahid.

The train began to roll southward. Agent Patterson alerted Chief Roberts using a small transmitter that Fahid was spotted. "Target spotted entering at Olney Avenue."

Coby checked her watch: exactly noon. She paid her train fare and walked down the most southern steps to be close to the front of the train. She estimated where the second car might be at a full stop. She checked her pocket to make sure the revolver was there. The people on the platform were all kinds of humans from those dressed in suits and skirts to those with ragged clothing.

The entire station was a cement jungle. The steps and the platform were made of cold and grayish cement. The tracks looked worn, and she noticed that there was a cement carve-out about six feet long between the tracks spaced every few feet apart. A loud horn sounded and it startled her.

There was a southbound side and a northbound side that shared the same platform. She could hear a train coming, and her heart beat fast. Looking at her watch, she saw it was 12:05 p.m. Way too early. A train sprang out from the darkness of the tunnel. It was a northbound express. It stopped and let out passengers, let in passengers, and just like that, the doors closed, and the train took off somewhere north of City Hall.

Chief Roberts conveyed to the rest of the team that friendly eyes were on Fahid.

A penetrating screech of metal wheels rubbed the metal

rails as the train turned into the station. A horn alerted the would-be passengers to stand back and make room for the train. Coby checked her watch: 12:10 p.m. *It's showtime.*

Inside the second car, the speaker announced, "City Hall station, City Hall. Next station Walnut."

The two agents moved closer to the center of the car behind standing passengers ready to exit. Fahid moved closer to the doors. The train began to slow down, and the passengers anticipating the stop edged closer to the door. On the platform, there were a dozen people ready to board the front two cars.

Coby was the closest to the tracks. People began to swarm behind her. The train stopped, and the doors opened.

The agents moved close to the door but were hampered by the many passengers ready to disembark to spend another day working at the many downtown stores and offices.

As the doors opened, Coby and Fahid made eye-to-eye contact. Coby entered the car as the throng of people were rushing in and out of the car. "Good afternoon, Coby. It has been a long time."

Coby said nothing, but her stomach was nervous. Once the crowd was settled, a bell rang, and the doors began to close. At the last second, Fahid pushed Coby back onto the platform and followed her pushing the door back with his hands to allow his exit.

The two agents could not reach the closing doors and were now in the car on its way to the next stop.

Coby lost her balance and fell to the ground. Fahid took out a gun and motioned for her to stand.

FBI agents planted on the platform observed this surprise move and reported it to Roberts.

Another loud horn, more screeching, and, like magic, the northbound train arrived. Coby was now standing with Fahid's gun firmly planted in her back. "We are getting on this train."

"And what if I don't?"

"Then you and your baby will die today."

Reluctantly, she entered the last car on the six-car train with Fahid.

The two agents on the platform entered the next-to-last car.

"Next stop, Spring Garden station, Spring Garden." The train moved.

Coby looked around the car. She thought, *I could kill this motherfucker right now, but I need to show restraint.*

She noticed a mother holding a little girl around the same age as little Dina. There was a priest across from where they were standing and a transit policeman at the far end of the car. In two minutes, the train pulled up to the Spring Garden station. Since most of the daily workers left at City Hall, the train car was only twenty-percent full.

The doors opened, and Fahid motioned for Coby to exit.

The two agents saw this and exited. One of the agents made eye contact with Fahid who now realized he was being followed. Fahid barked an order to Coby to move toward the steps, and hurry.

The agents were now close enough to grab him.

Fahid, seeing this, fired his revolver at one of the agents, hitting her in the arm.

Coby was in a quandary: run or follow him up the stairs?

The second agent rushed Fahid, who panicked, and in his escape to the stairs, pushed Coby onto the tracks with an oncoming train entering the station. Coby looked up and calculated she could not get up in time.

The agent stopped the pursuit of Fahid and tried to catch her, while Fahid ran up the stairs and into a waiting stolen car driven by Josef.

The train engineer saw Coby trying to get up and blew his

horn. The engineer closed his eyes not to witness the slaughter.

Then miraculously, an old friend appeared, unseen by those around.

Out of Coby's body emerged a gray figure that pushed her into the carved-out receptacles between the tracks that could protect a human when the train raced across the top of them.

The Engineer, following procedure, slowed the train but did not stop until the train exited the station completely.

Coby stood, shaken but relieved she was not hit and that she was saved once more by one of her souls.

The agent called into the control base that an agent was down then reached for Coby and helped her back onto the station platform.

CHAPTER 45

THE RING TIGHTENS

Josef waited until the three men entered the car, then he sped up from the place where he had parked.

Fahid was out of breath. "There were FBI agents on the platform. She went against the rules and now she knows the consequences. Drive about a mile or two and let me off. I'll take a taxi. You return the car right where you picked it up."

"The owner won't know a thing," Josef chimed in. "He doesn't get back from work for hours yet."

"Good. I must punish her for disobeying. Have a cutting tool ready for me when I get back. We'll send Mommy a tiny present. There's a public phone. Leave me off here."

"Yes, sir."

At the Four Seasons, Chief Roberts returned and immediately spread out the subway system map on the coffee table. He took a pen out of his pocket and circled Olney Avenue. Agent

Donnelly entered the hotel room and grabbed a Coke out of the refrigerator and sat next to Chief Roberts.

Roberts said, "This is the station where he entered the subway." Then he took out a map of Philadelphia and found where the Olney Avenue and Broad Street interchange was located and asked if Donnelly would point to where he thought one mile was from the train station.

Donnelly placed his finger on the one-mile mark and Roberts put a pen point there and drew a circle with the subway station as the center. "Now we need to alter the circle. The south end covers the next couple of stations, so squeeze the circle east and west. The north was where you guys got on. That's Erie. So we'll squeeze the circle more east and west." He took the pen and altered the circle. "Now look east, not too many houses, a hospital, and a large park, so again I'll squeeze the circle and skew it more to the west."

Donnelly noticed that now the west edge of the circle covered Central High School, Girl's High School, and La Salle University. "I'll need to expand the circle to allow for the schools." He then drew and redrew the circle into more of an obelisk covering an area that included Germantown, Wister Hills, and Chestnut Hill. "He came from one of these areas. Instruct our men to take the sketch of Pinto to all the stores in the area. Maybe we'll get lucky."

Coby and her military security entered the hotel room. The agent that was with her on the platform walked in and immediately said, "I thought she was dead. That train came within inches of hitting her. Don't know how she was able to find the ditch to lie down so fast, but thank God she did."

Coby added, "Yes, it was a very close call."

"Major, we think we have identified three areas where there is a very good probability that Fahid and his boys are hiding little Dina. Fahid entered the train here." Pointing to

Olney Avenue. "And these areas are the more likely place where they are hiding."

"Chief, entering the train at that point could have been a diversion to throw everyone off," Coby said, throwing them a curve ball.

"Yeah, we thought of that, but right now it is all we have to go on."

"I hope you are right. I am terrified he will harm my baby. Having agents present just might have killed my little girl. I told you to let me do it alone. He is vengeful and will harm her for disobeying his instructions."

The phone rang and caught everyone off guard. They all ran to their stations while Chief Roberts checked the status of everyone and nodded to Coby to pick up the receiver.

"Yes?"

"I did not expect to hear your voice. I was sure you were beheaded by the wonderful Philadelphia transit system. For you not following my rules, you will be punished. Tomorrow at one p.m., my courier will deliver to you a package. Same thing. No agents, no harm, and no following."

"I am sorry, I wanted to go alone. Please do not hurt my little girl."

"You knew the consequences, Major. Put on the FBI Chief Agent."

Coby looked at Roberts and handed him the receiver. "He wants to talk to you."

Chief Roberts got on the phone. "Chief Roberts."

"Hell, I'm impressed. Well, listen, Chief Roberts, your stupidity will get this baby in a body bag before she pisses her next diaper."

"Fahid, tell us where the baby is and we will go get her, and you and your posse can be long gone. It is that simple."

"Now that I know Coby is alive, I will only give the

fucking kid to her. Directly to her without you or any of your people around." He hung up.

The FBI technician said, "We have a lead on the connection. It is a public phone at Temple University."

Donnelly chimed in, "That is not close to where the circle is."

Roberts added, "Remember, he was way downtown. From what we know, he jumped on another subway car and got off to throw us off. He knew he was long enough on the call to get a good trace. Go there and search the area. My money is still on the three areas, or close to them."

Donnelly left with the car keys in his hand.

"Can I see Sergei now?"

"Too late," Roberts said.

"Just want to see him."

"The technician at Cooper is gone. We'll do it in the morning."

Agent Poore entered the room. "Well, I hear it was a pretty close call." Looking at Coby, she said, "Glad you're still with us. I have some interesting news. Our pigeon Fasbottom was shivved at Lewiston. D.O.A. Guess our Fahid guy had tentacles in more places than we thought."

"Did they get the guy who did it?"

"No. One supposed witness said there were two lines of men passing each other in the hall, then Fasbottom dropped to the ground. This happens often there. We probably should have had him secluded."

"Too damn late now."

"Jesus, what are we dealing with?" Chief Roberts exclaimed then went to the sink and splashed water on his face. "It has been a long and frustrating day." He took a towel and dried his face and sat on the sofa. "We need to get that sketch circulated."

"Agent Pattison, make sure that a team of twenty agents get the sketch. Recruit the police to help. I want every store surveyed."

"Yes, sir," Pattison said.

"I need to rest my eyes and think a bit. I'm staying here tonight. I'll call home and tell my wife. She won't be happy. She doesn't feel safe if I'm not there." Roberts took out his cell phone and called home to tell his wife he would not be home and not to worry. He promised to put a car outside the house to keep an eye on things. He then fluffed a pillow on the sofa, sat back, and closes his eyes. Eyes still closed, he said, "Who is ordering dinner?"

Agent Poore responded, "I will. Get some rest."

The next morning, Chief Roberts was in the same spot. "Guess I needed the rest. I missed dinner. Could we get some breakfast and have them hurry on the coffee?"

His cell phone rang, and he noticed it was from his wife. "Everything okay?"

"Yes, but I did not sleep well," his wife, Molly, said. "I had a terrible, frightening nightmare. You were shot and you died. It was awful."

"I'm okay. Just a little hungry. I missed dinner last night and breakfast will be here soon."

"Okay, sweetheart. Just be extra careful today."

Coby came into the room. "When can I see Sergei?"

"At ten." Chief Roberts, after checking with the communications person, answered Coby's question.

"Sorry, good morning," Coby corrected herself. "I am not usually this rude, but I am scared of what Fahid is sending me today. I have imagined many terrible things. I swear to you, if he harmed Dina, I will find him, no matter where he is in the universe, and kill him most painfully."

"I understand," said Roberts.

A knock at the door was a military person with breakfast on a wheeled serving tray.

There were two pots of coffee, and Coby and Roberts grabbed one each simultaneously. They recognized their mutual addiction to coffee, and both smiled.

The time was 9:30 a.m. at Cooper Medical Center. Sergei's room was quiet with the sound of the monitors keeping track of his vital signs. The security outside his room was tight. Up to as many as six law officers were watching out for his safety. No one could go in or out of his room without vigorous scrutiny, including a pat down.

The FBI technician arrived, cleared security, and entered the room ready to transmit a video signal to the Four Seasons Hotel where Major Coby Rodriguez awaited eagerly for the televised sight of her husband. Sergei's doctor joined the technician to make sure Sergei did not get so excited it could do harm.

Fifteen minutes before transmission, the silence was broken by, "Dina, Dina, I've got you!" The loud statement came from Sergei who was waking from his days of silence. The doctor called in a nurse who hovered over Sergei and calmed him down. "Dina, Dina, I love you. I will save you!"

The doctor ordered the FBI man out of the room. "This morning's transmission is canceled."

The word was conveyed to the hotel room. "Major Rodriguez, the doctor has just canceled this morning's transmission."

"What, why? What's going on? What did they say?'

"Just five words: 'This morning's transmission is canceled.'"

Agent Poore offered her help. "I'll call our contact there and find out what is happening."

"Dammit. I need to go there right away."

"Don't know if we can get you there and back by one."

Coby ran into her room, brushed her teeth and hair, and entered the common space, ready to go.

Agent Poore, on the other side of the room, ended her conversation with the command at the hospital and approached the others. "Sergei is awake and delirious. The doctors have given him something to settle him, but he woke up yelling for Dina. They feel that is a good sign, believe it or not."

"Now I know I must be there. Let's go!"

"Donnelly, get the car ready and alert the Philly police."

At 11:00 a.m., they reached the hospital. Coby ran to the elevator bank and after what felt like the slowest elevator ride, exited on Sergei's floor.

She ran to the room. When she opened the door, she was surprised.

Sergei was sitting up in the bed, wide awake, and when he saw her, he flashed a giant smile.

"Oh my God. You are going to make it."

They embraced and the doctor intervened. "We have some work to do. After all, he has a new hip and a new knee. We just can't rush this."

Sergei said with certainty, "I'm a strong Russian."

"That's my Sergei!"

"Any news on Dina?"

"When they hit you with the car, they took her. The FBI believes they have narrowed the area where they were keeping her."

"In a day or two, I'll be ready to help. You'll see."

"It is time to leave, Major. We are taking very good care of our favorite comrade."

"I'll be back later." She turned to Donnelly for permission. "Okay?"

"Depends."

Coby kissed Sergei one more time and exited the room walking backward.

They got her back to the hotel room at 12:45 p.m., fifteen minutes before the package was to be delivered.

In the lobby, everyone was in place. The cameras, the agents outside, the agent behind the counter, and the toxicologists were all waiting for the delivery.

At 1:00 p.m. sharp, the same man with the cap, sunglasses, and mask entered the lobby with a small, white box. The box was handed over to the agent, then he left quickly through the automatic doors leading to the street.

The box was cleared, then it was opened.

The white-gloved FBI agent opened the box and there was a wad of blood-soaked cotton. She carefully lifted the cotton and saw what appeared to be a tiny baby's little pinky toe. She reacted with disgust and had trouble holding her vomit.

Chief Roberts took the box and now had to decide whether to show Coby or not. He decided to take it to her.

He entered the hotel room, and his face gave away the prospect of something gruesome. "Major, please sit down."

Coby obeyed but was visibly shaking from fear of the unexpected. "What is it? What is in the box?"

"Coby, the bastard has amputated Dina's little toe."

Coby tried to stand, but her knees were so weakened by the news, she collapsed to the ground.

"Get her some water."

Agent Poore grabbed a glass and filled it with water from a pitcher on the coffee table.

Coby did not touch it. She began to sob deeply into her hands. "That monster has disfigured my daughter. I will go after his family and murder each one of them."

"Coby, he will meet his justice. Right now, you are full of hate and revenge."

The team of FBI agents left her alone forming a ring around her. None of them were sure what to do to make such a heinous experience better.

After a few minutes, Coby stood. "Let me see it."

"Not sure you should."

"Chief, let me see it."

Roberts took the box over to her and lifted the lid revealing the tiny digit.

Coby picked it up and examined it. "The green nail polish is still on her pinky toe. Can we save it and reattach it later?"

Agent Poore said, "Give it to me, I will pack it in ice and personally take it to Hahnemann Hospital and order them to preserve it until the time is right."

The toe was packed in ice and Agent Poore left the room. She was given a police escort to the hospital where the nurses took the toe and assured her that the toe was supple enough to be saved, as long as it was done within a week.

When she returned from the hospital, she told everyone the prognosis. "I wish I could turn back the clock and kill that monster back in Russia. We were all fortunate to have left there with our lives intact. I need to lie down for a few. Any word of the canvassing?"

"They are out there. As soon as we get some reliable news, I will let you know."

"Thank you."

CHAPTER 46

SHOE LEATHER

Running through Philadelphia's Germantown Avenue was a trolley track that was the longest of its kind in the world. It could take a passenger to downtown Philly then to the southern point of the city miles away. The Germantown area was founded by the Mennonites in 1683, making it one of the oldest neighborhoods in the colonial days.

A variety of stores lined Germantown Avenue, and the dutiful police and FBI agents were walking the street, visiting each store with the sketch of Fahid's designated nanny, Pinto. One by one the store owners responded "No" to the question, "Have you ever seen this individual?"

Josh Murphy, from a long line of policemen named Murphy, had only four more stores to visit on the block. The Germantown Drug and Pharmacy Store had been around for decades, and it looked like it. Inside, the place was well lit with a battery of fluorescent tubes shining brightly from the ceiling.

Officer Murphy approached the counter and an older

woman in a druggist frock addressed him. "Hello, Officer, is there something I can do for you?"

"Yes, ma'am. My name is Officer Josh Murphy." He gave her his contact card. "We are looking for a person of interest, and I was hoping you might have seen this individual." With that, he took the sketch and showed it to her.

"Yes, he's been in my store. It was so odd. A big man was embarrassed to ask for pull-up diapers, baby powder, and wipes. I found it odd and funny."

Murphy removed a notepad from his pocket and began to write down her responses. "What else did he buy?"

"I think a quart of milk. He asked for oatmeal, but I told him we do not carry a full line of groceries. Only the staples."

"What is your name?"

"Millie Van Buren. I am a descendant of Martin Van Buren, you know, the president."

"Yes, ma'am, I'm familiar with his name. If you were to see this man again, would you recognize him?"

"I could spot that big ugly galoot from a mile away."

"Do you remember how he paid?"

"Cash. I was so leery of him that had he showed me a credit card I would not have taken it."

"Can you recall what direction he went in when he left or if he had a car?"

"No sorry."

Officer Murphy pointed to the card. "Miss Van Buren, if he should enter the store again, please call this number right away. Ask for the Detective in charge."

"I will, Officer Murphy. Do you want me to hold him here?" With that, she removed a pistol from under the counter. "I know how to use this thing if I have to."

"Millie, now don't get crazy. Just let us do our job."

Officer Murphy took out his wireless and reported the finding. That word got to Chief Roberts in minutes.

"At 775 Germantown Avenue? I know where that is, and it is smack dab in the middle of our target zone. We are tightening the noose. Please send a big thank you to the officer that made the connections. It proves that good ol' shoe leather sometimes is better than all the sophisticated technology we have at our disposal."

"Officer Murphy did have one additional comment. He says he spotted two FBI choppers in the area flying above the target zone you described."

"Thank you, dispatch, the helicopters are a big no-no. I will send in a commendation to the mayor over Officer Murphy's keen awareness and dedication."

Chief Roberts called the FBI Headquarters at Fifth and Market Streets.

"Federal Bureau of Investigation, how can I help you?"

"Barbara, this is Chief Roberts. Please connect me with aviation."

"Certainly, sir." The call connected.

"FBI Agent Amie Tanchak."

"Yes, Tanchak, who ordered choppers over the space I denoted as the area where Major Coby Rodriguez's baby is being held?"

"Sir, that is Base Commander Lewis."

"Please ground those birds until further notice from me and only me, you got that?"

"Yes, sir."

"You can tell Commander Lewis those helicopters will spook the bad guys and they may overreact."

"Yes, sir, I will certainly convey the message and get those choppers back to base."

"Thank you, Tanchak."

He knocked on Coby's door. "Come out. I have an update."

Coby exited the room, ashen and despondent. The spunk in her was fading.

"I have some news that cheered me up a bit. We have a hit on the sketches."

"Oh really? Where?" She perked a bit.

"A store dead center of our target zone. Assuming Pinto walked there, we can narrow the search even more."

"Chief, I've given this some thought. I'm going to give myself up. He wants me and Sergei more than my little girl. Next time he calls, I will offer a trade: me for Dina."

"Major, I cannot begin to understand the pain you are experiencing. He is now toying with you and will wear you down. Please don't let him win. Look here." He took out a map of the area and placed a dot on the location of the drugstore. "Now we'll draw a ten-block radius and if we have to, we'll go door to door."

Donnelly, looking over the chief's shoulder, said, "There are about four hundred homes in that area."

"Let's see, twenty men, each get twenty homes. We can cover that in a day. Call the task force together."

Inside the house, Fahid was pacing the floor.

Pinto told him, "The kid is still bleeding."

"What the fuck do you want me to do?"

"Just thought you ought to know that if we do not stop the bleeding, she will die."

"Then do something! Tie a tourniquet around her thigh and cut off the blood supply. Go get some gauze and bandages."

"I have no money."

"Then take money out of the pool and go, you idiot."

Pinto had no idea that his picture was being circulated around the city, so he left without fear.

Two minutes later, Mo, the only member of Fahid's team with blond hair and green eyes, entered the house with a piece of paper in his hand. "Look what I found on the street." It was the sketch of Pinto.

Fahid, seeing this, ran out of the house and caught up to the slow-moving big man.

"Pinto, come back with me. I have something more important."

"What about the kid?"

"She'll be fine. We'll tear off some shirts and use that as a bandage. We'll pour whiskey on the wound to kill the germs. Come back with me."

They walked back to the house and when they entered, Fahid asked Pinto to wait for him in the basement.

Pinto, as a good soldier would do, headed for the basement. He turned the light on and descended the steps.

A few minutes later, Fahid joined Pinto. Fahid asked him to sit down, and Pinto obeyed. Fahid spread the flyer with Pinto's sketch on the table. "Your beautiful face is plastered all over the city. You cannot be seen outside this door again. Do you understand?"

Pinto nodded.

"You have already been exposed. Tell me all the places you have been."

"I got the diapers and baby stuff and a quart of milk from a drug store and the oatmeal from the grocery store."

"How do you think they got the sketch?"

"From the two guys, I hired to kill the Russian?"

"One was killed in that farce; the other is now dead too.

He had a mishap in prison. Our brother there took care of that. Too bad he lived to describe you beforehand. What do you think I should do?"

Pinto was wise to this line of questioning that usually led to death. In this case, his death. On the offensive, Pinto upended the table, knocking Fahid to the ground. He then bolted for the stairs, but halfway up, Fahid aimed his silencer and fired. Pinto fell backward tumbling down the steps.

The noise from the gun woke up baby Dina. Fahid climbed over Pinto's body and when he reached the top of the stairs, Josef and Mo were there ready to come to his defense.

Mo asked, "You okay, sir?"

"I am fine. He was going to run to the authorities. I had to do the right thing and stop him."

Josef said, "Would never have thought he'd be a traitor. You just never know."

Fahid ordered, "Dig a hole in the yard and take his body and plant him. Meanwhile, I will appoint someone in our team to be the new caretaker for the baby."

Josef responded, "Sir, when the girl started crying, I went to her and picked her up. She has a fever. The wound must be infected."

"Pour more whiskey on it. I can't have her die without her mommy watching."

"Yes, sir. If it helps you, sir," Josef offered, "I will be her caretaker. I am good with little children. With the money from Denali, I wanted to build an orphanage."

Fahid nodded. "Then the duty is all yours. Go to the drug store and buy some baby aspirin. That will keep the fever down. But take care of this mess first. I demand loyalty!"

"Yes, sir."

CHAPTER 47

QUID PRO QUO

General Matthews had been reeling over the situation that Coby, Sergei, and baby Dina were experiencing. "Please get me in touch with Major Rodriguez," he asked his assistant. After a few minutes, his phone rang. "General Matthews here."

"Hello, General, it is Major Coby. It is so good to hear your voice."

"Likewise. How are you holding up?"

"Lately, not very good. They hurt my—"

"Yes, I heard. Barbaric. I was scheduled to retire at the end of the month. However, I have delayed it until little Dina is found and you and Sergei are safe and sound."

"General, you have always looked out for me, and I owe you so much. Why the delay? I don't see the connection."

"I am working on a hunch," Matthews said. "I've asked military intelligence to locate any and all relatives of those who were killed in the Denali bombing. Collectively, they are all working in unison to get their vengeance out on you and those you love. We did find that there is one individual who is not a part of the hit force against you. Ironically, it is the daughter of Fahid himself."

"Interesting."

"As we speak, she is being flown here to the US and has committed to working with us in finding and capturing Fahid. We plan to use the press to make sure Fahid hears the news that we have her in custody."

"So," Coby summed up, "the plan is a quid pro quo? Give us Dina and we will give you the daughter. What is her name?"

"Lidia. Now remember, she is working with us, so what you will see in the news will make it look like she is captured under duress. Once she arrives, the press and cable networks have said they will work with us. I still have a little pull with many of them."

"General, this is good. Who else knows about this plan?"

"Just you, military intelligence, and me. When she arrives, she will be thoroughly vetted and rehearsed. She hates her father and calls him Satan."

"I cannot disagree."

"She is single. No kids, for reasons she can tell you herself. I will be escorting Lidia to Philadelphia so you can meet her."

"Hmm, Lidia, nice name."

"You may inform your FBI agent but in confidence. We cannot take the chance of any of this leaking out."

"Yes, sir. I will wait to hear from you with further information."

"Heard about the subway incident. How many times now have you cheated death?"

"Too many times."

"Remarkable. Well, I'm glad you survived that harrowing experience."

"Thank you, General, for this. Let us hope your idea works."

Later, Coby gave thought to how to properly phrase the general's message. She took Chief Roberts to the side and explained what the general was planning to do.

"And he wants this to be hush-hush?"

"Correct, he is a smart man and I believe we need to give him a chance. He is owed much respect"

"That is not going to deter from the plan for a house-to-house search."

"When will that begin?"

"As soon as we can select the twenty agents, suit them with vests and parse out their respective zones. Maybe as soon as the day after tomorrow."

"Meanwhile my baby may be bleeding to death, and with no anti-bacterial care, may suffer from gangrene and later sepsis. She is so little it won't take much to hit her heart."

"Major, we are spending every moment working toward saving Dina."

"I know, Chief. Sorry if I sound despondent."

"It's understandable."

At Cooper Medical Center, Sergei had made a remarkable recovery. He was now standing and walking. Albeit in tiny steps, he was mobile.

The FBI technician there called his counterpoint at the hotel to inform him that they could go live on the video hook-up in fifteen minutes.

The fifteen minutes passed by like they were fifteen seconds. Everyone was in place for the transmission.

Curtains back, the receiver on...three, two, one...the snowy picture morphed into a rather clear picture of Sergei standing with the help of crutches.

Coby screamed, "Oh my God. You are standing!"

"I told you I am a strong Russian." He was able to laugh at his physical strength. "I'll be up and around soon. The doctors say I will need crutches and a wheelchair for a long time while rehabilitation takes its sweet time."

"I don't care. I'll carry you on my back if I have to."

"And the baby?"

"She can ride on your back while I am carrying you."

They both found this rare moment an opportunity to smile.

"Anything new?" Sergei asked.

"Yes, but I am not allowed to say a word."

"I get it. I saw the rosary you left for me. I don't know all the prayers, but I will use them and make up my own prayers so we can get our daughter back safe and sound."

"Sergei, I am contemplating sending a message to Fahid that he can swap Dina for me."

"Don't you dare. In Russia, many babies die, and the philosophy is so clear...have more."

"She's not going to die. I have lived my life, and you are a great daddy. That is where the future may lie."

"Then it will be me who is the bargaining chip in a swap. Me for Dina. Or do you think you still have life-saving souls ready to save the day again? We cannot count on the supernatural for help."

Chief Roberts was close enough to eavesdrop and had a visceral double-take reaction to the word "supernatural."

"I really don't want to talk about that here. I will come over to the hospital so we can talk alone."

"When can you come? Now?"

"Not sure. I'll get a message to you when I am clear to travel."

"I can't wait to see you. I can even hold you with my arms."

"That sounds wonderful."

"Dosvidaniya."

"Dosvidaniya, my sweetheart."

With that, the transmission ended.

Chief Roberts was curious. "Major Coby, can we talk in private?"

"Sure, let's go into my room."

They entered the room and sat down on the chairs facing each other in front of the curtain-pulled windows.

"Would you like some tea?"

"I'd rather have something a little harder." He laughed.

She laughed because she had never seen him touch anything with alcohol. "I'd like to go see him."

"Major, we are entering a critical phase of the search. Your presence here is vital in case we need your input."

Thinking a bit, Coby responded, "Then bring him here."

"Let me think on this one. I'll contact his doctors. My bet is they'll say no."

"Chief, we can give him every bit of comfort—"

"Major, there is too much going on here. If this goes another day, we'll look at it. However, I will contact his doctors."

"I guess that is about as good an answer I can get at this time."

"What was the reference to the supernatural?"

"It's a long story," she said, but managed to sum it up quickly. "These souls would act as game changers, either protecting my life or giving a window to open for a better life."

"That's the craziest story I ever heard. Hmm, wait a sec,

the subway incident. Is that one of the special soul-saving situations?"

"I'm not telling. Just let's leave it up to good living." She smiled.

He smiled. "Well, we may need the help from above, or within or from wherever to give us a leg up here."

At Fahid's place, the tension was running sky high. Fahid was getting frustrated over not fulfilling his mission. "I need to come up with a new plan. I was thinking I'd go to her. No one would suspect me capturing her in the hotel."

Mo contributed, "Sir, the officials are covering that hotel everywhere."

"If we can get to her in her room, we could get her out right under their nose."

Josef suggested, "Food deliverer?"

Mo shot down that idea. "No, they have that secured."

Josef added another concept. "Cleaning people?"

Fahid perked up at that thought. "That could be part of it. Those big laundry carts. Drug her, throw her in the cart, and take her down the utility elevator and into a van waiting outside."

Mo played Devil's Advocate. "Fahid, sir, I would believe they have the cleaning people under security too."

Fahid agreed, "Correct, but what about maintenance?"

Mo objected, "They fell for that trick back at the hospital. Don't think they'd fall for it again."

Fahid said, "Yes they would. They would never expect it. We need to find a place to get a maintenance uniform."

Josef suggested, "We are really close to La Salle

University. I could sneak in and steal a maintenance uniform real easy like."

Fahid said quickly, "Do it tonight."

"Yes, sir."

La Salle University was a liberal arts institute of learning located at Twentieth and Olney Avenues, just six blocks west of the Olney Avenue subway station. The ivy-walled university was over one hundred years old, and this Catholic University was taught by the Christian Brothers. To the south of the educational buildings was a field used for myriad sports, including football, soccer, and track and field.

Cutting through Wister Woods, the walk for Mo to the school was fifteen minutes long. When he arrived, there were a few athletes practicing track and field events. The lights on the field were on, and Mo noticed a man in a maintenance uniform walking across the field into a building labeled "Explorers' Athletic Building."

Mo carefully walked up to the door and opened it to look inside. He saw nothing, which allowed him to hide until the actual maintenance man left and shut down the building for the night.

Two hours later, the man was ready to leave. Mo observed the fact that the man had showered and changed clothing. The man opened the door, stepped outside, and yelled, "Lights out!" giving notice to those still in the field that if they want to continue, they'd have to do it in the dark.

He re-entered the building, walked over to a light switch labeled, "main field lights," and flipped it off. Then the man turned the inside lights off and left the building.

Mo heard the distinct noise of a key entering the lock that would seal the door for the evening.

He was now alone and ready to steal the uniform. He found a used uniform in a pile on the floor and unlocked the door from the inside and walked out with the uniform under his arm.

When he returned to the house, Fahid applauded and asked him to try on the uniform.

Mo changed, and Fahid exclaimed in a happy mode, "It fits perfectly. Now we need to look at the hotel and find the weak spot. They all have weak spots."

The next morning, Fahid and Mo traveled to the hotel, incognito. The streets were busy with cars and pedestrians going to and from work, stores, or just sightseers headed to the many museums along the Benjamin Franklin Parkway.

To the rear of the hotel was a loading dock. The cop positioned there stood out like a sore thumb.

Fahid and Mo did not want to stand in one place, as that would be too noticeable, so they walked past the dock three times when Mo noticed something. "Fahid, look at the door to the left of the dock. There is no way the cop there can get a clear view of it. The perfect entry point. Once inside, we can access the stairs and get to the room."

"Good. Now we need to locate a laundry bin and get a van."

"Josef can get the van. Once inside, the laundry area can be located."

"Josef is in charge of the baby. We'll have to get one of the other men to take over that duty."

Mo said, "Watch, I will get in and find the laundry room."

"If you get into trouble, just play ignorant."

Mo and Fahid walked together to the corner of the back of the hotel.

Mo then walked back close to the wall and entered the dock area, at first hiding behind a Sysco Food Service truck then walking up the steps to the dock as though he belonged there. He even waved hello to one of the workers unloading the truck. Using the workers as a shield, he opened the door and entered the building unnoticed. He could hear various sounds while inside, but one sound over the others caught his attention: the unmistakable sound of large clothes dryers whirling in a syncopated rhythm. Following the sound, he could see the laundry area. Slowly he approached the room and there they were: five laundry bins, two empty and three full of sheets, towels, and bed coverings.

A rather rotund woman exited the area and said to him, "You would think with all the steam and heat, I'd be able to lose some weight." She continued her walk, grabbed one of the bins on wheels, and moved to the utility elevator.

Mo backtracked his steps and worked his way back to Fahid, who was in a coffee shop catty-corner to the hotel, reading the Philadelphia Daily News.

"No problem getting in, Fahid."

"Good, but now look at this." He folded the paper to show Mo the front page. Above the picture of his daughter, Lidia was the headline: "Daughter of Kidnapper, Bait?"

"Mo, they are going to try to trade little Dina for my daughter. Very clever."

CHAPTER 48

CANVASSING THE NEIGHBORHOOD

It was dinner time in the hotel. Chief Roberts was checking to see if all the men were ready for the door-to-door search and that they were all wearing vests. "Looks like we are ready to rock and roll. The men are ready, and we have assault teams at four intersections in case we need to use them."

He turned to Coby and said, "We are ceasing the video transmission. You two will have to communicate by phone in the future. I am close to getting the okay for Sergei to come here."

"Chief, that would be wonderful."

"The canvassing should start in an hour. Let's hope for the best."

FBI agent William Conti had just celebrated his second year on the force. Many of the assignments for those considered new to the bureau were grunt jobs: the stakeouts, the person taking notes while someone with seniority did the investigative work, and now this canvassing assignment. One of the streets to cover was Williams Boulevard.

Each canvasser had a copy of the Pinto sketch and photos of many of the suspects who had close relatives killed in the Denali bombing. Door after door, there was no luck. Some of the people were not home. Those addresses would be noted and visited later that same day or the next.

His list showed that the next house was owned by Kenneth and Ida Jones. The first thing he noticed was the number of newspapers on the front porch. He picked them up and proceeded to knock on the front door. No answer. He then became aware of the stack of mail in the outdoor mail holder. He deduced that they just were not home. *Possibly on vacation*, he thought. As he did with the other houses that did not answer, he left a card in the crack between the door and the jamb. As he was walking away, a dog inside the house barked. He left thinking about how badly some people treated their pets. He wrote notes about the entire experience at Ida and Kenneth's house.

Next house: 3625 Williams Boulevard.

As Agent Conti moved from one house to another to compare the condition of the front yards, porches, and window dressings, he could tell who lived inside the house by observing the outside. This talent was honed when, as a teenager, he sold cable TV door to door. The first irregularity he noticed at this house was that the front yard was unkempt with long grass and weeds. It was the oldest-looking house on the block. The porch was in desperate need of repair and paint.

The gray wood under his feet on the porch did not feel secure. Certainly not on solid ground. The screen on the screen door was torn and the glass on the door needed a serious bath. He knocked. No one answered. He knocked again.

The four men inside were not going to violate Fahid's orders to "not open the door for anyone."

The agent took a few steps to his right to look into the window. He did a double take when he saw a shadow well into the body of the house. He tapped on the window with the ring on his left hand.

Inside, one of Fahid's men thought he had been seen when the man moved in front of the window. "I think he saw me."

The agent again moved in front of the screen door, opened it, and knocked much louder this time, then announced he was with the FBI.

Inside the house, the men were in a tizzy. "I think we better answer it."

"No, you are crazy and signing a death warrant for each of us."

Whispering, Sayid stated, "I do not agree. He will report suspicious activity and come back tonight with an army."

Sayid, the bravest of the lot, said, "I'll get rid of him." He opened the door. "Hello, can I help you?"

Flashing his credentials, Conti said, "Agent Conti, FBI. I'd like to ask you a series of questions. We are searching for a kidnapper who may be in this or the surrounding neighborhoods."

To paint a benign front, Sayid offered the agent to come into the house.

"That will not be necessary. I can ask you here." Agent Conti removed the notebook from his jacket and flipped to an empty page. He took a pen from his shirt pocket and clicked the top.

"What is your name?"

"Sayid Kim."

"Are you the owner of the house?"

"No, the owner stepped out."

"What is the owner's name?"

"We call him Philadelphia Sam."

"Does he have a last name?"

"Funny, I never heard his last name."

"When is the owner expected back?"

"He never said."

"Do you reside here?"

"Just temporarily."

The agent removed the sketch and photo out of his jacket pocket and showed them to Sayid. "Have you seen these people?"

"Let me take a closer look. Ah no."

"How well do you know your neighbors?" Pointing to the Jones house.

"I said I am staying here for a short period of time. I don't think I have ever seen anyone living there."

"It looks like they have not been home for some time. And they have a dog locked in the house. I will have Philly's Pet Services come by tomorrow to see if anything has changed."

"Anything else, Agent uh..."

"Conti."

"Yeah, Conti, sorry. I have a bad memory. Is there anything else I can do for you?"

"No thank you."

"I'll tell Philadelphia Sam you were here."

"Good. Also, tell him I will be back tomorrow. Here is my card if you see anything suspicious. And, oh, if your neighbors return, call me right away."

"Okay, have a good day."

Before the door was closed, one of the men in the kitchen dropped a cup on the floor.

The noise did not escape the agent. "Is there someone in the kitchen?"

"No, no, there is a cat in the house who has a mind of its own."

"Oh, yeah, pets can be frisky. Have a good afternoon."

"I will, sir. I hope you find your criminals."

Agent Conti left the house and moved to the next house on the street.

Under the label of good timing, Fahid and Mo entered the house less than an hour after the FBI was there. Sayid gave Fahid the complete report.

Fahid was furious. "I told you not to answer the door, but not only do you answer, but you also invite an FBI agent into the house. Are you fucking crazy? Now we need to act quickly. Tomorrow, we make the capture at the hotel."

In walked Josef with a bag of items bought on Germantown Avenue.

"Here is the baby aspirin and other things needed for the baby, and some snacks for us. There was something I saw when I was in the drugstore. On the counter next to the register, I saw a picture of Pinto. She saw me staring and asked if I knew him. Of course, I said, 'No.'"

Fahid believed the authorities were getting close.

Sayid added, "The agent also was asking about the couple next door. He mentioned that the Philadelphia pet services would be checking on their dog who is trapped in the house."

Fahid, thinking out loud, said, "Is the house clean?"

Josef exclaimed, "I did the best I could. But the blood on the bedroom rug I could not totally clean."

"Leave me alone. I need to think."

Fahid left the room and entered the baby's room. She was up and quiet, and her face was flush. "Josef, bring me the aspirin." When he got the bottle, he took two of the tiny pink pills and inserted them in Dina's mouth. He then got a glass and filled it with milk. He gently lifted the baby's head, and she sipped from the glass. "Thatta girl. You need to get well. Josef, change her and give her a cool bath. That's what I would do whenever Lidia had a fever. I know it is hard to believe, but I was a good father. I left my family to build a career in arms trading. They never understood. Now she is here, and they will use her to taunt me. Good tactic. Never saw this coming."

Josef took the baby out of the makeshift crib, undressed her, and took her to the bathroom to bathe her in cool water to combat the fever. When the water hit her toe stub, she winced and cried.

Fahid reentered the living room and asked everyone to leave except Mo. "Mo, try on the maintenance uniform, I'll wait." Fahid sat, then stood and sat again.

After ten minutes, Mo entered the room dressed as a La Salle University maintenance man. "Nice fit," remarked Fahid. He handed Mo a brown satchel that held a hypodermic needle with a sleeping formula ready for injection. "When you enter the room, she will not be alone. Kill the security and inject her anywhere on her body. Carry her to the utility elevator and put her into the laundry bin. When you get to the bottom floor, roll the bin out to the van which will be waiting for you. Do you understand?"

"Yes, sir."

"The van will take her here for a wonderful reunion with her sick child."

In the hotel, Agent Conti reported to Chief Roberts, who read out loud the results of the first day of canvassing. "Seventy percent of the homes were **occupied** and deemed clear. There were six vacancies with no one in the home. There were some just not home and have to be revisited. Over on Williams

306

Boulevard, there was a home whose residents were absent for days, but the dog was trapped in the house. A side note here asked that Philly Pet Services check on the dog. Tomorrow, we'll do the second pass, but so far, no luck. Okay, Agent Conti, good report. I will wait for your report tomorrow. Two more agents need to report but seems this wretch and his band of creeps were elusive."

Later, the hotel room was silent. Coby was in her room. Chief Roberts had gone home for the evening. The military security people were playing gin rummy on the dining room table which had been cleared of all the microwave electronics. The FBI technician was reading a novel.

A little after 9:00 p.m., the phone rang. The technician swapped his book for earphones. He turned on the recording and tracking devices and gave the nod to Coby, who had entered the room.

She picked up the receiver. Controlling her temper, she said, "Yes?"

"You don't sound so happy."

"Get to the point."

"You know the drill. Tomorrow, one p.m., another instruction will be delivered. Just instructions. No body parts."

"You are cruel. Life means nothing to you."

"Goodbye."

Fahid hung up.

CHAPTER 49

THE MAINTENANCE MAN

Everyone in the City of Brotherly Love was waking up to heavy rainfall. Coby peeked outside the window and could see a parade of umbrellas being carried by the multitudes.

Agent Poore arrived with another bag of clean clothing for Coby. "Here you are, darling, and don't worry about the cost, this is on Uncle Sam. Oh, and there are some fresh undies in there."

"I cannot get this out of my mind. Can we confirm how much time we have to reattach Dina's toe?"

Agent Poore volunteered to find out the answer.

This time Coby's phone rang. "Hello."

"Hi, sweetheart, I miss you so much that the thought of being with you again is giving me the strength to walk and feel better."

"That's wonderful. He called again."

"What did the bastard say this time?"

"That he is sending a messenger over to deliver new

instructions. I am sure he will want to meet me, and I must be alone."

"Coby, you need to have protection."

"Sergei, the last time I did not obey, it cost Dina her little toe."

"Coby, I cannot lose you. I feel like I am choosing between you and our girl. Understand, I will move mountains to save Dina, but you must live."

"Sergei, I have to do this. If I don't, Dina's death will destroy my life, well, our life forever. I must take every chance to save her."

"The doctor said one more day here and I can come to stay with you at the hotel."

"Oh, that is wonderful."

"The nurse here is giving me a hand sign. I need to go. Call me as soon as you get the new directions."

"Will do, baby. Love you big time."

"Love you."

The evil residents of the Williams Boulevard house were preparing for the next move to capture Coby. Josef reported there was a van he could steal that was parked in the church parking lot about a half mile away. Mo had put on the maintenance man's uniform and had tucked into his pants the satchel with the hypodermic needle. He also had a Beretta in his pocket. It was now 11:00 a.m. They would begin to move at noon.

The camouflaged courier had just put a note written by Fahid and little Dina's blue bow in a plain cardboard box. Everyone checked the time. This delivery had to be done without a hitch and with precision timing.

The FBI was used to the delivery routine. Everyone was in place.

Chief Roberts arrived on the scene and gave a pep talk to the agents assembled in the lobby.

Coby, Agent Poore, and the two military security people were alone in the room.

Josef and Mo walked to the church to get the van.

Fahid and the rest of the team waited for Coby to be delivered. All of this was to happen in the next two hours.

It was noon and Josef cracked the targeted van's window, reached in, and unlocked the door, then he used a screwdriver and some wire and was able to start the van. Mo got in and they were off to the hotel.

At 12:45 p.m., Agent Poore left the room to see the hand-off in the lobby. At the same time, the church van backed up to the dock. One of the dock workers shouted to Josef, "We'll be right with ya. Maybe fifteen, twenty minutes."

Josef said to himself, "That works perfectly."

Mo began his sly moves to the door, grateful he rehearsed this already. The first stop was the laundry room. He took one of the bins and moved toward the utility elevator. It seemed easy. He entered the utility elevator and exited on Coby's floor. He pushed the button that kept the elevator car from moving. This was where he was greeted by a cleaning lady. She did not recognize him and looked quizzically at the bin. "Who are you, and what are you doing with that laundry bin?"

Realizing that this was something they did not plan Mo became panicked and removed the Beretta from his pocket.

The cleaning lady reacted swiftly, running down the hall toward Coby's room screaming, "HELP!"

Mo chased her for a moment and fired his gun three times. They all hit the cleaning lady. However, the sound alerted the military men inside the room. A gun battle ensued in the hallway. After three more shots, Mo's gun was empty, and he made a break for the elevator and frantically pushed the button to release the car. As the door was slowly closing, the military man was there and fired his pistol, squarely hitting Mo in the head then the heart.

Coby exited the hotel room and was yanked by her arm back in by the other military man. "Major, please stay inside."

In the lobby, the delivery person was intentionally late with the hope to give Mo more time to kidnap Coby and take her down to the docks.

At 1:03 p.m. the messenger arrived. A different person this time, he was taller and walked with a limp. He handed the brown box to the agent with the white gloves and left.

Chief Brown was buzzed and with that, he placed his earpiece in and learned about the intrusion upstairs. "What!? Jesus Christ, these fucking people are relentless. Donnelly, alert the team that the hotel room was violated, and the perp is dead thanks to military security. Order the police to form a perimeter around a three-block area."

Josef was getting nervous in the van. "He should be back by now." In a matter of a few seconds, he heard the unmistakable sound of many police sirens. He took that as his cue to leave.

The worker on the dock yelled, "Jeez, I told you fifteen minutes. Some people are just impatient."

Josef ditched the van and ran to Broad Street to take the subway.

Back at Fahid's place, the television was on, and the regular programming was halted for a breaking news story by reporter Jackie Jackson. "This is Jackie Jackson at the Four Seasons Hotel on the Parkway. This afternoon, a would-be assassin was gunned down in a utility elevator. His target was international hero Major Coby Rodriguez. Chief of the FBI Roberts had this to say."

Roberts' face was now full screen on scene with the reporter, capturing Fahid's total attention.

"Today at one p.m., an assassin was bent on killing Major Coby Rodriguez who was in her hotel room with military and FBI protection. She and her husband, Sergei, have been the target of a group of mercenaries who have a vendetta against them for their part in spoiling the plot against the free world on Denali Island near Turkey in 1995. This same group is responsible for kidnapping the child of the heroic couple and the FBI is determined to save the young girl before they harm or kill her."

"Chief Roberts, do you have a good idea of where they are keeping the baby?"

"I'd like to keep what we know as confidential as possible," Roberts told the reporter.

"Thank you, and as always, stay tuned to this channel for continuous updates on this unfolding story. Now back to your regularly scheduled program."

Screaming at the TV set, Fahid said, "Shit, Mo is dead, and where the fuck is Josef?"

At the hotel, a team of investigators was searching for clues. One of the agents approached the worker at the dock and the policeman on duty.

When asked if he saw anything unusual, the policeman said, "I saw nothing out of the ordinary."

The dock worker had a different story. "About one p.m., a white van backed into the dock area. I alerted the driver that it would be awhile before we could tend to him. He nodded his head like he understood my words, but later, I guess right after the incident, he took off like a bat out of hell."

"Did you note the direction he took?"

"Yep, that way." The worker pointed west.

"Those video cameras work?"

"Yes, want me to pull the tape?"

"Can you take me to the surveillance room so I can see it now?"

"Sure, follow me."

They entered the building using the same door Mo used to enter the building then into a small room with a series of television monitors depicting all the entrances into the hotel.

"Here is the machine with the video you need." After the worker turned the dial to the proper time code to match the time when the van pulled up to the time the van left, the two could clearly see the white van with lettering on the passenger door.

"Stop it there," the agent said. "Can you enlarge the picture so I can read what is on the door?"

"All I can do is double the size." The worker pushed a button, and the enlarged picture revealed the lettering to be "Mount Vernon Baptist Church" plus a phone number.

The agent wrote down the information. "Please continue with the video." The video showed a man dressed in a maintenance uniform exiting the passenger side and crouching low along the van to the steps leading up to the dock. "Good, now can we see the other angle?" He saw the van but could not see the passenger until he reached the top of the steps and disappeared inside the same door the agent just used to get inside. "Reverse the tape and blow it up. I can get a look at the driver." After looking at the driver, he asked the worker to give him both tapes for further examination.

Inside the lobby, Agent Donnelly opened up the "clean" box to examine the contents. The note inside was accompanied by a flowered bow. The note read, "Please put this on my mommy's grave."

CHAPTER 50

LIDIA

That evening, Agent Poore and Major Rodriguez were sitting in the space at the dining room table now cleared of the TV and microwave equipment.

Agent Poore commented, "You look shaken."

"I am. To think that guy got this close is nerve-shattering. I was under the belief this place is secure."

"Nothing is one-hundred-percent secure. If the hate is deep enough, some people are zealots."

"So that means Fahid won't stop until his mission is successful, or he is killed."

"Yes. He and his team of fanatics need to be eliminated. Think about the balls of that guy who made it up to the front door. Something is motivating them to do things that normal people just would not do."

On the table were several plates protected with a stainless-steel cover.

"I'm not hungry. You can take these away."

"Major, you must eat. I may not know much, but you may

need energy, and food will help." One of the covers was removed. "Just eat the protein. This salmon doesn't look too bad."

Coby picked at the food, then excused herself, and went into her bedroom. Lying in bed awake, she begged God to let her sleep.

The next morning just seemed like a continuation of the previous hyper-motion day. After a shower, Coby got dressed, took a deep breath, opened the door, and when she entered the common area, to her absolute surprise there was Sergei. She rushed to him and threw her arms around him.

The accompanying nurse asked her not to hold him too tight. Coby backed off. Her eyes were tearing with joy.

Behind Sergei was Chief Roberts. "Major and Sergei, please sit. I have an update."

The two move toward the sofa. Sergei was helped to bend and sit.

"The man we killed in the utility elevator is Mohammed Allen and is one of the right-hand men for Fahid. The driver of the van is not positively identified, but we think his name is Josef Poland a relative of one of the people killed at Denali. He was driving a stolen church van from a church in our targeted zone. We believe they were desperate. To try a stupid assault yesterday was a sign of desperation. We are examining the avenues a desperate man might take next. He is losing his men and I don't see any new recruits coming to his aid. We are monitoring every relation to Denali. They all share in his vengeance except his daughter Lidia. By the way, Lidia will be here today."

With that statement, Coby said, "Let me get this straight. We are bringing his daughter here. Wasn't she also denied wealth because of our actions in Russia? Based on the line of thinking proposed here, how can anyone trust her?"

"General Matthews and our team of phycological experts do not believe she is a threat. Trust me, we will be watching her every move."

Sarcastically, Coby said, "Just like you were watching the hotel?"

Sergei added, "Relax, honey. Let's listen to the chief."

"The second wave of canvassers have already started their scrutiny of the neighborhoods. We will be calling on every house that did not have anyone home, and a few special homes where we did not talk to the person who resides in the home."

"We can only pray," said Agent Poore.

The anticipated knock on the door finally came. When the door opened, Coby laid eyes on the daughter of her nemesis' daughter, Lidia Fahid. Tall, with dark hair and eyes, she was a beautiful woman whose beauty seemed impossible as the daughter of a monster. Two agents escorted her in.

Chief Roberts welcomed her in. "Is the general with you?"

One agent responded, "He sends his regrets but was called back to the Pentagon."

Lidia entered and saw Coby. "You must be Major Rodriguez?"

"Yes."

With that, Lidia approached Coby and extended her hands.

Coby hesitated but held her hands in exchange for a peaceful posture.

"May I call you Coby?" Lidia asked in broken English.

"Yes."

"I cannot tell you how hurtful my heart is over what my father has become. In the beginning, he was a simple man driven by money. He took chances to go into a business that at first was not belligerent, then he met people who showed him how to make a fortune in trading arms."

"How was he as a father?"

"He loved me most. Many of my family were killed in war or after war." Stumbling for the right words she continued, "We were unlucky, born in an area that never knew what peace was like. My mother was killed in the most horrific way, which only made him more bitter and lose any compassion for life. He saw the Denali move as a way for him to gain wealth and power that he would only dream about. And you took that all away from him."

"How do you feel about what we did?"

"I'll answer that, but you asked how he was as a father. Under the duress of where we lived, he was about as good a father as anyone. He put his family above anything." Lidia paused and assembled her thoughts. "He would make little puppets and put on a show for me and my brothers." Tears were now rolling down her pure ecru and blemish-free cheeks. "About what you did, well you had no choice. You saved the world. How could anyone feel negativity toward you and Sergei's heroic actions? Think about how many people would be dead today if you did not risk your life. For that, the world owes you much."

Coby questioned her motive. "Why are you here?"

"Knowing him, he will call again. When he does, I would like to talk to him, in private if possible. I must take this opportunity to talk to him. Perhaps if he hears my voice, he'll give himself up."

Chief Roberts interjected, "Sorry, Lidia, that will not be possible. We are recording every phone discussion."

"I see."

The Chief added, "Maybe you can make a miracle happen here."

Lidia's security person saw Lidia becoming emotional and asked if she would like some tea.

"Tea sounds good." Lidia moved over to the table and her military protector brought her hot water, a cup, and a tea bag.

Coby leaned over to Sergei, grabbed his hand, and whispered in his ear, "Well, what do you think?"

"I'm no expert, but I want to believe her. Hopefully, she can talk her father into giving us our baby back."

Chief Roberts' phone rang. "Yes, I see, unbelievable." He hung up and addressed the room. "Seems we have a report from the Philadelphia Pet Services Department that the house where the dog was trapped is owned by the Jones family. They contacted the son and daughter-in-law in Allentown, and they were en route to the house. They report that a closer look inside the house shows a shard of porcelain on the floor. Then they walked around the backyard and noticed what they called, and I am using their words, newly dug graves."

Coby summed up her feeling in one word: "Jesus!"

"One of our agents has notified Agent Conti, the man surveying that street, about the discovery. The city was sending a coroner and a forensic team to the location. Conti will be there within minutes."

As if on cue, the hotel phone rang. The team knew the drill. Lidia was asked to stay where she was seated.

Coby answered the phone. "Yes?"

"You are a very lucky person, Coby. Once again you escaped death. You must be related to a cat," added Fahid.

"It is your luck that is running out. We are close to you. So close we can smell your rank odor."

Chief Roberts motioned for Coby to give the receiver to Lidia.

Lidia said, "Father?"

Hearing this, Fahid hung up.

"Guess he is not ready to face me."

"The technician says not on long enough," Roberts said.

Sergei commented, "I would have liked to have seen the expression on his face when he heard Lidia's voice."

"Me too," quipped Roberts.

Agent Conti reached the Jones house and was greeted with a sidewalk, front yard, and backyard array of yellow "Crime Scene" tape. He approached the police captain on the scene.

"Good day, Captain. I am FBI Agent Conti. I am the one who called in the animal cruelty inquiry."

"Good day, Agent Conti. My name is Captain Daniel Zinn. I was told you are canvassing the area looking for the missing, I mean, kidnapped little girl, correct?"

"Yes, sir. The FBI believes she is holed up in an area that consists of four hundred homes. A team of agents was going door to door to weed out any suspicious activity."

Pointing to the Jones house, Zinn said, "Do you believe this might be associated in any way with the kidnapping?"

"Not sure about that, but anything is possible. I talked to the neighbors, and they knew very little about the couple. I am headed to that house next." He pointed to Fahid's house.

They observed a man wearing a brown hoodie leaving the house. He began walking down the street away from the crime scene. Agent Conti shouted, "Sir, sir!" but the man did not respond. He kept on walking. The man was now too far away for Conti to catch up with him.

"Excuse me, Captain, I need to finish my survey."

"Good luck. I hope you nab those creeps."

"Hope all goes well here. Here is my card. Contact me if you see anything that might be a clue in my case."

"Roger that!"

Agent Conti moved to Fahid's place and knocked on the door, this time announcing in a very loud tone, "FBI!"

No answer.

He moved to the window and tapped with his ring on the glass, loud enough to get anyone's attention inside.

No response. He thought, *Should have chased the guy in the hoodie?* On his list, there were only three no-contacts. He eliminated the Joneses since they could be victims of foul play.

Conti called into Chief Roberts. "Chief, Agent Conti here."

"Yes, Conti, do you have a report?"

"Yes, sir. I had four homes unresponsive but took one off when it appears the residents could be victims of a double homicide. I am somewhat suspicious of their neighbors, which includes a temporary resident. When I asked about the now deceased neighbors, he said he knew nothing about them."

"Describe the temporary neighbor."

"Tall, seemed friendly, wearing a t-shirt. I did notice a strange odor coming from the house. Smelled like a dirty hospital room."

"Thank you, Agent, good work."

The man with the hoodie walked east toward Broad Street to a café across the street from the Olney Avenue subway station. He entered the phone booth outside the store and began to dial.

In the hotel room, the phone rang. Coby answered, "Yes?"

"Is Lidia still there?" Fahid asked.

"Yes."

"Put her on."

Coby handed the receiver to Lidia. "He wants to talk to you."

Lidia talked into the phone, "Father?"

"Lidia, I figure what I am doing will probably lead to my death. Before that happens, I just wanted you to know I started on this path for you. I wanted to see you so wealthy that you and your children would not ever need anything. Do you have children?"

"No, Father."

"Why?"

"I carry your seed. It is an evil seed that needs to be stopped and ended for all time. Your son feels the same. And now what you have done to shame our name, even more, is unthinkable. Your sick ways have harmed a baby. A BABY, FATHER!" Lidia began to cry, sobbing with every word.

The FBI technician was getting a good track of where the call was originating and motioned to keep it going.

"Do you even know what you are doing? You are run by hate, an emotion I never saw as a child. You make me sick to my stomach."

"I wish I could say I am sorry," Fahid said, "but you are right. Hatred and vindictiveness have brought out a devil that I cannot change. I will not be satisfied until the three of them are tortured and beg for mercy during the entire time. They took away all I wanted for you and your brother. There is nothing left for me to live for..."

The FBI technician handed Chief Roberts a piece of paper. Written on it were the words, "Pay telephone southwest corner Broad and Olney."

Chief Roberts stepped out of the room and called on his phone to headquarters. "Alert the Philadelphia Police to send all available cars in the vicinity of Broad and Olney. Fahid was currently there on the phone." He then continued, "Alert our units to speed to that location and report to me when you get there."

The Chief re-entered the room.

Fahid was still on the phone with Lidia. "Lidia, I wish you were not here. These people are using you to get to me."

"Father, I have allowed them to use me. You must be stopped once and for all time, even if that means your death."

Fahid hung up, aware of the time he spent on the phone, and instead of going back to the house, he entered the subway station. Seconds later the area was swarming with law officials, and Fahid was headed south on a subway car.

CHAPTER 51

THE END GAME

Lidia was visibly shaking, and it was Coby who now tried to settle her down. "That was a tough and brave thing to do. Hopefully, he will see the light and give us back our baby."

"Very little hope for that. You see he is reckoning with his failures and understands the hatred for you and your family inside him. For that, I am sorry for him. He is ready to die. He said after this there was nothing to live for."

Roberts' phone rang, and he picked up.

"Chief, this is Agent Brown reporting that the targeted phone booth is empty. We have sent a squad of agents to patrol up and down every street to spot him. Witnesses say he is wearing a brown hoodie and may have gone into the subway system. Obviously, that will make the search much more difficult."

"I see. Order all to continue the patrol. We might just get lucky."

On the police and FBI radios, the announcement was made. "Suspect in the baby Dina kidnapping was last seen at a phone booth at Broad and Olney. He left on foot and may have entered the subway system. He was reported to be wearing a brown hoodie. Please proceed with caution. He is considered armed and extremely dangerous."

After the canvassing, Agent Conti received a call from Police Captain Zinn, who said, "Agent Conti, you would be interested in knowing that we have unearthed two bodies. Elderly people, presumably Mr. and Mrs. Jones. We are completing our forensic sweep and will take the bodies to the coroner's lab for an autopsy and exact identity. I can say that the woman was strangled, garrote style, and the man was shot several times. The dog was in surprisingly good shape considering all that went on. The next of kin should be arriving from Allentown within the hour."

"Thanks, Captain. Please continue to keep me informed. Is the neighborhood prone to murders like this?"

"Nope. That is what makes this intriguing. This area is a very quiet neighborhood."

"I see. Thanks."

The Four Seasons room was somber. Everyone in the room was contemplating the conversation Lidia had had with Fahid. The military man entered the room with a tray of sweets, a coffee urn, and a stainless-steel pitcher of hot water. "Help yourselves."

No one moved.

"Okay, then. If anyone wants anything, just let me know."

Sergei spoke up. "I would like a cup of Earl Grey if you have it. Then I need to lie down. The medication tires me."

The tea was served, and Sergei drank it black. Then retired to the bedroom.

Coby commented that she would be in there soon.

The nurse added, "Before you doze off, you need to take these antibiotics."

Agent Conti drove downtown to the FBI building housed in the Federal Government Center in the most historic section of town. He parked his car in the above-ground lot, meandered to the elevators, then traveled to his office floor. He stopped in the men's room to freshen up after a long day of canvassing. The workday was almost over for him. He just had to fix a cup of coffee and write up his report.

From the breakroom to his desk, he passed a bulletin board with a sketch of a man wearing a hoodie. Under the sketch were the words, "wanted for kidnapping."

He thought back to just a couple of hours before and in his mind's eye saw the man with a brown hoodie walking away from the house that supposedly belonged to a man called Philadelphia Sam. He walked fast to his desk spilling coffee along the way.

He called Chief Roberts whose phone went straight to voicemail. He then texted, "Agent Conti has a good lead on the kidnapper. 3625 Williams Boulevard. Code red!"

Seeing this message, Roberts hung up and called Conti.

Conti answered, shaking from an adrenaline flow. "Chief Roberts, we have them. When I was canvassing today and came across the crime tape on the Jones house, I saw a man with a hoodie—I believe it was brown—leaving the neighbor's house. I called him, but he just kept on walking. Then I saw the sketch and realized he was seen at a phone booth shortly after I saw him leave the house."

"Thanks, Agent, you epitomize what a good agent is all about. Diligence and intelligence are the hallmarks of a great detective and a solid investigation."

Roberts immediately put out a directive to surveil the suspicious house on Williams. The FBI headquarters had a series of vans with various company names on the outside. The one used most often was the phone company. A surveillance team was now in overalls similar to what a phone pole worker would wear. They picked up the faux phone company van and drove it to the site. They parked on the street two houses to the south.

Fahid, on the run, exited the subway at Temple University, removed his hoodie and threw it in the trash, then hailed a taxi that took him to the Williams Boulevard address.

Once inside, Fahid was excitable. "The FBI will be here soon. Get packing our tools and ammunition and be ready to leave this place behind."

Josef asked, "Fahid, what about the girl?"

"We'll take her. Has her fever broken?"

Josef claimed he had been giving her baby aspirin regularly. "But her foot looks bad, really bad."

"What do you mean?"

"Swollen and red. The toe part is turning black."

"We don't have a way to leave," said Sayid.

Looking out the window, Josef turned to the men and let them know there was a suspicious telephone van two houses down the street.

Fahid said, "We have been made. Okay, now we need to change course. Assemble all our weapons and ammo. You must know we could all be killed today."

All of them bravely responded, "Yes."

The two stakeout agents reported activity at the house. "A man just entered the house, no description." They also reported the police were working on the murder scene.

The report was given to the people at the hotel. Agent Poore took Coby, Sergei, and Lidia in her car to the site. Roberts, Donnelly, and the technician left in their car headed for the Chestnut Hill-Germantown area and the suspected hideout of Fahid.

One of the stakeout men noticed a second-floor window

open and a person was staring right at them. "They know who we are. Better let HQ know and see what they want us to do."

Out of the window, a sniper rifle was aimed and fired. The bullet shattered the van window but missed the driver and passenger by inches.

The police and forensic people working on the Jones murders scattered and took cover. They were looking up but did not know which direction the shot came from.

"Better send in the SWAT team. Active shooter. Repeat, active shooter." That was the directive given to Roberts who was in the car racing to the scene.

Within minutes a host of armored police vehicles, police cars, two ambulances, and the news media arrived on the scene. The FBI directed the news media to stand their ground because there was an active shooter in the building.

All the television stations went live. The local CBS affiliate news reporter, Jackie Jackson, stood at a distance wearing a flak jacket and helmet. She was caught off guard when the signal was first beamed across the entire Delaware Valley. "Are we ready?" she asked the cameraman.

"We are live," he responded.

"This is breaking news... If you can get a shot of that house next to where there is yellow crime tape..." She stepped out of the frame. "This is the house on Williams Boulevard in Chestnut Hill where the FBI and Philadelphia Police believe little Dina Rodriguez-Billicoff is being held. The details are sketchy at best. The law officials have kept most of this case secret presumably to not tip off the kidnappers. Our news source also tells us that the house next door, the one with the yellow tape, was the scene of a double homicide. We will try to get more information on whether the homicides and the kidnapping are connected. Once we get more information, your CBS local news will cut in and inform you of the latest."

She touched her ear, listening to studio producers speaking in her earpiece. "The police are asking people in the neighborhood not to come out since there is an active shooter in the house. This is Jackie Jackson live on the scene in Chestnut Hill. Now back to the show already in progress. We will interrupt with any breaking news."

Chief Roberts arrived at a scene right out of a movie. Dozens of police cars parked in a circle: a large SWAT vehicle, firetrucks, various city cars, and two large command RVs, one for the City of Philadelphia and one for the FBI.

Everyone was keeping a low profile due to the sniper in the second-floor window. From that vantage point, the targets were easier to aim at and shoot.

Roberts entered the FBI command RV and addressed the tactical team. "Hello, everyone, I am Chief Roberts, and I will be the one in charge here. I know the city has its teams here too, but remember, this is a federal case and, therefore, the FBI is in charge. Let me tell you what we will not do. We will not indiscriminately answer any shots fired from the building. We will not introduce tear gas, and finally, we will not enter the property. There is a young girl inside the building. Violating any of the rules I just laid out will put that girl in jeopardy. Are there any questions?"

No response.

"Also, understand that nothing, I repeat nothing is done unilaterally. Every action we take will come from my orders and no one else. So please stand pat. Thank you." He then donned a bulletproof vest, grabbed a bullhorn, and exited the RV. Roberts approached the police commander. "Good day, Commander. I am FBI Chief Roberts."

"Good day, Chief Roberts. I am Commander Johnson, here to support the efforts of the FBI."

"I just want to make sure you understand the nature of the

situation we find ourselves in. Since this is a federal crime, the FBI took the priority role here with your officers as backup. Nothing will be done unless I say it is done. Okay?"

"Yes, sir."

"Here is what we know." Roberts proceeded to fill Johnson in on the details and history of Fahid and Coby

"I see. Do you know if the child is alive?"

"We really don't know. Fahid did amputate her little toe and sent it to Coby after the subway incident, as I am sure you are aware."

"Yes, she was fortunate to escape. How many are in there?"

"We estimate three or four. Fahid, the driver of the church van, the man who answered the door, and possibly a guy named Philadelphia Sam."

"I know a Philadelphia Sam. He's a wannabe conman with a long list of misdemeanors and one or more felonies based on forgeries. I think they made that name up. Not saying there is not another person in there, but I am willing to bet it isn't the Philadelphia Sam I know."

"Then how would they come up with the name?"

"Lucky guess. However, his name was in the papers recently. The obits I believe."

"Regardless, we must proceed as though the child is alive."

"I understand. Where do we go from here?"

"I am waiting for an FBI negotiator and psychologist from New York. They should be here in thirty minutes or so."

"Fine, Chief. If there is anything we can do to assist, we have your back."

"I was counting on that."

A few seconds after that exchange, another rifle shot emanated from the open window. Shouts of "COVER!" could be heard a dozen or more times.

In the car with Coby, Sergei, Lidia, and Agent Poore the tension was very high. Sergei broke the silence with, "I cannot believe we are this close to Dina and cannot do anything about it but hope."

"You mean pray," Coby corrected. "I know our little girl is alive. I can sense it."

Lidia added, "I feel terrible. I'm nauseous over what my father has done. I am glad I spoke to him. I know it will be the last time."

Agent Poore said, "They will try to capture him and bring him to court to collect what justice is coming to him."

"I hope they kill him honestly. He was in pain," said Lidia.

Coby started to exit the car.

Agent Poore grabbed her arm and said, "Where do you think you are going?"

"I need to be there."

"They will target you," Agent Poore said, "and then little Dina won't have a mother to help her and guide her through the years."

Reluctantly, Coby stayed put.

Chief Roberts took the bullhorn, checked the battery level, and pushed the button to amplify his voice. "Fahid, it is time for you and your people to come out with your hands up. This will ensure that no harm will come to you and your people." He waited a few minutes and began to talk again into the bullhorn. "Fahid, if you are not willing to come out, let us come in and take the little girl. It is right thing to do."

With that statement came another shot from the rifle. The bullet was directed toward chief Roberts and ricocheted off the hood of the FBI's car.

"This is no game, Fahid. Let us know the girl is alive."

A voice from inside the house responded, "Why? So, you

will know whether to storm the house and kill us all? You fucking think I'm stupid?"

"Not stupid, Fahid. You are enraged with hatred and you will die with that hatred eating your soul."

When the chief received no response, he sent an order to one of the two helicopters overhead. "Drop a percussion bomb set to explode over the house."

He turned to Agent Donnelly and explained, "The percussion bomb is so loud it can wake the dead, but in this case cause a baby to be scared into crying. Aim the audio receivers at the house to see if we can pick up any sounds of a baby. But, by all means, tell the technician in the RV to take his earphones off until after the explosion."

In Roberts' earpiece, a chopper pilot said, "Sir, we are ready with the bomb."

Just as he was ready to give the order to release the explosive device, he saw one of the TV news helicopters cross in front of the FBI chopper. He used the bullhorn, but this time directed it toward the television people. "Tell your stations to keep a safe distance of one mile from this active situation!"

His request worked. He saw the intruding copter take flight away from the area, then he called up to the agent in the FBI bird. "Drop it."

"Roger that."

Everyone could see something tossed out of the helicopter on its way to the roof of the house. Seconds later, the house, the cars, the RV, and the people could *feel* the explosion. The FBI audio person then put his earphones on, and he dialed and aimed the parabolic dish toward the house. He was giving an account of what noises he could pick out coming from the house. "I hear screams of men yelling profanities, objects breaking from the vibrations, and, wait, yes, the undeniable sound of a baby crying." He turned to Chief Roberts. "Your idea worked. The baby is crying."

"Thank God. Let me see if I can talk sense into Fahid." Engaging the megaphone again, his resounding voice was so loud, it created an echo. "Fahid, it is that time that you understand, you will not survive."

Fahid retorted, "you must realize that I will not come out. I have a precious little tot here, and if you try anything, you are signing a death certificate for her!"

Commander Johnson crawled over to Chief Roberts and explained that he could send in his best man to surveil the inside of the house. That way they could send in the correct number of men and give each of them a target as their assignment. Roberts thought about the idea. Being a Libra, he always tried to weigh everything and every decision he needed to make. *If something goes wrong, what is the consequence? What if one of the men is close enough to the baby, and they will use the girl as a shield?* The number of ways this could go wrong was weighing on his decision.

"Commander Johnson, I think your plan is doable, but we need to use ultimate caution."

"Of course, Chief."

"I'll let you know. I want to use an infrared heat wave scanner to spot where the humans may be first. To do your plan correctly, we need to know exactly how many are in there and approximately where they are located."

The Chief used a low-profile sprint to the FBI RV. Inside, he asked the technician to scan the house with heat sensors. "I need to know how many adults are in the place. Start with the sniper."

The agent moved to a set of controls on a panel and threw a switch and aimed the dish toward the house. The screen was similar to a green radar screen. Aiming at the sniper, a white figure of a man could be seen clearly on the screen. He marked down on a pad and said, "One upstairs front room."

Then he aimed the device at the front part of the house's lower level. He then wrote down, "Two in the downstairs." He then asked the RV driver to move farther south so he could get a look at the house from a side view. The driver carefully maneuvered the RV to the left of the house. This time he wrote down, "Two in the kitchen area." Then he threw a lever that gave him ultimate x-ray penetration. He wrote, "Two in the room next to the kitchen, one figure is small." He said to himself, "Must be the child."

"Chief, the heat probe sees six adults and one child."

"Where is the child?"

"In the room far side to the left of the kitchen."

Just then the fire chief, Commander DeFranco, entered the RV with a paper rolled up under his arm. "Chief Roberts I presume?"

"Yes."

"I am second battalion Commander DeFranco and I have the blueprint of the house."

"Thank you, Commander, this will come in handy."

Chief Roberts opened the door and got the attention of Police Commander Johnson, and waved him over to the FBI RV.

"Commander Johnson, I do not think it is necessary to send a man in for a body count. The heat sensors show six adults."

"I see. I can have six men rush the house and go to the locations you mark and kill them within seconds of each other."

"Let me give one more try to talk Fahid out."

Coby took a moment when Agent Poore was not looking.

She grabbed the car handle, stepped outside, and moved in the direction of the FBI RV.

Lidia followed her.

To stay out of the shooter's line of sight, they crouched while walking over to the Command Center.

Chief Roberts saw them and became angry. He ordered them, "Get back in the car! NOW!"

Coby defied the order and approached Roberts. "I have an idea. See if Lidia can make a difference."

"Major, this is too far gone," Roberts said. "The longer we wait the more dangerous it is for your daughter. He might succumb under the pressure and lose it."

"I think it is worth a try."

Roberts thought for a minute and handed the bullhorn to Lidia. "This is how you use it. Push this red button when you are ready to talk, then let go when done. Speak clearly. If too loud, it can become distorted."

"Okay." Lidia took the bullhorn and called out, "Father." The moment was still. "Father." She became louder and said, "FATHER!"

To everybody's surprise, Fahid opened the door and stepped out on the porch. Upon seeing Fahid, many of the law authorities aimed their weapons at him. Chief Roberts instructed all not to shoot. "hold your weapons!"

Fahid spoke. "Step out in front. Let me see you."

Lidia put down the megaphone and moved out from around the car that was giving her shelter from the sniper.

He did not speak at first but stared at his daughter. "You have grown up to be a very beautiful woman, just like your mother."

Lidia could not control the tears generated by this poignant moment in her life. She feebly said, "Thank you."

"Don't be afraid. Come here and let me see you close."

Lidia took a series of steps to where she was ten feet from her father.

Coby turned to Sergei who managed to hobble over on crutches while keeping a low profile. "This is what he did at Major Burka's house. He knows no one will harm him as long as our baby is inside."

Fahid stepped to get very close to Lidia. He wrapped his arms gently around his daughter.

In a low tone so that only Fahid could hear, Lidia said, "Father, would you want these people or any people to harm me?"

"Have they?"

"No. So please do not harm their daughter."

"Lidia, I have nothing to live for." He kissed her forehead and turned to re-enter the house. Before he closed the door, he directed his words to Lidia, "I am sorry, but I must show the people who have entrusted me to take revenge that I am a man of my word or die trying."

With that statement of finality, Lidia fainted.

Police and agents rushed to her side and took her to shelter where medics revived her.

Standing next to Chief Roberts, a man identified himself as Dr. Perry Friedberg, FBI staff psychologist. "Dr. Friedberg, it is a pleasure, but as you can see, things here are chaotic."

"Yes, Chief, that is apparent. However, what is not apparent is the mental condition of Fahid."

"Go on."

"If he feels his back is against the wall, he will have no other recourse but to kill the baby."

"Go on."

"The longer this stand-off goes on, the greater the chance that the baby dies. You need to find a way to end this impasse now."

"Thank you, Doctor."

Convinced he was doing the right thing, Chief Roberts approached Commander Johnson and said, "Send your men in."

The five men and one woman exited the Philadelphia Command RV in full battle gear. They were hidden from the view of the sniper in the window.

The commander explained the plan to them. "You six will take your places this way." He showed them the interior blueprint of the house. "You and you enter from the rear porch and when you reach here, turn right, and take out the two in the kitchen. You go into the front room and blast the two immediately." Now he pointed to the woman swat member. "You climb the steps and take out the sniper. Use your silencers so as not to arouse any reactions. You have the job of going to the room with the baby. Obviously, be careful and remember, these maniacs will murder her if they panic. Do you all understand your assignment?"

All answered, "Yes."

"Okay, proceed with caution. I suggest going over to the Jones house and entering their backyard by climbing over the fence. All six will enter the house here." Commander Johnson pointed to the back door. He took out his communication device and informed Roberts that the plan was in action.

Chief Roberts said a silent prayer.

The six were extremely trained officers with a history of experience. They managed to crawl next to the police cars and firetruck unseen by the upstairs sniper. They were greeted by an officer who led them around the left side of the Jones house and into the yard.

The sun was going down, and the RVs turned on their spotlights filling up the front of the house with enough light to ensure a daytime appearance.

The television crews were using their ultra-zoom lenses to capture every moment at the Williams Boulevard house.

The helicopters were ordered to fly low to create noise to help create a cover for the six brave officers.

One by one they climbed over the fence and into the backyard of their targets. With stealth, they reached the top step, and the lead officer stepped on a hidden trigger device, which caused a blast throwing three officers back into the yard. One was out of commission. Two got up and joined the other three and made their way to the door. Knowing they were now detected, they altered the plan and rushed into the house.

A firefight ensued.

One of Fahid's men was killed when he stupidly tried to cross the room for protection.

Outside, Coby and Sergei were panicked. Sergei yelled, "Stop! Stop! Call them back, now!" But he was not in control and the gunfight continued.

The police and the bad men were moving in patterns to outfox their adversaries. The female officer saw the stairs and knew her job was to take out the sniper. She climbed the stairs and was greeted by the rifleman who fired three rounds. Two hit her vest, but one pierced her forehead. She dropped dead on the spot and fell back down the steps.

The Police Commander heard the voice of the lead officer inside the house. "We have two officers down and one of them is dead. They also seem to have an unending supply of ammo, and we are running short."

"Then, abort, abort!"

The officer led the others out the back door in a hail of bullets. One of the shots grazed the helmet of the last one out.

The team of three took the officer lying in the weeds from the porch blast and carried him to the fence. They handed him over to a team of police personnel waiting to bring him to medics.

"Chief Roberts, we had to abort the action. One of our people was killed inside, and one is unconscious from the IED. The current report from the team leader is two maybe three of the hostiles were killed, but we do not know if Fahid was one of them. We are also sure that the baby was unharmed. They could hear her crying during the entire fight, even when they were leaving."

"The FBI shrink warns us that Fahid when he feels defeated will kill the baby. It may not fully satisfy his thirst for total revenge, but, in his mind, it will cause a level of pain that gives him some solace. That his actions were not a total failure."

"Do you have another plan?"

"Unfortunately, no."

The sniper took his rifle and fired it at various targets in the street below. Roberts ordered his best sniper to fire back. One shot and the enemy sniper was down.

Roberts thought to himself that they were down to two. Charging the place would solve the problem unless Fahid was still alive. He would take the baby out before he'd fight them.

Coby, Sergei, Lidia, and Agent Poore were inside the FBI RV.

"Sergei, you know I love you—"

"He's coming out again," the agent manning the video feed interrupted.

Fahid stepped out the front door again.

Coby opened the door and ran to the crowd standing behind the shielding police cars.

"Get down, Coby," yelled Sergei.

"Fahid is by himself. Let me take him out," the sharpshooter exclaimed.

"No, he's about to say something."

All eyes were on Fahid. The television cameras were focused on the story of the century.

Fahid said, "People, we are at an end. All but one of my men have been killed by your police. That man is currently standing over the child. He has the point of a knife touching her sweet little throat."

The psychologist looked over to Chief Roberts and nodded like this was the moment when he could begin the "scorched earth" climax of a long and harrowing nightmare.

Fahid continued, "Is Major Rodriguez here?"

Coby broke away and confronted him just thirty feet away.

Sergei was being held back by two police officers.

"Ah, my nemesis, my nightmare. I will make a deal with you."

Coby was staring at him with steel-cold eyes.

"Cat got your tongue?"

"Speak, Fahid."

"Oh, that voice, it brings back such bad memories. The deal is simple. A trade. Your life for your daughter's life."

Coby showed a moment of confidence and began to walk toward the steps where Fahid was standing. He smiled at her. She stopped, now ten feet away. "Before I accept my death sentence, bring her out. I don't go in with you unless you show the baby."

"Dearie, I am not stupid. The split second I give this baby away, your friends here will open fire and I will go down a failure. No, no, I will give up the baby once you are inside, and not until we have had that long-awaited, shall I say, date of destiny."

Coby turned and looked directly at Sergei. Her eyes were telling him she was ready to perform the greatest sacrifice. The eyes sent a message of love and the hope that Dina would grow up to be a wonderful daughter who would never forget her mommy. Coby turned and headed toward Fahid.

He waited until she passed him and the two of them were in the house.

The people watching this drama play out were in a frenzy. Half the people were crying. Some were wailing from spiritual pain.

Chief Roberts told the police commander to ready his SWAT team. "If the baby is not out in a minute, we need to charge the house."

Coby and Fahid were in the kitchen looking at each other. Fahid turned to his last comrade and said, "Get the child."

Coby's heart was racing. Her mind was spinning over what her last words would be to her daughter. Then it happened. She saw Dina in the arms of Fahid's last soldier.

"Take the child to her."

Coby extended her arms, and her daughter was placed in her care. Her hand touched baby Dina's face. "My baby. Someday you will be told a story that will sound so unreal that it will take time to fully sit in your mind. I hope that if you remember anything of this final moment you will know I love you. I love you so much." The tears were flowing down both cheeks.

"How touching. You see, Coby, my dreams were killed when you destroyed them." He removed his revolver and aimed it at the baby. "Now you will witness the death of your child, but your pain will not last long, because I will kill you too."

With those words, he cocked the gun.

Coby's motherly instinct was to protect the baby with her body. Covering Dina's face and head, Coby looked at Fahid and shouted with every morsel of strength and animus, "Leave my baby alone!"

With that, all the souls inside her exited the body and formed a head-to-toe shield over both mother and child.

Fahid's gun was fired once.

The gunshot was heard outside, and the FBI and the police reacted swiftly.

Fahid and his comrade could not believe their eyes. The bullet was repelled by the protective shield. Fahid fired again, and again the same protection.

Coby was still standing, hugging her daughter.

The lawmen entered the house and drew their weapons on Fahid and his man.

Chief Roberts entered the scene and saw Coby and Dina unharmed, embracing each other.

CHAPTER 52

THIS LITTLE PIGGY

The ambulance raced from Williams Boulevard to Hahnemann Hospital. Inside, Coby held baby Dina, and Sergei rubbed Coby's back with gentle strokes. Coby unwrapped the crude bandage around Dina's little toe and was horrified and began to cry over what she saw. The foot was red where the toe was separated from the foot, and a black clot of dried blood and discoloration from infection was apparent.

It seemed like they arrived at the emergency room at lightning speed. The group was greeted by a series of nurses, doctors, orderlies, policemen, and FBI agents. The baby was taken from Coby, and they all proceeded to Emergency Room One.

The doctor examined the wound. He then injected medicine into the affected foot. "We just administered an antibiotic."

Coby felt relaxed when she was told Dina did not even wince from the needle. From that point on, Dina was injected two more times, and the wound was thoroughly cleaned. The doctor looked at the wound and turned to the parents. "There is a very good chance that the toe we have protectively packed in our lab can be sewn back on. The only thing I am concerned about is the infection. It is a race between the complete elimination of the infection and how long her toe can last in the preservative protocol."

Coby and Sergei left the emergency room, and baby Dina was moved to her room where she would be readied for the operation to reattach her little toe. Before leaving Dina with the hospital staff, Sergei pulled a policeman aside and said, "You'll watch her, huh? Please don't leave until we return."

"Sir, my partner and I are here for the next five hours, then a new shift comes in. We will never leave her side, I promise."

Satisfied, Sergei and Coby walked over to the cafeteria.

Back at Williams Boulevard, Chief Roberts was in the FBI RV giving a postmortem over what just transpired. "Thank you for your diligence today. I am going over to Commander Johnson to console him and his team over the death of the brave woman who knew what she was up against and was just doing her job. God rest her soul."

A YEAR LATER

Inside their home in Malvern, Pennsylvania, Coby, Sergei, and four-year-old Dina were together in the living room watching an animated film on the television. The doorbell rang, and Sergei, with a lingering limp, got up and answered the door to see FBI Chief Roberts.

"Chief Roberts! Come on in. Coby, it is Chief Roberts."

Coby entered the room and saw her savior. She hugged him and planted a kiss on his cheek. "Oh, it is so nice to see you again. Only this time in much calmer times. Would you like some coffee? I even know how you like it." She laughed out loud.

"Nice hearing the laugh. Really, I did not hear anything like that a year ago. Yes, I would love a cup of coffee."

"Come sit down here." She led him into the kitchen and offered a chair at the breakfast table. "Sergei, join us and bring the baby. She needs to meet her liberator." Turning to the chief, she said, "He won't leave her alone for a second."

"I can understand that."

Sergei placed little Dina in her special chair. Roberts stood and kissed Dina on her forehead. The child looked up at him and giggled.

Coby put the coffeemaker on, and the slow dripping of the java entering the carafe stopped, and they heard a subtle "ding." "Sergei, you'd like a cup too?"

"Yes, sweetheart."

"She's adorable," Chief Roberts said to Dina's parents with his eyes now fixed on the little girl. "You are adorable."

They all sat around the table.

Chief Roberts asked, "How did they do with the toe?"

Coby stood, went to where Dina sat, and removed Dina's shoe and sock. "Look, Chief, you can hardly notice."

The Chief held the foot in his hand and examined the little toe. "Remarkable. Amazing what modern medicine can do. I can see a small scar, but that is expected I presume."

"Yes, she has the scar, but other than that she has complete mobility and in time she will be walking like a normal little girl. We even have her enrolled in preschool."

"That is fantastic. You might know that Lidia has filed for US citizenship. You might also want to know that your old buddy Merlino has hired her as an assistant in his office and is spearheading her citizenship."

"That is wonderful."

Chief Roberts added, "He is ready to retire, but he likes being the oldest member of the House of Representatives. He told me to tell you that you should run for his office. I have asked him to train Lidia well while he is still in office. She will have a position in the FBI someday. We could use a worldly person who is strong enough to confront evil and live to talk about it. By the way, she has met a man. It sounds like it is serious."

"That is super about Lidia, and I am flattered about the political future, but I am still active in the Army."

"Do you have another cup handy?"

"Sure, why?"

"I have a surprise for you."

He got up and walked to the door, opened it, and let in three people, one carrying a professional television camera, one carrying a small wooden case, and the last one an old friend, General Matthews.

Coby, surprised, rushed over to salute then hugged and kissed the general. "This is like a reunion made in Heaven."

The general asked Coby to stand while he opened the wooden box and proceeded to pin a gold bar on her shirt's lapel. "Major Coby Rodriguez, I am honored to announce that as of today, you will be addressed as Colonel Rodriguez."

The photographer snapped a dozen pictures, and they all applauded Coby for being a brave heroine and being the first Hispanic-Lebanese colonel in the US Army.

"I am speechless. Not sure how you pulled all this off, but I am eternally thankful."

General Matthews left with the entourage. The chief, Sergei, and Coby sat for their coffee and reminisced. Chief Roberts said, "Major, eh, I mean Colonel, I need to ask you a question."

"Okay, shoot."

"When the forensic team swept through the Williams Boulevard house after most of the crowd was disbursed, the head of the team showed me three slugs that were discharged. To me, it looked like they hit something so strong that the slugs were compressed to the point that they look like a flat dime. They are puzzled because they found no marks anywhere in the room that could cause that compression. I recall what you told me about the supernatural. Not sure if this fell into that category."

"Chief, my eyes were closed, and my arms were holding Dina so tight, I can't honestly tell you what occurred."

She and Sergei looked at each other, smiled, and grinned from ear to ear.

EPILOGUE

Coby remained in the Army and led a command of Army Rangers into major clandestine operations in the Middle East. Her record was impeccable.

Upon returning to the US, the president called her to the White House. He thanked her for her bravery and surprised her by bestowing on her a promotion to Brigadier General.

The president added, "Congratulations. You deserve it. Now that you have achieved your lifelong goal, perhaps you should think twice about running for Merlino's seat in Congress. It is for real now. He is resigning. We need someone like you in Congress."

Later that year, Coby found herself decked out in her general's garb and medals, sitting on the trunk of a convertible winding down 17th Street in a parade, thanking the people in her district for giving her the biggest margin of victory in the district's history.

Late afternoon one day, Coby and Sergei were in the living room with Dina. Ever since Dina had her toe reattached, the family began a tradition that lasted well into Dina's pre-teen years. Her little legs were each held by Mommy and Daddy. Coby took her thumb and index fingers and gently grabbed Dina's big toe. Together they sang, "This little piggy went to market..."

THE END

ABOUT THE AUTHOR

In 1983, Michael N. Ruggiero founded ATV Broadcast, a media consulting firm. He later joined Perennial Pictures Film Corp., an animation studio that has produced 14 television specials and a feature direct-to-video. The studio also created www.crawfordthecat.com, which has amassed over 12 million web viewers. Worldwide, 22,000 teachers use Crawford the Cat in the classroom.

Michael sits on the Board of the Mozel Sanders Foundation, a 51-year-old organization that feeds the hungry. In 2021, the Foundation served its one millionth Thanksgiving dinner. Born in Philadelphia, Michael N. Ruggiero now resides in Carmel, Indiana, with his beautiful wife, Carol. They have three amazing children and four grandchildren.

You can contact Michael at www.the7thsoul.com.

COMING SOON — 7TH SOUL - APOCALYPSE